STUPID GIRL

BOOK FOUR IN THE FAÎTE FALLING SERIES

MARY E. TWOMEY

For Jennifer Thomas,

Who has never, ever been a stupid girl.
And who loves me, even when I'm sure that's all I am.

MY DARK DAYS

I'd thought I'd known my fear maximum when Rigby took my dress and lowered me down into the abandoned well on the back end of my mother's vast property. It turns out I was capable of a whole additional layer of panic when they moved a cover over the top, sealing me in the dark.

I cried as I carefully balanced myself in the gently rocking wooden tub, knowing that if I tipped myself over, it might be the end for me. I worried that Lane and Draper would never find my body, that they'd think I'd run off or something. The incredible woman who raised me to be fearless would never have the closure a dead body provided. For that reason alone, I knew I needed to calm myself down and form a plan.

Only the problem was, there was nothing to plan with. I didn't have a ladder I could climb up, and precious few tools to make my grand escape. The terrible soldiers had even cut the rope they'd used to lower my bucket down. I carefully splashed my hand in the water, moving myself to the side of the well to see if I could feel anything I could use to climb up with. I had about three feet of space on either side of the bucket, and tried not to feel the claustrophobia I knew would start clawing at me if I let it.

This was the price I paid for pissing off Morgan le Fae, my birth mother and feared Queen of Avalon. She and her eight sisters had each been given a Jewel of Good Fortune, blessed by the immortal warlock, Kerdik. The gem made their respective provinces more fertile, so of course, a war ensued between the sisters. One by one, Morgan slowly began absorbing her sisters' lands when she stole their gems and left their land bereft. She would come in as the benevolent queen and offer the famine-ridden people a place to stay, if only they surrendered their region to her. Province 1 was now the largest in all of Avalon, though a few of the provinces still managed to hold onto their independence and fight the good fight. Morgan was feared, hated and beloved, depending on who you asked. She was ruthless, but provided for those in her care. With stolen resources, of course, but whatever.

King Urien, my dad, had worried when Morgan's obsession over the gems started taking over her life. Kerdik had blessed me when I was born with the ability to understand unknown languages, and also with a unique ability to find stuff. I could locate pretty much anything, if I concentrated hard enough. Morgan was chomping at the bit for me to take my first steps, so I could lead her to the remaining jewels. My dad sent me away with Morgan's youngest sister, Lane, who'd been my caretaker since birth. Lane ditched Avalon and ran me to Common (that's what the peeps down here call earth), keeping me away from even a mention of Avalon.

Boy, had that been a shocker.

I ran my finger over the large square-shaped aquamarine stone, tracing the three diamonds on either side in the white gold vine-looking setting. Kerdik had given the most beautiful ring I'd ever seen to me when we were becoming friends, and he was just learning how to be one. I'd been warned about his temper, but to see it up close was chilling. Though I'd called for him over and over in the way he'd taught me to do if I needed him, Kerdik didn't come for me. No one came. I was stuck in the bottom of a well, several stories down in the ground, enveloped in the suffocating pitch black. The darkness felt like it was seeping into my pores, strangling me and daring me to have a mental breakdown. Morgan wanted the ring because she guessed Kerdik had blessed it. When I hadn't given it to her, she banished me here until I cracked. A Daughter of Avalon, still doing everything she can to get her hands on a jewel that was never hers. Some things never change, I guess.

Bastien will find me. I repeated the promise over and over again.

I don't know how long I floated with nothing but my thoughts and not enough sanity, but the time passed slowly, keeping me in the dark with my mind in panic mode.

Panic mode had never really been my thing. There was always a plan, always a way to figure things out. Between Lane and Judah, I'd never been permitted much space to freak out before one of them would redirect my mind to something more productive. I took a deep breath and reminded myself that I'd just shimmied up an elevator shaft. This was nothing.

Well, it was probably a similar fall from top to bottom as the elevator shaft, but whatever. I hadn't fallen then. I waited until my crying subsided and my pulse steadied before reaching around to find a spot on the wall to try and climb up. The stones were slick from rain, but a couple jutted out just enough to give me hope. All I had to do was wait for the sealed well's walls to dry a little, and I could try my hand at climbing. Of course, that meant I also had to wait for my hands and feet to dry, so I had a little time to kill. If only Andre the Giant was here. He could've climbed up with me on his back like it was nothing. Dude was fierce (which reminded me to stop being a baby).

It turns out, time spent at the bottom of the well is the trickiest part, if you want to stay sane. I don't know why my brain was being a jerk, but suddenly all my failures came flying out at me, slamming themselves in my face so that they were all I saw in the pitch black.

Failed papers I'd worked all night on, failed tests that were so far below a D, one of my teachers had actually written the grade "Z" on it. I heard three of the cool girls on the playground in the second grade telling me they didn't want to play with me because I was stupid. Then there was the star football player I'd had a crush on all through the ninth grade that Judah encouraged me to talk to. When I finally worked up the nerve, eleventh-grader Luke McCrary was nice enough, asking me how I did my spin kick on the soccer field. When I got the guts to ask him out, he thought I meant for tutoring. He showed up with Chemistry and History books, plus the girl he was planning on taking out after our study session. I showed up with nice shoes Lane let me borrow, and a hopeful smile that quickly crashed and burned when I realized I'd never be more than Remedial Rosie to most of the kids I knew.

Add that to the fact that Lane had given me a necklace that changed my appearance to a girl with a hump, a lazy eye and acne, and I didn't stand a chance at getting a date.

Nobody ever asked me where I wanted to go to college, except for Judah and Lane. Not even my guidance counsellor, who pushed trade school brochures at me and told me there were lots of good options for "kids like me."

It didn't matter that I studied harder than Judah. It didn't matter how much effort I put in. The day I came home with Lane from our meet with the principal and my scowling teacher, ruling that I should repeat the third grade, I didn't think life could get any worse.

Lane hadn't yelled. She hadn't said anything to cheer me up or make me feel worse. She rented all my favorite eighties cheesy cult films, the whole John Hughes collection, and held me while we watched movies until we passed out in each other's arms. I'd wanted *The Princess Bride* for the millionth time, but she ruled it was too perfect a movie to sully with a bad memory. The next morning, she helped me make a plan for a better third grade experience for the next year.

I loved Lane, and knew I'd done nothing to deserve a mom as solid as her. She didn't lavish only me with her love, either. When Judah didn't get into MIT, she busted us both out of school and took us to an amusement park for the day, ruling that we were about to go off and conquer the world, so Judah and I should spend a little time being kids first. She even Googled all the things about MIT that didn't fit into Judah's master plan, and famous people in his desired field who'd graduated elsewhere. We'd eaten elephant ears and carnival hot dogs until all three of us were ready to puke. By the end of the day, Judah had a new plan, a more optimistic attitude and a sore stomach to distract him from his emotional pain. The next morning, he was at our kitchen table, college applications spread out while he and Lane filled out a new batch with all of his best qualities.

I loved Lane for so many reasons, but taking Judah in as her own was one of the greatest on that list. I wanted to be like her, to love fiercely, even when it was hard, even when plans fell through, and even when there was no way to not repeat the third grade.

I tightened my fist and resolved not to lose it down here. I would not forfeit my sanity to the darkness, or lose my mind to loneliness. I would not repeat the third grade ever again. I would be strong and courageous, even if I was sitting in my underwear in a bucket at the bottom of a forgotten well.

LYING TO MY MOTHER

*W*hen the lid overhead opened up however many hours or days later, I couldn't open my eyes – the light was so painful. My blood boiled when I heard Morgan shouting down to me, her voice echoing off the walls and creating a confusing dissonance. "Are you ready to give me the ring?"

More rain entered the well, frustrating me that I'd have to keep waiting longer now for the walls to dry. They'd almost been sturdy enough for me to make an attempt, but not quite. "I can't get it off!" I shouted, trying my hand at lying to see if it would work.

"Then I guess you should make yourself at home down there," she spat back. "Enjoy your meal for the day."

I squeaked when something came flying down at me, hurling at a speed I couldn't counter, banging off walls and landing with a bloody splat in my lap. I shrieked at the dead quail that had been skinned for me, and still had lines of blood sliding down over its body. I was horrified at the lifeless creature in my arms, and unsure what to do with it. Without thinking, I tossed it over the edge of the bucket, letting it splash in the water as the well closed overhead. Then I panicked, guessing that an animal carcass would pollute the only water supply I had. Quickly, I tipped the lip of the tub I was hugging my knees in, filling it with rainwater to the point where it was almost non-buoyant. Though I could go without food for a while, I knew depriving myself of drinkable water would ensure I died quicker.

I had to stay alive. I had a new brother I was only just starting to get to know. Draper had recently been adopted by Lane, and the two of us had hit it off right from the start. Draper was desperate for family, and I didn't want him to finally get a sister who would fight for him, only to lose her so soon.

Lane and I were best friends. As much as I would never survive without her, I knew that same desperation existed on her end, too. She would find me.

I heard Morgan's cruel laughter above the relentless rain. Then I was sealed in the darkness, unsure if I would ever feel the grass beneath my toes again.

REUNITED

For the millionth time in four days, I wondered what Judah was up to. If he'd gone back to his normal life, or if he'd up and done something crazy after learning about a whole new universe that fit so easily into his D&D passions.

I was surviving on water, afraid to eat an animal whose thoughts I might've heard in passing. It's the downside of the birth blessing Kerdik gave me. If I didn't have the ability to hear animals, I probably wouldn't be so unmoving in my vegetarianism. Taking a bite out of Thumper once you've had a conversation with him feels more akin to cannibalism than a tasty meal.

I went over my Spanish lessons, and my chemistry notes Judah had recorded himself reading so I could memorize them. I recited every lesson I could remember, and then took to telling myself grand stories from Judah's *Lord of the Rings* imagination. I couldn't remember which one was Saruman and which was Sauron, so they were renamed "Bad Guy" and "Super Bad Guy". I knew Judah would throw popcorn at me for forgetting.

I hugged my knees in the cramped tub that was growing more buoyant with every passing day. That meant I was running low on drinkable water.

I spent my sleeping and waking time with my knees curled to my chest in the wooden tub, marking the passing of the days with a visit from Morgan. When she opened up the well on the fifth day, I was expecting another dead animal hurled down on my head. I ducked and shaded my eyes, the small golf ball-sized hole above casting painful light down on me. My eyes were too used to the darkness. Though I wanted the light, now I recoiled from it, hissing like an underworld leper.

Morgan's voice echoed though the stone well. "Are you ready to give me the ring yet?"

"I'll be dead soon, so you can cut it off my finger then," I replied nonchalantly, as if fading away with no one who loved me around was no big deal. I would not cry in front of Morgan. I would not ask for a thing. I would not be less than the woman Lane raised me to be. I rubbed my naked sternum, repeating Lane's mantra that had seen me through many a downward turn: *Remember who you are.*

I managed to catch the bowling-ball shape Morgan threw down at me before it plunged into the water below, hoping it was a cantaloupe or something I could actually eat.

I turned the shape around in my hands, letting the light fall on it so I could make out what I was holding. A scream like none other shot out of me, giving Morgan exactly what she wanted. The tears I promised myself two days ago I would stop altogether bloomed in the corners of my eyes and slid down my face, streaking my filthy cheeks and dropping onto the treasure I knew I couldn't part with.

"I thought you might like some company, my sweet. Give me the ring, and the deaths will end at Demi."

"Screw you!" I roared, shaking with rage. "You're twisted! I can't believe we're even related!"

"The ring, Rosalie." She sounded impatient, like I was holding her up from tea time or something.

"It's staying with me until I die, you wench. And right before I die, I'm throwing it into the well, so you'll never find it. Two can play at this game!"

Morgan sealed me in again, today with not even the pretense of feeding me. The darkness concealed my tears and wrapped me in a hug as I shook, alone and very afraid in the well. The darkness burned into my brain the closed-eyed look of a simple nap that Demi's face was frozen in. I sobbed as I cradled my boyfriend's head, murmuring his name over and over again. "Demi, Demi, Demi…" The sobbing turned to horrified, heartwrenched screaming, and I feared my sanity had slipped past the point of no return.

He'd been my *soumettre*, which I'd originally thought was a personal attendant or something, but quickly learned that Demi's services also extended to the bedroom. I was devastated when I learned that he'd slept with my mother and a few of my aunts, being traded like a baseball card when things needed to be smoothed over with tensions that always grew too high in Avalon. I'd developed a crush on Demi, which he easily reciprocated. Everyone told me it was an act – it was what Demi was expected to do for the royalty he served. But I knew it wasn't. I knew Demi had loved me – he told me as much. He'd kept things PG with me, though he was used to far faster advances. He was sweet to me, kind and thoughtful. He kissed me like I was delicate, so I remembered to be. Demi looked at me like I was something special, warming me so that I felt like I was cool enough to flirt with the hottest guy in the room – even if he was a slave.

Demi read to me. In my land of dyslexia, that was no small thing.

I blubbered uncontrollably, unable to part with the last bit of him. I hugged his head, the sticky innards and pointy vertebrae resting against my bare stomach. I couldn't be repulsed by him; it was Demi. He'd stayed with me when I was a mess, was kind to me when I was a jerk, and loved me when I wasn't sure. If this was all that remained of the man who'd held me while I slept, then I would treasure it. Our bodies would go down together, buried in the water like lovers with no happy ending. He was my Romeo, and I would be his Juliet, stretched out over what remained of his lifeless body.

"This isn't how your adventure ends," I promised him. "You are not this awful place. I'll get you out of here, Demi. We'll run away together."

My lips trembled from starvation, fatigue and grief as I kissed his hardened cheek. My fingers smoothed back his black hair from his forehead as I apologized over and over to him, as if that could fix anything. "It's all my fault. If I'd stayed up in Common, none of this would be happening, and you'd be going about your normal life." I clung to Demi as horrible, painful sobs retched from my soul and polluted the dank air.

I don't know how long I blubbered for, but as my cries gave way to quiet hiccups of grief, I clung to Demi, praying there was a way to make it all better.

MY NEW SHRINK

I recounted the entire *Princess Bride* movie to Demi, pretending he was alive, and that he was fascinated I knew every single line by heart. We were on day eleven of no food, and the water in my tub was only an inch deep. I didn't have long to live, so I gave in to my crazy, not bothering holding on to the false hope that Bastien could find me down here.

I winced at the thought of his name. I hadn't allowed myself to dwell on him all that often, knowing it was too painful. There was so much unsettled between us, and I wondered if he would stay unsettled after my death, or if he would find peace. His pretend fiancée and family friend had just died, and then I would be gone shortly after. If he wasn't a hermit before, that ought to do it.

I held Demi to my chest and rocked him like he was my baby, singing to him like Lane used to do for me when I'd had bad dreams. I would never graduate from college, though I'd been close before my life was stripped from me by Avalon. I would never get an apartment next to Judah, so we could be separate when he finally settled down with Jill, but still together. This was the longest we'd been apart since we met, and the distance was painful, the loneliness clinging to my filthy skin in ways not even the brightest day could shake. I would never play another soccer game. I couldn't even move my legs, so stuck was I in the tub that served as both my harbor and my prison.

I would never get married, though I'd never given that much thought. I would never have children, and raise them with the same courage and kindness Lane had worked hard to instill in me.

By the twelfth day, Demi was my shrink. He listened to every mistake I'd made, all my insecurities and the details of my childhood that no one except Judah and Lane knew. Demi was my very best friend now, and I told him so as I cradled him to my scabbed chest like a teddy bear.

The rotting animal carcasses Morgan had thrown down into the water around me made the whole well stink, the decay seeping into my pores. I thought at some point I would grow immune to it, but with every inhale, all I knew was the rotting chicken smell that plagued me. After a while I *became* the smell, the air permeating my skin and making me one with the macabre scent.

On the thirteenth day, I ran out of clean water.

I laid down with Demi in my tub on the fourteenth day, when there was nothing but darkness.

On the fifteenth day, there was light.

THE CAVALRY

I ducked my head away from the light that shone down on the sewer creature I now was. Morgan hadn't been back in a long time, though admittedly, time was something that was difficult to measure. The rain hadn't stopped during the entire period I'd been down here, and it fell on me now like a punishment that was mixed with a blessing. I expected Morgan's cackle. I expected my cracked lips and dry throat to muster up some sort of "screw you" that hopefully was more triumphant than it felt.

But Morgan's taunting didn't come. I knew I'd gone crazy when Lane's frantic voice called my name. "Rosie? Rosie, is that you? Rosie, baby, are you alive?"

My rasp was barely audible, but the acoustics of the well did me a solid and carried my weak response up the chamber. "Mom?"

Lane broke into sobs. "Baby, I'm here! We're coming! Hold tight for a few more minutes, and we'll get you out of there."

"Mom?" I rasped, confused. "Am I dead?"

She didn't hear me, but two shadowed figures dipped down into the well, obscuring some of the painful light that felt like a slow death to my already fried senses. Two men were lowered on ropes that were tied around their waists.

"Demi! Demi, wake up!" I shook the head in my arms and kissed his cheek. "Demi, we're saved!"

"Hold on, Daisy! Just stay right there."

Like there's anything else I can do. Bastien's voice was the sweetest sound, though I still couldn't open my eyes to see him. The light was so painful, I could feel my heartbeat behind my eyes.

I shivered as the fresh air wafted down toward me. I'd been cold for so long; I was surprised my body was still making a fuss about it.

Draper's cadence was fearful when he neared me. "Oh! Rosie, are you naked? She threw you down here without your clothes?"

I was too relieved to be embarrassed. "Draper? You came for me?"

His voice turned soft, and I could tell he was finally right next to me without looking. "Of course I did. You're my sister. Can you lift your head, pumpkin?"

Bastien tugged twice on the rope and called up for the other part of the team to stop lowering them. "Rosie, take my hand. Then Mad, Link and Remy are going to pull us out."

I tried to raise my arm, but it wouldn't go very far. "I can't really move!" I admitted, panicked that I might be stuck down here forever. "My limbs are too stiff."

"How long have you been down here?" Bastien asked, as if we had time for conversation.

"Fifteen days, I think. Since I last saw you."

Draper took charge when Bastien let out a pained cry of rage and punched the stone wall. "Bastien, grab one side of the tub, and I'll take the other. Rosie, get down low in there so the basin doesn't wobble on the way up."

I did my best, but there wasn't much space to move. I bit my dry lip and whispered a fearful, "Are you real?"

Draper's fingers flitted over my head, gripping my skull with a fierce protectiveness. "I'm real, Rosie, and I'm getting you out of here."

My weakened pulse rallied at the sound of my brother's promise. I clung tight to Demi, curling my body around him. "We're saved, Demi. We're saved," I rasped to him. Then I closed my eyes as the two men hoisted me up.

6

PARTING WITH DEMI

I whimpered from the light, and the sensation of being rained on. I hadn't been touched in so long, and the rain felt like a hard whack instead of the gentle snuggle I needed. I could feel the light on my skin. The quiet burning made me recoil and cover myself when the tub finally broke through the mouth of the well.

I heard a cacophony of voices shouting my name and asking me questions that piled on top of one another as they lowered my wooden bucket onto the grass. All of my muscles were constricting and writhing as they tried to recoil from the painful intrusion. I banged my free fist to my head and begged, "The light! It's too bright."

Draper's shirt was thrown over me, covering my nakedness and my eyes. My muscles relaxed in a gust of relief. I reached my fingers to the edge of the tub, silently asking for anyone's hand to hold onto. "Can't move!" I whispered when Lane dropped to her knees and threw her body over the tub.

"Oh, honey. I'm here! We've been searching for you for weeks! I'm here now, and I'm never letting you out of my sight ever again."

Remy pried Lane off of me and peeked under the shirt to show me his face. *"Where are you hurt?"*

"I'm not in the well," I answered, as if that wasn't obvious. "I'm not in the well." My brain was skipping, unable to process much other than that. "I told you I'd get us out," I said to Demi. "I told you your adventure wouldn't end in this awful place."

Lane and Bastien worked in tandem to pry me out of the basin, but even after they lifted me out, my legs were stuck curled to my chest. I let out a raspy howl at the pain the small movements caused me. My bones felt thin, and grated against each other as my joints protested the freedom I'd been begging for. Remy was shouting at them to be careful, but of course, no one heard him.

When Lane tucked my stiff arms into Draper's button-down shirt, Demi rolled out of my grip and landed with a splat onto the mud-soaked earth. "No!" I eked out, scrambling as much as I could to gather Demi back to me. We'd been through too much; I wasn't about to let him be alone now.

"Shite! Is that a head?" I heard Madigan nearby, but kept my eyes shut as I clung to Demi.

"Honey, who is it?" Lane's voice was tense, but she still wore the front of trying to be brave through her tears.

"Demi," I whispered, my body curling around him in the mud. "He's my boyfriend. He can't be alone. He gets sad when he's alone. He needs me."

I heard everyone take a collective step back, but I didn't budge, clinging to my treasure for all I was worth.

"Is tha what's all over her legs? Is it his brains?" I heard Link ask in horror.

I didn't feel anything on me, but then again, I'd been too cold and numb to feel much. "His brains are fine! He'll be fine!"

There was complete silence, except for Remy's errant thoughts. *"She's cracked. She's absolutely lost her mind."*

It was Draper who finally broke the silence, kneeling by my

side and placing his hand on my shoulder. The simple touch was painful, but the lonely ache in my chest longed for it. "Rosie, I'm going to pick you up now. It might hurt, but we've got to get you out of here." He turned his head over his shoulder, and his voice caught on emotion he'd been trying to keep at bay. "She's too thin, Lane! She's been starved down there."

Lane was loudly weeping now. "Okay, then. One thing at a time. Let's get her out of here."

Link reached for Demi. "Here, let me take your friend. I'll give him a proper burial, Rosie."

"No!" I roared, my voice cracking horribly. "We don't like the dark anymore! You can't bury someone in the ground if they don't like the dark. Then he'll be scared forever. His adventure doesn't end here!"

I felt horrible when I heard the sound of Lane retching. She didn't understand. She thought I was holding a severed head, but Demi wasn't dead. I'd spent over a week with him in the well, talking with him and trusting him with my blackest secrets.

Bastien's voice was wobbly. "I can't watch this! Rosie, honey, he's dead! His face isn't even there anymore. You've got his brains all over your legs!"

"I cheated on him!" I confessed, unable to get ahold of my swinging emotions. Draper propped me up while Madigan poured a few swallows from his canteen down my throat. "I kissed you while I was with him! I'm a whore!"

Bastien's voice was husky. "That's not worth thinking about right now. Let's get you and Demi somewhere safe, okay? Can I hold his head? Would you trust me with that?"

I considered trust, and how much of it I had on tap. "You'll bury him. You'll hide him in the dark, and he'll be afraid."

"No, baby. I'll carry him and keep him safe until you tell me otherwise."

"Promise me."

"I promise."

Mad's voice was grave. "Ye don't have to do this, Bastien. I can hold it."

Bastien was firm. "She doesn't trust you like she does me. I can hold it."

I hiccupped through my tears as I let Bastien slowly pry my treasure out of my fingers. "Promise me," I said again, needing to hear the words again.

"I promise." Bastien indulged me as often as I needed.

I heard footsteps running toward us, Link's excited voice breaking the tension. "Berries! I found a handful in the bush over there. Here, lass. Down the hatch."

The first food in over two weeks hit my stomach with an acidity that made my guts roil. Draper waited a few seconds to make sure I didn't puke, and then gently hoisted me up in his arms. I bit back a scream as everything in my body jarred when I shifted against him. "I'm here, I'm here," he vowed. "You're safe now. We're going to say hello to the fine people of Province 9, who've been waiting to greet you."

"Huh?"

"Lane's province. They've had their time to pack, and they're ready to leave Province 1 behind. Duke Lot rallied them, along with a few other sympathetic provinces, and they marched on the castle, demanding Morgan produce the princess. They need to see you now, and then we'll go home."

Draper was strong, though not as ridiculously bulky as Bastien or the other Untouchables. I shuddered against him, clinging to his undershirt as the rain pelted us through the late afternoon sun. "I failed the third grade," I whispered only to him, my face close to his jaw. "I can't…" I wanted to confess my deep insecurity that I couldn't read – a secret I didn't part with unless there was no other option. I tucked the confession back inside, worried he might drop me if he knew I was stupid.

I don't know why my brain was betraying me like this, but it was stuck, and spewed more truths at my new brother. I was certain one of the things would make him recoil from me or drop me in the mud, but he walked steadily onward, repeating after every admission, "I'm here."

"I ran away once when some kids at school were picking on me."

"I'm here," Draper vowed, tucking my secrets tight in his heart as the rain pelted us.

"I stole a test in Algebra class so I could memorize the answers and pass."

"I'm here."

"I cheated on Demi with Bastien twice!" I fretted, ashamed as I clung to Draper, afraid that this would be the part where he dropped me.

He hefted me higher in his arms so he could press a kiss to my filthy forehead. "I'm here. No matter what, I'm here. You're coming home with us now, and you're never coming back to this place." When I didn't answer, he made himself vulnerable and sang me the song he'd invented for me when I'd been a baby. "Climb all the mountains, run off when you're grown, but for now, little girl, my song is your home."

"Please don't leave me," I begged.

Draper's firm cadence had the note of a promise to it that I clung to as if it was the only thing anchoring me to the planet. "Never, Rosie. I'll never leave you."

I HADN'T BEEN PREPARED for the noise that was hundreds of thousands of people shouting their victory when Draper brought me to the front of the castle and crossed over the bridge. Remy and Lane walked in front, making a path that everyone scattered from. Link and Madigan walked in silence on either side of me, shoving a few villagers who grew too zealous and tried to touch my trembling body. The nonstop rain paired nicely with the exuberance of the moment, making everyone rampant for a new life, a new day.

Lane's voice was triumphant as she called out to the people, "Do not be afraid of your own voice, Avalon! See the good you can do, if you only work together. Remember who you are, and don't let Morgan take that treasure from you! It's because of you that the Lost Princess lives! Master Kerdik gave me a Jewel of Good Fortune, but you are the thing that shines brightest!"

I shuddered against Draper like a cornered animal as the cries grew to deafening heights around us. Lane was born to rule a nation. I was only just beginning to understand how much she'd been holding herself back.

"I'm here," Draper promised again as we continued forward.

"Look on your daughter and see how black Morgan le Fae's heart is! This is what she does to her own daughter, her own flesh, her own blood. What more would she do to you, if it served her purpose?"

The crowd cheered and jeered, and then commotion started to splinter as a horse galloped toward us. I heard Damond, Draper's younger brother, calling out to Lane. "Wait! Wait, Aunt Elaine. I'm coming with you! I've brought many from Province 2 who want their freedom from Duke Henri and from Morgan. Can we come with you?" It always made me sad that Uncle Henri had the kind of relationship with his kids that warranted them using his formal title, instead of simply calling him "Dad".

Draper gripped me so tight, I was certain I would have finger-sized bruises on my thigh. I could tell he didn't want Damond making such a public separation from their father and risking his wrath, but he said nothing, letting Damond make his own choice.

I didn't need to see to be able to feel the smile in Lane's voice. "Anyone who wants freedom from Morgan la Fae can make their new home in Province 9. Province 4 has already merged with us, making us all a stronger front against the enemy. Welcome to your new life, Prince Damond."

7

CLEAN START

The procession to Province 9 stretched on through the night, while the ceaseless rain beat down on our heads. Hundreds of thousands of people packed up their meager belongings and marched with us out of Province 1 and into the quickly healing Province 9. I was offered bread, nuts and apples from fellow travelers, and tried not to chew like a wild animal as I choked down the few bites I was allowed. Remy was strict in only permitting me small amounts, so my delicate stomach didn't revolt. When Draper's arms started to shake, he handed me to Madigan, who shot Bastien a look of brotherly determination that he would get the job done, no matter what. People were so kind as to offer us their wagons for the journey, but Lane wanted my devastation visible, since it clearly showed Morgan's shriveled heart.

My eyes were given grace by the nighttime sky, and when the sun rose in the east, my vision was starting to adjust to the intrusion of light. Madigan hadn't said a word to me the entire time, but kept his eyes on the path until his arms began to spasm. "I need a break."

Remy, Link and Draper all volunteered, but Bastien had had enough. He smacked Demi's skull into Link's hands, wiped his palms off on his pants and arrested me from Madigan. "I've got you," he promised.

"P-people are watching," I warned him.

"I don't care. No one carries my girl over the threshold but me. We're not far from Lane's mansion now. Don't worry. I won't kiss you in public. They'll just think I'm your *Guardien*. It's my job to keep you alive and safe." His voice wavered. "I failed you, Daisy. I was so turned around. I thought the jewels mattered. *You* matter. I never should've left you alone with Morgan."

"I'm alive," I assured him. "You saved us."

"You're too thin. I'm afraid I'll trip on a rock and break all your bones." He closed his eyes for a brief handful of seconds, and I watched the rain drip through his lashes. "She starved you?"

I nodded slowly, the movement achy, but worth it to not have to stretch my raspy vocal chords with words.

He leaned his head down and whispered, "I love you. From this moment on, it's you and me. I'll take better care of us."

I snuggled closer to him in response, feeling right in his arms. I hadn't felt safe in so very long, but something told me that with Bastien nearby, the solace I craved wouldn't be completely out of my reach. He carried me without anyone else's help straight into the Ninth Province.

The housing here was mostly long stretches of two-story apartment buildings, broken up by a smattering of single-family huts. While one might see a roof over their heads and leave well enough alone, that wasn't my Lane. She had flare, and there wasn't any point in trying to hide it. The apartments were multi-colored, the outside brick walls going for teal in stretches, then lavender, and then red. Each color had its own set of balconies on each door: the teal had curly wrought iron gates on the balconies and porches, the lavenders were more forbidding and straight, while the red part of the building went for a minimalist look, with lower railings painted blue to add a pleasant accent. "Amazing," I rasped.

"See that there?" Draper pointed to a plaque that seemed engraved onto the outer walls where each new color began. "That's where the artist marked their portion, along with the year it was painted and designed."

My mouth fell open, confounded that architects were given the freedom and nobility to sign their works of art. "It's gorgeous."

"It is. Lane wants the people to make this land their own, which is exactly how it used to be when she ruled decades ago. It's part of why they love her so much; it's not *her* province, it's *ours*."

Morgan's stone castle was far larger than Lane's. Hers was more the size of a roomy mansion, and far less hostile. The interior stone walls had been painted white and beige to make the place feel more chipper and less like an enormous dungeon, as Morgan's had been. There were even flowers etched in red, green and yellow along the crown moldings, making the whole place seem whimsical with its loveliness. The ceilings were tall and vaulted down each hallway, showing off the majesty of the building without seeming pretentious.

Bastien didn't part from me when we reached what was apparently supposed to be my new bedroom. He showed me the mahogany bed with four tall posts that had emerald curtains hanging between them. There were matching swirls painted along the baseboards of the walls, glittering up at us as if to announce that magic lived here, and this place would give me pleasant dreams.

Even after Remy ordered the servants to fill the ivory bath tub with warm water to scrub the filth and dried brains off me, Bastien still didn't let go. He shot Lane a look of warning when she argued that she could help me bathe. "I'm done assuming she'll be there whenever I turn my back. I'm through taking chances with her life. I'm not leaving."

The two went back and forth until I gave Lane a small nod to let her know I was okay being naked in front of Bastien. "Okay" might be a stretch, but it was more like I couldn't let go of him if my life depended on it. The insane part of me worried that the second he was out of my sight, I'd find myself back in the well, hoping anyone would come and rescue me.

The two were careful with my fragile body as they lowered my emaciated form into the warm water. Lane had a steady, reassuring voice, but tears in her eyes as she scrubbed my back. "This is your new bedroom, baby. You like it?"

I looked at her, my eyes haunted and vacant. I wanted to put on a brave front for her, but the well had stolen my stellar acting abilities. "Kerdik hurt me," I said, as if this was an appropriate response to what she'd asked.

Lane moved to my right arm with the soap, going over the skin four times before the filth was removed. "I know, sweetheart. Bastien told me everything. Kerdik's a very powerful warlock, but he doesn't know how to be a friend. He spends his too-long life alone, which isn't good for anybody. He doesn't have those normal filters most people have. We learn to take turns, to share, to listen, to be understanding. He doesn't have much practice with that. Plus, he's got too much power for a person with so little self-control to be able to handle. He's a two-year-old driving a Mack truck." She lowered her voice. "Kerdik is not your great adventure. *You* are your greatest adventure. Never forget that."

I went back to staring vacantly, my brain taking its time to chew on the information. I kept losing my focus, my mind skipping all over, and landing on a fog of nothing. Lane passed the soap to Bastien, who washed my left arm with great care, as if he expected the bone to break if he scrubbed too hard. "I can't believe Morgan didn't even feed you. I thought I got how awful she was, but starving her own daughter? What did she expect would happen?"

"She wanted my ring. One of her guards tried to yank it off me, and somehow the ring killed him." My eyes flitted over to Bastien. "*I* didn't kill him. I'm a vegetarian. I don't kill people. It wasn't me."

"I know, honey." He kissed my filthy forehead, and something about that simple act made it dawn on me that I wasn't too much of a mess for Bastien. That revelation sunk deep inside my heart, to be digested later.

I blinked twice. "Dead quails."

"Huh?" Lane asked.

"Once a day, Morgan would throw down a dead, defeathered, raw quail on me to eat."

Lane hung her head. "Oh, baby. You could've eaten it. No one would've thought anything bad about you breaking your diet in those circumstances."

Slowly, my head craned to face Lane, and I saw the hurt there. "'Know who you are.' I wasn't about to change myself for Morgan."

Lane hung her head in self-loathing. "I instilled that in you to make you stronger, not to push you closer to death. Rosie, you should've eaten the quail."

I shook my head, firm in my conviction. "'Know who you are.' Now I'm sure she can't break me."

"Yes, but she broke *me*! If you're hurting, it *destroys* me, baby."

"I'm not hurting." I stared vacantly ahead, not caring that I was filthy, naked, and that my body was protesting my very existence. "I don't feel anything."

Lane's arms were gentle as they wrapped around me, scared and protective. "I need you to be alive."

"Know who you are," I told her. "We always have that, and we have each other now. Morgan can't touch what's inside of us."

Lane gulped, scrubbing the dried brains from my knees. She turned to retch a few times, so Bastien took over. His firm hands didn't tease or play around; he washed me from head to toe like a pro. Then a fresh steel tub was brought in, and I was scrubbed all over again with non-brain water.

When I was finally clean, Remy was brought in to treat my fungus and pus-riddled cuts. He gave the pronouncement that yes, I was dehydrated and nursing too many well-borne infections, and that duh, I needed food, water and rest.

Lane wrapped me in a pink velvet robe, tying the belt around my thinned waist. Then Bastien carried me to the enormous bed that had to have been bigger than a king-sized. I was used to sharing a bunk bed with Judah, so the luxury felt like sleeping on my own personal island. The mattress was somehow both firm and fluffy, and the sheets were soft and buttery, cradling my skin as if it hadn't been in the bottom of a well for over two weeks.

"I'm haven't been sleeping," I informed them, my grammar taking a vacation. As the days had stretched on in the well, I wasn't even granted the mercy of sleep to pass the unending hours, since there were no animals to wear my magic out.

"I can fix that." Lane wiped her tears away and poked her head outside. "Can you go get the animals?"

Draper came in with a tray of food and a face I hadn't seen in too many months. Reyn was thinner, his cheeks sunken in and his smile pinched. "Reyn?"

He cleared the distance between us and leaned over the bed to hold my hand. "Rosie, I'm so sorry I couldn't go with them on the search party to find you."

"What's wrong?" I asked, my tone making it clear I wouldn't tolerate skating around the elephant in the room anymore. I'd known something was wrong with Reyn when Bastien had offered to give him a magic transfusion back at Draper's whorehouse.

"That's a story for another day. It's quite harrowing, and I'll want you fed and rested so I get the loudest gasps and most thrilled reactions from you." Even in his weakened state, Reyn was still charming. You couldn't not love a guy who tried to lighten the mood when the topic of his own mortality was brought up.

Bastien shifted me to lean against the headboard. It was rich, deep-colored wood, and had angel wings carved in it. Not angels themselves, just the wings. I couldn't decide if it was artsy and dark, or whimsical and beautiful. Either way, I was grateful not to be in the well anymore. Reyn and Lane pulled the sheet and comforter over my lap, the two of them working in perfect synchronicity to tuck me in. For the briefest of moments, I had the surreal feeling of being their child – not just Lane's, but Reyn's as well. Their eyes met over my body, and they shared a sweet smile of togetherness that warmed my fragile insides.

Draper shifted the tray on my nightstand, and made himself comfortable on the edge of the bed. He gave me a reassuring smile as he popped something that looked like a green grape into my mouth. It tasted like oranges and strawberries, but had the grainy bite of a pear. "Whoa. What is that?"

The corner of Lane's mouth drew up. "It's a *frai*. They haven't grown here in decades, but a month of the gem being where it should, and the bushes are already sprouting again."

Draper fed me dozens of *frai*, and I let him do it without protest, while Lane took her time brushing the knots from my hair. I drank water, ate a few pieces of bread and a handful of nuts before Remy returned and ruled that was all my stomach could handle for now. I wasn't sure if I was still hungry or not; the shock was still rolling through me. "Am I in the well?" I asked my brother.

Draper blinked at me, looked at Remy, and then produced a brave smile. "Nope. You share a house with Mom and me now. How it should've been all along."

I heard Link and Madigan shouting in surprise down the hallway, and stiffened against the headboard. "Don't worry," Draper assured me. "We're safe here."

When Damond came in, he brought a sight with him that was too wonderful to be real. My squirrel I'd snuck down here from life in Common was riding on my baby bear's back like a cowboy. Only Abraham Lincoln wasn't tiny anymore – he was a mid-sized bear. I didn't hang out with many bears in my world, and didn't realize how quickly they grew. Or maybe the growth spurt was an Avalon thing. "Hamish? Abraham Lincoln?"

"Mommy!" Abraham Lincoln cried, letting out a loud roar that brought Mad and Link into the room with their weapons drawn.

"Come here, guys. I missed you." I didn't have enough moisture to spare for tears, but my heart cried all the same. "You didn't come with me," I accused my bear, remembering back to when he'd decided to wait it out for Bastien in the Lost Village so many lifetimes ago. "I needed you guys. You've been here with Lane?"

Hamish jumped from his perch on Abraham Lincoln's shoulders straight onto my lap. He scampered up my body and sat on my shoulder, giving my face a squeeze. He started in on his adventures, including a harrowing story of him standing up to one of the two-headed pit bulls. His recollection was far different than Abraham Lincoln's, but I let Hamish paint himself as the hero he'd always pictured himself.

Mad and Link watched the exchange warily while Remy started his examination. The Éireland Untouchables reluctantly agreed to leave the room with Draper, Damond and Reyn when Remy needed to take off my robe so he could re-salve the cuts from Kerdik's ice prison. Apparently, they had become infected in the well, and that required two different kinds of salve that had to be applied five minutes apart. There was also a fungus on my toes and fingertips that required a different kind of medicine, which actually worked quite quickly. I could feel the grayed areas fizzing the moment the cream was rubbed in. Remy wiped it away, and a good ninety percent of the fungal growth was gone.

I couldn't follow Hamish's lightning speed chatter, though I tried my best while Remy worked. I caught the highlights, which was all my mind could latch onto with the holey net I had to work with. When he realized I wasn't talking back much, he brushed my cheek with his tail. *"You don't look so good."*

I didn't have the strength to bravely reassure him that I would be okay. Hamish seemed to understand, and took up residence on my shoulder, wrapping his tail around the nape of my neck to warm my skin. I couldn't seem to hold onto my body heat. "Thanks, Hamish. You're a good friend."

I was startled to find Remy writing things down and handing the note to Lane. I hadn't heard his thoughts until they broke through my foggy brain however long after the examination was already done. Then he turned my head so he could look into my eyes, testing their focus. *"I can't tell anymore. I've been talking to you this entire time, but you're not answering. Can you hear me?"*

I stared at him a few beats too long, but then gave him the relief he needed when I finally nodded. "I don't feel so great."

Bastien helped fashion my robe around me after Remy finished working his medicinal mojo. He tugged the comforter up over my lap and tried to rub a little friction into my spine to warm me.

Remy exhaled, as if he'd been worried we'd somehow lost our special connection. *"I know, Princess. I'm shocked you're upright at all, after everything. I think it's time you got some rest."*

"Morgan's not just going to let this go. She's not going to leave me alone."

Remy thumbed my chin sweetly. *"That's for us to worry about.*

You've restored enough kingdoms for now. It's time the warriors rest, and you, my dear, are the bravest of warriors."

I didn't have a response, so I simply blinked at him. "Demi. See what you can do for him."

Remy glanced up at Lane warily, who closed her eyes before giving him a curt nod. *"He's not alive, Rosie. There's nothing to be done for him. I can bury him, if you like."*

Panic welled in me, my sudden mood swing chasing Hamish off my shoulder. "No! Demi doesn't like the dark anymore. We were in the well for so long and couldn't see each other! You can't put him back in the dark!"

Bastien turned away and walked to the corner of the room to get some breathing space. Lane placed her hand on mine, using gentle but firm pressure to reel me in. "If we can't put him in the dark, what would you like us to do with him?" She cleared her throat. "He can't stay here, Rosie. I don't allow *soumettres* to work in my house. We have servants, but none of them... *service* us in the way most of my sisters allow." She tried to find a polite way to skirt around the issue, but her nose was still pinched in distaste. It was probably pretty similar to how my face looked when I found out about that little custom.

I tried my best to force my brain to focus, and finally came up with an idea that would suit everyone's wishes. "He has family in Province 8. Could he go live with them? He always wanted to go back home."

Bastien turned around with a mix of determination and hope in his raised eyebrows. "I can take him right now, if you like."

Lane nodded, but the fear on my face couldn't be concealed for the sake of my pride. Pride was one of the things that had been stripped from me, along with my dress. I didn't have the need to protect my desires from public view anymore. Life was too short to pretend I didn't want what I needed. My heartbeat drummed in my ears when the truth I'd been trying to shove under the rug burst out of me, raw and unpolished. "I don't want you to go," I admitted.

Bastien's resolute expression melted into a reverent affection I'd seen in passing, but was never able to study up close without it running off his face completely if I got too near his exposed heart. He rubbed his hand over his chest to let him know I'd touched him in his soft spots without lifting a finger. "You have no idea how long I've waited to hear you say that. I won't go, then."

Lane cleared her throat, glancing uncomfortably between us. "I can send one of my riders out."

Though I couldn't give Demi a good life here, I could at least return him to his brothers and sisters. It wasn't enough, but given my current state of deterioration, it was the best I could do. His adventure wouldn't end in Morgan's castle.

"Get some sleep, Princess. I'll come check on you in the morning." Remy gave my newly cleaned fingers a reassuring squeeze, packed up his bag and left.

"I need to go check on Reyn," Lane said, touching her eyebrow in concern as she glanced at the door.

"Go ahead. She won't be out of my sight. If Reyn needs more magic to try to get it all to stick again, you might want to purge from Roland this time. I don't want to compromise myself when Rosie's been attacked so recently."

I was touched that Bastien was thinking about my safety, and taking it more seriously than either of us had before. There was something about his focus that made me feel more secure than his hulking muscles alone could.

Lane had a different reaction. She crossed the room and placed a hand on either side of Bastien's face, pulling him down so that his forehead was pressed to hers. She closed her eyes, and I could see her fingers digging into his cheeks with barely contained fury. "I swear to you on all you hold precious in this life and the next, Draper and I will tear your bowels from your screaming body and use them to strangle you if you have sex with my daughter." She squeezed his face harder, her fingers trembling. "Remember that I am Morgan le Fae's sister. I have real darkness in me that wouldn't bother to blink if you dare defy me under my own roof. Untouchable or not, you'll obey my rules for my daughter, or you'll die screaming your regrets. You are not Untouchable, but as far as you're concerned, my daughter is until her wedding day."

Bastien gulped, and though he could turn her over in a hot second, he nodded his submission. "Yes, your majesty." The title was a banner of respect he didn't have to pay her, and had never paid to Morgan. Lane deserved the honor, so he gave it to her, not caring about his own pride in the moment. I thought I understood how much I loved him, but then he lowered his voice to a pleading whisper. "Please don't send me away from her. I love your daughter."

I swallowed hard, unable to look away from the fierce mama bear who loved me enough to say the uncomfortable things. Morgan had sent me a guy to screw to my heart's content, but Lane was protecting my heart at every turn. "You can stay, but you're done being a child. You're done being an angry old man. Your relationship learning curve is officially over. You'll be the best thing that ever happened to my Rosie, or you'll be thrown out with the trash, and no one in this house will shed a single tear for you. You are not her great adventure. Do not forget that." She pursed her lips, and I knew the gavel was coming by the flash of fury in her green eyes. "You are not worthy of my daughter. If you truly want to be with her, you'll see to remedying that immediately."

Bastien carefully held Lane by the wrists and pried her hands off his face. "Understood. Tell Reyn I'll check on him tomorrow if Rosie's feeling better."

Lane nodded, and then moved back to the bed to kiss my

cheek with a playful smile that told me she knew what a badass she was. "Get some sleep, baby. I love you."

"You're not leaving the castle, right? You and Draper are staying here?"

Lane softened, taking in my childlike insecurity with compassion. "We'll stay in the mansion, and we'll all be here when you wake."

8

MOMMY AND DADDY AND HOME

*H*amish skittered over my lap, and scampered up onto my shoulder, scolding me for getting cold again. He worried that I hadn't smiled yet.

"Sometimes you have to wait out a smile. It'll come, Hamish. Just not today."

Bastien lowered the lamplight and drew the curtains, but the room was still too large to feel homey. The four-poster had drapery I hadn't noticed when I'd first come in. Then again, there was probably a lot that would be a surprise by morning. Without a word, Bastien helped me lay down in the bed after feeding me a few more bites of a roll and another sip of water. I only spoke when he started closing the curtains around the bed, making it three-quarters of the way around before the panic burst out of me. "I don't like the dark!" I blurted out. "Can we leave one of the curtains open?"

Bastien paused. "Of course. How about the one facing the door, so I can make sure I see anything trying to come inside?"

"Okay. Do you have your knives?"

He displayed his belt, which had his leather sheath on the side. "Never leave home without them."

"Will you keep them nearby?"

Bastien examined my face before nodding. "You don't have to worry in here. If I'm around, you're not in danger. You keep getting messed with when you're out of my sight. I won't make that mistake again. Get ready to be closer than you've ever been with any other guy. How long until you think you get sick of my face?" He crossed his eyes just to make me smile, and whataya know, it worked.

Hamish hugged my cheek, overjoyed that the smile he'd been wishing for had returned to him.

"Too late, I'm already bored. If only you were handsome." I sighed dramatically.

I expected more banter, but Bastien leaned across the mattress and pressed a kiss to my lips. "You made a joke," he explained of his affection. "You're still in there."

"It wasn't a joke," I teased. His body felt right, hovering next to mine.

"I missed you." He kissed me again, melting us both. I couldn't help the yawn that swept over me, though I did have the grace to turn my head away from the kiss and clumsily cover my mouth halfway through. "Sorry."

Bastien leaned down and snorted a laugh into my neck. "Man, if you ever wanted to tell me I'm not pretty enough to look at, yawning in my face mid-kiss is the way to go."

I grimaced, patting the back of his head with a weighted hand. "I didn't mean to! I'm sorry, Bastien. I take it all back. You're completely lust-worthy. You're sexy and handsome and..." I yawned again, making Hamish and Bastien laugh together. "I can't help it!"

Bastien sucked on my lower lip before pulling himself off the mattress. "Get some sleep, honey."

He observed a shiver that rolled through me, despite the fact that I was buried under a thick down comforter. "Come here, Abraham Lincoln. Up you get." Bastien patted the mattress, bringing good old Abe up next to me. My teddy bear was a big boy now, and sank like a rock on the left side of the mattress. He positioned himself between me and the door, just in case.

My body rolled to his, and I breathed contentedly at the warmth his brown fur radiated. "Oh, I missed this."

Bastien gazed down lovingly at us. "I know you did."

I waved Bastien to come around and snuggle with Abe and me. There was plenty of room at my back. An unfathomable look crossed his features before he nodded, going around the closed curtain to come in behind us. He shed his boots, socks, signature flannel, and his belt, though he tucked the sheathed knife under my pillow to make sure we weren't unarmed.

Bastien sunk down behind me, his arm wrapping around my torso to pet Abraham Lincoln. Now I had heat in front of me, and heat from behind. My body sighed as the cold finally started to seep out of my bones.

Bastien shifted a few times, trying to get comfortable. "Sorry. I'm afraid to take off my jeans. Lane's speech scared me a little."

"Smart guy." I giggled softly. "She's the best."

Hamish wouldn't tolerate being left out of the reunion, so he dove down under my chin and curled himself into a ball that rested over my heart, his tail draped on his teddy bear. I heard Abraham Lincoln's contended coos of *"Mommy"* and *"Daddy"* and *"home"*.

I sighed, letting much of my anxiety go as a wave of exhaustion swept over me. "That's right, baby. Mommy and Daddy are home now."

Bastien's intake of breath told me he hadn't been expecting me to settle so easily into a rhythm with him. He lowered the edge of my robe so he could kiss my naked shoulder, giving us both the shivers. "You're my home," he promised, "and I'm your safe place. I've got you."

The gentle lantern light barely reached us, only highlighting small details as I turned my head to glance over my shoulder at his striking features. I knew I needed to sleep, but he was just too stunning to look away from. Watching him promise me things I'd never thought him capable of, and looking at me like… well, no one had ever looked at me like that. "Thank you for rescuing me. Thanks for not giving up on me."

"Never," he vowed. His hand wound around my stomach, tracing my ribs and pressing his palm under my breast so my torso elongated. "I love you, Daisy."

9

INMUNIS

$\mathcal{M}$y imagination wasn't a safe place, but Bastien's arms were. My dreams were haunted, plunging me back down into the well. Carcasses rained down on my head, but they weren't just quails. Demi's whole dead body was thrown down on me again and again. It was a long night for all involved. Bastien woke me any time my fear grew palpable, and didn't pull away when I wailed out Demi's name. Lane's room wasn't too far, and each time she heard me cry out, she was in our room in the next minute, coaxing water into me and reminding me that I was safe, and that we were together again.

It was two days and two nights of my grieving the loss of a man who had been kind to me when the world was mean and ugly. The worst part of that was that I cried for Demi in Bastien's arms. Most puzzling was that Bastien was unselfish every step of the way as my heart bled for Demi.

"I know, Daisy. Let it out."

I didn't deserve how kind Bastien was being through all of it. As often as I woke, he held me gently, soothing me back to sleep. Not once did he leave. Not once did he get frustrated with my lack of progress. He loved me, and it turns out, Bastien's love was the kind that was learning how to heal the brokenness around him. He was a builder, though everyone labeled him a destroyer, what with his Untouchable title.

When Draper came in with breakfast, Bastien kissed my lips in front of my sort of brother. The corner of his mouth turned up at the sight of my blush. "I'm going to do a check of the grounds. I need to make sure Demi's been taken back to his home, and I also want to put in a few extra security measures for you and Lane." He pulled back the curtains to expose my bed to the room, and then sat down in a nearby chair to shove on his socks and boots.

Draper cuffed Bastien's shoulder when Bastien hesitated at the door, looking like he didn't want to leave. "I'll stay with her until you come back. Go on."

Bastien still looked uncertain. "I'll send Mad up. He'll keep you safe, Rosie."

"Take Abraham Lincoln. People will listen more if you have a tamed bear backing you up." I kissed my teddy bear and sent him off with Bastien. Hamish promised to hold down the fort with me, even going so far as to salute Bastien.

Draper rolled his eyes when Bastien left, as if Bastien was being overbearing. The truth of it was that the second Bastien left the room, I felt uneasy, exposed and worried. "Is it safe for him to leave the mansion?"

Draper's upper lip twitched in amusement. "I think he'll be just fine. Lane's land was reserved for shepherds and farmers until the famine chased most of them away. They've come back in the past couple weeks, though, ready to take their land back."

"So Lane has like, people and land and all that to rule over?"

Draper handed me a bowl of strawberry-scented porridge, watching me carefully for signs of duress. My hands got the occasional tremors still, and the effort that it was for my joints to bend to hold a simple spoon made me feel like a wuss. It had been a couple days since my rescue. I mean, shouldn't I be doing jumping jacks already? Draper studied my movements as he spoke. "She has many subjects. Even more now, thanks to you and the Untouchables. People from all over are still coming in, claiming old plots and making them their own. It's kind of amazing to see. We merged with Province 4, and that's been going over smoothly."

Madigan let himself into my room and pulled up a chair between me and the door. "Bastien said I was to sit with ye until he came back. Are ye well?"

I didn't know how to answer that, so I simply blinked at him. I was turning back into Remedial Rosie, I guess, unable to answer simple questions.

Madigan lowered his chin, seeming to understand that sometimes there weren't words. "Aye. You're safe now. Ye should get my ring sized so it's actually on your finger."

I touched the chain around my neck that had Mad's engagement ring fashioned on it. "I don't think Meara would be okay with me doing that. She gave it to you, and probably wouldn't like me making changes to it. One day I'll give it back to you, and it'll be like this never happened."

Mad met my eyes, seeing with gratitude the respect I paid his deceased wife. "Aye. Link's out screening the people who want to live close to the mansion. He's sending the troublemakers toward the center of the province to give ye and Lane a safer home."

I pulled back, confused. "That's awful nice of him. Did Lane ask him to do that?"

"She didn't have to. It needed to be done, so Link's taking care of it."

Hamish laid out on my lap, belly-up so he could get a good tummy rub from me. I set the bowl down on the bed, and stroked his torso with two fingers while I thought over Mad's words. "Huh. I didn't realize he cared so much about Province 9. You guys aren't even from Avalon. That's super way nice of him."

Madigan shook his head. "You're Bastien's lady, and my

fiancée. The Brotherhood takes care of our own. Your job is just larger because of who your family is." He waved his hand like what he'd said wasn't a big deal. "You'll see. Once ye get marked, people will meet ye and see tha you're one of us. If ye ever travel to Éireland, you'll have protection."

"Marked?" I questioned as I reached for the cup on my nightstand. My fingers were trembling, and I worried that I might spill the water, but I was too stubborn to ask for help. I'd needed help escaping the well – fine. I didn't want to be so weak that I required assistance just to drink a few swallows of water.

Draper didn't say a word when his hand coiled around mine, steadying my grip on the cup. My pride took a serious hit when my brother pressed the cup to my lips. He remained quiet, meeting my eye every now and then as he listened to the customs of the tightly-knit group of Untouchables. I could tell he had opinions, but he was keeping them to himself for now. He set the cup back down on the table, and then picked up my bowl, spooning out a bit of oatmeal, as if I was too weak to even feed myself. When I took the bowl from him, I nearly dropped it all over Hamish. My squirrel did me a solid and coiled himself in a circle on my lap, beckoning me to rest my bowl atop his body. My squirrel could hold a bowl steadier than I could. It was a tough blow, but somehow less humiliating than letting my big brother feed me, as he'd done when I was a baby.

Madigan stood and moved closer to me, reaching up his meaty hand to pull down the collar of his black shirt. The neck tattoo was displayed proudly, along with the matching wrist tattoo he held out for me to see. There was some word written across a tight fist on both tattoos. I noticed a small raven inked below it that Bastien didn't have. "What's the bird mean?"

"'*Inmunis*' means 'Untouchable', and the bird's for my Meara when we were wed. It shows people tha I'm watching over someone, and tha she's under my protection. My freedoms extend to her."

43

I wanted to trace the bird's wings, but I knew how much Madigan loathed being touched. "That's really beautiful." My eyes widened in understanding. "Wait, I'm supposed to get that on me?"

Draper spoke up at this. "No, Rosie. You don't have to."

Madigan eyed Draper. "Aye. When you're ready. If you're Bastien's lady and my fiancée, ye belong with the Untouchables. The sooner everyone sees ye marked, the less Bastien will have to worry about ye getting messed with by Morgan's soldiers."

I shivered when I recalled the red-haired soldier who'd grabbed me in the hallway at Morgan's mansion. "I don't think that'll work on me. I don't look like you, Link and Bastien. I can do some damage, but I'm not a trained fighter or anything. Being a princess didn't keep me safe. I don't think the mark will change things as much as you're hoping."

"Aye, but it will. People fear Morgan for her ruthlessness and her magic, but they revere us. The soldiers wish they could be us. It's a fraternity thing. We fought alongside them, went through training together. They tried to murder each of us when we decided we'd had enough, and they carry that weight with them. Turning on their brothers in arms. The soldiers respect the code of the Untouchables above all other orders."

I wanted to believe in the safety Mad was promising me, but there were a few too many too-good-to-be-true gems on the ring. Though my robe was cinched closed, I tightened it around me and backed into my pillow that had been propped up against the headboard. I saw red-hair guy in my imagination and felt his eyes combing my body, his sweaty breath filling my nose. "It'll keep them from putting their hands all over me? Like, they'll see that mark, and I won't get cornered anymore?"

Madigan and Draper both stiffened. "Who put their hands on ye?"

I swallowed hard. "One of the soldiers in Morgan's mansion. He was pissed I told on his buddy. They wanted to lock me in the stocks and, you know, do stuff." I tugged the comforter up over my chest. "Then there's the dudes who took my clothes before putting me in the well."

Madigan's jaw was tight. "Do ye know their names?"

I shook my head. "It doesn't matter now. It's done. But that *inmunis* mark will keep it from happening again? Like, no one's going to molest me or try and take my clothes anymore if I have it?"

"Aye. And don't be worrying about the ones who took your clothes. I'll find them easy enough."

A solitary tear formed in the corner of my eye, and in the back of my mind I was relieved to know I was on my way to getting hydrated again. "I know you don't like to be touched, but just so you know, I'm hugging you in my mind. I don't need the vengeance stuff, just the mark. Just something to keep the hands off me."

Madigan nodded once. "As soon as you're better, I'll bring someone in to mark ye."

I stroked Hamish's tail idly. "How many other girls are there in the Brotherhood?"

"Katya's the only one alive," he stated flatly. "My Meara's gone on into the mist now, but she still counts." Then he shrugged at my questioning stare. "We don't settle down easily. Not exactly a loveable bunch."

Draper warned me with a quiet, "That means you should take some time to think about this first, Rosie. Talk it over with Lane."

I met Draper's eyes that were saying more than his mouth was, and nodded. "Okay."

Mad waved his hand to clear it of our caution. "It's done. I'll not have my fiancée unprotected."

I stared up at him, mouth agape. "You really care that much about me?"

Mad shook his head, as if "care" was a weird cuss word I shouldn't be using. "It's strategy, Rosie. It sends a message of weakness to Faîte if one of our women gets messed with. It's bad enough they all saw ye when ye came out of the well. I don't want anyone thinking it's grand to go taking swings at our women."

I fed myself a few more bites of my porridge, the passing minutes giving the room enough time for the tension to die down.

"Is it still raining?" Draper asked.

Madigan moved to the window, pulled back the beige curtain that had emerald swirly embellishments scattered across the fabric. He pushed open the glass, revealing gray clouds and fat raindrops pelting the earth. "Aye. Hasn't stopped for weeks. Link and I were working with the soldiers to put sandbags around the mansion to keep the foundation sturdy."

"Is this normal for Avalon? Raining for weeks?"

Mad looked over his shoulder at me. "No. If anything, it's the other way around. Not enough water for the plants to grow as they should. Hope it lets up so people can see the plots of land they're reclaiming."

"Huh?"

Draper filled in the gaps for me. "People are catching wind of the outlying provinces merging and coming back to life, so they're migrating back to their homes. Add Morgan throwing the Lost Princess into a well, and no one wants to be near her castle. Province 9 is coming back, but other provinces that Morgan absorbed are leaving her, too. They're all coming here to start over. Now Lane's got almost as much land as Morgan, and probably as many jewels to sustain us."

"I guess that's some silver lining in all of it. At least Morgan got exposed for the mom-ster she is. Good to know Avalon has a heart." I dropped my spoon twice in the bowl before I managed another bite.

"Some of them do, yes, but it's not that. They're scared to be near her castle because you're Master Kerdik's..." He cast around for the right word. "Special friend?"

I scoffed, fingering my ring. "Kerdik doesn't have any friends."

"Well, whatever you are to him, you both made it clear at the coronation that he would move Avalon into the ocean if you asked him to. Morgan threw you into a well, and they all saw how broken down you looked coming out of there. Much of Avalon doesn't want to be within a thousand miles of Morgan when Master Kerdik comes to avenge you."

I pursed my lips, doing my best to keep my attitude to myself. "The hype will die down when they see that Kerdik isn't coming." I gave up when my hand shook too noticeably for me to work another bite of porridge into my mouth. My mind kept going in and out of focus, letting me listen to bits of conversation before my battery started to power down. It wasn't sleepiness that weighted my smile into nonexistence, it was an utter break from reality, though I was desperate to cling to the small bits I could grasp.

"Draper?" I said, only realizing after I opened my mouth that I'd interrupted the two of them talking about… something.

Draper turned back to face me, his frown of concern fixed firmly on his features. "Yeah, Rosie?"

I couldn't remember what I was going to say, only that I was glad he was around. I wasn't sure how to tell him I'd always wanted a big brother, and that I was so glad he was it. I wanted to tell him how happy I was that he got to have Lane as a mom. She was the best mom in the world, and the universe was better off giving her another lost soul to watch over. I didn't know how to say all of that, though, so I mumbled a confused, "I love you, man."

Draper blinked twice, no doubt just as perplexed as I was that I'd interrupted the conversation to tell him what was perfectly obvious. He rested his hand atop mine, and didn't give off any impression that I was an inconvenience for him. "Thanks, pumpkin. I love you, too. Always tell me that any time. Four in the morning, you wake up and it dawns on you that you love me? You come find me, and tell me exactly that."

I wanted to tell him everything, but my mind drifted off again, my eyes moving to the window to stare out listlessly into the province that was now my new home.

10

BROTHER, COUSIN, UNCLE, DAD

I ate until I couldn't stomach another bite, and then Draper sent out for some juice to perk me up. The fresh-squeezed orange juice did the trick, helping me to stay in a conversation for at least a few minutes before my mind wandered.

Draper and I sat in my bed and shot the breeze for a while. Madigan remained at the window, keeping himself on the outside of our conversation so he didn't have to pretend like he enjoyed being around other people. "So, you've got a mom again. Prince Draper, in the flesh. How's that feel?"

"Like every day is my birthday. Like no matter how many messed up things happened along the way, Faîte somehow landed me somewhere good. Man, I bet old Duke Henri's boiling right about now. He hates seeing me at all, much less when I'm happy. With all those people Damond brought over from Province 2?" Draper shook his head with raised eyebrows. "I feel sorry for Gwen being stuck there with him."

"Not to be a jerk, but I don't so much like your dad. That he was in bed with Morgan, forming plans and whatnot? It's gross."

Draper set down the empty bowl, his face twisting. "He wasn't in bed with Morgan. He wouldn't risk having an heir with her. She didn't care for you from the start."

I flinched at the blunt words. "I didn't mean it like that. It's a saying in Common that means they're in cahoots."

"Oh. That makes more sense. I can't imagine what he was thinking, putting his token in with your other suitors."

I'd almost forgotten Madigan was there until he spoke, still staring out the window. "He wanted to put a baby in Rosie."

I buried my face in my hands, wishing that little phrase wasn't so common in Avalon. So caveman-ish. It made me blanch every time.

Draper let out a bray of disgust and slunk off the bed onto his knees, like he was melting or something. "Gross! Why would you say something like that?"

"Seriously, Mad. Say Uncle Henri wanted to 'knock me up,' like a gentleman."

Draper covered his face with his hands and let out a tortured howl. "Oh, you're making it worse, Rosie! That's disgusting!"

Mad was unperturbed at Draper's theatrics. "Duke Henri wants to align his kingdom with Morgan's. Before the missing jewels were found, tha was the only way to guarantee his people's safety. Ye should know tha."

Draper looked like he was going to be sick. He reached up and gripped my fingers. "On behalf of my father, I'm sorry, Rosie. You're not a pawn. You're a person. What he did... unforgiveable." Then Draper stood up and crossed the room, gripping Madigan in a tight hug that the gruff Untouchable pushed off one whole second into the embrace. The simple force moved Draper much farther than he'd been anticipating, but then again, Madigan was a big dude.

"What was tha for?" Madigan looked offended at the unwelcome affection.

Draper was unbothered that Madigan had shoved him away. "You stepped in so Rosie didn't get handed over to Duke Henri.

Even though you didn't love her, you still saved her. She's my sister, and you saved her from being raped by him." I could almost see the bile rising in him as he choked out the words. He held his stomach as he made his way back to me. This time when he climbed into the bed, he sat next to me, his arm around my shoulders with a note of protection.

"Hug me again, and I'll take it all back," Madigan threatened. "She needs more juice. This is the longest she's been able to pay attention to a conversation in a while. Tha's the ticket."

Draper refilled the cup with more orange juice from the pitcher and molded my fingers around the glass, so I could drink as much as my stomach could take.

I grimaced when I recalled the day Madigan fake proposed to me, how scared I'd been when it looked like I might be married off to Uncle Henri. I pinched the bridge of my nose, my chin lowering to my chest. "Mad, I'm sorry. At the coronation, I got a little carried away. I know you don't like to be touched, and I was all over you. Part of me was trying to sell it for the crowd, but the other part of me was just plain terrified, and clinging to you so I didn't fall to pieces up there. I wasn't thinking about you, only my fear in all of it. Totally not cool of me."

Mad turned back to the window to watch the rain. "You've no need to apologize for tha, Rosie. We had to sell it."

A knock interrupted us, announcing Remy come to check on me with Lane. Lane looked like she had too much on her mind, her eyebrows bunched and her lips taut with tension. "How are you feeling, hun?"

I echoed her words back onto her. "How are *you* feeling, hun?"

Lane's frown broke into a softer expression. "It's been a long one." She sat down on my other side, the three of us in the bed and snuggled like one weird, pieced-together family. It felt about nine kinds of wonderful. "Even though you're here, I've been in worry mode for so long; I don't think it's dawned on me yet that you're safe. I'm sure I woke you up too many times last night, coming to check on you."

"Not at all," I lied.

"Breaks my heart when you cry, kid. How's my girl looking, Remy?"

"Well, if I could get to her, then maybe I could tell you." Remy had to reach over Draper to examine me, but my brother made no attempt to move.

Something pinged in my brain, so I turned my head to look up curiously at Draper. "Are you my brother or my cousin?"

Draper leaned his cheek to my temple. Some might find his closeness and Lane's fawning claustrophobic – those people have clearly never been in the bottom of a well before. "I guess that depends on who Lane is to you – your aunt or your mom."

I answered without hesitation. "Lane's my mom." Though she'd fit both roles so seamlessly, I always knew who she was in my heart.

Draper's grin spread wide across his face, and beamed itself onto Lane's, as well. "Then I guess that makes me your brother." He squeezed me with a gentle pressure that made my emotions rise in my throat. "Wouldn't have it any other way."

Lane shooed the guys out once she realized Remy needed to check my infected cuts. She stayed with me the entire time, holding my hand, brushing my hair and trying unsuccessfully to pry out every last tidbit she could extract from me. "You need to talk about it, babe."

"I really, really don't. Especially not to you."

Lane flinched like I'd slapped her. "Why would you say that? You've always been able to tell me anything. Did I do something?"

"Of course not. It was all just pretty awful, and you don't need those thoughts in your head. I love you, and I know it hurts you to think about bad things happening to me."

"You don't need to protect me, Ro. That's the thing about being a parent. It's *my* job to protect *you*."

I couldn't bring myself to meet her eyes. "It's too late. Damage is done."

Lane swallowed whatever retort she wanted to make. Remy deemed me on the mend, and instructed me to keep up with lots of water and steady, small portioned food. My muscles were still a little shot and unstable from being cramped in the tub for over two weeks, so a massage was recommended, as well. "Best doctor ever, Remy. Seriously. No shots and a massage script? You're the best."

Remy held my hand to his heart before leaving, and I realized how out of practice I was at speaking to animals and healers. The simple exchanges between Remy and I during my examination, coupled with Hamish's idle chatter were starting to wear me out, and it was barely noon.

Lane rubbed my arms, hands, legs and feet for me, trying to force circulation. Hamish did his part by pounding his tiny fists into the meat of my shoulder. It wasn't all that effective, but I made sure to give him plenty of "that feels great" noises to boost his ego. He tired of the task quickly, and gave me a snuggle before scampering off after Remy, whom he'd taken a liking to. He told me that the two often went searching in the woods together – Remy for herbs, and Hamish for nuts.

"This robe isn't warm enough. Let's pick out something for you to wear." Lane moved over to the corner of the large room, to the beige wood wardrobe with emerald borders. When she threw open the doors, there were dresses on one side and jeans and t-shirts on the other.

My eyes widened. "I get to wear jeans?"

Lane smirked at me over her shoulder. "You get to wear whatever you like. You're a princess, Ro. You could wear a shoe on your head, and the next day everyone would be wearing one, like it was the height of fashion."

I started singing to her, "'Did you ever know that you're my hero?'"

Lane whirled around, her simple emerald dress belling out at the half-twirl. "You made a joke. You sang! Oh, baby. Sometimes a mother needs to hear her girl sing. Best sound in the world."

I yodeled a little off-key just to make her laugh. Though truly, I wasn't sure the difference between yodeling on-key and off.

She held up different matches, and we finally landed on jeans and a form-fitting tank top, with a sheer purple tunic over top. It would look cute, even in Common. I quickly realized I couldn't stand when I tried the grand feat and fell in a heap on the wood floor. My knees jarred worse than when I played two soccer matches in one afternoon. My bones felt out of place, like a marionette puppet who hadn't been given the proper strings.

Lane picked me up as she choked back her tears, and set me on the bed. "Slower, kid. We've got to take everything slower than you're used to. This is the time to lay back and be glad we have servants here."

I shook my head, resolute. "I don't need men to help me get dressed. Bastien's fine, but no one else."

Lane quirked her eyebrow at me, but then threw her head back when realization dawned on her. "Right. Because Morgan only employs male servants. We don't do that here. It's a mix. And I don't think Bastien would be cool if I had some dude in here buttoning you up." She was hinting, but she didn't need to. She could always just ask; I had no need to hide anything from her. "So, you and Bastien," she said as she helped me into the clean clothes, so I didn't have to risk the hazards that came with standing.

She was so bad at this, mainly, I realized, because this was uncharted territory for us both. I'd never had a boyfriend in Common, much less a man who I was living with. Granted, we were under her roof, but still. This wasn't exactly Judah we were talking about. "Me and Bastien. Still pretty new. We've been on opposite pages too many times before. Now we're finally on the same one. Hopefully it lasts."

"Oh, it'll last." Her eyes darted to the door, and she lowered her voice conspiratorially. "He asked my permission to mark you with the Untouchable tattoo."

"Oh, right. Mad mentioned something about that earlier. Care to weigh in? Draper didn't seem all that thrilled."

Lane's face broke out into a goofy grin. "Well, Draper hasn't forgiven Bastien for running out on you after your first kiss. He's your brother, kid. It's his right to make every guy miserable who wants to catch your eye. Keeps Bastien on his toes."

I let out a soundless snort at Bastien being bossed around. "You cool if I get the 'don't mess with me' tattoo?"

Once I was dressed, she started braiding my hair, parting down the middle and doing two French braids on either side of my head, the same she used to do for game days when I lived back home. "It's more permanent than a wedding ring, so I really don't feel like I should weigh in on that." She took a few seconds of silence to twist a ribbon around one of my braids. "There's magic in the ink they use, you know."

"Oh? Will it turn me into an enchanted fairy?"

"You're already Fae, so damage is done there, babe. No, it's a tracking ink. Not quite as powerful as your Compass ability, but pretty useful. It's how they keep tabs on each other. It's hard for them to live alone, to feel safe after all they've been through. Knowing they've got their brothers to look for them if they go missing is a little thing that puts them all at ease. Cushions the blow of living alone, which most of them do."

"They'll always be able to find me?"

"It's got its perks and drawbacks. Being found is a good thing if you love the man who's looking for you. It can be a dangerous thing if he turns out not to be a great guy. The ink never fades, and it connects you to the entire Brotherhood. They treat their women like gold once they're inked, that's for sure. It's just..." She sighed and started rubbing lotion into my arms after she finished with my hair. "They're a hard bunch to love, Ro. Been through a lot, all of them. Think it through, is all."

"You're fine either way?"

"Fine with you permanently tying yourself to Bastien? That might be a stretch, but I can accept it. You're an adult, and I'm in your corner. I trust your judgment. We have to let each other make the big decisions. Much like the conversation we're about to have concerning Reyn."

My eyes widened as she steadied herself by blowing out her breath. She stared at her knees and bobbed her head to a tune only she knew as she psyched herself up. It was the same nervous tick she'd gotten when she'd broken the business of the birds and the bees to me. That was one long night.

I put on my best parental tone to scold her. "Don't tell me there's been kissing under this roof, young lady."

Lane snorted, grateful I'd made a joke. "There may have been a few stolen kisses, I admit."

"For shame."

Lane kept her eyes on her knees. "This is big, Ro. We've never had this conversation before, so brace yourself."

I raised my arms in a defensive karate move that only the coolest Power Rangers could pull off. "Braced. Hit me with it."

"I'm in love. Like, deep over the moon, too many stars in my eyes kind of love. *Princess Bride* kind of love." She cleared her throat three times before continuing. "I'm going to marry him. Like, in a church and everything. No one knows yet. Not even Bastien. I wanted you to be the first to hear it." She closed her eyes against my response. "Say something, Ro."

My mouth hung open in shock. "Um, that's crazy awesome! You're really getting married? He's your Sweet Wesley?" The farm boy from *Princess Bride* was our shared dream hunk.

Lane's head jerked up in my direction. "You don't mind? You're not mad?"

"I'm a little mad at Morgan for keeping me holed up in the

well all this time, so most of my rage is directed at her for the moment. But no, why would I be mad? I like Reyn. He's great."

Relief lit her face, lighting her up as if she'd swallowed the sun. "You have no idea how worried we've been to tell you. Everyone else can go screw themselves if they don't like it, but you? You're the one person I need on my side."

My hand was tired, but it managed to find hers. "I'm always on your side. If this is what you want, go for it."

Lane wrapped me in a tight hug that squeezed my aching ribs. "I love you all the red Skittles in the universe."

"I love you all the double-stuffed Oreos in all the galaxies."

Lane and I giggled together, holding on as long as we could before questions started bubbling up in me. "Am I supposed to call him 'Dad' or 'Uncle Reyn'?"

Lane belted out a belly laugh that did us both some good. "Can I please, please be there when you ask him that?"

"You got it, sister." I fiddled with the hem of my gauzy lavender tunic, searching for the right words. "Can I ask you something?"

"Anything and everything."

"Reyn seems a little... under the weather. Like, all the time under the weather. I feel like if he's going to be my uncle-dad, I should know what's going on there."

Lane sobered, threading my fingers through hers. "Reyn's sick. He's got something called *mortel magique* sickness. It's a disease that happens when you share too much of your magic. He used a large part of it to preserve his sister's body, so she didn't die when she was beaten and left for dead. His magic gave Rachelle's body time to heal, though in the end, it didn't bring her back. It's sort of like living with a severe vitamin deficiency. Every time Reyn used his magic, he got weaker. He looked so normal in Common because earth doesn't require magic for simple things like, say, staying healthy. When his sister passed away, the portion he gave Rachelle was supposed to return to him."

"Why hasn't it come back to him, then?"

"It is, it's just taking longer than usual because he's stubborn."

"You ended up with a stubborn guy? I don't believe it. I guess opposites do attract," I teased.

"Ha, ha. He needs a few months of not using a ton of magic to get better, and living down here isn't exactly helpful with that. People in Avalon use magic without realizing it." She pressed her thumb on each of my fingernails, studying them as she went down the row. I was grateful Remy had gotten all of the fungus off me. Lane bit her lower lip before she spoke. "I want to take him to Common when this is all over, where he can't use his magic. He could really heal up there. Plus, you know this isn't my bag." She motioned around the large room that was clearly nicer than anything we'd ever had. "You could come with us, or you could stay here."

My body was achy and stiff, but I managed to fling my arms around Lane and squeeze her with my pitiful force. "Get me out of here!"

"Oh, thank God. I was hoping you'd say that. We've got some things to deal with before we can take off, but it's all in the works. I'm hoping in the next six months or so, we're splitsville."

I hadn't heard the door open, but I heard Bastien's intake of breath. "I'm going with her," he decreed. I turned around to take in his soaking form. He was head to toe drenched in rainwater and mud, but he'd never looked more handsome. Though, I'd had that thought about him at least a dozen times, so maybe I was a poor judge of it all. Bastien held my gaze. "Avalon or Common, I don't care. I'm staying with Rosie."

Lane kissed my temple before she stood, rolling her shoulders back to face Bastien. "That's up to Rosie, but you'll get no complaints from me. Any of you Lost Boys are welcome to come with us, so long as you can fall in line and leave your

Untouchable status in Faîte. Might be a good fresh start for you all."

Bastien waved off that stipulation, as if it was a done deal. "How are you feeling?"

I wasn't sure how to answer that. "Like a dork for being so useless?"

Lane tsked me. "You're neither useless nor a dork. You and I will talk more later. I've got to go be a duchess and pretend like I'm some big deal." She blew it off like it was all a joke, but she paused when she reached Bastien. "How goes the sand wall?"

"Almost done. Link loves a challenge. We've been helping people sort out where they should move, keeping the loyalists closer to the castle, and the people who are just here because they're mad at Morgan in the middle, with the shepherds and larger farmers in the back where there's more unclaimed land."

"Very good. And no sign of Morgan retaliating?"

"Not yet, but we're still rallying the men, just in case. I'm guessing she won't try anything largescale in weather like this. She likes to make a show of her battles, and she won't get the awe and shock she needs in rain like this."

It was strange watching Lane be a duchess. She was sharp with her tone when she needed to be, but not an inch more than what was required to get the job done. "That's good. Thank you, Son."

Bastien whipped his head to gawk at her, his eyes asking hers silent questions. She merely smiled and bowed her head in answer, but Bastien needed verbal confirmation. "You approve, then?"

"I approve up until the second Rosie tells me not to. Then it's your testicles in a little glass jar in my trophy case. It's her you should worry about pleasing. I merely follow my daughter's smile. The second it fades in your presence," she clucked her tongue in threat and moved her head from side to side. "Time for your A-game, boy."

11

THE PERFECT THING TO SAY

*B*astien didn't bother with modesty once it was just the two of us, since he'd seen every inch of me too many times already. He stripped down to his black cotton boxer briefs just to give me a nice show before he washed himself in the tub behind the partition. After he dried off and dressed, he latched the door and settled into the sheets next to me the second he caught my yawn.

"I'm sorry I'm being boring. I want to be helping you all out there to get everyone sorted, but I'm totally useless. Can't even really walk yet," I admitted, ashamed.

He broke a roll in half and handed me my piece. "Slowly," he warned. "Remy's worried about you not getting enough food, and then worried your stomach can't handle much. Totally vetoed my idea to shove lard down your throat. But I guess you can't exactly afford to go puking up what little's managed to stay in you."

I finished chewing and snuggled up to him, my head resting over his outstretched arm. "Bastien, do you think…" I wanted to ask him a million questions, but his lips were too plump and inviting. I interrupted my own thought so I could kiss him, sucking on his lower lip to bring him closer, though it was still never close enough. He hadn't shaved in weeks, and the usual stubble had turned into half an inch of actual growth. It made him look rugged, like a sexy lumberjack, wrapped in the flannel that always smelled like comfort and pure him.

Our kiss took on a mind of its own, transforming my weak and tired body into a voracious makeout machine. Our limbs and lips tangled with each other, until Bastien rolled over atop me, and froze. He quickly retreated, getting clear off the bed as he ran his hands through his hair to get a grip on himself. "Sorry. I shouldn't have been on top of you like that."

"Yes, you should. I'd like a double order of exactly that. Get back here."

Bastien took a step toward me, longing burning in his eyes, but he stopped himself. "I'm afraid I'll crack your ribs or something. You're so thin now. I want you, but I don't want to be the one who breaks you more."

I let out an exasperated sigh. "Darn you and your selfless reasons." I yawned for the millionth time and stretched my arms over my head.

Bastien tentatively approached the bed, as if sudden movements might cause either one of us to pounce on the other. He handed me the other half of the roll after smearing too much butter on it. "Eat, and then take a nap. I'll lay down with you for a few before I go back out to help the guys."

"Give me another day of being lazy, and I'll be out there with you."

"No, you won't. It's moving sandbags that are heavier than you, and building retaining walls. Then showing rain-soaked families to abandoned houses around the province so they don't have to build new ones in this weather."

"I can do that. I should probably meet the people who left their homes to follow Lane."

"You should probably rest. We've got this. Link and Mad are

great at this kind of stuff, and I've got Roland and a few of his guys showing people where to settle in."

I wanted to argue further, but knew he was probably right. "Could you start thinking of a job for me to do? I don't want to be the useless princess who lays around all day in her mansion. They'll burn me at the stake."

Bastien knelt on the bed next to me, leaning over with a fist on either side of my head. He steadied himself so he could capture my lips without crushing me. "I love when you say stuff like that. I'll find you a job once Remy says you're well enough to help out. Until then, you stay here. I'll keep Hamish out of the room, too. Otherwise you'll be sleeping all day and night."

I gazed up at him, confused and pleased at the unfettered adoration he beamed down at me. "You're nicer now. All the fighting we were doing before – what was it about?"

Bastien kissed my lips again, this time with the measured pace of an unhurried seduction. "Pure denial and stupidity. We're done with that, though. I'm in this, Daisy. I want to be with you for all of it, even when you fight with me."

"What changed?"

"Nothing changed. I just stopped resisting what was there all along. Saw what life without you was like, and decided it wasn't for me. I'm done being without you. It feels right, being together. Being separated? It killed me, Rosie. Killed me."

I ran my fingers through his short beard along the edges of his cheeks. "Well, we can't have that. How sure about us are you? I mean, we've been through kind of a lot."

Bastien's eyes searched mine, and I could tell he was debating how brave he wanted to be with his answer. "So sure that I flagged down a man with the tools to mark you when he came through to settle in Lane's province. You don't have to, you know. I just thought it would be good for everyone to know you belong with the Brotherhood."

I gulped. "I've only met Link and Madigan. You sure the

others want me in their group? I don't want to piss off your friends."

Bastien studied my face with barely contained hope that I hadn't shut down the idea altogether. "Each of us has the right to mark someone. They don't have to meet you at all to respect the code. One of them never met Meara, but that doesn't matter."

I fiddled with his flannel shirt. "How can you be so sure about us? I was just with another dude, like, less than a month ago." That was probably the wrong thing to say, but I didn't want to skirt around anything.

Bastien pecked my lips. "I've tried being without you, and it didn't take. I told you, we're done being apart."

"What if I decide not to take the mark?"

He shrugged, as if I hadn't just hurt his feelings. "That changes nothing. The mark's for your protection. I'll still want to stay with you, no matter what."

I pulled him closer when I tugged on the edge of his shirt. "What if I decide to wait for a while and think about it?"

"Take as long as you need."

I hissed. "Stop saying all the right things. It's too sexy."

The corner of Bastien's mouth lifted in that self-assured way I missed. "Can't help it." He brushed his hand down my face from my forehead to my chin, so I closed my eyes. Then he gave me a heart flutter when he pressed a kiss to both my closed eyelids. "Get some sleep, and dream about me."

"Will you be naked in my dream?"

A low growl snared in Bastien's throat as he buried his nose in my neck to inhale the scent of me, like I was the best kind of drug. "I could be naked right now, if you like." Then he pulled back, frowning at me. "Lane's no doubt plotting my murder as we speak. Though it might just be worth the risk if I could make all your dreams come true."

I reached up and clumsily twined my fingers through his.

"When you have to go after I pass out, could you leave your shirt or something that smells like you?"

He sunk down atop the covers, rolling me on my side so he could spoon me. "How about I stay in here with you. Don't worry about me leaving. I know you get nervous sleeping alone. I won't go until you wake up again."

It was the perfect thing to say, and I couldn't help myself from sneaking one more kiss from his willing and tempting lips.

12

WUSS, LOVELY AND SWEETHEART

$\mathcal{I}$t was another day before I could walk around, and another few days before I didn't need someone with me to help with every little thing. When Remy finally gave me the all-clear, I was able to help the guys outside. Granted, I don't think I was all that helpful, but I was trying. I didn't have all my strength back, and I didn't know the territory at all, so I mostly just helped the guys move sandbags to reinforce the retaining wall around the mansion. The first day when I was helping, no sooner would I pick up a sandbag, then one of the men would take it from me. The chivalry was sweet, but it rendered me useless, which wasn't a good label for me.

The rain hadn't relented the entire time, going on almost a month of nonstop torrential downpour. The clouds had opened the day before I was thrown in the well, and hadn't relented since. It made progress slow, and spirits dampened (dampened, get it? I'm funny).

A few days later, I finally found my calling. I noticed the absence of children running around, and commented on the oddity to Lane over breakfast. "It's the rain, Ro. What else can they do, but stay inside and wait out the weather?"

I perked up at this. "Could I watch them here?"

Lane quirked her eyebrow at me over her cup of tea. "Here?" She wore simple emerald dresses these days, but still looked regal. Then again, I would imagine anyone with servants tending to their every need might look royal. The dining room for royals consisted of a long mahogany table that could easily seat fourteen, though it was just the two of us that morning. There were dainty green and gold leaves painted on the walls in sporadic dots that made the room feel quirky, yet elegant – just like Lane.

"In the mansion. I mean, your staff's only a dozen or so people, plus all of us staying here. We've got a whole floor that's basically unused down below." I tapped my foot to the ground, indicating the basement.

Lane gaped at me, as if praying she'd heard me wrong. "You mean the dungeon? You want to bring children in here to play in the dungeon?"

"You got any bad guys down there?"

"No, but still. Is that weird? 'Hey parents, bring your kids over and let them lock themselves in my dungeon.'"

"Better than locking themselves in a single-room hut for weeks on end. They're probably going bananas all cooped up. I could keep them busy."

Lane mulled this over. "I'm sure everything they're bringing into their homes is filthy with mud. I could offer for the children to bring their household's linens and whatnot to the mansion to wash. I could provide the soap, and while the clothes are drying, they could play together in the dungeon."

"You know, if you call it a dungeon, people aren't going to want to play there. It's a basement." I tapped my forehead sagely. "It's all about the marketing."

Lane held up her hand in surrender. "Okay. If you can watch the kids and make sure no one actually locks themselves in a cell, that works for me. It's got to be cleaned, though."

"Thank God. I've been looking for a chore anyone will actually let me do. I'm totally useless out there with the retaining wall. As soon as I pick up a bag, someone takes it from me. What the crap? They think I'm useless."

Lane smirked into her cup. "You can thank Bastien for that little maneuver. Before anyone joins them to help, he pulls them aside and makes sure they know you're not to do any real work."

I frowned. "Are you serious? I can help! Why's he treating me like I'm useless?"

"He's treating you how an Untouchable treats his woman. They're revered, Ro. About as much as a princess, if you can imagine. Only instead of only Avalon, the entire world of Faîte bows to you." She studied my reaction as she bit into her scone. "It's heady, but comes with a certain amount of letting Bastien be good to you in the only way he knows how. This is his culture. Some things you two can compromise on, but some are just who he is. You've gotta decide what you can be cool with."

"Well, he doesn't need to send the message that I'm a wuss."

Reyn chose that moment to venture out of bed. He was similarly stir-crazy, but less ready to conquer the world just yet. He paused by my chair to kiss the top of my head. "Bastien doesn't think you're a wuss; he thinks you're valuable. Big difference." When his eyes fell on Lane, they both sighed the same contented breath. "Good morning, lovely."

"Good morning, sweetheart. Come have breakfast with us."

Being around the two of them was a bit like watching pre-mating rituals at a very polite zoo. There were flirty hand touches, too many public kisses, sweet giggles and gooey eye gazes that made you feel like you were intruding on their falling in love moment. Only they were falling in love every day, every time they got near each other. It was precious, if not totally freaky. I'd never seen Lane with a dude before. As Lane explained my idea of inviting the kids into the dungeon, she did even this with "honey", "sweetheart", and "love" thrown in every other sentence.

Though Reyn's skin still looked sunken in, and his movements weren't as lithe, he perked up at the idea. "I love it. I'll help. I'm so tired of resting."

Lane's eyebrows pushed together. "But you're supposed to be healing up, Reyn. I want you whole."

"I want me whole, too. I promise not to use any of my magic."

"You know it's not that simple."

He jabbed his finger at me. "It is if this one's watching me. She's tough." He kissed Lane, lulling her into going along with his idea. "I'll just sweep, and the second I feel fatigued, I'll go straight back to bed."

"Liar," Lane accused. "I don't like you doing too much."

Reyn crossed his left ankle over his right knee, taking a bite of her scone. "Now, what's that you just got done telling our Rosie? Something about compromise and letting people be who they are? I'm not a waif, Lane. I'm a man. I'm a man who wants to help rebuild your kingdom, however I can."

They kissed for the millionth time, so I shoved the rest of my scone in my mouth and washed it down with the dregs of my tea. "Peace out, lovers. I'll see you in the dungeon, Uncle-Dad."

Reyn raised his cup to me, while Lane choked on her tea at my phrasing. I wasn't sure I'd ever get used to the two of them, but seeing Lane that happy was well worth the effort.

13

THE CHEAT SHEET

"*R*emind me again why I said I wanted to help sweep?"

"Because you wanted to be treated like a man." I dipped the rags in the bucket of soapy water and scrubbed another line down the wall. The bubbles trailed down the drab, gray concrete, chasing each other toward the freshly swept floor. "It's already looking loads better than it did when we started. We're not too far off from being finished."

"You truly have no idea how vast this dungeon is."

"Nope, but if I keep telling myself we're almost done, one of these times it'll be true."

Reyn kept his eyes on his broom, but never ceased to run out of conversation. "You want to talk about taking Bastien's mark?"

"Not really. Still haven't made up my mind. Too many things are in flux to make a big decision like that. We only just got back together. I feel like we need a solid month of not breaking up before I tattoo the guy's name on my butt."

Reyn's nose scrunched. "That's not how they do the mark."

"I know. I was kidding. My whole life lately kind of all feels too good to be true, but still too terrible to be real."

"Hopefully Bastien's the good part."

"He is. Model boyfriend, actually. Better than I deserve, for sure. The terrible part is the fact that I'm not done finding the jewels. My dad's still holed up in the castle, and I can't get to him." I mentally kicked myself for the fifteenth time that week. "He didn't even know it was me. I should've told him."

"Cowardice never did suit you."

I bristled. "All that bedrest sure put a mouth on you. How're you feeling? You sneaking any magic past me I don't know about?"

Reyn moved from one cell to the next, sweeping the gray pile of too many decades of abandonment out into the center aisle. "You don't have to worry about that. I want to get better more than anyone else." He paused his work to study me. "I want to marry Lane, Rosie. And I want that as soon as I can possibly have it."

I swallowed down the nerves that came with such adult conversation. "That's what Lane wants, too."

"I know. Is that what *you* want?"

I kept my back to him as I washed the wall. "I want Lane to be happy. If you're the guy for the job, then yeah, marry the crap out of her. I've got no issue with you two happily-ever-aftering each other until the end of time."

Though I'd already told Lane as much, he seemed to have needed this confirmation direct from the source. "That's a relief."

"Honestly, my opinion doesn't matter in this equation. I'm the kid. Lane's a big girl. She knows how to make good decisions."

"Ah, but you're her best friend. She abandoned her kingdom and her mansion for you. She gave up her title and ran away to Common to face homelessness and poverty because of her love for you. Your vote is almost as high as her own, so I'm grateful to have you in my corner. I love her very much."

I still couldn't bring myself to look at him, but continued

scrubbing the wall. "Then you should know she says she hates extra tomatoes on her pizza. She actually really likes the way it tastes with too many tomatoes, but refuses to order them because she says it makes her pizza generic."

"Okay." Reyn answered me slowly, unsure what to do with the totally useless information.

"And she portions out her root beer floats, because if you add too much root beer, there's not enough ice cream to balance it all out. So let her add her own. Just give her a mug of ice cream and a cold root beer in the bottle still."

"I'm afraid I don't know what a root beer float is. Is it something important?"

"To her, it is. You'll learn, and when you do, pay attention to the little things that make her a gem. She dances when she cooks. Did you know that?"

"I admit, I've never cooked with her in a proper kitchen. There are servants here, and every other time we've shared a meal, it's been on the road."

"You should cook with her. She likes eighties pop girl bands when she's making dessert, and nineties female divas like Mariah Carey when she's making a dinner she loves. If you don't switch the stations between the two, she'll get irritable while making dessert and not know why."

Reyn was quiet while he swept. "I don't know the details yet, but I want to. I want to be around for all of it. The broad strokes I've learned so far have been enough to captivate me. I can only imagine the details will draw me in that much more."

I kept my eyes on my work. "Women are about the broad strokes, sure, but they're more about the details. Learn to love Lane's details, and she'll never lose that goofball glow she has for you. Just a little tip from me to you." I swallowed as I scrubbed the wall. "The next time you bring her tea, put a wedge of a lime on the side. She has a theory that tea with lime makes her brain open up to see new things. It's totally ridiculous, but if you do that, she'll look at you like you're the only guy in the universe, sent from Heaven just for her."

"Keep them coming, Daughter-Niece."

I snorted at the term, and proceeded to spend the rest of the day cleaning side-by-side with Reyn while giving him the cheat sheet on Lane. He soaked in every tip, mentally taking notes on everything I doled out that clued him in to the wonder that was our girl.

Reyn and I were a good team, switching off tasks when one of us grew too tired or bored with our current job. We were both on the mend, so we kept an eye on each other. It didn't feel patronizing, which was a relief on both our ends.

When Bastien came stomping down the steps, I nearly laughed at his livid bear face. "What do you think you're doing?"

"Clearly I'm building a rocket ship. What does it look like I'm doing?"

"It looks like you're not resting at all, which is what I thought you were doing this entire time! How long have you been out of bed?"

I glanced over my shoulder at Reyn, who grinned at our sparring. "I dunno. How long ago was breakfast? Since then."

Bastien was soaked to the skin. He stomped his soaking foot to the floor, and I half expected steam to billow out of his ears. "Are you kidding me with this? You could've at least come to get me for lunch."

"Lunch? What time is it? Did we miss lunch?" I dropped the rag in the bucket and stretched my arms over my head, giving my spine a satisfying twist.

Bastien seemed to choke on too many acerbic retorts, and finally jabbed his finger at Reyn. "You. This is your fault."

I sauntered over to Bastien without a care in the world. I'd had a great day with Reyn, finally feeling like I was pitching in.

"Sorry I missed lunch. You hungry? You always get crabby when you're hungry."

Bastien stammered through Reyn's laughter. "I'm not crabby, and it's past dinner time! You skipped two meals? We're trying to put meat on your bones, Rosie. Considering you don't eat meat, it's an uphill battle, and one you can't go skipping meals through. Am I the only one taking this seriously?"

I leaned up and kissed his cheek. "Yes, you are, and I love you for it. It's a good thing we have you around to yell at us." He'd finally shaved that morning, and man, had I missed his face.

Bastien's shoulders slumped, his cheek brushing against mine to savor the closeness. "I shouldn't be yelling. Just don't skip meals. And don't work yourself to death. You have actual servants who can clean this place for you." He pulled back to look at me, his eyes filled with a hollow emotion. "I don't like the look of my girl in a dungeon."

"Why not? I was thinking this would be a great place for Lane to marry Reyn. White paint on the walls, pink tulle and ribbons on the cell bars. A rolled carpet down the aisle. Cute, right? It'd be unique. No one else would have a wedding like it."

Bastien narrowed his eyes at me. "I'm not marrying you in a dungeon."

My mouth fell open in shock. "I wasn't talking about us. I was talking about Lane and Reyn."

"I know, but when we get married, you're not talking me into this, so don't get any ideas." He motioned around the dungeon.

Reyn stifled a gasp that was mingled with a choked laugh. "And on that note, I'll leave you to your ensuing debate." On the way out, he clapped Bastien on the shoulder. "You know, I always wanted a son exactly like you." He laughed and scurried up the steps when Bastien's grimace stifled any intelligible response.

I waited until Reyn disappeared up the steps before putting my hands on my hips to address the elephant in the room. "Marriage is serious, Bastien. You shouldn't go making jokes about it like that. Especially not in front of Reyn, who's actually getting married."

Bastien's face contracted, like he'd eaten something sour. "What makes you think I'm joking? Of course I want to marry you."

My cheeks flushed, and the basement felt suddenly both cold and too hot. "We're still getting to know each other. This is the longest we've managed to stay together without breaking things off. You can't possibly be this sure."

"I'd marry you yesterday, Daisy. Without a blink, I know it's you I'll want forever."

I squinted one eye at him, trying to see any false angles in his intentions. "Yeah, okay. Let's give that subject a little air so it can breathe and decide how it feels being in the same room with me." I walked back to my bucket and picked up the rag again to give the wall another swipe.

Just like that, Bastien's bark was back. "Do you think I'm screwing around down here? Get upstairs and go eat something! Skipping meals isn't an option anymore."

I dropped the rag in the bucket, rolling my eyes at his over-protective rant. "Sheesh, fine. I was going to come up after I finished this wall. It's the last one."

Bastien crossed his arms over his broad chest. "March it on upstairs before I lose my temper and carry you up there."

"I've got news for you; if you think this is you keeping your temper, you've got another think coming, pal."

I thought Bastien had another few rounds of sparring in him, but apparently he'd hit his limit. He charged at me like a bull and flipped me up over his shoulder. "If you want to keep up this fight, you'll do it upside-down, screaming my name."

"Bastien, put me down!"

He mocked my tone, and I could hear the smile in his voice. "'Bastien! Bastien! You were right and I was wrong. I'm sorry I was reckless. Bastien, you're the king of all the things. You're always so wise."

"Oh, shut it."

He was soaked to the skin, and now my front was wet, as well. I was filthy, covered in dust and cobwebs, so the two of us were quite the sloppy pair as he tromped up the stone steps toward the kitchen. His spirits soared along with his volume when he boomed out to the kitchen staff, "My bride needs dinner!"

The three sisters who worked in the kitchen giggled and clapped, as if the whole thing was the best show they'd seen in ages. Mercy, Hope and Faith were the cutiest of cuties, each with round faces and deep dimples they didn't hesitate to show off. "I've got vegetables roasting for her now, Sir Bastien."

"Perfect. What of a wedding cake? How soon can you throw that together?"

"Give us a couple hours, and you'll have yourself a cake the likes of which Avalon's never seen before! Oh, the princess is marrying Bastien the Bold!"

"He's joking!" I protested, bringing the sisters back to reality. I beat on the small of Bastien's back for him to shut up. Though Lane had made an announcement throughout the house that my engagement to Madigan was off, I didn't know how I felt about Bastien's unwavering devotion. It was such a switch; the whole thing still felt like whiplash. I wanted to give it more time to make sure it was real. "Would you knock it off? I have to actually say yes, and you have to ask me for real before you go blurting everything out to the world."

"Married?!" I heard Roland's voice above the usual clamor of kitchen chatter. "You're marrying her for real, Bastien?"

I stiffened, and Bastien sensed that the teasing moment was over. He let me down, and I didn't waste a second before I ran out of the kitchen, and scampered up the stairs to go wash up. Though I knew Roland was a royal, and lived in the gigantic annex next to our mansion, I hadn't run into him yet in the week or so I'd been staying here. I kept my door locked mostly because of him, and stuck near Lane, Reyn or Draper when Bastien was working, to make sure Roland didn't try to kill me again. Though I hadn't sensed a threat or hostility from him during my stay here, I wasn't willing to chance it.

14

IT'S NOT EASY BEING GREEN

*M*y body was overly tired, and I guess skipping two meals hadn't been my best decision, but I made it to my bedroom and locked myself inside without Roland trying to kill me, so you know, bonus.

I scrubbed my body until my skin was pink, and then moved out from behind the partition with a towel wrapped around me to hunt for clean clothes in the wardrobe. The blur of green caught my eye in the lamplight, and I nearly dropped my towel in shock when I took in the figure I never thought I'd see again. "You! Get out of here!"

Kerdik looked lost, tired, and oddly enough, weak. I'd never seen him be any of those things, so to find them all painting his features at once was a shock that temporarily stayed the scream in my throat. "Rosie, you have to listen to me." His voice was dry, and sounded pained when he spoke. He swayed on the spot, grabbing onto the post of my bed with unsteady chartreuse fingers. "She's never going to… I'm not…"

The scream I'd been saving to alert the others was repurposed when Kerdik collapsed in a heap of limbs on the ground. I ran to him, horrified that such a powerful being was so very mortal and pitiable in the faint lamplight of my bedroom. I didn't think about our fight, or how he'd attacked me when we'd seen each other last. I thought only of the fear in his usually haughty eyes, and the pained bleat before he hit the wooden floor. His sky-blue hair was messy, which was something I knew he wouldn't tolerate under normal conditions. I picked up his hand, abandoning my anger at him for the moment. "Kerdik, honey, what happened? What's wrong?"

"Safe," he murmured, his eyes rolling back. "Keep my body safe. Too much magic. She never lets up. Do you have the Darkness? Keep it safe. Keep the Darkness safe, Rosie."

I ran to the door, unlatched it and flung it open, belting out a frantic message through the mansion. "Bastien, help me! I need you!" My hands were shaking when skipping a meal and overdoing it in the dungeon combined with my peaking nerves.

I returned to his side and scooped his upper half into my arms, worried that I couldn't fix all the bad I didn't know how to undo. I pressed his cheek to mine and realized it was cold. "What happened to you? Tell me how to help you. I don't know what to do! I don't know anything about magical diseases. Are you sick?"

"*Magique Fatal.*"

"I don't know what that means!" I was scared, so I cried out for the one person who I knew would know what to do. "Lane!"

Bastien's boots pounded the stairs, but the second he burst into the room, he hopped back out. "What's he doing here?"

"He's sick! He's got *Magique Fatal?*" I didn't understand what it was, but Bastien sure seemed to.

He gasped, and his gaze climbed from Kerdik's barely breathing form up to mine. "Do you want me to help him?"

"Yes! I don't know what it is. How do I fix it?"

"He needs magic. A transfusion, just like Reyn gets, and then lots of rest." He rubbed the back of his neck. "What he could've possibly done to exhaust the deep magic he's got is beyond me. Something big, Rosie."

Lane came in with Draper on her heels. "What the... Oh! Get out of here!" she yelled, furious that Kerdik would dare show his face after what he'd done to me. I kind of loved her for that.

"He's hurt, Lane!"

"Good! Let him remember what it feels like to be scared, to be mortal."

I glared up at her. "You don't mean that."

Her shoulders slumped. "No, I don't, but I want to mean it. The gems are tied to his life. If he dies, Avalon doesn't stand a chance."

I growled up at her, "You can do better than that! You can't be like everyone else and just use him."

Lane's mouth was drawn in a tight line. "He attacked my daughter! He's lucky I don't take my window of opportunity and bash his freaking head in!"

"If you forgave Roland, then you can help Kerdik. This is my call, Lane. We're better than revenge. Know who you are."

Lane ran both hands through her hair, frustrated. "Shut the door, Draper. No one can see him like this. People need Master Kerdik to keep them afraid enough to fall in line. If he's compromised, there's no telling what chaos will go down."

Draper locked the door, his gaze wary when it fell on me. "Go get some clothes on, kiddo. We've got it from here."

I shook my head. "A magic transfusion? You just gave Reyn some of yours this morning, Drape. And Bastien, you're helping people move into the province. It won't do any good to drain you. And forget about using yours, Lane. You can't use yours – any of you. You're all needed, but I'm not. No one needs my magic right now. I only use it to talk to Remy and the animals. You have to use mine."

Bastien, Draper and Lane shook their heads as if their chins were tied to the same string. "Not a chance," Bastien ruled, his palm migrating to the small of my back – a thing he did to stake his claim when he was feeling territorial. "I'll call Link up here. You can use his magic, or Mad's."

"They're needed out there, but I'm not. And seriously? How many favors do you think you can ask of them?" I examined Kerdik's jaw that fell slack against my arm. "Hurry! He needs help now!"

Draper moved over to Kerdik, and helped Bastien lift his body up onto my mattress. Lane crossed over to the wardrobe and yanked out underwear, a fitted white t-shirt and some teal cotton shorts out for me, sending me behind the partition.

I changed in lightning speed, coming out, readying for a fight. "Okay, guys. Teach me how to help him."

Bastien shook his head. "No way. I'll do it. I can take a day or two away from everything out there. Mad and Link can handle it."

Lane pinched the bridge of her nose. "Rosie's right. She doesn't use most of her magic because she's never been trained. It won't affect her the same way it would you. Plus, you gave to Reyn yesterday. It would wipe you out for a couple days, at least, if you did this. It's not a small transfusion, like what you do for Reyn, Bastien. Kerdik needs more than you're used to giving."

Bastien shrugged and rolled up his sleeve in preparation. "So what? So I'm out of commission for a day or two. Big deal."

Lane's voice rose in pitch, and she started gesticulating animatedly. "You're responsible for her! You can't protect my daughter if you're too weak to get out of bed. Trust me, Bastien, this decision is in her best interest."

I could tell Bastien wanted to argue, but I didn't care. "Let's do it. Now." I glanced over to Kerdik, whose breaths were so shallow, I could scarcely tell they were there. "Hurry!"

Draper stood by my side as Lane ran out the door toward her room. She returned a couple minutes later with a small, clear medical tube sticking out of a black bag. "Remy's out helping

Madigan and Link, so we've got to be quick with his supplies. I don't want this noise spread to anyone else."

My heart was pounding, scared that I'd agreed to something I understood nothing about. "How does this work?"

Draper offered me a reassuring smile that was tight with tension. "You let us worry about that. Sit down on the bed and relax. You'll just feel a little pinch, and that's that."

Something told me it was a little more complicated than Draper was making it sound.

Lane's words were clipped. "Just like a blood transfusion. This needle pulls out magic as well as blood, so both will flow into Kerdik."

"My magic will come back?"

Draper's arm coiled around my shoulders. "Of course. Sometimes it only takes a couple hours. Might take a little more, since you're a little under the weather still. Just makes you sleepy, and you won't be able to access your magic for a few hours."

"A day, at least. Maybe more," Bastien grumbled. "Don't lie to her. Master Kerdik's teetering on the edge. Can an immortal even die? I mean, how serious is this? Can't we just let him wait it out? Won't he regenerate?"

"He'll regenerate, but his power is tied to the gems, Bastien. If we want Avalon back on its feet, Master Kerdik has to be functional. Otherwise Rosie risked her neck for a handful of useless rocks. *Magique Fatal* can take someone out for weeks if they're not tended to. We can't risk that. We can't go weeks without the blessing from the gemstones. We can't have led these people into a barren wilderness, which is exactly what will happen to the land without the gems!"

Kerdik moaned, which made me more frantic to get this going. "Hurry! Just shove the needle in me already. Don't let him die, Lane!"

"I won't, baby." She hooked the rubber tube up to the needle and jabbed it hard into Kerdik's forearm, not bothering to hide her disdain for him. She was far gentler with me, kissing my temple as the slight pinch bit my skin. Then she began muttering a string of nonsensical syllables, and I realized she was doing some sort of magical spell to make this more than a simple human blood transfusion. The magic needed that extra push from her to come out of me through the tube.

I watched the blood flow from my arm into the clear rubber tube with a sick fascination. It circled around and wound its way into Kerdik. His sharp inhale burst his lashes upward, revealing fear and wonder in his eyes that scared me. He mouthed something and reached out into the air before his arm collapsed on his belly.

I expected the red in the tube to be mixed with like, glitter or something, but it was just normal looking blood. The magic was incognito. Draper turned my head from the tube, so I didn't pass out from the sight. He cradled my upper half in his arms, rocking me gently back and forth while Lane held my arm steady. I didn't roll my eyes at the babying; Draper needed to find his role in our family, and this was what soothed him.

My breath came out in puffs across Draper's neck, eventually growing shallower as the minutes passed. When an invisible hand felt like it was gripping my stomach, I let the foreign sensation take over, knowing I couldn't resist saving Kerdik with any portion of my being. I let the hand wring my stomach out like a skeleton squeezing a sponge. I could feel magic, or something important, flowing out of me through the tube. I tried not to worry when a cold ice started creeping into my arm.

"Stop the drip!" Bastien ordered. "She's starting to fade. It's enough."

Lane removed the needle, and Bastien took me from Draper's arms. Instead of laying my limp body in the bed, he took me to a chair and plopped down, cradling me like the floppy noodle he loved. "I hate this. I hate this. I hate this," he chanted over and over. "I don't want her around Master Kerdik. I'm going to go lay her down with Reyn."

Kerdik moaned in frustration when Bastien stood and walked my body toward the door. "I didn't fail!" he managed to cry out. "Give her to me!"

Bastien turned with a snarl. "Not a chance. She's been better to you than you deserve. The least you can do is leave her alone now."

An animalistic roar burst from Kerdik, scaring me with what little nerves I had left. "Give her to me!" I wanted to cling to Bastien, but my hands were numb and useless.

Bastien cried out in anger and borderline fear, his forearms shaking. It was as if something was yanking on his arms, though Kerdik hadn't moved off the bed. "No!" Bastien roared through gritted teeth, his fingers biting into me to stop whatever psychic tug Kerdik was using on him. "You can't have her like this! You can barely take care of yourself! You could've killed her the last time you lost your temper."

"Mine!" Kerdik thundered, going from weak, to sweaty and feeble, but somewhat stronger in his magic.

Bastien cried out in shock and panic when my body somehow lifted out of his arms and was yanked by an invisible force toward Kerdik. Draper and Lane dove for me, but it was too late. The second Kerdik touched my arm, the room vanished from my sight. I found myself sucked into a tornado of sensations, fearing the worst as my body gave up and my brain jumped ship. I passed out in Kerdik's arms, and the last thing that filled my ears was the sound of my own screams.

* * *

I CAME to however long later in a meadow I'd never been to before. Stranger than that, for the first time in over a month, it wasn't raining. The sun was shining down on thousands of fuzzy yellow daisies. The sunshiny flowers wore petals that looked like felt. I examined them as I lay in the meadow, the furry flowers bending over to tickle my nose and bless me with a breath of pure beauty. There were no houses or anything around in any direction as far as I could see, and barely any trees. It was too eerily quiet to be Heaven, so I was pretty sure I wasn't dead. I tried to sit up, but my head swirled, knocking me back down again. The grass and yellow flowers cradled me, keeping me snuggled in their softness for as long as I would have them. "Where am I?" I moaned, feeling like my head had been kicked.

Kerdik's voice was equally worn when he answered. "My place. It was too noisy at your house. Had to get out."

My chest jumped in time with his, unsteady and frail. "You stole me?"

Kerdik nodded from his supine position next to me. "Bastien was going to take you away from me. I needed... I needed..."

"You need your head checked. Bastien's going to kill you dead, immortal or not."

Kerdik chuckled, as if I'd told a cute joke. "I had to show you something."

I carefully turned my aching neck so I could look at my captor. He didn't have the same "I'm about to die" look about him, but he definitely looked sick. His forehead was coated in a thin sheen of sweat, his lips parted and his eyes going in and out of focus as he turned his head to gaze at me. I frowned in concern, putting aside my anger for the moment. "What happened to you?"

"Morgan's spell. I tried to break it, and she put... I didn't... I wasn't expecting the..." He waved his hand to let me know he wasn't with it enough for speech yet. "Sleep. I need to sleep. My magic needs to recharge."

I nodded. "Take me home, and you can crash in one of the beds in Lane's castle."

"No. Bastien will take you from me. Here. Just a few hours of sleep together."

I wanted to protest more, but I was barely awake myself. My eyelids drooped as I snuggled into the soft, pillowy grass in the meadow. The sun behind us shone over our bodies, warming us pleasantly. I was so tired that I didn't even protest when Kerdik's fingers threaded through mine, clasping my sweaty hand to his. I knew I should run, but my legs were too weak to commit to the effort. "Just a few hours, then I'm mad at you."

"Don't leave. I don't want to be alone when I fall asleep." He sounded afraid of rest, foreign as it was to him. He gazed into my eyes with such regret that I couldn't doubt his sincerity. "I'm sorry, Rosie. I'm sorry I hurt you."

"You should be," I murmured, my mouth falling slack as exhaustion and blood loss took me under, my head falling to the side so my temple rested to his.

15

GROVELING IN THE MEADOW

I have no idea how long we slept for, only that we both seemed to need the release. I awoke in the same meadow, but was rolled onto my side instead of laid out flat on my back, as I had been when I'd closed my eyes. Kerdik was spooning me, his body coiled around mine. His arm was stretched out beneath my head, and his fingers were studying mine with slight sweeping touches. Our contrasting skin was curled up over my chest, so I was tight in his embrace.

His lips pressed to my hair. "Are you awake yet, little dove?"

I yawned and stretched, too comfortable to delve straight into pissed just yet. "Yeah. You sleep alright?"

"What would make sleep not alright? I only know one way."

"Oh, like if you have bad dreams or something."

"I don't dream. Or if I do, I don't remember them. I only sleep every few decades, if I use magic that costs me too much effort. I was long overdue, and I'm afraid I stretched myself past the breaking point. I didn't know where else to turn. Not many can be trusted to care for me when I can't protect myself."

I stretched against him like a cat, arching my spine and throwing my head back over his shoulder. Then I curled into a ball, his body wrapping around mine like we were two kittens from the same litter. "That was a risky chance you took. How'd you know I wouldn't hurt you the way you hurt me while you were snoozing?"

Kerdik buried his face in the nape of my neck. "Because you're beautiful."

My mouth popped open in disgust. "Screw you! So you're saying that if I was still the ugly girl, you wouldn't have bothered coming back to me? Being beautiful has nothing to do with what kind of a person a girl is." My fists tightened. "You're just like everyone else, judging me by what I look like. You were supposed to be different!"

Kerdik groaned at his poor choice of words. "That's not what I meant. You wouldn't understand. I meant that I can see your heart. You're lovely on the inside and out, so I knew I could trust you." He dragged in an unsteady breath, and let it fan over my skin, giving me goosebumps. "You're the only pure soul I know. You're their princess, but you're my queen."

Though I got the eerie sense he was saying more than his words were communicating, I wasn't willing to let him off the hook for his superficial assumptions that being beautiful meant that you were automatically worth someone's time. I squinched my eyes shut at the memory of Morgan gripping my face, digging in her nails as she ordered me to "be beautiful." "You mean I'm a pushover. I'm a giant sucker. You knew you could take advantage."

"You've lost weight," he observed, thumbing my ribs in dismay. "I don't like there being less of you."

I swallowed hard, wishing I hadn't been so very wrecked by my mother. I kept my lips shut tight in lieu of a response, lest I open them and buckets of tears come flinging out of me.

I felt Kerdik's lashes flutter against my neck. "I'll never be able to explain how sorry I am for what I did. I lost my temper, and when that happens, the elements sometimes bend to my state. I didn't mean to hurt you, but I couldn't turn it off." He wrapped his arm around my torso. "I thought you were like Morgan. She trapped me once and tried to pry information from me about whether I'd been born or if I was always like this. I knew the spell she wanted the information for. I knew what she intended to do."

"Jeez, what?"

"If I was born, I can die. If I always was, then I couldn't cease to be. She wanted to know if she could kill me. I admit, I thought she was working through you to get that information."

I gulped at the answer I hadn't anticipated. "You thought I was trying to find a way to kill you?"

"Why else would you have asked me such a specific question?"

Sadness weighted my soul, and I wished life wasn't so complicated for either of us. "I wanted to know if we were the same. If you were lonely, like me. If you'd been orphaned. You never mentioned parents, so I wasn't sure. You think I was trying to kill you? I wanted more of you, not less," I said quietly, turning his own words back on him. "Now I don't want any part of you."

"Of course your questions were as innocent as you." He buried his face in the nape of my neck again, and I could feel his shame through the connection of our skin. "It occurred to me after the fact that I may have overreacted. When I realized your reason was as blameless as you are, I freed you from the ice and disappeared. I knew I couldn't show my face again until I made it up to you." He sighed into my flesh, giving me the shivers. "I'll tell you the truth, if you want to know. Only one other person knows, and he's not in Faîte anymore."

I reached behind me to grip his hair, relishing the thickness of the handful of light blue I'd always been fascinated by. "No. Don't tell me. I don't want you uncertain about me like that ever again. I didn't mean to ask you such a loaded question. I thought we could have a heart-to-heart. I wasn't trying to kill you. Jeez."

"I know that now. You really don't want to know if I was born or not?"

"Not anymore, no. That's what you get when you lash out at people; they don't want to know you. Someday you'll want to be known, and it'll be too late. You scared me, K."

"I scared me a little bit, too. It's why I didn't come when you called. I was afraid to show my face without some sort of peace offering. You're the only... You're the only true loveliness left in Avalon. I can't risk something bad happening to you."

"*You're* the something bad that happened to me." I closed my eyes, my senses filling with the dank stink of the well. I remembered clearly the desperation I felt when I called out for him, and the devastation when he didn't come. I quickly inhaled the fragrance of the meadow – a purity so lush and perfect, it smelled like freshly mown grass, joyful flowers and love, all sprinkled with a smattering of dew. I wasn't in the well anymore – it was a lesson I needed to remind myself of from time to time still. "I needed you, and you weren't there."

"I'm here now." He gripped me tighter to him. The pressure of his hold threatened to jerk the tears from me, so I held my emotions in as fiercely as I could. "You needed me? What happened? I assumed you were angry, and looking to get an audience with me so you could tell me how badly I hurt you. That wasn't it?"

I chewed on my lower lip, unsure just how much I could trust Kerdik with the new information factored in. Good excuse or not, I'd needed him, and he let a misunderstanding keep me at the bottom of a well. I cleared my throat and tried to calm myself down, so I didn't lean on Kerdik more than our fragile friendship could handle. "It was nothing. It got taken care of. I survived. But you were a jerk to me, and then you hurt me on purpose. Don't feed me that crap about your emotions being tied to the elements. You knew what you were doing, and you didn't stop. You left me bleeding and screaming, and you only came back because you needed help. That's not friendship. Stupid me for ever thinking it was."

Kerdik's thumb traced up and down my ribs, ignoring my correction. "Why are you thinner? How much weight have you lost?"

I squirmed and struggled out of his grip, rolling away indignantly. I propped myself up on all fours, my eyebrows wrinkling toward the center, and my frown stalwartly in place. "You don't get to hold me like that. Not after attacking me like you did."

Kerdik sat up, his eyebrows pushed together to mirror my own. "You're hiding something. What happened? Is Bastien not watching you?" He groaned and shook his head. "What's the point of giving him those enhancements if he's completely incapable of keeping you safe? Taking away his social obligation was supposed to make him tied tighter to you. I thought it was working, but you're a skeleton!"

"My body is amazing, thank you very much. And Bastien rescued me not long before I was about to die, I'll have you know. I'm safe and alive, thanks to him. Not you. Him."

Kerdik's full lips tightened. "And what danger did you fall into that almost killed you?"

"Morgan," I hissed, sitting back on my heels to face him. "She's not too thrilled about the ring you gave me. Had some of her soldiers try to yank it off my hand when I wouldn't give it up."

Kerdik leaned back on his elbows and chuckled unexpectedly. It was a chilling sound that held no remorse. "How many of them died before she realized her mistake in crossing me?"

"Just the one."

"One? Wow, she's learning quicker this time around. Good for her. I thought her far more stubborn and foolish than that."

"Well, she switched tactics real quick." I debated between glossing over the details with an "I dealt with it" vibe, but part of me wanted Kerdik to understand just what happened when you ignored someone who counted on you. The blood loss was getting to me, so I took a few extra heavy breaths before delving into the truth. "I wouldn't give her the ring, so she ordered a few of her men to take my clothes and lower me into an abandoned well. She wanted me to rot there until I got so desperate I gave up the ring."

I was expecting some kind of a "how dare she" sort of reaction from Kerdik, but when the yellow daisies underneath me withered in a breath, I grew worried. Then they spread their death like a foul breath that rippled across the entire meadow, killing off every single flower in this gorgeous haven, and leaving it bereft of beauty. "I'll handle it," Kerdik promised in a low threat.

I stood, backing up as I surveyed the death that rippled out from where Kerdik sat, peering up at me with a fierce promise in his eyes. "I don't need you to handle it. I needed you to get me the crap out of the well, but you didn't answer me. What's the point of being able to call you if you never pick up? Were you that pissed at me?"

"No! I didn't understand, and I overreacted. I was angry with myself, not you."

I didn't have all that great a hold on my emotions, so my voice came out pinched and hurt. "All I did was ask you about your life! I didn't deserve to get yelled at by you, then sliced up by your ice, and abandoned because you were being a brat. We were supposed to be friends, K, but you treated me like you didn't know the first thing about what kind of a person I am."

Kerdik stood, his hands raised and chin lowered in surrender to my temper. "I would have come for you, had I known."

"I was in the bottom of that well for more than two weeks! I was freezing, starved and scared." Angst rose up in me, so I pinched the skin on my knuckles to keep myself from shedding tears in front of him. "She killed Demi! Her or Avril, I'm not sure who. They killed him and then Morgan dropped his head down on me! Demi's only crime in this was loving me, and it got him beheaded! Who does that? How does this get to be my mom?" My breath came in heavy gulps as I motioned to him with a clumsy hand. "How do you get to be one of my few friends here? You were terrible to me the second you got scared!"

Kerdik cleared the distance between us and wrapped me in his unsteady arms, knocking me back a few steps with his passion. He seemed unperturbed that I pounded my feeble fists on his chest. We were both weak and sweaty, and together we were an exquisitely flawed mess. "Darling," he cooed, his softness a sharp contrast to my anger. He was trying to soothe me, but I was beyond reason. I knew the second I confessed the awfulness, the tears would spill out of my control.

My fury at the unfairness of Morgan, Avril, and just plain life welled up and exploded all over Kerdik. More than my mother and my twisted aunt, I was mad at Rigby, whom I'd trusted and befriended – as I'd cared for Kerdik – yet he turned snake and bit me. "You left me! You hurt me, and then you left me!"

"No, my darling. I didn't know. Do you think I would've left you if I'd known you were naked in the bottom of a well?"

"Yes! Yes, you would because you're selfish, just like all of them! You were supposed to be my friend. You were supposed to understand how hard it is to only be used as a tool – a means to an end – because that's how they treat you! You weren't supposed to be this walking landmine, making me tiptoe so you don't explode. Do you think I have the time for your PMS? The cuts your ice gave me got infected in the well, you jag!"

His sweaty hands gripped my back and my hip, desperate to make things right when it was far too late for any of it. "I'll heal them, Rosie. Show me where I hurt you."

"No! I'll heal on my own, without your help."

"If I cut you, I should fix it! Please, how can I make this right?"

I punched his chest over and over, hoping I'd push him too far, and he'd snap. I don't know why I wanted him to break me, just so I had a reason to stay down, but I longed for a permanent push so I didn't have to feel conflicted. "I'm so tired of trying! It's never enough, and you made it worse! I wasn't supposed to have to try with you. We were supposed to be easy – friends that fit nowhere, but somehow fit with each other. Don't you get how rare it is to find someone like us? And then you threw it away the second I stopped looking all shiny. I would never have turned on you like that." When his hands mutated from a desperate grip to a sweet embrace, my posture started to slump in his arms. Somehow, he found the strength to hold me, and somehow, I found the grace to let him. "You were supposed to be different! Man, I'm so stupid for falling for it, and I hate being stupid!"

He shushed me, but surprisingly didn't lose his temper or fight back. He let me wail on him in my weakened state, his expression pained but patient. "I'm sorry, darling. I'm so sorry. I did. I hurt you. I didn't come when you called. Then I show up at your aunt's home, expecting you to take care of me."

"If I were like you, I would've left you to rot! I had no one but Demi's severed head!" Admitting that Demi was, in fact, deceased pushed a petrified scream from my lips. The sound escaped before I could shove the crazy back down into the denial box I'd locked it neatly in. My erratic outburst made me want to punish Kerdik for forcing these emotions to the surface, when I knew bringing them to light would do nothing to bring my boyfriend back. My temper flared as I shouted in his face, "Demi's dead body was a better man than you!"

I guess that was one too far. His hands turned hard, crushing me to him so tightly, it smooshed the breath from my lungs. "Listen to me," he worked out through clenched teeth. "I had no idea you were in a well, or that Morgan hurt you like that. No matter how furious I was with you, thinking you were trying to find a way to kill me, like your mother did, I would have saved you still."

"No, you wouldn't!"

His eyes narrowed with passion that made him shout in my face. "I would, because I love you!"

I gasped, scandalized. "Words! Stupid, useless words. I called you, and you didn't even bother to answer me! If not for Lane and Bastien finding me, I would've died!"

He kept me crushed with one arm, his other hand reaching up to brush a few of my wild curls back so he could meet my angry eyes with his repentant ones. "I was trying to give you a grand gesture. I knew I couldn't come back to you without one. Give a man some time to grovel, *Fleur*."

"I don't need your stupid gestures. I need you to not attack me in the first place! I need someone in this awful world to be good! My mom throws me down a well, my only friend left in the mansion takes my clothes from me, and you just... I needed a friend, but you couldn't handle it. That's not love."

"What friend took your clothes?"

"He's not a friend anymore, obviously."

"What's his name, darling?"

"Rigby? He was just following orders, like every other soldier who's ever carried out a psychotic dictator's rule."

Kerdik shushed me, kissing pure sweetness into my forehead. "Rigby is Morgan's pet. And she took your pet from you? This Demi boy?"

"Demi wasn't a pet, he was a person! Why does no one understand that?" Panic rose in my chest, causing my fingers to wrap in Kerdik's shirt. "She killed him, and he didn't do anything wrong! She killed my boyfriend so she could take my ring!"

"Take a breath. I'll handle it."

"Can you raise the dead?"

"No, but I can take her pet away. It's a good place to start my vengeance."

I shook my head, so turned around and distraught that I didn't know which way was up anymore. "I don't need vengeance. Vengeance doesn't do Demi a lick of good now."

"It's for me to decide how Morgan should be punished for her many crimes. I'll send her his head on a silver platter. There's something poetic about carnage on a silver platter, I've always thought."

I shook my head, disgusted. "Don't. Rigby was following orders. He wasn't happy about any of it. Even told the soldiers not to get too handsy with me."

Kerdik's grip around me turned tender, and he slowly started swaying us from side to side as we stood together, my head tucked under his chin. "All he did was buy his life an extra month. He'll die, and that's all there is to say about it. You may not need vengeance, and that's good. Keep your pure soul – it only adds to your beauty. My darkness allows your light to stay untouched." He lifted my hand to his lips and kissed my knuckles, before returning it to rest on his chest. "I need that light, darling. Being in your glow, and then losing that warmth? It's a cold, long life without your affections."

"If you need my light, then don't go out of your way to put it out. Rigby should live a long time with the memory of what he did to me." I looked up at Kerdik with unconcealed sadness. "You can't fuel my light with darkness." I wasn't sure why I wanted Rigby to have a free pass. Maybe I was just tired of all the deaths, and didn't want to be part of yet another.

Kerdik's body wobbled slightly, but he didn't release me. He held me, even when I was angry, even when I was bossy, even when I had no hope we could find a way to work through the sea of angst we were both trying frantically not to drown in. Despite my insistence that we were doomed to lose each other, Kerdik found the steadiness to be tender with me, his lips brushing my ear as he spoke. "When you greeted me at your coronation, not caring who saw or what they thought?" He held me to him as if I was precious, as if I wasn't the naked, filthy girl covered in fungus at the bottom of the well. I could practically feel his heart swelling as his words cradled the broken parts of me, treating them more gently than I thought him capable. "I loved you that day. You were their princess, but in that moment, you were my queen. Every day without your brightness has been a sea of dark." He kissed my fingertips, letting me touch the fullness of his lips. "Rigby will die, and Morgan will see that you're to remain unharmed."

"There you go again, not listening to me. You are the worst friend in the world. I have no use for your kindergarten temper."

Kerdik rolled his tongue along his teeth, frustrated that he was trying to give me some big gesture, and it was the wrong one. "Fine. If you wish this Rigby spared, then I'll let him keep his head."

My voice came out small and insecure, muffled in his white dress shirt, which was damp from dew and sweat. "Why does she hate me so much?"

"Pure darkness can rarely understand pure light, and people fear what they do not understand. Morgan does not hate you. She's afraid of you."

I didn't know what to make of his response, so I stayed quiet, letting the stillness of the dead meadow around us lull me into a calmer state of mind.

Finally, Kerdik broke the silence with a cautious whisper. "I'm sorry I lost my temper. The power I have… it's not always easy to control. It's one of the reasons I don't get close to people anymore. It's why I've stayed away – for everyone else's safety."

"Why'd you come back?"

He brought my knuckles to his lips again and kissed them. I felt his tender affection for me blooming between us. "A man can only live for so long in his own darkness." There was a softness in the way he held me that gave me hope he would work on all the things that had gone so very wrong.

16

KERDIK'S SECRET MISSION

*K*erdik and I spent a fair amount of time talking quietly in the dead meadow, calming from our fight and breathing in the air that was so fresh, it felt like each inhale regenerated long-dead parts of me. As our connection returned to us, the yellow daisies slowly started to resurrect, blooming and standing with beauty I'd thought was lost forever. I managed a few smiles, but was overall cautious of the quick-turning temper I didn't trust him to control.

"You ready to tell me what happened to you to get you so sick?" I asked, more at ease when I tossed an orange back at him. I'd needed the simple game of catch to bring something familiar to my life. He'd grown a full-blown tree from scratch just so we'd have a ball to play with.

"I found a way to undo one of Morgan's spells."

"Yikes. You weren't looking so hot when you came to me. You sure you're feeling alright?"

"Better than I was, though, I admit, I'm still on the mend. That nap did me a world of good. Thank you for the magic transfusion." He dipped his head to me politely.

"No problem. I figured you probably wouldn't trust anyone else's blood in you."

"You figured correctly."

"Which of Morgan's spells got you so twisted?" I threw the orange to him, winding up like a Major League Baseball pitcher.

"The one outlined in the paper you gave me."

My eyes widened as the orange landed back in my palm. "Huh? You mean the paper I found with the jewel?"

"That's the one. I figured you didn't take the time to read it over. It was basically her confession of what she'd done to Urien. Her dirty little secret, and the map of how she poisoned him. It wasn't just Hemlock, but a binding curse that made the poison stay in him for prolonged periods of time."

My mouth went dry as I sucked in a breath filled with trepidation. "You... Did you... The spell holding my dad hostage in his mind. Did you break it?"

"I almost did, yes. I stole Urien's body and delivered it to one of Lane's rooms in her mansion with explicit instructions on the next steps to take. They're rudimentary, really. Any healer could perform them, now that the spell is broken. I wanted to do it myself, but breaking the binding charm took more out of me than I'm afraid I had to give. She armed the spell with several traps, which injured me beyond what I was anticipating. I don't know why I underestimate her spell work. It was the fault of my own pride that I fell victim to her tricks."

I dropped the orange, crushing one of the yellow velvet daisies. "How could you keep something like that from me this entire time? Let's go back! I need to see him!"

"We will, darling. Be patient. My magic takes time to regenerate. I'll bring you back soon enough. He's not awake yet, anyway. Besides, your magic's been drained from the transfusion. I doubt you'll be able to communicate with him so soon."

I cringed at my own dumb choice that might mute my father's

voice from me. "Seriously? How long until my magic comes back?"

Kerdik picked another orange from the tree and tossed it to me. "That one's for eating, not throwing. It worries me that you're so thin now." When I was not amused at his coddling, he replied, "Patience, love. These things take time. Come and rest with me. Play awhile. The world's got work enough for us when we return."

When he drew near, I tilted my head up to gaze at him, chewing on my lower lip as I attempted the impossible task of figuring Kerdik out. "Bringing my dad back was your grand gesture?"

"Of course. I knew I couldn't come back to you unless I presented you with a reason not to turn me away."

I mulled over his assumptions that put a disproportionate amount of power in my hands. I didn't quite understand it all, but that didn't change the possibility of hope. "Thank you. Having my dad back? That's a super big deal."

"I was hoping it would be. Give his body some time for the charms to set in, and he'll be ready for your smile soon enough. Until then, we rest here. We play. We stop fighting."

"Well, if you insist."

"I'm afraid I do."

Kerdik extended his hand to me, and again I saw that signature note of fear that I would recoil from the contact. I slid my palm across his, sifting his fingers through mine and giving him a reassuring squeeze. "Alright, K. You convinced me. Let's take a break together."

17

SAFE WITH YOU

Of all the things I never needed confirmed about Kerdik, one point was clear: Kerdik was a filthy cheater. "Alright, I know you mind-melded that one. You're really just terrible at playing catch. And you're not supposed to be using your magic! We're supposed to be letting our mystical amazingness recharge, which means no tapping into it."

Kerdik examined the orange in his hand, as if wondering how he might manipulate it without the use of his magic. "You're no fun."

"Actually, I'm tons of fun. You're just a dirty, rotten cheater. Toss it for real this time. I don't care if you miss." I held both hands out to give him a wider target. "Pitch it here."

Kerdik frowned, and then tossed the ball with aim that suggested I was two feet to the left of where I actually stood. "Well, that's embarrassing."

"Not embarrassing," I lied to cover over his pride. "You're new at this. Who's there to be embarrassed in front of? It's only me and the daisies here." I picked up the orange and trotted over to him, letting the flowers kick up their tantalizing scent as I moved through the lush greenery. The air smelled like peach jam, freshly mown grass and possibilities. I stood behind him and lifted his arm, bringing it back and around, like my softball coach had taught me when I'd been much younger. "Just like that. Aim with your elbow, and your pointer finger will follow suit." I helped him through the motion a few times.

He turned to smirk at me over his shoulder. "You seem like you know what you're doing. You certain you aren't using magic? You've barely dropped the ball at all."

"Most magic doesn't transfer up in Common. Your blessings did, but nothing else." I leaned up on my toes to peck his cheek, and darn it, if he didn't blush. It was totally precious. The pink flooding the green made for a sweet color contrast. "Thanks for my birth blessings, by the way."

Kerdik's smile turned bashful, his neck ducking into his shoulders as the tips of his ears pinked. "It was no trouble."

"Well, I appreciate it. I appreciate it so much that I'm not leaving this meadow until you learn how to throw a decent pitch."

He tossed the orange, and a little straighter this time, though his focus was so much on the aim that there wasn't much muscle behind it.

"Good, but a little more power now. You can do it, champ." I slapped him on the back and moved to my post across from him, so I could give him something to aim at.

This time, his pitch sunk truer, making it to my hands. I only had to stretch a little to the right. "I think that was better," he ruled.

"You'll be a pro in no time."

"So this is what Commoners do to pass the time?"

"It's what I like to do. Softball wasn't really my thing, though – not enough contact and running around. Soccer's my sweet spot, but I tried them all. Lacrosse, basketball, rugby, tennis, and one excruciating summer of golf." I rolled my eyes. "That was a waste of my life. I don't know why I thought I would like it. My lacrosse coach said I didn't have the patience for golf, so I signed up for a semester of it just to prove her wrong. Lamest rebellion ever."

Kerdik chuckled. "You're a stubborn one, that's for sure. I'm not sure if you get that from Morgan or Lane." He caught the orange and considered his words. "Really, I think you get that from your father. Urien doesn't come across as stubborn because he doesn't make a big fuss when he doesn't get his way. But if he feels strongly about something, he's immovable. And he plans. Oh, how he plans. I had great fun with him when he was upright. He was one of my dearest friends. It was because of my friendship with Urien that I blessed you in the first place."

"You really think you can get him back?" I was afraid to let myself trust the hope that made dormant parts inside of me bloom with new life.

"I know I can. The hardest part's over. My magic isn't healed yet – it took a bigger hit than I was expecting, but it was worth it. Urien was good to me. Looked at me with the same acceptance you do."

"Aw, I'm sure you're selling yourself short. If you didn't parade around your ground-shaking abilities so much, people wouldn't be so afraid of you."

"Yes, but the fear is what keeps them in line."

"So does love. They love Lane, and that's why they followed her to Province 9. They fear Morgan, and they ran out on her."

"I'm certain Morgan crossing you had a little something to do with that. No one wants to be on the wrong side of my wrath. I'm almost glad my magic is a little broken, so she can wait out her days in fear, trembling in dread of the day I come for her."

I tossed the ball from one hand to the other. "But you said yourself, you can't kill her. You put a protection on the Daughters of Avalon so that you can't kill them."

"Ah, but there is so much more to dominance than killing. So much more to fear than the final blow. There are the millions of blows that lead up to the finale. It will be my finest orchestration, composing Morgan's demise."

I frowned at him. "I don't like this kind of talk. I don't want someone to have to die for the world to be right again."

"What you don't want is evil like hers roaming about unchecked."

"What I don't want is for my mother to be so terrible. Isn't there hope that she'll change? Isn't there a way that someday she'll be a better person?"

Kerdik caught the throw I lobbed at him, his eyebrows puckered in my direction. "She let your boy toy be killed, tried to marry you off to your uncle, threw you into a well and starved you, and yet you hold optimism for her redemption? Why? What possible use could her redemption serve?"

"I don't feel happy thinking about revenge. I want what all girls want – for my mom to look at me and be proud, be happy at what I've become. I don't waste my wishes, hoping for her to die. That's grim, dude. I don't think I'd want to live in a world where I didn't have hope that people could change for the better."

"It's naïve," he warned, "and it's never going to happen. Morgan's center of the universe is her own desire. She cares nothing for your life, only that it doesn't outshine hers. And darling, there's no chance for your light to bow to hers. You have faith in good things, and she has trust only in herself."

"You shouldn't encourage me not to forgive her. You shouldn't push me toward revenge. You hurt me, too, you know. If I didn't forgive you, then where would we be now?"

I could tell Kerdik wanted to defend himself, but closed his mouth instead, showing us both that he was capable of growth. He dipped his head in my direction, humbling himself instead of arguing. "You're a princess, if ever I saw one."

I tossed the ball to him. "We should get going, if you're feeling up to the trip. I'm sure Lane's freaking out right about now."

He caught the orange, but instead of throwing it, trotted it over to me. "Eat this first. And when we get back, you're sitting down to supper first thing. There are some maladies even my magic can't fix, so take better care of yourself."

I dug my thumb into the orange, ripping it open and tearing out a segment. The juice ran between my fingers as I handed him a section. "Here. It looks real good." I shoved a bite into my mouth and savored the light citrus that coated my tongue with pure sunshine. It was the fourth orange I'd eaten to appease him.

He looked at the dripping fruit, and then at me, as if I was joking. "I don't need to eat to live; you do."

"Sure, you don't need this to survive, but what's the point in living forever if you never enjoy the fun things? Eat a bite. It's warm from the sun. Super way yummy." I didn't take no for an answer, but kept the orange piece outstretched to him.

Instead of taking it from my me, Kerdik wrapped his fingers around my wrist and brought my arm closer so he could eat straight from my hand, like a giraffe at the zoo. He tilted his head to the side, considering the flavor that danced in his mouth. "Wow, that is better than I remember."

"When's the last time you had an orange?"

"I want to say ten years ago? Fifteen? Time doesn't mean the same to me as it does to you."

My mouth dropped open with a loud guffaw. "Are you serious? You can straight up grow fruit trees from nothing in a blink, but you haven't had an honest to goodness orange in ten or fifteen years? That's bonkers. Seriously, K. You need to live a little. Have another bite."

Kerdik grinned at me, and then held his mouth open, silently asking for more. I fed him another piece, letting his plump lips close on my fingertips. "That's delicious. My, I am talented."

I chuckled at his self-compliment, but then noticed his forehead was slick with sweat. "You alright? You were looking better for a minute, there, but now you're going downhill again. What gives?" I walked with him over to the orange tree to get him under the shade. We sat beneath it, our knees pulled up and resting against each other's.

"Regeneration takes time. A few more days, perhaps."

"Days? Um, not to be a child about it, but Lane's probably freaking out that I've been gone this long. I should probably be getting back."

"Then I'll come with you."

I chewed the orange segment. "Are you sure about that, chief? Lane's not going to be as forgiving as me about the whole leaving me bleeding in the tub thing."

Kerdik nodded. "If you need to get back, I'm the only one who can take you."

"Oh, right." His shoulder pressed to mine while we ate, polishing off two more oranges before I begged off. "It's so good, but I'll get sick if I eat another one. Too much citrus for one meal."

I made to wipe the juices off on my teal cotton shorts, but Kerdik motioned for me to give him my hands. With water he produced from his palms, he washed me off, and then thumbed a few stray lines of juice from my chin. He took a chance and kissed my cheek, warming the skin before his arm wrapped around my shoulders. "I like it here with you."

"Where exactly are we?"

"This is my meadow. It's my special place." He leaned his cheek on my head while he trilled his fingers up and down my forearm. "I've never brought anyone here before. I didn't know where else I'd be safe."

"You're safe with me," I promised. I craned my neck to glance up at him. "Am I safe with you?"

Kerdik's expression grew solemn. "On my honor, I'll never hurt you again as long as I live."

18

CRASHING AT MY PLACE

I'm not sure what state I was expecting the mansion to be in when we returned to it, but out and out panic wasn't in the forecast. The servants were rushing around the house, one of them screeching to a halt at the sight of us near the entrance with a shrill, "The princess has been returned to us!" Then she shrieked at Kerdik's close proximity, and tore down the hall to escape him.

A collective noise of relief echoed in the nearby hallways, and one of the servants ran through the mansion shouting the news. This place really needed an intercom system. Lane bolted toward me from up the stairs, wild-eyed and ready for a fight. Her finger flew in Kerdik's direction. "You! Make off with my daughter again, and you don't want to know what! Rosie, are you okay?"

My answer didn't matter because I couldn't get out word one as more people poured into the foyer. They wanted to come near me, but were too afraid to get near Kerdik. Lane crushed me with a fierce hug that showed me exactly how scared she'd been. "I'm fine, Lane. Honest. We just went away for a little bit so I could rest. Kerdik was afraid someone would mess with my body while it was weak." I shot Kerdik a look that told him I wouldn't rat out his secret that it was he who'd been too weak to defend himself.

In response, he threaded his fingers through mine and squeezed, like we were two children with a secret. "I returned her safe and sound. You've no need to worry, Elaine."

Lane ripped her body from mine, furious that he was speaking calmly when she'd been so clearly freaking out. "Don't tell me not to worry when my only daughter vanishes into thin air! This girl is my world! You don't just make off with somebody's world and expect everything to be cool. Get upstairs!"

Kerdik rolled his shoulders back, letting Lane know he would tolerate her mouth only so far. I tugged him along so things didn't get any worse. His hand was turning clammy, and his grip was slackening. "Come up to my room," I urged him, noticing when he stumbled slightly. Then I lowered my voice to speak into his ear, "Can you make it?"

He nodded, though none too convincingly.

Draper came bounding in from outside, mud up to his knees. "Rosie!" he cried, clutching his chest as if he might have a heart attack.

I waved him over, and did my best to take charge of the situation. "Everyone, I'm real sorry to have made you all worry, but I'm back now. I'm just tired, so I'm going up to my room to sleep, if that's alright." I shot Lane a look that told her to get the staff out of there quick.

She caught on, though not without an inquiring look that demanded an explanation sometime soon. She shooed everyone out while I waved Draper toward us. He kicked off his boots and ran to swallow the distance between us, sweeping me up in a hug that told me how scared he'd been. "Never again!" he roared. "Never disappear like that ever again. I can't tell you how out of my mind it made me to have you gone all over again."

I kissed his cheek and squeezed him, taking the opportunity

the closeness provided me to whisper in his ear. "I need you to help me get Kerdik to my room."

Kerdik glared at me for betraying his secret, but said nothing as he clung to the banister, his chest heaving. "I'm fine."

I spoke quietly to Kerdik. "We can trust Draper and Lane. Bastien, too. If you collapse on the stairs, then everyone will know. This way, your secret's contained."

The fear on Draper's face was plain as day. He was wary to touch Kerdik, but managed a hand on his elbow. "Easy, then. One step at a time."

Kerdik jerked his arm from Draper, indignant at having his wounded pride so closely examined. "I said I'm fine. I don't need help up the stairs. I'm Master Kerdik. All of Avalon bows to me."

Draper quirked his eyebrow. "Would you like me to bow right now, or would you like me to make sure you don't fall down the stairs? Your call."

I wrapped his green arm around my shoulders and moved us slowly up the winding steps. "For all the power you have, you are such a guy. Seriously, dude. We're helping you, and you'll stop being a baby about it."

We made it up eight more stairs before Kerdik's eyes grew panicked. "My body isn't safe here! We need to go back to my meadow."

I shook my head. "Draper and I will watch your body to make sure nothing bad happens. I won't leave you the entire time. I'm getting you up the stairs without everyone watching. See? Your secret's safe." I had one hand on his taut abdomen, and the other around his hips, knowing he only trusted me to anchor his body.

Draper shot me an inquisitive look that was laced with apprehension, but I shook my head to tell him now was not the time. "Whatever you need, Master Kerdik. Our home is yours."

"Of course your home is mine. I can have anything I wish," Kerdik grumped.

"Man, you suck at being helpless. Slow your roll. He meant

that our home is yours because I love you, so you're welcome to stay here as a guest, not as a tyrant douchebag who takes what he wants."

Kerdik swallowed his pride. "Oh, that is better. Yes, I should like to stay as a guest, then."

We made it up two more steps before I prodded him with a gentle, "Tell Draper 'thank you for the offer.'"

Kerdik glared at me, but I refused to shrink.

My fingers tightened on his hip. "Thank my brother, or you sleep on the floor."

Finally, Kerdik caved. "Thank you for the offer, boy."

"His name is Draper," I reminded him.

"Why should I care what his name is?"

"Oh, you are such an asswagon right now. You care because he's helping you up the steps, and if he gets fed up with your attitude, then you could fall. I know I talk a good game, but I'm a little beat still. We actually need his help here."

Draper warned me with a glance that I was pushing too hard. "It's really fine."

"Thank you for the offer, *Draper*," Kerdik finally managed. There was too much attitude laced in to be truly indicative of gratitude, but whatever. His legs were rubbery, and the right one started dragging when we reached the third floor where my room was.

"Almost there, sweetie. Don't worry." When we finally made it into the bedroom and shut the door behind us, I heaved a sigh of relief. "No one else saw. Now let's get him to the bed, Drape."

"What's going on, Rosie? I mean, what broke his magic this much? You two have been gone all night and part of the day, and you come back like this? What happened to him?"

I shook my head, unsure how much I was allowed to spill. We were almost to the bed when Kerdik collapsed. I closed my mouth through a bleat of distress, panic welling in my throat as I scrambled to test his pulse.

109

Of course, I couldn't remember if Kerdik had a pulse to begin with, so I tried not to freak out even more when I couldn't find one. "Get Remy!" Draper ordered, hefting Kerdik's body up in his capable arms, and depositing my friend on my bed.

I bolted out of the room and stumbled down the steps, calling for Remy. He poked his head out from Reyn's room down the hall, shooting me an inquisitive look. He was probably saying something to me, but I couldn't hear him. My magic wasn't totally healed yet, but no one needed that information. "I need help in my bedroom. Grab your doctor bag, quick!"

I tripped as I moved back into my bedroom with Lane hot on my heels, asking questions along the way. I shut the door with the four of us in there, gawking at Kerdik, who was still unconscious. My hand went to my forehead, trying to decide what needed doing first, and which secrets were worth divulging. "Okay, something happened to Kerdik when he was trying to wake up my dad."

Lane let out a gasp of hope. "Did it work? Is Urien awake?"

"Not yet, but he's closer than he's ever been. Kerdik stole his body from Morgan and hid it somewhere in the mansion here. Draper, grab Reyn and quietly search every room until you find my dad. Just the two of you, no one else. Don't try to move him or touch him, just find him, make sure his body is comfortable, and lock the room. No one can know he's here."

Draper made to move, but stayed in the doorway. "Why not? The whole kingdom will want to throw a party."

I cut the flat of my hand through the air. "No one can know. Promise me. It would start a war between Province 1 and us if Morgan found out, and we're in no position to fight her right now. The staff can't know. Only us." I looked around the room. "Where's Bastien and the guys?"

"Damond rode out with them. They split into two parties to search Province 9 to try and find you. Bastien's a little out of his mind." Lane chucked my shoulder. "Well done on nabbing yourself a psychotic protector. I sent him into the province just to get him out of here. He was driving me nuts."

I rubbed my temples, trying to part with only the most useful information. "Okay, first, can you send someone out to let the guys know we're back?"

Draper nodded. "On it." My sweet brother gave me a squeeze before disappearing out the door.

I latched it behind him, my voice low as I spoke to Lane and Remy. "Our magic isn't quite back yet. Kerdik took me to a safe place so no one would hurt our bodies while we healed. He was getting better, but then he transported us back here, and it sapped him dry again. He needs to rest, and he's afraid someone's going to mess with his body while he's out, so I'm not going anywhere for a while. Remy, can you help him at all?"

Remy stared at me without moving toward Kerdik, and it dawned on me that he was probably trying to talk to me the entire time.

I shook my head in dismay. "I'm sorry, Remy. My magic's not quite back yet. I can't hear you." A wounded look crossed his face at losing the one connection he'd needed so badly. I couldn't hold myself back, but flung my arms around his neck to let him know that I wasn't leaving him, and our special link hadn't deserted us for good. "It's temporary," I assured him. "Can you help?"

Remy's face twisted into a grimace of uncertainty after I released him, but he moved to Kerdik's bedside to give the all-powerful being a look.

"What are we supposed to do to help him?" Lane whispered. I detected notes of dread in her voice I hadn't expected. "Rosie, what happens if he dies in here? Can he really die?"

I patted her hand, doling out what I hoped wasn't the last of my optimism. "He'll be alright. Just give him some time."

Kerdik stirred when Remy touched his wrist. An angry whine escaped his lips, and I knew no good could come from this. I darted to the bed, climbing atop the mattress next to his supine body so he could see me if he opened his eyes. I smoothed back the haphazard blue hair from his sweaty forehead, relieved when he leaned into the touch. "It's okay, sweetie. I'm right here." A smile played on my lips when his tension seemed to dissipate, his exhale relaxing his torso in a gust.

"Rosie," Lane cautioned. There was so much she wasn't saying, but I heard it all in her anxious tone. "This is... Master Kerdik is... Be careful."

I didn't tear my gaze away from Kerdik, but took my opportunity to study his features up close. His black lashes contrasted dramatically with his sky-blue hair and green skin. He didn't look so authoritarian in sleep, but more like a younger man who'd worked too hard that particular day. I felt the strangest desire to trace the outline of his curvy lips with my fingertip, but wasn't sure that was something friends did. Instead I drank in his face, hoping that he awoke to better things. "Everything will be alright," I told myself more than Lane.

I cooled Kerdik's heated cheek with the back of my hand, hoping all would be well when he opened his eyes again.

19

YOU'RE MY HOME

"Where is she?" Bastien demanded, his voice booming through the mansion. My spine stiffened, and Lane manned the door to make sure only members of our close-knit circle came through.

I wanted to get up and run to him, but Kerdik moaned when I moved toward the other side of the bed. I slunk back to his side, holding his hand to my chest to reassure him. He stirred infrequently, but always reached for me in his lost moments to anchor him. It was the best kind of precious, so I tried to treat our friendship tenderly. There was also the added concern that he might get worked up and accidentally bring the house down on our heads with his oft-swinging temper. Lane was acutely aware of that possibility, and reminded me of it often.

Lane called Bastien upstairs, and he didn't bother taking his filthy boots off as he charged up to my room. Lane let him in before he broke the door down, warning him to calm down. Bastien gripped the doorjamb as if using the frame to hold himself back. His desperate eyes pored over me, taking in my features as if searching for a severed limb or something horrific. "You! What happened? Where were you?" Before I could answer, he thrust his body into the room, beelining for the bed. He was covered in mud, but that didn't stop him from scooping me off the bed and wrapping my legs around his waist. He didn't pause for decency, or hesitate because of the company. Bastien kissed me as if he'd thought he never would have the chance again.

Guilt washed over me that I'd been shooting the breeze and playing baseball with oranges while Bastien had been freaking out.

His kisses were hard, almost painful, and filled with earnest devotion. He was frantic to get me near and keep me in his arms. Even after I assumed he would deflate and set me down, he only held me tighter, mashing his body to mine and squashing my belly to his. "Never again!" he roared between kisses. "I blinked, and you were gone!"

"I know," I worked out, his lips smearing to my cheek before he was drawn back to my mouth like a magnet. "I'm so sorry."

"Are you alright?"

I nodded, inhaling sharply when he bit down on my lower lip.

"Then never do that again! What happened?" Before I could answer, he covered my mouth with his again, not bothering to taste me, but conquering me with his tongue, taking no prisoners. Then he pulled back to study my features. "Don't tell me yet; I'm too angry." His hand squeezed my thigh roughly, making me yelp in his arms.

"I'm here now. I'm okay."

"*I'm* not okay!" he bellowed, taking his hand from my thigh to give my backside a smack. I jumped in his arms at the slight sting I hadn't been expecting.

That was right about the time that Lane decided we'd carried on enough. "Other people are in the room, Bastien. Put my daughter down."

Bastien seemed to come to himself gradually, slowing the kisses down from their frantic pace until they melted into a languid tasting he couldn't cut himself off from. "You scared me," he admitted, his eyes closed as he pressed his forehead to mine. He finally let my feet touch the floor, and lifted my hand to press it to his chest. "Never scare me like that again."

I nodded, rubbing my hands across his chest so I could give the taut pectoral muscles a covert rub. My back was to the audience, who vacillated between averting their eyes and peeking like naughty children at our display. "I'm sorry, Bastien. I'm home now."

"*I'm* your home," he told me, staking his claim on the heart we both knew couldn't deny him for long. "Tell me."

"You're my home, and I'm your safe place."

Lane cleared her throat. "Go clean up, Bastien. You can use the tub down the hall. Rosie's going to use this one."

Bastien shook his head. "No. I'll wait here. Not out of my sight, Rosie. I won't risk it."

Lane huffed, like Bastien was being dramatic, but really, I couldn't blame him. I'd been abducted too many times for either of us to feel secure when we were apart from each other. I leaned up on my toes and pecked his cheek. "I'll be quick."

When we were clean twenty minutes later, and food had been brought up. I munched on my dinner while the search party huddled quietly in the bedroom. Through much indignation and fear, everyone was brought up to speed. Draper was firm that Damond not be welcomed into our secretive circle, to keep him safe. I was resolute that Roland not be allowed anywhere near me or my secrets, and though I could tell Reyn and Bastien didn't like discluding their friend, they let it be my call. Lane had moved him into the grand house next door after I'd been brought to live here, ruling that though she'd forgiven him, Roland wasn't to live under the same roof as me after all he'd done.

Kerdik was still in and out of consciousness. Each time he came back to us, he fumbled around like a blind man for me, settling down only when he found my hand. His body was hot, and no matter what herbs and spells Remy used, Kerdik continued to sweat.

Madigan stood at my open window, arms banded over his chest as he stared out into the darkness. "The sun should've been up a while ago."

Link crossed the room to peer out into the midnight. "Aye. I thought so, too. But it doesn't even look near dawn. The cattle are getting restless. They know something's amiss. But at least the rain stopped."

My eyebrows pushed together, wondering if there was yet another ridiculous thing I was supposed to be worrying about. "Is that normal for Avalon?"

"About as abnormal as it would be in Common. I don't understand." Lane moved to the window to stand between the Untouchables, and shook her head. "It's Kerdik. It's got to be. He's the only one in Avalon who can control most of the elements, though I've never known him to have power over the sun. I'm guessing this is his doing. Are we any closer to waking him, Remy?"

"How should I know? This is way beyond my expertise. Treating someone who never gets sick? A man on the brink of death who can't die?"

I perked up, my head whipping around to Remy. "I heard that! Remy, my magic's starting to heal."

Remy gusted out a tornado of relief. *"I thought I might never be heard again! You can really hear me?"*

"Oh, thank God. How can I help you?"

"No one can do much, but you need to stay near him. You're the only thing that's keeping him calm. His body is going to work this out, hopefully. There's nothing else that can be done for him right now. Just keep him peaceful, as much as you can. Otherwise, I fear the mansion might come down on our heads." Remy sighed contentedly. *"How I missed you, Princess."*

I smiled at my official healer and unofficial knight from my spot in the middle of the mattress. Though everyone had assured me my gifts would return, I'd had my doubts, and was relieved to have my old self back. "I missed you too, Remy. You're the best knight I ever had." I was sandwiched between Kerdik and Bastien on the bed, though every now and then Bastien would inch closer to me, so now I was practically on his lap. He'd gone from Mr. Boundaries to Mr. I've-Never-Heard-of-Boundaries.

Remy burned his fifth bundle of herbs over Kerdik's body before packing up his bag. *I need to go back to Draper, Damond and Reyn to check on King Urien.*

"Be careful, Remy. Kerdik said a lot of Morgan's magic that was used to keep my dad frozen had fail-safes built in. It's how he got so hurt in the first place. Just try to keep my dad comfortable and healthy, if you can. Nothing more. I don't want Morgan's magic making you sick like this. If it can do this to Kerdik, you need to tread lightly."

"I need to go out into the village," Lane said while Remy packed up. "I have to be present when people start to realize that the sun isn't coming."

"I'll go with ye," Link offered. "T'won't do to have ye getting snatched at. Can't afford to be down a duchess right now."

"Thank you, Link. That's very kind of you."

I thought Link would be out the door, but he paused by the bedside, leaned over Bastien and kissed my cheek. "Stay with Bastien," he said quietly, a note of concern in his voice at the prospect of leaving the mansion.

"I will. Be safe out there."

He shot me a wide grin. "Now, what's the fun in tha?"

Mad didn't say a word, but followed his friend, offering my Lane protection without being asked. When they left with Remy, Bastien and I were alone with Kerdik, who was basically not really there.

Bastien's kisses were slow, and looked like they caused him physical pain. His eyes were squinched tight, pleading silently for me to stay with him in the dim flicker of the lamplight. Though I was twisted in his arms, lifting and turning my chin to kiss him over my shoulder, it still wasn't close enough. He pulled me more fully onto his lap, thumbing my jaw and brushing his knuckle across my cheek.

I was completely entranced by his scent, his body and his earnest need for us. It wasn't just *me* he wanted – it was *us*. The two of us were finally working in synchronicity instead of fighting, as we usually did without hesitation.

"I love you, Daisy," he murmured, making my heart stutter in my chest. I knew without a doubt that I loved him, too. That no matter how many times I tried to deny it, to separate my heart from his, I always came back to the steady thrum that drew me in. Oh, how I loved the draw he had on everything that was me. Though Kerdik was right next to us, it felt like we were on our own personal island.

His fingers moved from my jaw down my throat, cascading over my shoulder to grip the skin possessively. Goosebumps and anticipation broke out over my flesh, thrilling me and setting my body on fire. I kept my lips locked on his, arching my back to get as close as I could to him.

The heat in my body balled itself up in my stomach. As our kiss morphed from good old American into French, the growing inferno rose into my chest. I was warm all over, so much that I didn't recognize the heat for what it was until I started choking.

20

LUEUR

"*I*'m sorry! I'm sorry!" I cried between bouts of gagging on my *lueur*. I hadn't meant to conjure up that bit of dormant light in my belly, but it was straining to get out of me and into Bastien as I coughed.

Bastien's eyes flashed with a breath of panic before they cooled into a bold determination that fixed his gaze on mine. "I want to be your *Guardien*, Daisy. Don't be afraid to give me your *lueur*."

I turned my head and coughed into my fist, sitting up so I could move onto all fours on the mattress, hacking away like the sexy beast I was. "You don't know what you're saying. I didn't mean for this to happen! Just give me a second."

Bastien rubbed my back while I coughed, rousing Kerdik. "Rosie? Are you alright?" Kerdik promptly fell back asleep after his hand found my ankle. Worst threesome ever.

Bastien leaned over and spoke low in my ear. "Let me be yours. I already am. This would make it easier for me to watch out for you."

I slapped my hand to the mattress, moisture pooling in my eyes. "You'll leave!"

Bastien shook his head adamantly. "No! I'll never leave us. I want this, honey. I want to protect us."

That he said "us" instead of just wanting to protect me was what clinched it. I wasn't the weak princess who needed saving, though sometimes I felt exactly that. It was us together that needed protecting. It was our connection, however simultaneously strong and fragile. It demanded nothing but our best efforts. "Are you sure?"

Bastien didn't answer right away, but pulled my shoulders up so I was kneeling on the bed facing him. He didn't care that I coughed in his shirt; he only cared that we were in the same boat. That even when we were lost, we would drown in the same ocean, choking on the same air. His arms coiled around my waist, thumbing the small of my back. "I'm more than sure. It's you and me. There's never been a chance of anyone else. Trust me to take care of us."

I didn't know how to answer; the whole thing felt like a marriage proposal. When I leaned up to kiss him again, I realized my chin was trembling. I wasn't sure if I was nervous or excited or scared, but all of my emotions bubbled to my tear ducts when I whispered, "I trust you," against his lips.

Bastien kissed me, holding me tight against him – partly out of desire, and partly because closeness was key for feeding him the heat that was still yearning to leap out of my body and give itself over to him. Part of me realized that it had belonged with him from the very first kiss. It was denying that truth for this long that had gotten us into so much trouble. "I love you," I whispered with a shiver.

"It's always been you, Daisy." Then his lips melted into mine, soft and needy with an earnest desire for more – always more.

The heat in me rose once again, no matter how many times I told it to go away. No matter how often I'd repressed the warmth Bastien coaxed into me, it was there all the same, rising up from my belly to my throat, choking me for only a moment before it migrated from my mouth and into his.

Bastien stiffened, letting out a cry that muffled itself against my lips. His body went rigid, holding mine just a little too tight before he fell away from me. Bastien landed on the mattress and bounced, falling out of my grasp with eyes wide open.

I realized then that I should've asked what would happen immediately after my *lueur* went into Bastien. His breaths came in deep gulps, as if the air was too thin for him to get in a decent pull. I ran to the door, unlocking it and flinging it open when his body started seizing. "Remy! I need Remy! Draper, help!"

Several servants ran to my aid, but I couldn't let any of them in with Kerdik lying there. I kept them at bay until Draper bolted up the steps, taking them three at a time. "What is it? What's wrong?"

I let only him in, apologizing to the others before I locked us inside. "He's freaking out! I don't know what's wrong with him!" I ran to the bed and tipped Bastien onto his side, hoping he wouldn't swallow his tongue or something.

The jostling roused Kerdik, who grumbled at the imposition like a jerk. "He's fine, Rosie. This is all perfectly normal."

"It's not normal! I gave him my *lueur*, and he started to spaz out! Help me, Draper!"

The urgency in my brother went down a few degrees. "Oh, I didn't know you were seriously considering doing that with Bastien. Wow. I guess I should probably stop giving him such a hard time."

"We can talk about that later. Help me calm him down!"

Draper gently pried my fingers off of Bastien, standing upright and holding me to his side while he explained the way of the world to me. "His body's adjusting to your *lueur*. It's a very old, powerful bit of magic. When a Brownie takes a Fae's *lueur*, part of the Fae goes into the Brownie. Makes them one, in a sense."

"He didn't tell me I'd give him a seizure! Get it out of him! Can I yank it out somehow?"

Of all things, Draper chuckled. "No. He probably didn't tell you because you'd refuse to give it to him if you knew. No Brownie who can handle the job of a *Guardien* dies from this."

"You're telling me there are Brownies out there who *have* died trying to do this?" My voice was shrill, my spine straight as a board.

Draper winced. "Only the ones who couldn't handle the responsibility. The *lueur* is smart. It knows not to move inside of a body that can't support it." He waved his hand at Bastien. "He's been watching out for you for a long time now. The *lueur* won't reject him. It's been trying to find its way into his body since your first kiss."

I tore away from Draper and climbed up onto the bed, throwing my arms around Bastien's chest to steady him as much as I could. "I'm sorry! I didn't know this would hurt you. I didn't know *I* would hurt you. Why didn't you tell me?" His flannel twisted around his torso as he jerked and twitched beneath me.

Draper pried me from Bastien again, drawing me back so I didn't get punched by one of Bastien's errant fists. "It won't take long. Bastien's worthy."

But it did take long. It took a solid hour of Bastien crying out and thrashing on the bed. It took an hour of my soul freaking out and my prayers spilling unintelligibly through my lips for everything to be okay. An hour of holding Kerdik's hand in a chair at the other side of the bed. An hour of my father still lost to us with me nowhere near him to offer any sort of solace. An hour of the sun still not rising.

21

PROTECTING US

𝓘t was midmorning, but still looked like the blackest midnight outside when Bastien finally stopped seizing. Draper had moved him to the ground so he didn't accidentally punch Kerdik and incur his sleepy wrath. We moved him back onto the bed when his body finally stilled. To his credit, Draper stayed with my crazy brain the entire time. He brought Bastien broth when my boyfriend's eyes finally opened, and rubbed a reassuring circle into my back as I fed Bastien spoonfuls of the golden liquid I hoped would make him better in a blink.

Bastien didn't say a word for a while, letting the silence build between us until he knew he would have to be the one to break it. "I didn't piss myself, so that's a plus."

My mouth set in a firm line while Draper sniggered. "That's all you have to say to me?" I raged, letting loose the anxiety that had somehow morphed into fury. "You didn't tell me any of that would happen to you! I had no idea my *lueur* would kill you if it decided you couldn't handle it!"

Bastien shrugged, wincing at the slight movement. "You wouldn't have given it to me if you'd known there was that chance."

Draper clapped me on the shoulder. "Told you so." He kissed my temple and stood from the bed. "I'll leave you to your fight. Maybe I'll see if Reyn or Remy needs any help. You want me to send Remy up here, Bastien?"

Bastien's posture was slumped against a stack of pillows, his body worn out from the nonstop workout of seizing for an hour. "Yeah, might as well. When he's bored. Don't rush or anything. I'm really fine."

My tone was clipped when I turned my head toward Draper. "That means he's really hurting, so unless Remy's actively resurrecting my dad, please send him on up with everything in his arsenal."

"Will do," Draper said, shutting himself out of the room.

Bastien had the gall to smirk. "You love me."

"Fat lot of good that did either one of us. You almost died!"

Bastien scoffed. "I nothing like 'almost died.' I was fine. Bored, actually. Thought about taking up knitting to pass the time."

I was shaking with anger, and spilled a few drops of broth onto the comforter. "You're about to be wearing this soup, you jackballoon. Don't act like everything's going to be simple when it's not. Don't let me hurt you! I just... And then you... I hurt you!" I'd thought all my tears had been worked out of my system, but apparently I had a few more for just such an occasion.

Bastien's smile was sympathetic and sweet. He patted the space between himself and Kerdik. "Come here, honey. You didn't hurt me."

I set down the bowl of broth on the nightstand and crawled in between my two guys. I wasted no time at all snuggling up to Bastien's side, feeling a deep sense of belonging when we connected like this. I'd felt it before, but this time the symphony in my chest was amped up to a ridiculous volume, drawing me in and captivating me. His arm fell around my hips, and though he tried to pull me to him, I could feel how weak his grip was. "How can I make it better?"

"Just keep looking at me like that, but with less pity. Honestly, Ro. I'm strong enough to handle a little struggle."

"You were seizing forever! It wasn't a little struggle, Bastien. You scared me. I thought I'd killed you!"

"Nah. It'd take a lot more than that to kill someone like me. It was nothing. I'm just milking it so I can get more sympathy. I like you close like this."

Kerdik groaned, whimpering in a childlike voice, "No, Father! Stop it! I don't like it out here!"

I sucked in my breath, hoping Bastien hadn't heard the unconscious admission that Kerdik had parents. I knew he wouldn't want either of us to know the secret he kept tight to the vest. "You didn't hear that. I mean it, Bastien. Forget he said that."

Bastien nodded. "I'm barely upright. Just tell me I hallucinated him saying something, and I'll believe you."

"You hallucinated." I reached over and tugged Kerdik's pillow closer to my other side, shifting his head so his temple rested against my hip. I combed my fingers through his thick blue hair, my heart clenching in my chest as he moaned in relief at my touch. Finally he mumbled something unintelligible and then fell back asleep. He breathed more evenly and was prone to fewer fits when he was touching me, so I kept my hand against his cheek.

"He loves you," Bastien remarked, his chest moving in a slow rhythm, his eyes barely open. "I don't know how I like that."

"He needs me. He has literally no one else. He stays until I say he has to go."

"I wasn't assuming I had a choice in any of it. Just be careful. Kerdik's love can be terrifying."

I shivered when I recalled the ice he'd used to imprisoned me. "I remember. But he doesn't know any better. He needs to learn how to be kind. Everyone needs someone to be good to them, and he has no one who speaks that language to him. He's so isolated. It worries me how alone he is."

"You're so predictable. Always taking in strays and loving too much. Though, I guess I can't complain. You took me in easily enough."

"You never needed me. You're so self-assured. I'm just lucky to be along for the ride."

Bastien worked out a light scoff. "When we were apart? Mad had to fish me out of a pub after I'd carried on with my misery a little too much." He shook his head, and then grimaced at mention of his drinking. "Never again. Never doubt that I need us." I loved when he said he needed "us" instead of "me". My affections only grew stronger for him that it was our connection he was protective of, the team we'd built, just the two of us.

"Where does it hurt?"

He turned his head to crack his neck and groaned. "Only everywhere. I'm glad I never have to do that again. It's all down-hill from here, right?"

"Let's hope so." Though something in me warned my waning optimism that we might not have hit the worst of things yet.

22

THE LAST WILL AND FREAKOUT OF BASTIEN

*T*hree days passed, and the sun still hadn't risen. It was pitch black, the province lit only by oil lamps hanging off of tall posts that had been provided by Lane.

Bastien was good as new, and perhaps even more so. His senses seemed sharper, hearing things before anyone else did, and putting smells to things and people to identify them without having to turn around. He'd gone from action star to supernatural action hero overnight. He'd paused over breakfast, his shoulders tensed, and then took off, abandoning his porridge mid-bite. His freaky *Guardien* intuition had alerted him that there were weak stones near the servants' quarters, and could be used as a possible break-in point, if anyone else knew. Within two hours, the weak stones were reinforced, and he was back to his cold porridge, breathing easier, now that a gap in my protection had been covered.

Our connection had never been stronger, adding a layer of intensity to the fire that was already there. It often caught those around us off-guard. I could sense when he walked into a room now, and felt the cold absence when he left. His rounds to make sure the mansion was secure every morning were done in haste, hurrying to return to me. I know it sounds dramatic, but even brief separations were painful for us both.

When Bastien needed to go out to see to adding extra security, he sent Link in to watch me – as if I was a toddler who might electrocute myself if left unchecked. Link wasn't too bad a guy to hang with, though. Lane found us a ball, and we kicked it back and forth in my bedroom while he drilled me with question after question about Common. Link was prone to laughing, and didn't hold the joyous sound back, but belted out levity at every opportunity. He'd even made up a song for me that he sang throughout the house when he wanted to announce his presence: "Rosie, I love ye. Rosie, I care. Rosie, without ye my heart's in despair." He was a goofball.

Bastien still hadn't slept, though we both knew it was coming. He was fighting it off as long as he could, using his magic sparingly to fend off the inevitable. Hamish scolded him over breakfast that it wasn't a weakness to be a creature that slept. In fact, in Faîte, it was sometimes an indicator that you'd wielded a great amount of magic.

Link and Draper teased us mercilessly the first couple days, making jokes about how we couldn't eat off two separate forks. When we shrugged and continued feeding each other like the gooey lovebirds we were, they gave up on their quest to call us out on the obvious. Every now and then, Link just stared at us in utter flabbergast, his mouth gaping open so wide that I debated shoving a roll inside.

I rarely left my bedroom, since every time I did, Kerdik started freaking out. When I'd gone to visit my dad and talk to him (as Britney Spears, of course. I was still too chicken to tell him who I was), and then headed down to the dining room for dinner with the crew, the house started shaking halfway through the meal. I'd thought it was an earthquake until Remy shouted to me that Kerdik was trying to reach me in his sleep. The second I bolted up the steps and held his hand, the ground calmed.

Province 9 lost eight sheep, one empty hut (thank goodness), and injured a few people in the quake. It was for all our sakes that I basically lived in my bed now.

It was hard to tell night from day anymore, but when I started yawning and Bastien caught a bout of the same sleepy cue, I knew it was time. He was nervous, and called Madigan and Link up to give them a talk. He pointed his flat hand perpendicular to the floor, meaning business. "No one comes into the castle that you two don't personally clear. I mean it, guys. I won't be able to help, and I don't know how easy it'll be to wake me up. I don't really know much about sleeping, other than watching Rosie." He ran his palms over his thighs, wiping them off on his jeans. "If anything happens, wake me up. If you can't wake me, then tell Lane. Her head of security's a joke."

Link nodded. "Aye. Nice enough lad, but I wouldn't trust him to guard a wee kitten. We've got Abraham Lincoln. Rosie's taught him to listen to us, so ye've no need to worry. People tend not to mess with two Untouchables from Éireland who come armed with a bear."

I moved over to Bastien and ran my hand over his shoulders, rubbing the tension and hopefully soothing a little of his fear. "It's alright, Bastien. Sleeping is nothing to be afraid of."

"The only thing I'm afraid of is something happening to you while I'm out." Bastien fidgeted on the side of the bed, shifting to keep himself awake for as long as he could. He met Madigan's eye with a brotherly trust that ran deep. "If something should happen to me, I want you to make sure Rosie's taken care of."

"You're not dying, Bastien! Honey, it's really okay." He sounded like he was writing his will.

Madigan didn't miss a beat. "Aye, brother. Ye don't have to worry about tha. I'll look after your lass with my life."

My mouth dropped open in shock, unable to hide how moved I was at Madigan's vow to be good to me. "Mad, you don't have to do that."

Madigan met my eyes with a certainty that told me there was no use arguing. "It's done. Untouchables take care of their women."

Bastien's eyes slid to Link. "Nicholai's locket is buried under the hideaway in my cabin. If I die, see he gets it back. But not until I'm actually dead. Otherwise keep it hidden there. He can't be trusted with that much power."

Link stood with Bastien, taking his hand and using it to pull him in for a tight hug. The sweetness touched me deep in parts I hadn't assumed needed softening, but melted all the same. "Aye, brother. Ye don't need to worry about a thing. Get your beauty sleep. Ye look like you've been needing about a week's worth for a while now." He slapped Bastien a few times hard on the back before he released him.

Madigan wasn't prone to such affections, so he kept his distance, nodding his loyalty to Bastien. "I'll keep the fort locked down for ye." Then he turned to me and gave me a look that told me to be gentle with Bastien when he was in this rare fragile state.

"Goodnight, wee Rose." Link smooched my cheek, and then blew a loud raspberry on my skin. He always doled out the adorableness before earning the slap he was constantly begging for.

"Alright, alright. Get out of here, Lucky Charms." After I shoved Link and Madigan out of the room, I locked us inside, turning to face Bastien. "Are you okay? I think you've got the wrong idea about sleep. It's not dangerous or anything. You'll be fine."

Bastien shook his head slowly, stretching his arm across his chest so he could pop his shoulder. "I need to go do another walk of the grounds. I'll be up in a few."

I spread out my arms and legs like a starfish over the door. "Not a chance. The guys have everything under control. You're going to hit your breaking point, and pass out in the mud somewhere along the way. It's still too dark to see anything, so it would take us hours to find you. You're stalling."

"You know me too well." He faced the bed and slapped his palms together, eyeing Kerdik with mild frustration. "So how do we do this?"

"Pajamas," I suggested, pulling out Avalon's version of sweat-pants. I'd had them made by the seamstress who worked for Lane. They were flannel, drawstring and would cup his tight butt like he was modeling the outfit. Rugged chic, for sure.

Bastien slowly unbuttoned his flannel shirt, holding my gaze as his turned smoldering out of nowhere. He took a few steps closer, tugging the bed curtain across the foot of the bed to separate us from Kerdik and give us the illusion of privacy. "I might need your help with those. You Commoners with your strange customs."

I knew he was putting the moves on me to fend off sleep, and darn it, if it wasn't working all over the place. My cheeks turned pink as my unsteady hands reached out to fiddle with his belt's buckle. It was a standard latch, but my hands started to forget the simple mechanics of such things. My fingers kept slipping on the metal, my face grimacing when I should've been giving him my best you-know-what-you-want-so-take-it eyes. "I'm having trouble with…"

Bastien kissed me, our lips moving slowly as he took my hand and used it to unfasten his belt. My heart spasmed in my chest until I let out a childish whimper when the button of his jeans came undone. I hopped back from him, spinning around with my eyes shut when his jeans fell to the ground. I winced when he chuckled, tugging up the pajama pants so I didn't have a panic attack. Part of me knew he was wearing underwear, which I'd seen him in before, but there was a new intensity to our relation-ship since he took my *lueur*. Everything was heightened, which made me more than a little nervous when I pictured the lusty and delicious possibilities that come with undressing a man. For all that I'd been through along the way in life, there were some things I just wasn't ready for. "It's okay, Daisy. I'm dressed. You can turn around."

I turned back to him, but kept my eyes to the side, holding myself to keep my bashfulness from vanishing me off the planet altogether. "Okay, um, you ready for bed now?"

"Look at me."

I shook my head once, my gaze still pointing to the left. "Not yet. I need a minute to pull myself together."

"Do I get to dress you in your pajamas?" His eyebrows waggled suggestively, making light while I was freaking out.

"No! Go lay in bed, you boy. I'll be there in a second." I ignored his chuckle and huffed while I snatched up my soft nightgown. Abella, the seamstress, had made me five of the same design in all different colors. It was loose cotton, low cut, but not enough to make me feel slutty. The gown had spaghetti straps, with soft lace around the bust and the mid-thigh hem. I marched behind the partition, tore off my jeans and t-shirt and slid on the sexiest thing I owned. I'd never been given to wearing sexy clothing, but there was something about the loose fit of this that made it feel like I was wearing a comfy old t-shirt. I gulped when I glanced down, taking in my cleavage that was barely visible, but definitely a feature that couldn't be ignored. I flipped my hair over my shoulder and tried (unsuccessfully) not to overthink it. We'd laid in bed dozens of times before. Somehow this felt different. Bastien was giving me this vulnerable side of him. He could have opted for one of the dozens of other rooms in the vast mansion that was now my home, but he wanted to share this new experience with me.

I took a steadying breath and moved out from the partition, rubbing a spot on my elbow as my nerves took over the use of my hand.

Bastien's muttered curse and wide eyes told me this little number was a hit, and that I had nothing to be nervous about. He was sitting on the side of the bed, gawking at me like a teenager. Kerdik was on the mattress as our unofficial chaperone, so I knew nothing would venture farther than I was ready for. Still, there was a highly-strung note of sexual tension that thickened the air between us. "Suddenly I'm wide awake. Come here. Let me look at you."

I moved closer, a shy downward tilt to my head as he pulled me to stand between his open knees. Bastien moved my hands to rest on his shoulders, looking up into my eyes that were trying not to dart away from his. "So, I bet of all the times you were hoping we'd be in bed together, you never pictured a second guy in the room."

Bastien's hands slid down my spine and stroked my backside, cupping the swell possessively. "I'll take what I can get." Then he tucked a lock of hair behind my ear, exposing my face to his. Oh, how very exposed I felt. "Kiss me."

I leaned down and brushed my lips to his, sinking into his body as he leaned back on the mattress. We really lucked out that the bed was so large. I would've been so embarrassed if we brushed up against Kerdik while in the throes. It was bad enough to be carrying on like we were, but some things just couldn't be helped. I mean, it was Bastien in pajama pants. Be still my heart.

Bastien had a rugged charm to him that had me crawling on top of him like a prowling jungle cat, my body practically purring with every brush against my skin. I couldn't get close enough, couldn't kiss deep enough, couldn't possibly want him more than I did in that moment.

It was as good a time as any for Kerdik to stir. He didn't open his eyes, but cried out for me as he'd been doing for days when he needed reassurance that he was safe, and I hadn't left him for scavengers to tear apart. I kissed Bastien once more in silent apology before rolling off of him to fumble my way over to Kerdik before he got too worked up. "It's okay, Kerdik. I'm right here. I haven't left you." I picked up his hand and patted the back to reassure him. "Deep breaths, hun." As quickly as Kerdik's fit started, it began to drift away at my touch. He mumbled something I couldn't make out, and then went back to sleep. I smoothed his hair back from his forehead. "Poor baby."

Bastien let out a low breath, adjusting himself before he sat up. "I guess sleeping with a third person in the room won't be too terrible. But as soon as he's better, I want a night alone with you in here. No Hamish. No Abraham Lincoln. Just us."

"You got it, chief." I pulled back the covers and tucked my feet inside, snuggling down next to Kerdik. I patted the space next to me, beckoning Bastien to lay down. "Come sleep with me."

The left corner of Bastien's mouth lifted wryly at my proposition. "Can't imagine getting a better offer than that." He turned off the lantern and slid in next to me, his weight tipping me toward him so I landed in his nook. My neck lay over his outstretched arm, and my hand rested on his shoulder. "I'm nervous," he admitted. "I don't like closing my eyes when the guy who attacked you is right in the bed with us. It's counterintuitive."

"Kerdik and I talked it all out. We're cool now. He's going to work on his temper."

"My body's exhausted, but I've got all this anxiety over him being right there."

"I have to stay in here, but you don't. Did you want to try finding a different bed?"

Bastien scoffed. "Like you could pry me away from you right now." He tightened his arm around me. "Come closer."

I snuggled into his firm body, my spine stretching when he looped my leg over his. His hand traced from my knee up to my thigh, tickling the underside until my back arched. My backside landed itself in his palm, and he wasted no time giving it a tight squeeze. We took turns nipping each other's lower lips, falling for each other all over again until the night took us under.

23

BED FOR THREE

*B*astien slept like the dead, making up for lost time, I guess. I roused in the night, so I got to just watch him sleep for a while. His scratchy cheeks made him look far older than me, and his perpetually grouchy expression melted into the face of a docile man who'd been through just plain too much. His chest moved slowly up and down, taking my hand along for the ride.

Kerdik rolled onto his side during the night, seeking out my body so he could touch my back while I was cuddled up to Bastien. It was hopefully the strangest sleeping arrangement I'd ever be in. Though, really, if I added Abraham Lincoln to the mix tomorrow night, that would be weirder. My bear had been growing an affinity for Link as of late, and was no doubt sleeping outside so he could be closer to Link if he needed backup.

I knew I should feel claustrophobic with Kerdik resting right behind me. Instead of anxious, I slept deeper than I had in ages. Bastien was facing me, his hand cupping my butt like it was his coveted treasure. At one point, he rolled onto his back, but instead of parting from me, he grabbed my leg and took it with him, stretching it over his lap so he could stroke it in his sleep. I kinda loved him for it, and dozed back to sleep with a smile on my face and my man in my arms.

In the morning, I awoke to someone's hand cupping the underside of my breast. I didn't look because I didn't want to know which one of them it was. I couldn't tell if either of them were awake, or if it was a sleepy blunder. Instead I stretched, giving myself just enough wiggle room to breathe. I heard birds singing a cheerful call to wakefulness that made me smile. They were excited to see the province filled with people for once. One of the birds chirped that he'd found a twig just the right size to help rebuild his nest, which had been damaged during the rain.

My eyes popped open, and I saw natural light cascading in from the window. Though three-quarters of our bed curtains had been shut, I could still make out a noticeable difference in the room. I gasped, relieved and excited that the sun had finally returned after days of darkness, and that it shone without rain marring the beauty. I heard no trace of the rain, only felt the possibility of new life springing from outside the mansion.

"Are you happy to have your birth blessing back, darling?"

I hadn't realized Kerdik had been awake. Bastien was still snoozing, so I tried to be careful when I turned over under the covers to face my buddy. "I am!" I whispered with a grin. "Plus, it's finally light out. While you were out, there were days and days of darkness. Like, the sun didn't rise. I'm glad you were out for that part."

"Oh, that was me." He said it with the bashfulness of excusing himself after blasting out a belch. "I don't sleep often, but when I do, I accidentally control some of the elements, so they usually keep themselves attuned to me."

"Huh. That's kind of cool. I guess it's a good thing you don't sleep often, then. People have been freaking out without the sun."

"How long was I out?"

"Days, Kerdik. Like, four days now. I'm glad you're back. Are you feeling alright?"

"Better now. I didn't... Did I hurt you in my sleep?" His eyes were wary, as if bracing himself for my outburst.

"Not at all. You were afraid, though. If you couldn't find me in your sleep, then the house would start to shake with an earthquake. Kind of scary." My nose scrunched. "Okay, I get why Avalon was dark, but what about the nonstop rain before that? It was weeks of nothing but rain. Was that you, too?"

Kerdik nodded, ashamed. His eyes darted away from me, but his hand curled around my waist to move my body flush to his. It was very intimate, and beneath the preciousness of the moment, the back of my mind wondered if perhaps we were a little too entwined. "I was upset that I'd hurt you when we had our little spat. I told you, the elements are tied to my emotions sometimes. I was devastated without you, so nature cried on my behalf. That kind of thing I can't actually control. I mean, when it happens, it's a fluke. I don't know how to turn it on and off on purpose."

I rubbed the sleep from my eyes and balked at him. "Are you serious?"

"Serious and sorry. I won't lose my temper like that again. I gave it a lot of thought while I was sleeping."

"I don't think sleep works like that."

"Mine does. It gives me time to examine my choices, which truthfully, is one of the reasons I don't often do it." He closed the breath of a gap between us and pecked my lips, as if we'd been married for decades and did that sort of thing all the time. He pulled back two inches and examined my face to make sure that was kosher. I was too stunned to weigh in. "I'm truly sorry I hurt you."

"I forgive you. Just like I forgive Morgan for what she did. Just like I forgave this one when he crossed the line a while back."

Kerdik's expression darkened. "You shouldn't waste your forgiveness on Morgan. It won't change her. Revenge is the better choice."

I brushed my nose across his, savoring the sweetness before

the world piled too many problems on our plates. "Forgiveness isn't meant to change Morgan. Forgiveness changes me. It keeps me from turning into someone who could throw her daughter down a well."

Kerdik's mouth popped open, as if I'd said something totally crazy. "Just when I think I've lived long enough to have heard it all, you come along and retrain all I thought I knew." He tangled his fingers through mine, kissing my knuckles and holding them to his chest. "Leave the vengeance to me, then. You should worry about only the things that are completely within your control, like this one, for example." He jerked his chin in Bastien's direction.

"Hello, I don't control Bastien."

"Darling, you hold power over every man who's ever touched the silk of your hand."

I'd thought Bastien was sleeping, but he murmured a lazy, "I'm not under Rosie's control. Unless she says I am, and then it's all, 'Yes, Mistress. Whatever you say.'"

I smirked and rolled over. "I like the sound of that."

Kerdik tugged the curtain that separated our bed from the window the rest of the way open, letting in a flood of light that brought Bastien up to a seated position so he could gawk at the beauty we'd been missing. Kerdik leaned over the mattress and lightly kissed my lips again in plain view of Bastien, marking his territory like a dog. "I'll go see to your father, darling. Then I'm afraid I'll be gone for a little while. Revenge on Morgan is best when it comes with plenty of explosions and surprises. I'll need a little time to prepare."

Bastien said nothing, but he went from pleasantly barely awake to all of a sudden on full alert.

"Okay. Let me know if you need me to help you with my dad."

"After you've had breakfast and dressed, come up to his room so you can talk to him for me. That would be most helpful."

"Sure, K. No problem."

Kerdik rested his hand atop mine. "And thank you for staying with me. I knew I could trust you to watch my body while I slept. Not many safer places than with you." He leaned in to peck my lips again, addicted to the new flavor.

Bastien cleared his throat, winding his arms behind his head as he leaned back against the headboard. "That you think I won't test the limits of your immortality if you make a move on my girl just shows how little you know me."

Alarms went off in my head at the two men in my life fighting over stupid stuff. I missed Judah.

Kerdik's face composed itself into mild amusement as he took in Bastien's relaxed body and tight lips. "This should be fun." Then he squeezed his fist a few times, and out of the bottom came a polished rock-like substance that was equal parts solid and liquid. As the air hit it, the solid shape took over while Kerdik corrected the curve, and hollowed out the center. It grew longer until he seemed satisfied with it, and then he set the flat bottom on my nightstand.

"Whoa. Is that a vase? Did you seriously just make a vase?"

Kerdik grinned at me, and then waved his hand over the foot-tall, teardrop-bottomed stone container he'd made on the fly. Fresh flowers sprang up in the vessel, blooming with purpose and unfolding their petals. The buds of the yellow roses aimed toward the sun, as if soaking in the light with human-like enthusiasm. "For you, darling. The scent deters prowlers. They'll never wilt, so keep them in your bedroom to fend off anyone who shouldn't be lurking."

"Oh, that's the sweetest thing! Thank you."

Bastien threw up his hands and rolled his eyes. "Give me a break."

24

SUPERMAN IN PAIN

"*I* don't like it. That's a hard 'no' for me." I replied not for the first time. I was standing outside my father's door because no one could keep it straight that I was, in fact, Britney Spears in front of my father.

Kerdik rubbed his forehead, as if my sticking up for Urien was giving him a headache. "I don't see many other options, darling. Yes, it'll be excruciating, but it's our only chance of getting him to wake. I've had plenty of time to ponder. This is the only option."

"Do you even hear yourself? I'm not going to say yes to anything that puts my dad in excruciating pain. Not going to happen."

Bastien remained stoic, his arms crossed over his chest as he mulled over Kerdik's plan. Sleep was good for Bastien, and in the week since he'd started snoozing regularly with me tucked in his arms, his temper didn't run quite as hot.

Lane asked questions, but refused to weigh in with an opinion. She was modeling a simple green dress that made her tanned skin look almost rose-hued when she stood in the sunlight that filtered through a window in the long corridor. Reyn couldn't stop looking at her with adoring eyes. Something told me he'd take whatever side she landed on.

Kerdik huffed. "It's not as if I wish pain on Urien. I have a handful of true friends in the entire world. Do you really think I'd hurt him if there were any other way?"

"Hello, you just came up with this plan not half an hour ago. Give it a little time for something else to dawn on us. Something less horrible. Something with a sure rate of success."

"This is the only way!"

I threw my arms into the air. "You just said you'd give this method a sixty percent chance of it working."

"Would it have gone over better if I'd said ninety?"

"Yes."

Kerdik shrugged. "Fine. Then I'm ninety percent certain this will work."

I growled my frustration. "You're making me crazy!"

Everyone took a visible step back from my outburst, except for Bastien, who inched closer to me. They all expected Kerdik to get pushed one shove too far and implode like the child he sometimes was. Kerdik narrowed his almond-shaped eyes at me until they were irritable slits. "I'm the one with the power, so what I say goes. Deal with it."

Panic welled in my chest. "I don't want you to hurt him for nothing!"

Kerdik studied the emotion I didn't bother to hide. "I would never hurt something I loved for nothing. But I'll break him a thousand times over if it gives me even a sliver of a chance to have him back. It isn't just you who's got a stake in this."

I glowered at him. "Let's put it to a vote."

Kerdik shrugged. "Do whatever you like, but I don't bow to the majority, whether they follow reason or not."

I thrust my hand into the air. "I vote we don't gamble my dad on a whim that has a less than awesome chance of working, but a perfect score that it'll put him in pain, possibly for nothing. I vote we look for another option."

To my surprise and disappointment, no one else's hands went up. I balked at them, but Kerdik's smile only grew. "Hmm. Perhaps I should invest in democracy after all. Yes, let's go with the majority here."

My mouth drew into a tight line, my arms akimbo as I glared at Kerdik. "Oh, you are so smug. I guess I'm the only one who cares about King Urien here."

Lane rubbed her temples, and it was the first time I noticed she was leaning heavily on Reyn. "Honey, we all care about Urien. We care enough about him to think long-term. The worst that happens is he's in pain for a short amount of time. He can handle pain. No one can handle being cut off from living for this long. We owe it to him to try every possibility until we've exhausted all the options."

"Fine. I'll go break the news. Let him know how painful all of your guys' love is."

Lane sighed, the sound lingering in the air as I spun around and pushed through the bedroom door. My dad had been laid on a bed near the window in hopes that a little old-fashioned Vitamin D might do whatever vitamins were supposed to do in this situation. I popped open the glass pane and let a handful of birds in, giving them someone to sing over. Hopefully it might distract my dad from his unending nothingness.

"Urien? It's R-Britney. Britney Spears. How are you feeling this evening, sir?" It felt off calling my dad "sir", but I wasn't sure how cordial a relationship he liked to keep. Morgan hadn't liked anything too familiar.

His voice came out in a desperate rush. *"You came back! I was worried something had happened to you again, and I would be trapped in here forever. I was shouting for you for days when you disappeared that first time."*

"Yes, well, Morgan's not here anymore, so you don't have to worry about anyone throwing me down a well anytime soon. She's back in Province 1, and I'm safe with Duchess Elaine in Province 9." It was the fiftieth time I'd told him as much, but apparently I wasn't the only one traumatized by the whole getting thrown down a well thing. Urien counted on me to listen to him, to give him a break in the abyss in which he was forever stuck. Each time I visited him after I'd gone missing brought forth another batch of relief. I knew part of that was circumstantial, but darn it, if my heart didn't leap at the sound of my dad being glad I was around. "You doing alright?"

He pfft'd. *"I hope one day I can answer that question with some amount of optimism. I'm stuck in here. I heard Kerdik in the room earlier. Is he any closer to breaking me out of this?"*

I sat on the edge of the bed as Kerdik, Bastien, Lane and Reyn came into the bedroom. I picked up my father's hand and patted the back of it, hoping one day it would be strong enough to hold me together when everything fell apart, as life had a tendency of doing. "Kerdik's here, along with Lane, Reyn and Bastien. Kerdik's got an idea, but ultimately you get to decide if you want to risk it."

"Whatever it is, I'll risk it." His answer came too quick for my liking.

Kerdik tsked me that I'd put the decision in the hands of my dad, and not in his own, which is where he assumed every important thing belong. He leaned over my shoulder, his hand on my spine for balance as he spoke to my dad. "Urien, can you hear me?" He sounded like he was testing a microphone.

My dad's voice came out grim and frustrated. *"Of course. It's only me no one can hear."*

"He can hear you," I confirmed for Kerdik.

Kerdik laid out his entire plan. There were so many technical magical details and horticultural elements. I knew I'd never be able to relay the message to Urien without Kerdik there to spell it all out. "It's what needs to be done, old friend. I wouldn't risk the pain if it wasn't the only option."

Urien didn't hesitate. *"I'll do it. Whatever needs to be done, let's start now. This very moment. I need to find my daughter."*

There was something so very Superman about the whole thing. He didn't wince from the pain, only faced the inevitable with a surety that he would do whatever it took to guarantee a bright future. He was a king if ever I saw one. My emotions stuck to my throat when I tried to piece together a response. "I'll take you to your daughter as soon as you're back to yourself."

"Can you bring her to me now? I should like to listen to her voice, even if she can't hear mine."

I pressed my father's knuckles to my cheek, closing my eyes while Kerdik gave my spine a reassuring rub. "You just focus on you for now. I'll make sure Rosie's here when you open your eyes."

Bastien and Lane both mouthed, "Tell him!" but I didn't want to risk it. He needed a clear head if he was going to make it through the searing pain. Kerdik didn't bother to hold back the details of it all.

I leaned back into Kerdik, turning and burrowing my forehead into his neck. "Okay, go ahead and start. He's ready." I stood and moved across the room to sink into Bastien's waiting embrace. He was so unbelievably open now. I didn't know what to do with my good luck. His thick forearms banded around me, crushing me to his chest with a loving protectiveness I don't know how I ever lived without.

Kerdik clenched his fist a few times, and out of the bottom squeezed a plant with five green leaves that had pink on the tips. "Take her out of here," he ordered Bastien. "I don't want her near these leaves."

"What's wrong with the leaves?"

"Poisonous if you do it wrong."

"Huh? No! Kerdik, if there's a chance you'll poison Urien, you can't do it!"

Bastien didn't waste any time hustling me out the door. He held me tight in the hallway, though I struggled against him to get back in. "Shh. Kerdik wouldn't risk killing your dad and pissing you off for all of eternity unless he knew what he was doing. He's doing all this for you, so let him."

I tried to stretch around Bastien for the door, but I was still more than a foot from my goal. "Bastien, let me go!"

A guttural howl started up from inside the room. It was too deep to belong to Reyn, and too agonized to belong to Kerdik. Kerdik mostly moaned and whined when he was in dire straits. "Urien! I'm here! I'm here! It's okay!" I struggled, and then let out a shout at the sound of my Superman crying out his pain.

"Can you hear him? Is he alright?"

"No! He's hurting, and you're keeping me from him!"

Bastien made an executive decision to piss me off when he lifted me off the ground and carried me like a bride through the mansion and down the steps. "You don't need to be hearing that. He wouldn't want you to see him in pain. You need to let Kerdik handle this."

"If you're wrong and he dies, it's on you that I'm missing my last moments with my dad!"

Bastien flinched, but didn't stop until we reached the kitchen. He plopped me down on the stool at the island in the center of the kitchen, unapologetic that he'd taken the choice away from me. Faith, Hope and Mercy were working on cleaning up from dinner as quickly as they could, but they stopped their progress to fawn over me like the aunts I wished they were. They never passed up an opportunity to be sweet to me. Their late-forties plump curves and grandmotherly chortles made the kitchen feel warm and welcoming, no matter how dreary the day. "What's wrong, Princess?" Hope asked, wiping her stained hands on her apron.

I wasn't sure how much I was allowed to say about any of it, so I shook my head. "Just a rough day."

Mercy seemed to flit to my side with a tray of colorful cookies. I mean, like, they were all the colors of the rainbow. "Here, Princess. Take a break with us. Would you like some?" She held up a blue cookie in her thick fingers.

"Okay. Thanks." I took the cookie, but before I could press it to my lips, Bastien sniffed it to make sure it was safe from all poisons, maladies, and Boogeymen. You never know.

Bastien eyed the platter with longing as he palmed the small of my back and rubbed the space lightly. "Mm. Those smell good. Can I steal one?"

Faith giggled, her dimples digging deep wells in her round cheeks. "Of course, Master Bastien. Take as many as you like."

"Haven't had a macaron in ages." He looked adorable, biting the dainty cookie in half, so I could eat the other part. The blue color was dye from super tart blueberries that hit my tongue with a burst of flavor. The outer edge was almost crispy, but the inner part of the sandwich cookie was fluffy, almost like marshmallow. Then the two cookies were stuck together with a blue jelly that tasted like love and candy and fruit.

"Oh, man. These are amazing. Did you girls really make this?"

Hope beamed at me as if I'd told her she was beautiful. The way she lit up at the simple compliment, she really and truly was. "We did. You like it?"

I reached for another one and bit into the dark red cookie, sighing at the delicious raspberry that had a hint of nutmeg or something to it. "Oh, man. You're only like, the queens of my dreams. Super way yummy." I gave Bastien the other half and reached for another, unable to help myself. "They're so good, I almost forgot that I'm mad at Bastien."

"Well done, ladies," Bastien said to them with a slight bow.

Mercy kissed my cheek and set the tray of cookies down on

the counter next to me. "Then perhaps I'll just set these here, in hopes they lessen your fight."

Faith and Hope each pressed a kiss to my cheeks before they vacated the kitchen. I kind of loved how they doted on me and Draper, treating us as if we were their children. Yesterday morning, they'd fawned over him for finishing all of his oatmeal, as if he was five. It was totally precious.

Once we were alone, I gave Bastien my most serious face. "You shouldn't take me away from my dad when he needs me."

Bastien leveled his face to mine, speaking low into my anxiety. "Listen up, Daisy. I'm doing this for your own good. When we have kids someday, no way would I want them to hear me cry out in pain. If I get hurt, you run them into another room. A kid needs to have faith that their dad can handle anything. I won't see you lose that right before you get him back. Urien can handle this. Have faith in your father's strength. Once that leaves a person? Well, it's a rougher road ahead for you both if you lose that."

I wanted to argue and give him a piece of my mind, but his reason was so unselfish and loving; I couldn't bring myself to be mad anymore. "That's... You really want to have kids with me?"

Bastien stood straighter, brushing off the front of his flannel, as if it desperately needed his attention. "Well, yeah. Eventually. You think I wanted to have kids with Reyn?"

"Well, I assumed. You two are awfully close." I don't know why I went with shtick. Bastien was doing and saying so many permanent and thoughtful things lately; I wasn't sure what to do with them all. "You're really that certain of us?"

He nodded, though he couldn't look me in the eye. I think we both knew he'd jumped a hair too far off the diving board, and now our relationship was plunging into the deep end. I hoped we could handle it. He cleared his throat, staring at a fixed point on the counter. "You know I want to marry you."

My skin felt cold and clammy, but my heart warmed to his

words. I wanted exactly that some days, but there was so much we didn't know about each other. To make a big life shift without Judah or anything from my world felt like making only half a commitment. We hadn't fared Common together successfully yet, and I needed to know we could make it in both worlds before I got too comfortable with how easy our love was coming these days. "How's it going to work with Mad being my fake fiancé?"

"When we move to Common, we'll start over. No one there knows the arrangement. Engagements are broken sometimes. Not often, sure. Duke Henri's daughter Gwen's been promised to a judge's son in Province 3, but she's been stalling on going through with the marriage for a year now."

"Hello, she's a teenager."

He smirked and mocked my valley girl lilt that sometimes came out. "Hello, that's pretty normal here. If a woman hits her mid-twenties and hasn't found a husband, that's when the stigma starts."

"Oh, rats. I guess I'm an old maid already." I frowned up at him. "You and Reyn are older than that, and you're both not married."

"Not for long," Bastien said, and then grimaced. "For Reyn, I mean. I know he's wanted to lock that down for a while now. I can't imagine them waiting a whole day after they move to Common before they exchange rings." He waved his hand. "It's different for men in Avalon. We outnumber women four to one. There simply aren't enough women for older, unmarried men to get a stigma. Plus, I'm an Untouchable and Reyn's a judge's son. We can do what we want without too much social judgment."

"Wow. What an amazing chauvinistic society I've stepped into. Excellent." I frowned. "I don't want to disrespect Mad, though. I know a few of the people in the household know the whole thing is a fraud, but not everyone, and certainly not the public. He did me a huge solid, offering to marry me so I didn't have to go off with Uncle Henri. I don't want to do something mean to him."

Bastien smirked at me. "I like that you're protective of my friends. Trust me, Mad will be relieved that you won't need to marry him. He'll take the stigma over forever tying himself to a woman who isn't Meara."

"Okay. If you're sure."

"We have to wait three more months until I can marry you. I have to wait, out of loyalty for Reyn's sister. I can't dishonor his family. They've done a lot for me over the years."

I scratched the nape of my neck uncomfortably. "Are we really talking about this now?"

"I guess we are." Then he grimaced and shook his head. "Maybe not. I'm supposed to ask your father for your hand. I want to do right by you. I don't want to take shortcuts."

My mouth went dry at the very serious conversation we were having. "Wow. I mean, I want to say something all refined, like a wife would say, but all I can think is a stream of 'holy crap, holy crap, holy crap.'"

"Well, you've got three months to work your way up to a solid, 'Yes, Bastien. I'll marry you.'"

"Thanks for the heads-up." I rubbed my temples, trying to get the ache out of my head. "You kind of threw my future plans for a loop. I was set on living the glorious gangsta life of a spinster."

"I've got big plans for the rest of our life together, Daisy." Bastien saw through my shtick and had pity on my ineptitude. He wrapped his arms around my waist and drew me in so my head could rest on its favorite support. The crook of Bastien's neck was entirely masculine, and I used it as my oxygen mask in times of duress.

"I should go check on my dad."

"Not now, babe. It's about time for the kids to show up," he commented after I inhaled a solid half-dozen hits of his scent.

"The kids?"

"Your soccer camp?" he reminded me.

I sat up straight, my eyes opening wider. "Oh, right! This whole not having a watch thing is really throwing me."

Bastien gave me a smile in a way that did nothing to quell the serious vibe between us. There was intention in his eyes, permanence that both scared and excited me. "I love that you do this. Taking all the kids from Province 9 into the dungeon to teach them to play soccer? It's genius, and exactly what everyone loved about Lane before she left. Her province was all about working, and then playing. Most of the provinces were about work and survival only."

"Lane knows what's important. Plus, how are the parents supposed to settle into their new homes if they're worrying about keeping an eye on their kids? Also, I don't want the same stigma that Morgan needed in Province 1. Royalty shouldn't be feared like that. They should be able to come to us if they need something."

"You are Lane's daughter, that's for sure."

I grabbed an apple from the bowl on the island. "I love when you get me. Help me round up the kids?"

"Whatever you like, Princess." His teasing tone always made me smile with a slight eye roll. I batted my hand at him, and he popped his elbow to me. Bastien was my welcome distraction, though as we walked through the mansion to the front door, my heart shook with the knowledge that while I killed time with the kids, my dad was in agony.

KIDS AND THE KEEP

"Just like that, Gaylord. Only try it with the inside of your foot next time. Kick it like you're doing too often, and you're going to break a toe one of these days." I caught a second, smaller ball I was tossing with a few of the littler ones.

Four days had passed since Kerdik started my father on the course of excruciating pain, and I hadn't been allowed near his chambers since. So far, there had been only pain on my father's part, and no healing to speak of. Kerdik assured me that sometimes things took longer than anticipated. I, in turn, assured Kerdik that if he let my father keep howling in agony, Urien would soon have a bunkmate who screamed louder than he did.

Two-hundred-fifty-seven kids were chasing the soccer ball around the basement. I kept insisting we call it a basement, but let's face it – no matter how I tried to clean it up and put a new smile on it, it was a dank dungeon. The undernourished children running around and giggling through it only made the image more stark in my mind. Some were from the outlying provinces that had risked everything – even their health – to stand apart from Morgan. Others were refugees from Provinces 1 or 2, and were well-fed, strong children. When Morgan had absorbed the other provinces, she gave them plots of land farther from the castle, which is where she'd stowed her Jewels of Good Fortune. So while they were provided for, their gardens were vastly different than those belonging to the original Province 1. It was hard to watch two nine-year-old boys playing together, one from Province 1 and the other from Province 8, their two sizes completely opposite. Yet they played together without division, laughing as if the life before this had not existed, and had no bearing on the fun they were determined to milk out of the dungeon. Only pure souls could see a dungeon and make it sing for them, but I guess that's the beauty of children.

Watching them play, I felt lucky to get to see such unity, kindness and sheer joy. People underestimate the value of play, but I've learned that you can't make that mistake in life. I don't know when adults go through that phase of forgetting their basest instinct, sacrificing it for the glory of achievement, but the very thought made me a little sad for the loss of the inner child in most adults.

The evening was setting in, which was when the kitchen staff usually came down with cookies and fresh milk for every single child. Faith, Hope and Mercy loved doting on the kids. They chortled often, shaking their enormous breasts and bellies with joy that came easy to them, now that Lane was back. Sometimes they even joined us and kicked the ball around, much to the merriment of the children. The sisters hadn't come down yet, but perhaps they hadn't felt like baking cookies tonight. Bastien had been mildly agitated that morning, checking over his shoulder and rechecking the mansion to make sure everything was secure. Perhaps he'd just needed a cookie.

Let's face it, *I* wanted a cookie. Or truly, like a hundred. The sisters made the perfect Parisian macarons, colored every hue in the rainbow, and flavored with just as much variety. Once they learned that I was enraptured with their macarons, a plate found its way to my bedroom every night with my tea tray. It's probably not totally healthy to eat ten cookies before bed, but I couldn't help myself. They didn't hold back, but flavored them with every weird thing they could get their hands on. My favorite so far was the coconut lime one, followed closely by the cayenne chocolate. I did not care for the black licorice variety, but muscled my way through it with a smile for the ladies who doted on my family.

I may not be able to keep track of the time all that well, but my stomach grumbled when the cookies did not appear during their usual time.

"Princess, is it getting late?" David asked me. David was the oldest of the teens who'd been sent to play in the dungeon with me. He was fourteen, and most of his friends were working the field with their parents. David had seven brothers and sisters, all younger, so he was their official shepherd, and my right-hand man down here when the kids needed wrangling. I'd probably bitten off more than I could chew. I'd envisioned a dozen or so kids I'd be watching, but it turned into two-hundred-fifty-seven children tonight. So many had signed up, that we did rotations, so every kid got to come one day a week, rotating out for five days straight. I told the parents that I could only take kids from age five and up, but perhaps I should've also asked for volunteers to help me. David was a good assistant, though.

"It is a little late, but it's probably because your parents all decided to get as much done as possible to make up for the blackout and rainy days. I wouldn't worry about it."

David bobbed his midnight-hued hair and went back to playing with the children. He always stayed near me, making himself my unofficial sentry. It was adorable.

Since the cookies were late tonight, I wondered if I should just dismiss the kids and take them all upstairs to wait for their parents without their usual treat. Avalon kids weren't spoiled at all, and had been introduced to hard farm labor early on in their lives. To be given cookies and play time did all of them a world of good. They were so grateful for the relief, that there were minimal bickering fights.

My mind wandered often to my dad, and I wondered how irresponsible it would be of me to sneak upstairs and check on him. *"Pretty irresponsible,"* I guessed, so I stayed put with the kids.

Babette came up to me and tugged on my thermal shirt sleeve after I kicked the ball to Selina. I knelt down so I was closer to her height. "Hey, girly. What can I do for you?"

Babette was five, and while I tried not to have favorites, I had a soft spot for this one. She'd suffered some kind of illness when she'd been a baby, leaving her blind in her left eye. Consequently, she had a more difficult time when we all played together. It was hard not to fall in love with Bastien when he took breaks from working outside to come downstairs and carry her around on his shoulders. Link and Draper sometimes joined us too, wrestling the boys, rolling around on the ground, and basically whipping the kids up into a frenzy. Mad was terrified of children, and gave the dungeon a wide berth whenever soccer clinics were in session.

"I think we're missing something," she said, her milky eye staring off to the side while her right eye was laser sharp on me. I wondered if I'd been similarly cute and pitiful as a wonky-eyed child. Of course, I'd had a hump to go with my lazy eye, so I'm guessing Babette was slightly cuter than I'd been.

My mouth drew to the side. "Hmm. I think you're right. I think Hope, Mercy and Faith might've forgotten about the cookies tonight. Oh, rats." I made a show of displaying how to throw a controlled fit.

She mimicked my downward fist that cut across my body, and my frown. "Oh, rats. Do you think they need help in the kitchen? I'm real good at helping."

I smirked at her. "I bet you are. Helpers are my favorite kind of people."

Babette beamed at me. "Princesses are *my* favorite kind of

people." She seemed to travel with her own light source, her sweetness taking all the bad in the world and dissolving it one smile at a time. She twirled her long brown hair around her finger and rocked back and forth on the balls of her feet.

"Well then that settles it; we were meant to be friends."

It didn't take much for the children to throw themselves into a hug. The teenagers had a harder time, but after a few days of soccer and cookies, their tough outer shells began to crumble, making them just as sweet and precious as the younger kids.

David trotted up to me, still giving me a slight bow before addressing me, as society dictated. "Your majesty, I think I hear something coming from up the stairs." David's face looked worried, so I kissed Babette's forehead and moved to the bottom of the steps to see what I could make out that was troubling David.

David followed me, his dark eyebrows pushed together in concern. His finger tapped to the wall of the stairwell in a steady thrum that sounded like a downbeat of a hard rock song. "Do you hear that?"

I strained, and then nodded. "What is it?"

Just then, Reyn burst through the door above us that separated the dungeon from the rest of the mansion. "Rosie, take the children into the keep! I'm sending the rest of the kids in the province down to you!"

"What?" I went from teaching soccer to hitting a peak of anxiety. Luckily, my nerves were slowly growing accustomed to the swing of the highs and lows the longer I lived in Avalon. "What's going on?"

Reyn didn't bother explaining, but repeated his command. "The keep! Go down there with all the children and don't come out until one of us comes to get you. Hurry!" As he spoke, dozens, and then hundreds of children came thundering down the steps in various stages of fright. Soon I lost count of how many were under my care.

Mothers were running their babies down the steps, swaddled and surprisingly still. "Don't worry," one of them said through her tears. "The babies have all been given a drop of *endormi* berry juice. They should sleep through the night for you."

"I don't have cribs!"

"It's okay. We'll line them up along the wall. It's safer in here like this than out there."

I whirled around, my mind going into overdrive. I didn't have the luxury of freaking out; we were in some sort of danger. I slipped into my danger-mode persona.

David was at my side, and Babette followed close on my heels. I clapped my hands three times to garner everyone's attention. "Okay, everyone! Uncle Reyn needs us to take a little trip further back. I want all of you to hold a hand and form a chain. Quick as you can, now. That means every single person is holding two hands. Older kids, make sure you link up with two of the younger ones. There are more of them, and they need you."

I'm not sure what I would've done without David. He barked out orders and made sure my command was carried out to a T. He met my eyes with a grave nod that told me something terrible was happening outside. I scooped up Babette and jogged along the quickly formed chain.

Some of the younger children started to cry, but I kept a brave smile on my face as I snatched the lantern off the hook on the wall. "David, can you take the rear and make sure we don't leave anyone behind?"

"Yes, your majesty!" David called, his chest puffing with pride that he'd been given such an important role. He turned the lanterns off along the way, leaving a trail of tears and darkness behind us as we journeyed into the belly of the keep.

26

PRETTY PICTURES IN THE ORC WAR

J didn't want to be scared, but there was no helping the anxiety that thrummed in my veins. I wanted to call for Bastien, but the fact that Reyn had been sent to warn us meant that Bastien already had his hands full. With what? I was afraid to find out.

I'd done a more thorough job cleaning the dungeon than I'd done with the keep, since we hadn't intended on putting it to use. The hallway that was at first concrete and relatively room-temperature turned into dirt floors with a chill in the dank air that you couldn't shake. I was scared that babies were put in their swaddled blankets on the floor, lined up like little hot dogs, side-by-side. They were sleeping, but I wondered how long that would last. I tried to keep my smile plastered on my face, but Babette started trembling on my hip, and I almost lost it. I didn't like when she was scared. She'd already been through so much.

Reyn and I had removed the larger spider webs and did a half-job of sweeping the packed-dirt floor, but we hadn't figured we'd ever need to use the underground hiding spot that was meant to hide the women and children while the men fought to defend their province.

The open room of the keep was really a better place to play soccer, with only a few pillars to interrupt the field. It was the size of two soccer arenas side-by-side. However, there was an ominous gloom about the keep. It felt somehow disrespectful to play games on ground that had seen untold terror. Not that a dungeon was much better.

"You guys are amazing! Let's all line up along the far wall over here and have a seat. I need to do another count and make sure we're all here."

I tried not to let anyone see my hand shaking as I patted each child on the head when I made my way down the row. I didn't want them to notice how fake my smile was, or hear the tremor in my voice. I wanted to reassure them. I wanted to reassure myself.

One of the little boys who was all knees, elbows and giant eyes whimpered up at me as I passed him, "Are we going to die?"

I rolled my shoulders back and looked him straight in the eye with a gentle smile. "Of course not. This is good practice for if anything bad should ever happen to Province 9. You're with me, hun. Do you really think I'd let anything happen to my kids? You guys are on my soccer team. That's like, sacred. No one messes with a team."

I tried not to panic when I started my count of all the kids. Each of them kept their backs pressed to the walls, their legs extended while I tapped them each on the top of their heads. A few of the teenagers offered to corral the toddlers over in the corner, so they could play or be held without having to obey stodgy rules like "sit still". It took a while, but the kids remained patient until I reached the end of the line, adding up each of the four-thousand-eight-hundred-fifty children, plus five-hundred-ninety-seven snoozing babies.

If ever there was a time to freak out, this would be the moment.

Without a word, David met my eyes and moved toward the

two-story-tall double doors we'd passed through. There were three sets of thick doors, actually, and he helped me bolt each one of them. We were trying to be brave for each other, but neither of us bought the act.

I brought him in for a hug before we rounded the corner to face the kiddos again. "I need your help keeping the children calm. Can you do that?"

"I can do anything you ask me to, Princess."

I rallied at his bravery, reminding myself that we were safe in the keep. It was here for a reason: to keep us from danger. I swallowed hard as a grim list of various types of danger flickered through my mind. Almost everyone I loved was out there, stuck in the middle of an Orc war (or something equally terrifying), and I couldn't protect them.

But I could protect the children Province 9 trusted me to watch over.

I put on my biggest smile and moved back out into the open floorplan, nearing the lamp light so they could all see me. "Okay, everyone, I think we should try writing our names in the dirt. I know most of you, but there are some new faces today." I couldn't actually read what they wrote, but it was something to occupy the time. Fear only brewed in situations like this if there wasn't a decent distraction.

David put his back to the kids so he could whisper privately to me. "I'll go get the weapons for the older kids."

"What? I don't know, David. I don't want to scare anyone."

"Being afraid is better than being dead. If we've been sent to the keep, there's no one too young to fight for their lives."

I hated how old he sounded. His battle wisdom wasn't that much different than Bastien's, but David still had an awkward squeak to his voice every now and then, and no facial hair marring his baby face. "You're fourteen," I muttered, sad beyond words.

"That's old enough to defend my family." He jerked his chin in the direction of his buddies, and five teens ran off after him.

The totally awesome activity of writing their names in the dirt took all of one minute. Then they were all blinking up at me with teary eyes, some of them crying for their parents. I slapped my hands together and pointed to the corner in the vast room that was furthest from the doors. "I think this place needs a little TLC. Who's good at drawing?"

Like clockwork, every single child's hand went up.

"Awesome! Let's start in that far corner, and I want you to cover every inch of this ugly floor with beautiful drawings. I know Duchess Lane is working hard to make sure we're safe, so I want you all to make her something pretty to show her how grateful we are. Sound good?"

There were various noises of assent muddled in with the tears, but they all moved to the wall that was an entire soccer field away, and started drawing with their fingers into the dirt.

I nearly lost my shiz when the six teenagers made it to the far wall, and started disappearing in the middle of it. I squinted, and then realized they'd gone into a cleverly hidden cabinet. The cement walls had a concealed tunnel, which was where the spare weapons were stored. They came back one by one, armed with spears, daggers, leather breastplates that were far too large and cumbersome, and synchronized expressions of doom they accepted without a tear.

I'd never known bravery like that from kids so young, but I vowed I wouldn't let them down. I kept my chin high and thanked David politely when he handed me a sword. It would probably do more damage to me than offering any real protection.

But I didn't need protection. Everything would be fine.

Everything would be fine.

Everything would be fine.

27

THE COLD HEART OF AN IMMORTAL

When Kerdik appeared out of thin air, the children – who had been quietly drawing in the dirt and calming themselves down – all screamed in unison. He was carrying my father's body, which didn't look quite as kempt as it had when I'd last seen him. My hand barely made it to my mouth in time to muffle my scream of distress at seeing my dad so worn. The children backed away into the far corner, most of them bursting into terrified tears at the sight of the revered monster they'd been taught to fear from birth.

"Kerdik! What's going on up there? Why are we down here?"

Kerdik's eyes were wild, which was never a good sign. "I need to store Urien's body with you in the keep. He's not awake yet, but the spell worked!" He carefully lowered my dad's body to the dirt.

I couldn't hear my father shouting in agony, which was the first time in four days he'd not been howling. "Oh, he's not crying out anymore! That's good news, right?"

"Very good news. I wasn't sure, but to have you confirm it takes a load off my mind."

It was then I realized Kerdik was sweating. "That's great!

Sweetie, did you maybe overuse your magic a little? You're not looking so hot."

I heard a man moaning in agony, but Kerdik was the only guy there. Then it dawned on me that the cries were coming from my father's closed lips. I gasped and dropped to my knees, scooping up his hand so I could hold it to my cheek. It wasn't an urgent plea for help, but more the groanings of someone who had gone through too strenuous a workout.

"It was worth it. I broke her spell." Kerdik grinned, though his eyelids drooped and his smile looked too tired to be pure. "That'll teach her to try and layer magic to keep me out. I did it. I'm smarter than Morgan."

"Was there ever any doubt?"

"More powerful is one thing, but brains are a different matter. Brains can overcompensate for shortcomings in the magic department, or any other shortfalls. But it doesn't matter. I won. Urien will wake as soon as the sun rises to greet him."

I gaped up at Kerdik, trying not to let tears flood me. I had too much going on to break down now. "You gave me back my... my King Urien?"

"It was you, too. That parchment you found filled in some of the gaps I was missing. I don't think I would've been able to make those leaps if I hadn't had that."

"Are you okay?" I whispered to my dad, my voice pinched.

The answering moan wasn't exactly reassuring, but he was responding, which was something.

"What's going on outside? Why did Reyn tell us to come down here?"

Kerdik leaned over, bracing his hands on his thighs to catch his breath. It worried me when Kerdik showed any signs of weakness. "The battle, of course. Do you really think children should be out in the middle of that chaos?"

"What?!" I felt over four-thousand sets of eyes on me, so I donned my reassuring smile and waved at all of them again, hoping they were far enough out of earshot to remain in the shelter of optimism. I needed them to believe that everything would be okay. "Go back to your drawings, kids. Kerdik's just stopping by to add a friend to the mix and hang out for a little while. Nothing's wrong. But I do see some empty spots in the corner still. Can somebody who's great at drawing flowers fill those in for me? The duchess loves flowers."

The kids were too scared to move. *Great.* I cast over my shoulder up at Kerdik, "Could you give them a little something to let them know they're safe around you? That you're not going to hurt them?"

"But they know that's not true. I am scary." He growled and bared his teeth as if they were gruesome fangs just to be a jerk. I winced when several of the children screamed and started wailing.

I shoved him, watching him break from his scary monster persona into a boyish snigger. "Knock it off! You know that's not doing anyone a lick of good down here. Be helpful."

"I don't care if children like me. Fear is more amusing anyway."

"I'm trying to keep them all calm, and you're not helping one bit. No one's given me any information, either. What's going on up there?"

"You've really got no idea? I mean, it's all about you out there."

"Huh? Kerdik, seriously. Why are we down here? Is Lane okay?" When he brushed his hand down my back, Babette screamed like she was watching her own personal horror movie. I realized *I* was the thing that was scaring the children. I was getting too close to their monster. "Hold on." I trotted toward the children with a smile on my face. "It's okay, everyone. Kerdik's my friend. He came down here to deliver a special guest, and let us know that everything's going okay up there."

This did nothing to assure anyone that all was well. Now that I was nearer, I could smell that one or more of the children had peed themselves. I didn't have any help to give them, other than the same hollow words that not even I was buying.

"Keep on drawing pictures for Lane, and I'll go see if Kerdik knows how long we're going to have to wait for our cookies."

I made my way back to Kerdik, shooting him a warning glare that told him to behave this time. Kerdik looked over at the children as if their crying was annoying. He waved his hand over the dirt floor and sprang up a lush meadow in the giant dirt-floored basement. "There. Is that better?"

The flowers were purple, with pistols that were almost translucent when you peered into the center. "Oh, how pretty! Thank you. That really is helpful." I called back to the kids, "Okay, everyone. It's time to pick some flowers for your parents. I think they'll love them."

Kerdik met me halfway and steered me from the field in a hurry. About ten seconds later, I heard small thuds echoing out across the keep. I whirled and shrieked as one by one, the children fell into the spontaneous meadow, unconscious before they hit the ground. "No! What happened?" I made to race toward them, but Kerdik caught me around the waist.

"They're fine. Just sleeping. Those are *somnolent* flowers. They have a potent smell that knocks you out. I don't like children." He waved his hand toward the field, and the flowers withered and bent over as if in obeisance to Kerdik, though the grass he'd grown remained stubborn and tall. He moved me to the far corner, away from the children.

"You can't knock out a bunch of kids! That's terrible!"

Kerdik was unperturbed that I was so upset over something he deemed logical. "I can do as I wish, and I wish to speak to you in private. Children are insufferable. You told me to help you with them; this is me helping."

I steamed at him, trying to block out the sounds of my father moaning in pain. They were now very easy to tune in on, since there was no other chatter. I led Kerdik further away from my dad and lowered my voice. "What's going on out there?"

"Morgan. She discovered Urien's body was missing. She must've put a tracking charm on it, because she knows he's here. Now would be a dandy time for him to wake up, march out there and tell her off, but that doesn't seem to be happening yet." He jerked his thumb toward the door. "She's got her whole army out there."

"Her whole army? We're not ready for that! The people have barely settled into their homes. They don't have the wherewithal to fight yet."

Kerdik shrugged, as if that mattered little to him. "I came down to make sure you were safe, and to store Urien here until he can return to us. If the house is overrun, it won't do to leave his body lying about."

"What can I do? How can I help?"

"Staying safe down here is the best help you can give me. Bastien's leading the men right now."

I gripped Kerdik's forearm to steady myself. "One of the teens gave me a sword." I motioned to the far wall, where I'd left my weapon. "Can you lock the doors to the keep behind me and zap yourself out? If the kids are zonked out, they'll be fine."

Kerdik rolled his eyes. "It's like you heard nothing I just said. Stay here. That's what you can do."

I reared back, affronted. "You don't know the first thing about me if you think I'm going to babysit while my boyfriend risks his life to keep everyone safe. I just need you to lock the doors behind me."

"Not happening. I'll put you in cuffs myself, if that's what it takes. You'll not fall to danger under my watch." He spread his fingers out, and up from the dirt sprouted a massive wall of trees in front of the doors to the keep. Like it was nothing, nature found its way into the basement of the mansion, blocking me from joining the fight. The trees were so thick and tight together that I couldn't squeeze through them if I tried. "There. I feel much better now."

"Lane!" I cried, utterly distraught. I held tight to his forearm, scared and overwhelmed. "You have to help Lane! If you won't let me out of here, then you have to go help her."

"Lane is standing for her people. The only ones who can kill her are Daughters of Avalon, nature or time, remember? I put a protection on them myself. They don't know that, of course, but they don't need to. I don't need them getting foolhardy. Lane will be fine."

"What about everyone else's moms? What about Bastien and the guys? Please, Kerdik! Let me out! I have to make them stop!"

It was only when tears moistened my eyes that Kerdik seemed to break out of his indifference. "It's alright, darling. Morgan wants what she can't have. She's bound to throw a fit. Frankly, I'm surprised it took this long."

"Yes, but you're acting like Bastien dying in battle is no big deal!" I turned to stare forlornly at the sleeping children. "Let me tell you the permanent ache it is to grow up without your parents. Don't do that to these kids!"

Kerdik shot me a quizzical look, as if wondering if he was allowed to say that the death of anyone wasn't a big deal to an immortal. "Morgan wants to wage war on Lane for too many reasons. Urien's body going missing is just the excuse she needed. She won't back down after the way Lane publicly shamed her and took half her people. Lane exposed her for the horrible witch she is. Morgan had two options: either convince her people she wasn't an evil queen, or embrace the stigma." Kerdik shrugged, as if relaying the plays of a soccer match for the viewers, bored by the game of it all. "Morgan will punish Lane. It's the price your aunt knew she would pay if she went up against Morgan. Best let her get it out of her system. Lane's been out of Avalon too long; she must be reminded of the way of things."

"Are you freaking kidding me with this? Help her! Stand up to

Morgan and help Lane! Show the people that you're on Lane's side, and Morgan will back down."

"For how long?" Kerdik's gaze sharpened. "You forget that I'm not on anyone's side, here. I don't serve the Daughters of Avalon. I'll not spend my time watching Province 9's borders, waiting for Morgan to attack again."

"Selfish!" I raged. "What's the good of immortality if you aren't making the world a better place?"

"I created Avalon! I gave them a perfect place, and they wrecked it with their greed. I have no interest in exhausting myself to restore Avalon to a mere portion of what it once was."

"You can't turn your back on someone, just because they disappoint you. I didn't leave you high and dry after you let me down. Avalon needs you! Don't you see that?"

Kerdik blew a loud, childish raspberry in my face. "You're growing predictable."

I don't know why I let Kerdik rile me up, but once the train got going, I couldn't stop it. "I'm disappointed in you. People will die up there if you don't let me out to help Lane stop this."

He shrugged – as if this were a shrugging moment. "People die every day."

I glared at him, not holding back how utterly ashamed I was at his coldness. "My family won't be next. I don't know what happened to you to make you like this, but it's ugly. So ugly, I can barely look at you."

Kerdik grabbed me and yanked my body tight to his, holding me there so I couldn't struggle away. "You don't seem to under-stand what it takes to endure immortality. I can't afford a heart that's easily broken. I feel affinity for Urien, Morgan spots it and takes him away. I feel deep love for you, and again Morgan threatens you every time my back is turned. I only risk having a heart every couple decades because I have to live for too long with the fallout. If we're apart, you feel the separation, what? A few days? Months? Years?" He squeezed me impossibly tighter as he shouted in my face. "I feel the slow death of being without the people I love for an eternity! I don't love carelessly, as you do. I can't afford the fallout of that kind of heartache."

His words started to thaw the ice in my chest, and slowly my heart started beating in the same rhythm as his odd one. I stopped struggling and wrapped my arms around his neck, resting my head on his shoulder, as if we hadn't just been yelling at each other. "I'm sorry," I whispered. "I was only thinking about me, not how getting involved would affect you."

Kerdik's anger melted under the warmth of my embrace. His hands started to move up and down my spine, instead of holding me too firmly in place. "No. That's the thing. You weren't even thinking of yourself. You were thinking about Province 9. You were thinking about your friends and the people you love." He pressed his forehead to mine. "One day I do hope you have a deeply selfish moment. I should like to see that."

"The kids will be asleep for a while?"

"At least another hour or two. Longer for the younger ones."

I pressed my cheek to his. "Then I need you to let me out of here. I have to go help Lane and Bastien however I can."

Kerdik's arms tightened around me again to hold me in place. "No. You'll stay right here."

"You know I can't. You're right that I shouldn't have asked you to care when I didn't understand the cost to you. But it's not right for you to ask me to stay when it's at too high a cost to me not to stand with my family." I kissed his cheek again. "I have to let you be who you are, and you have to let me be who I am."

I saw a flash of anger in Kerdik's eyes that made me nervous. I didn't protest or fight him when he backed me into the wall and pressed my shoulders firmly to the concrete. He said so many things to me with his eyes that neither of us could put words to. Then he lightly kissed my lips before slapping his hand to the concrete in frustration. Again he pecked my lips, making my stomach flutter. "Damn you, Rosie. Stop making me care."

Before I could react, two vines sprouted up from the dirt and wrapped around my ankles. The thick brown cords of nature acted with intent to keep me exactly where I stood. "Kerdik, what are you doing?"

Two additional vines twisted around my wrists, jerking me to the ground, bringing me to sit on my butt on the packed dirt floor. Kerdik knelt down to press a kiss to my cheek, unworried that I was freaking out, and tugging fruitlessly on the vines. "You'll stay here with the children. I'll fight in your stead. If you're intent on standing with your people, and I'm intent on keeping you from harm, then I'll take your place. Then we both win, and we still have each other."

Panic welled in me. Though I'd just been pushing for Kerdik to go out and help Lane, now that he was doing as much, I feared the worst. "No! I don't want you to get hurt while I sit here like a dummy!"

Kerdik quirked his eyebrow at me, and then pulled back a few inches, touched. "You're worried about me?"

"Of course I am, you jerk! Morgan hates you as much as she's afraid of you. All her guns will be aimed your way! You can't go in without me! She hates me just as much, so I could divert some of the fire." Anxiety was too high in my throat, choking me with nerves and regret. "We should go together, or you'll get all her fire!"

Kerdik dropped to his knees and locked me in a hug, kissing my cheek five times before words came to him. "No one ever worries about me. I love you, beautiful girl. Always their princess, but always my queen."

I gaped at him, dumbfounded that he was growing, and that I was learning to communicate change to such an immovable creature. Some part of me still scrambled for a way to do right by my province. "I can fight, Kerdik. I should be with my family."

He didn't answer right away, only stood while giving me a

long, unfathomable look that stayed any further arguments I had on standby. "You're my family now."

Deep, long dormant parts of me started to move in my chest, swelling with emotion that birthed out of me in a panicked cry of, "Don't leave me!"

In true Kerdik fashion, he didn't listen. He ran his fingers through my hair like he was petting a dog, and then vanished, leaving me bound to the floor with nothing but my own desperation.

28

THE PSYCHOTIC MEN I LOVE

J'd fallen asleep at some point in the night after the lamp's oil had run out, and I could do friggin' nothing about it. My dad had finally calmed from his torment, and we'd been enjoying a docile back and forth, though I had to shout to be heard across the way, far as we were from each other. Kerdik's guess of his sleeping potion flowers lasting a few hours on the children was a gross miscalculation. The snoozing went on far longer than that, allowing the little bodies to recharge their magic that was still so young and untarnished. Blessing in disguise, I guess.

My spine stiffened when I heard my name being called from the other side of the series of doors. "Bastien? I'm in here! Get Kerdik! Only he can let us out." I heaved a sigh of relief that the bindings would soon be cut from my wrists and ankles. I leaned my head against the wall. "Help is on the way, Urien. Hang tight."

"'Hang tight.' You amuse me. Your phrasing sounds much like Lane. She picked up a few Commoner words I'm unfamiliar with, but they suit her well. Do you come from Common, as well?"

"Kerdik?" I called, trying to pretend I hadn't heard him. I

didn't want Urien putting it together that I was his daughter. I couldn't reason with myself why at this point, but I was still nervous of the rejection I was certain was coming. I knew I couldn't handle the blow, so I fended it off as long as I possibly could.

After a few minutes of Bastien pounding futilely on the door, Kerdik appeared before me with a whoosh of air that set the lantern glowing again. His hair wasn't ruffled, but his shirt was untucked and had dirt on it. It was a sure sign that he'd won, but only just. He glared down at me without a greeting, as if I'd been the one to incite the battle. "Well, it's done. Now everyone assumes my gauntlet's been thrown, and I've taken up Lane's mantle. I've assured Lane no such thing has happened. I told her this was a one-time assistance, and that I wasn't going to involve myself again."

I blinked up at him, my head tilted to take in the man who traveled with the ability to create his own light. "You saved my family. You love me."

He threw up his hands in exasperation. "That's only what I've been trying to tell you this entire time! I've got news for you: if this little display has exhausted my magic again, I will take you wherever I please so I can rest peacefully, and I won't endure a word of protest from you or anyone else. You owe me for this. I used magic on a grand scale that I didn't want to have to do."

"Then why do it?" I asked stupidly. I didn't want him questioning why he'd helped me, but I needed to know.

"Because if I didn't, you would've done something reckless. I fear my temper losing all control if you get another mere scratch on you." He frowned again, as if caught in the act of being sweet to me when he'd wanted to scold. "But now Morgan knows I'm capable of carnage like that on a grander scale. She can take countermeasures for the next time, plan around my abilities that were mere myth to her before today. She's a chess player, and now she's seen what my queen can do.

She'll spot holes in my defenses. When I tell you no, it's for a reason."

"Yes, boss."

Kerdik's eyebrows were pushed together in concern. "And that boyfriend of yours? He's a lunatic. I'd never seen someone with no shred of self-preservation until I watched your crazy boyfriend hurl himself into the thick of the battle."

My mouth went dry. "Bastien's okay though? He lived?"

"I'm afraid there's no cure for the insanity that plagues his mind and makes him ridiculously foolhardy, but yes, I enhanced his body when we first met in that field, remember? He can endure far more than the average soldier, and he was never that. Plus, you gave him your *lueur*, which added to his prowess. I think he's only just becoming aware of all he can do now." He leaned over and jerked on the vines that ensnared my wrists and ankles. Easy as if they were made of yarn, the binds shredded and fell to the packed dirt floor. "Better?"

"Much. Thank you." He massaged my sore wrists for me. His touch was gentle to contrast with his stern gaze as he pulled me to my feet. I tilted my head up to stare at him. "Hey, Kerdik?"

"Yes?"

"Thanks for helping, even though it wasn't your battle." I leaned up on my toes and wrapped my arms around his neck, pecking his cheek to let him know I was grateful he'd fought for me, and grateful he'd survived.

"You're always my queen," he whispered to me like a promise. Kerdik rocked us side to side for a few beats, looking at me like I was someone worth going into battle for. "Let's gather up the children before their parents have a conniption, yeah? I'm afraid I can't take another person screaming."

"But how do we..." I didn't get out the entire sentence before Kerdik tsked me for questioning his awesome power. He turned us and waved his arm in the direction of the children who had all fallen asleep on the grass he'd grown them. My eyes bulged when tall, violet-colored sunflowers rose up from the grass, their stalks stretching taller than me. Then he pursed his lips and blew a puff of air that multiplied as it wafted toward them, building into a slight breeze that carried the scent of the sunflowers over the children.

Slowly, the kids started to stir. The pounding on the outer door to the keep was resumed by none other than my zealous boyfriend, who was shouting my name. Kerdik rolled his eyes at Bastien's tenacity, and clicked his fingers at the wall of trees he'd erected to hold me inside, and keep the bad guys out. The trees melted into the floor like they were being sucked down through a straw. The kids awoke to confusion, and then terrified screams broke out when they saw Kerdik's arm still around me.

Kerdik's eyes narrowed after I caught a glimpse of hurt at their immediate negative reaction to him. He made to move away, but I kept him glued to my side and cleared my throat to garner everyone's attention. "Hey, kids. I want everyone to line up along the wall and tell Kerdik thank you. He let you all take a nap so that your magic would be stronger than ever. Kerdik believes in you, and knows you can do great things for Avalon. He invested in each one of you, and I want you to keep that in your heart. You are worth an immortal taking his time to restore your magic to full power." I was tucked into Kerdik's side with his arm around my back. My hand reached over and rubbed his chest to soothe the ache I knew was there. "Kerdik went out to fight with Province 9 against Morgan la Fae. She attacked us, but Kerdik cared so much about you all that he fought with your parents to keep us safe."

Kerdik raised one eyebrow to question my blatant lie. "That's certainly a remarkable story you're telling them."

I moved my hand over and pinched his side to shut him up. "Before we go out to see your parents, I want each of you to say 'thank you' to Kerdik for being our brave hero today."

David was my right-hand man, so he set the example by going

first, his younger siblings trailing close behind him, glued to his shadow. "Thank you, Master Kerdik." He bowed his head, and then trotted over to the doors to the keep, thrusting up the heavy latch and opening the first set of doors.

I didn't want to leave Kerdik's side, but David was having trouble with the second set of doors, so I jogged over to help him. I could hear mothers on the other side of the barricade, their cries rising in time with their fists that banged on the outer doors. I gave David a quick hug before we pushed open the last of the series of doors.

The mothers and fathers flooded into the keep, stopping short when they saw Kerdik. He braced himself for the shrieks he was used to, but they never came. The men and women gave him jerky, terrified bows in gratitude for fighting with their province before moving on to find their children. The parents scooped up their kids with tearstained faces. They had filthy hands and blood on their shirts and aprons. Adrenaline was still ebbing, so tears flowed freely as mother, father and child alike were overjoyed at being reunited.

Bastien and I were holding ourselves back, staring into each other's eyes like bulls ready to be released from the pen. I knew that if I touched him at all, it would be the PG-13 kiss unsuitable for the thousands of children who ran around us. Bastien had streaks of blood in his hair that ran down his face and neck. He had too many cuts and red marks to count, but none of that seemed to bother him. His eyes were locked in on mine as his nostrils flared with desire.

A few of the mothers shrieked at the sight of King Urien, still lying supine towards the far end of the keep. They bowed to him, even though he could not see the gesture, and then made their way to the exit where I stood. I tried to be gracious when the parents got down on their hands and knees to thank me for keeping their children safe, but the whole thing really wasn't my bag. I hugged each of the mothers after they rose to their feet, and shook each dad's hand, hopefully making it clear that we were in this together, and that I was grateful to look after their little treasures.

I was holding it together pretty well until Babette's mother came to collect her sweetheart. I'd met her a few times when she'd dropped off her daughter to play, and knew the dark-haired mid-thirties beauty well enough. Of all the moms I was glad to see, Babette's mother gave me the most relief. After bowing to me, I gave her the standard hug I'd been doling out, expecting to quickly move onto the next parent in the long line. Only Babette's mother didn't let go. She sobbed on my shoulder, squeezing emotion out of me like an overfull tube of lotion. Tears were squished out of me when I imagined Babette being left an orphan to fend for herself with so much of life already stacked against her. I saw myself without a mother to watch over me, and tried not to completely break down.

"Thank you for coming back to Avalon," she gulped out as she held on too tight. "We've never had the strength to stand up to Morgan la Fae before, but now? Now we can do anything, with the Avalon Rose by our side."

The other women nodded with enthusiasm at the nickname I'd been given at my coronation. The rest of the women did the bow and hug with me, but then tacked on for their children to thank "the Avalon Rose."

Yeah, I was a tear-streaked mess after that.

Kerdik's mere presence kept the mothers and children from lingering in the keep. Once they were all gone, Kerdik made his way over to Urien to give Bastien and me a moment of privacy.

I wanted to say something cool and sexy, but all that happened was me bursting into fresh tears. "Kerdik said you were fighting like a maniac! You're not allowed to do that ever again. I was stuck down here, terrified for you! I didn't know if I'd ever see your face after this!"

"Honey," Bastien started, his hands up in surrender.

I didn't want to hear it. "You're not allowed to go into any more battles, do you hear me? If you die, then what? I don't care if I'm being selfish, I need you alive!"

Before I could shout another word, Bastien closed the distance between us in a few long steps taken at a run. He scooped me up in his arms that felt strong and capable, lifting me so that he had to raise his chin to kiss me. My arms draped around his neck, and my legs gripped his waist so I could keep myself right where we wanted me.

"Never again," I worked out between kisses. We were desperate to get closer to each other, clawing at material and scratching the skin beneath. I tugged hard on his hair, but then paused when my hands were coated in something warm and wet. I gasped into his mouth when too much blood coated my fingers. "Bastien! You're hurt!" I really should've put that together earlier, but my brain wasn't processing things in the right order. I unlocked my legs and slid down his body, horrified at how much damage he'd endured up close.

Bastien had the gall to shrug. "It's a few scratches. Looks worse than it is."

I balked at him. "Are you kidding me with this? You're going straight to Remy. Let's go." I called over my shoulder. "You coming, Kerdik?"

Kerdik hefted up my father's body. "I'll take Urien back to his room."

Bastien shot over me at Kerdik a sarcastic, "Hey, thanks for ratting me out to my woman. She doesn't need to know what happens out on the battlefield."

"You're welcome, you psycho. Next time you try to take on an entire army by yourself, be sure to invite me to the massacre. You do put on a good show."

Before Bastien could spout back a fiery retort, Kerdik vanished with Urien, leaving us alone in the keep. Bastien waggled his eyebrows at me, suddenly playful and seeming to think this was the perfect space for a reunion. He grinned at me, but the gorgeous smile I adored was marred when a trickle of blood dribbled from his nose into his mouth, dying a few teeth red. "Straight to Remy," I ordered, turning him around and shoving him toward the exit.

29

ERRANT PERVY THOUGHTS

*R*emy had been spreading the word about my gift to his community, so perhaps the influx of healers who'd sought refuge in Lane's province shouldn't have been all that much of a shocker, but when the numbers totaled over a hundred, I couldn't help but gape. Healers from all over had apparently been told that the Lost Princess could listen to them, so they came in droves.

In the aftermath of the battle, it turns out that too many healers is the best problem to have. They set up on the steps of the mansion, treating people on the wide dais as the injured were brought to them by the dozens. The sun still hadn't risen completely, but there was a promise of natural light on its way that could replace the lanterns' glow.

The children made themselves useful searching out herbs and roots the healers needed to take care of the wounded, and thanks to the quick response of everyone, no farmer, weary deserter soldier from Morgan's Army, or layman was made to wait all that long for treatment. The older kids helped wash strips of cloth that were used for bandages, and brought the wounded warriors water. It was kind of amazing to watch the province in action, tending to needs without being asked for the sacrifice. Everyone was on their way to getting back on their feet.

Except my stubborn mule of a boyfriend. Bastien insisted the other men and women go before him, giving up his space in line over and over again. I would be pissed at him, but it was so sweet that I couldn't maintain my frustration.

Finally I pulled Remy aside after he'd finished stitching up the leg he'd been working on. I led him over to Bastien, giving him a look that told him not to test me. "I don't need a healer. It's a few scratches, Rosie."

"This is more than a few scratches."

"You're telling me. You got anything in your doctor bag for being bull-headed, Remy?"

"Just the usual torture devices," he replied with an evil grin.

I snorted in response. "How can I help? He sleeps now, and I know he's probably tired, but should he be going to sleep with a head wound like that?"

Bastien rolled his eyes. "Oh, brother. You're making a big deal out of nothing."

Link made kissing noises, followed by "Aw, is my wittle Bastien sweetie baby not feewing well?"

Damond smirked at the needling, his uniform basically untouched. I'm guessing Draper put his foot down that Damond was to stay back, instead of fight too near the front lines. "Sit down, Bastien the Bold. You look utterly destroyed."

Bastien glowered at me. "See what you did there?"

"The battle's been over long enough for me not to worry about damage to his brain. He seems lucid enough, though watching him fling himself into the fray like that..." Remy shuddered. *"If you ever doubted that he's loyal to your cause, take in every gash on his body as proof that he loves you."*

I shot a look of warning at my faithful healer knight. "Don't stick up for him, Remy; it'll only make me madder."

Remy smirked as he started mopping off the blood from

Bastien's head so he could better assess the injuries. *"Apologies, Princess. After I finish up here, I'd like to take another look at King Urien. Is he still in the keep?"*

"No, Kerdik took his body back to his room."

"Very good. It's cold and dank down there. Not fit for a king."

I tried to hear Remy, but so many other people were talking. When a man came to stand next to Remy, looking like he wanted my attention, I realized the healers were all thinking to themselves. I was hearing not only the thoughts of the healers, but the conversations between the men and women getting patched up, as well. *"Is it true you can hear us, your majesty?"*

I nodded at the red-headed man who looked to be about five years older than Remy. I closed my eyes and put my hands over my ears. "Sure, but it's a little overwhelming. I mean, I can hear all of you talking at once. What's your name?"

Bastien tugged my hand from my left ear. "You're shouting, Daisy."

"What?" As more healers started to react to the confirmation of me being able to hear Remy, plus a second healer, individual people grew impossible to pick out.

The healers stood, migrating toward me to get a word in, but that consequently meant not a word was getting to me, since they were all talking over each other.

Of course, to the other people of Province 9, I no doubt looked like a lunatic, shouting responses to questions they couldn't hear and covering my ears while a hundred silent grown men and women surrounded me. I cringed when errant thoughts they hopefully hadn't meant for me to hear intruded my mind. Apparently, I had good birthing hips and supple breasts with pert nipples that would be good for nursing a baby. Good to know. A few of them had... ungentlemanly things to say about my butt. This was the raw thoughts of dozens and dozens of people, uncensored. I guessed that most of the men were single, judging by the errant lewd thoughts and lack of wedding rings. They'd been isolated from society, being called on when they were needed, but largely ignored until there was a problem for them to solve.

The healers kept up their rapid thoughts, moving closer and closer until I was starting to feel a little claustrophobic. Madigan stood and beelined for me, seeing that I was starting to lose my cool. I shouted above the commotion. "Okay, I want to hear all of you, but I'm literally getting every thought that's coming into your minds. You might want to clean it up before bringing it over here. Whichever one of you wants to see me naked and bend me over your knee, I can hear you, and it's gross." I stood straighter when they balked at me, stupefied. "You're going to have to do a lot better than *acting* like gentlemen and ladies. You're going to have to actually *be* gentlemen and ladies. I'll know the difference."

Bastien stood from his spot on the porch when I was backed down the steps out onto the grass. Draper had been on the far corner of the porch, but rose unsteadily to move towards me, feeling his way along the banister. "Healers, back to your posts. Best behavior around the princess."

Damond frowned at the mute crowd. "My cousin will not be objectified, especially not after keeping all the children of our kingdom safe."

"Oh, you guys. Go back and sit down. I'm alright." I breathed a little easier when Draper was lowered back to his spot on the porch. A healer set to work mending a cut on his leg.

Damond reached out and gripped my fingers, meeting my eyes before he went back to organizing supplies for the wounded. "I'm just over there, if you need me."

"Thanks, man." We shared a smirk, being two young'uns with too much authority in a world that was set up to devour us whole.

"The Avalon Rose will listen to each one of you, once you're all finished helping Duchess Elaine by treating her people. Now, go on back and let my charge breathe." Bastien put his hand on my shoulder and let out a long, intrusive whistle, which made everyone wince. Not fifteen seconds later, Abraham Lincoln came bounding down the field toward me with Hamish on his back.

When a few men cautiously drew their spears, I held out my hands to stop them from impaling my sweetheart. "Stop! That's just Abraham Lincoln. He's my friend, and he won't hurt anyone."

"You want us to stand back and hope a bear doesn't maul the Avalon Rose?" one of the farmers asked.

Link stood on my other side, enforcing my rule. "You've all seen the bear brawling alongside us out there on the field. He's a mite more loyal to her than the average beast."

The same question was repeated around me: *"What'd he say?"*

"He said that Abraham Lincoln's cool, so don't hurt him."

Link frowned. "Jays, my accent's not tha thick."

"Of course not. You're a total native." I motioned for the healers to go back and finish their jobs. Then I waved Abraham Lincoln over so I could run my fingers through his thick fur. "Hi, baby. You weren't fighting, were you?"

He whined under my touch. He'd been spending a lot of time outside helping Mad and Link secure the grounds. I hadn't had much cuddle time with him as of late, and I could tell both of us missed it. *"Of course I was fighting. Daddy was in danger. I wasn't going to do nothing while they killed him."*

Hamish chimed in with a fierce, *"And we'd do it all over again. Bring back the soldiers who tried to get at Lane. I'll show them all!"*

I whirled on Bastien, all pretense of sweetness gone. "You let him fight? He's just a baby!"

Bastien grinned at me. "He's a year old now. That's hardly a baby for a bear."

"He fought because he was scared for you. You just led a one-year-old into battle. A child. Is that the kind of daddy you want to be to our..." I stopped short, my nose scrunching. I blanched, horrified at how far my imagination had run away with me.

Bastien leaned his head back to bark out a loud laugh. "You just said he was our baby." He smiled down at me with more love than my scowl was willing to accept. "You want to have babies with me."

"Oh, jeez. Go back up there and let Remy deal with your brain damage. Clearly you're not thinking straight."

"Kiss me, Rosie."

My cheeks heated, so I ducked my head and shoved my hands in the pockets of my jeans. "Hello, I'm engaged to your friend. We can't do that in public."

All the levity in Bastien's face hardened. "Sorry. I forgot. In like, just over two more months, you can call the engagement off."

Madigan stayed out of our awkward conversation until it was over. Then he turned to me with his head lowered so he could speak quietly. "Which one of the lads wanted to bend my fiancée over his knee?"

I covered my face with my hands. "Sheesh. I dunno."

Mad moved my hands so he could read my lips. I wondered if anyone else knew he was hard of hearing. He hid it pretty well. "Which one?"

"I don't know. They were all talking at once. It's fine. It was a random thought. You've never had pervy musings about a woman who didn't belong to you?"

Mad's eyebrows furrowed, unable to stab at my solid logic. "I don't like it. Princesses aren't toys to be played with."

I nodded, trying to do damage control. "Well, like I said, I don't know who it was, so there's nothing to do about it. It's fine, Mad. I'm not upset. I just wanted them to know I could hear them."

I nudged Link with my elbow. "Dude, hottie checking you out over there."

Link slapped me on the shoulder. "Speaking of pervy thoughts..." He eyed the girl maybe two years younger than me who was helping the healers tear up rags to be used for bandages. She had big boobs, a flirty eye for him, and no wedding ring. I'd fallen into dude friend zone with him, which was my most comfortable default mode. "Excuse me, lads. I'll be rolling tha lass in the hay tonight."

"Enjoy."

Before Link left to settle in on his conquest, he smacked Mad on the back and nodded to Bastien. "You've got her?"

"Aye," Mad replied, leaning over to pet Abraham Lincoln, who apparently was one of the few who was allowed to touch Mad without him recoiling from the contact. They were actually kind of sweet together.

Hamish planted himself on my shoulder, his arms crossed over his chest. He started chittering at errant healers who walked past, angry at all of them for the few bad seeds.

"You guys don't have to do this, you know. Seriously, I'm not in any danger."

"Did ye not hear Morgan's threats on ye? Of course you're in danger. One victory means nothing to tha witch."

Bastien hissed, motioning for Madigan to shut up.

"What threats? I was in the keep with the kids the entire time."

Madigan eyed Bastien warily. "Uh, nothing. Just stay close. I don't fancy fishing ye out of another well."

Though the sun was starting to peek over the horizon more fully, I felt cold all over. "I think I'll go inside and see if Lane needs help with anything."

"Aye, me too."

I paused and stared up at Mad's hulking form. "You're not going to let me out of your sight, are you."

"Do ye need me to lie to ye and give ye some promise tha Morgan will leave ye alone?"

"No. I guess not. You don't have to follow me, though. I'm sure I'm not in as much danger as you're thinking. I'm just going inside."

"I need to go inside, too."

I sighed, glancing up at Bastien, who tried to keep a stoic expression while Remy stitched up a gash on his arm. As I made my way up the steps with Abraham Lincoln, Hamish and Mad in tow, I flinched at the barrage of errant thoughts that hit me all at once. My shoulders sunk inward and my arms crossed over my breasts to deflect the comments about my body I didn't need to hear. Guys were never like this when I had my hump and no boobs. I idly wished for the days when I was the ugly girl, and life was simpler.

Madigan understood and whirled around to the nearest healer, gripping his jaw in one of his massive hands. "Is this the lad who wanted a go at my fiancée?"

The dude was horrified, begging me for his life to be spared and swearing that he didn't have those thoughts about me.

"No! Jeez, Mad. I never should've said anything. Leave this poor guy alone. He's helping fix up the wounded. Inside now, before your temper gets the better of you." I rubbed my temples as too many voices cried out that they didn't think pervy thoughts about me, either.

I yawned, hoping I could make it to my bed before the overuse of my magical gifts took the last of my energy.

30

SUPERMAN'S DAUGHTER

"*I* don't know why it's not working," Kerdik admitted, holding my hand while we stared at my dad. He'd been standing with Lane and Reyn over the stretcher King Urien had been brought outside on as soon as the sun rose. Now that the entire day had passed and the sun had set with no hint of movement from my dad, we were all more than a little discouraged.

"It's been all day of him in the sun, and still nothing." I cleared my throat and voiced my dad's worries. "He's starting to get anxious."

Bastien and Reyn bent down and lifted the stretcher from the grass, and moved him into the mansion. Kerdik locked us inside, sending an ominous chill up my spine. The guys had been doing that a lot. Wherever I went, they locked the door behind me. It was a small thing, but didn't give me any kind of solace that the threats on my life from Morgan could be ignored.

They brought Urien to a room on the first floor that was down several hallways, and away from the hustle of the house. The stretcher was set on the bed, but no movement was made to take the stretcher from beneath him. We all just stared at him, stumped that our plan hadn't worked.

"Tell Kerdik that I have more sensation now. I can feel when he touches my foot. Whatever he did helped, but any progress seems to have stalled."

I harrumphed when the message didn't give Kerdik or Lane any kind of cheer. Urien's mind was going in and out of focus, sometimes tuning in to the conversation, and other times I had to shout his name to rouse him. Reyn patted Lane's hand to reassure her. "It was a long shot, and the fight's not over. We'll figure this out."

Lane didn't respond; she was too far gone. She'd been through enough in the past twenty-four hours. We'd lost twenty-eight people, and though we'd buried far more of Morgan's soldiers, the loss hit her hard. "I was supposed to keep everyone safe," she muttered again. She'd been saying the same thing on and off all day. "They trusted me."

I held tight to her hand while Reyn brought her into his arms. He kissed her lips, since it was just us in the room. "You did a great job. Twenty-eight is a small number to lose, Lane."

Both Lane and Urien said in unison, "One body is too many to lose." Lane sniffed, and then turned to Kerdik. "We were unprepared. We still had people crossing our borders and settling in when her soldiers marched on our land. That you..." She looked up at the ceiling to steady herself before she met Kerdik's eyes once more. "That you showed up for us means the world to me. You saved Province 9 from total destruction."

Kerdik's mouth was in a tight line. "I didn't do it for you. I owe the Daughters of Avalon nothing."

Bastien shook his head, his arms crossed over his chest. "Man, you're a tool. She's trying to thank you."

"I don't care about that. All I want is to have my friend back." Kerdik pulled a chair close to the bed and leaned forward to rest his elbows on the edge of the mattress, hands flat together while he pressed his fingertips to his lips. "I don't understand why it didn't work."

Lane's hand was hesitant when she reached out to rest it on Kerdik's shoulder, giving several false starts before touching down on him. "If I can repay you somehow for your kindness, I will. Until then, I'll do all I can to keep Urien's body safe. Would you like guards posted outside his bedroom?"

Kerdik turned his head to stare at her hand on his shoulder. "You don't have to do that. I know people don't like to touch me." His tone wasn't petulant, but more humble than I was used to hearing from him. I watched Lane swallow hard as she kept her hand on his shoulder to give him a squeeze of solidarity. Kerdik turned his attention back to my dad. "I don't need help guarding him. Use your soldiers to guard your borders. That's where they're most needed."

I could tell Reyn didn't like Lane so near the monster, but he let her make her own choices, and for that, I respected him.

Lane took her hand from Kerdik and moved toward me, wrapping me in a hug I prayed I would never stop needing. "Tell me everything's going to be okay," she whispered, trusting me with her moment of insecurity.

I held her tight, treasuring that every now and then, she stopped being my mom and my aunt, and let herself be my best friend. She didn't often need to lean on me, but when she did, I made sure not to screw it up. "Hey, everything's going to be okay. There's no way for it not to be." I rubbed her back while I hugged her, and slowly rocked her from side to side, her dress swaying slightly. "You've got this, Lane."

"I want to leave Avalon so badly, but how can I now? The plan was to instate Roland in my place, so I could get out of here. But they don't trust Roland after he left for the Forgotten Forest. I can't abandon them when they've only just started to come together." Her eyes squeezed shut. "I got twenty-eight people killed."

"Hey, now. Morgan got them killed, not you." My grip on her

was firm, and I could feel Bastien and Reyn's eyes on us, studying our weird bond. "You make everything better."

At this, Lane started to cry softly on my shoulder. "This is moving us to Common all over again. I didn't know what I was doing, didn't have a penny to my name, but somehow thought I could handle a world I didn't understand while I was responsible for a whole other person. Sometimes all I can think about are those nights we spent in the homeless shelter, Ro. I was so scared I would ruin you somehow. And here I am, more than twenty years later, totally out of my element and responsible for people who would be better off without me in charge."

"Hey!" My voice turned sharp, unwilling to let that kind of nonsense go on a second longer. "You can turn that noise right off. Do you think Avril would really be better at standing up to Morgan? What about Roland? You're it, kid. You're exactly the curveball Avalon needs. Morgan won't know what hit her when you get through with her." I took the handkerchief Reyn offered over her shoulder and dabbed at her tears with it. "And all that worrying you do about how we started out? Take a look at me, Lane. I'm exactly the girl you raised, and I turned out alright, thanks to you being one heck of a curveball."

"I love you, Rosie. You're the best thing I ever did." She caught her weird words and let out a laugh. "You know what I mean."

"Rosalie? Rosalie? Is that my daughter? Are you my daughter?"

I cringed and turned my head to look at to Urien. "Oh, crap. I didn't mean for you to hear that. Britney! My name is Britney Spears!" My eyes shut in dread. "I forgot you were listening." I glanced around nervously. "I, um, I've got to go check on something." I made to bolt out of the room, but Lane held me in place while Bastien blocked the door.

"Wait!" Urien roared in desperation. *"Stop her! Britney, are you really my Rosalie?"*

I begged Lane with my eyes to let me run, but she stood her ground. I would've put up a bigger fight, but she needed the win more than I did. "Urien, let me introduce you to your daughter, the biggest chicken in the whole province. Rosie's been pretending to be a random girl because she was afraid you wouldn't like her if you knew who she was."

Urien's voice came out choked with shock and a flood of too many emotions. *"Why? Why, would you hide from me? Don't you know how long I've ached to have you home? I tore my heart in two the day I sent you off so you could live away from Morgan's plans for you. Every day without you has been a death far worse than the one Morgan's kept me suspended in."*

I was wringing my hands, totally blowing it all over the place. This was not how I wanted him to find out. I was supposed to be doing something cool, making him proud of some big accomplishment he just so happened to see. I would wait until he was impressed, and then I was going to tell him. "I wanted to see what you were like – if we could get along without you knowing who I was. You don't understand. Morgan hated me from word one. I couldn't take two blows like that."

"Get me out of this prison!" He bellowed, making me flinch. *"I need to see my daughter!"*

My fingers wrung themselves as my gut twisted with anxiety. "We're trying, but we can't figure it out yet. Give us a little more time. We're all working on it, sir."

His voice came out angry and mournful. *"Don't ever call me 'sir'! I'm your papa! I sang to you and carried you around the castle to show you off to anyone who would look. You were my rose, not my subject. My beautiful, sweet rose."*

I tucked my hair behind my ear, shy under the grand words. "You don't know that I'm beautiful now."

"She is," both Bastien and Kerdik replied in unison, and then scowled at each other.

Urien started shouting orders and basically freaking the crap out trying to get to me. The little girl I never liked to admit was still inside of me wanted to burst into tears, but the adult I knew

I had to be lurched into action. "Okay, he's having a meltdown, so let's figure this out. I mean like, now."

Lane snapped to attention. "I'll go get Remy. And Draper. Draper should be here for this, in case Remy can think of anything to wake him." She moved out of the room quickly, shutting the door behind her.

Kerdik reached into the breast pocket of his standard gray charcoal vest and drew out the piece of parchment I'd stolen from Morgan's special box. Without tearing his eyes from Urien, he handed it to me and then rolled up the sleeves of his white dress shirt. "Read it to me. Maybe I'm missing something important. I have to be. The clue has to be in there somewhere."

My mouth went dry at the request, and my heart took on a terrified rhythm I was all too familiar with. This was worse than being called on in front of the whole class to read a paragraph. This was meeting my dad for the first time, and waving a big banner that screamed out a declaration that his only daughter was stupid.

I swallowed hard and opened the letter with shaking fingers, staring blankly at the tight and scrolly cursive that may as well have been written in a foreign language.

31

THE DUMBEST GIRL IN AVALON

$\mathcal{M}$y hands shook, which only made trying to read that much worse. One of the great things about Avalon was that I hadn't been exposed to all that much signage, so the topic of me not being able to read all that well hadn't been discovered. I needed Bastien to leave. If I couldn't go, he had to. I couldn't have him looking at me like we weren't equals, like I was stupid. I wouldn't be Remedial Rosie in Avalon, so help me. "Bastien, could you get me a glass of water?"

"Sure, babe. Read us the letter first, though. I haven't gotten a chance to look at it. We've all been pretty curious."

Not in front of my dad. Not in front of my dad! Come on, Lane! Why'd you have to pick now to leave? I cleared my throat so many times, I'm sure they probably thought I was coming down with something. I tried to work out the first word, but my voice vanished into a croaky whisper.

Trying a different tact, I handed the letter back to Kerdik. "I'm a little tired. You mind reading it to the guys?"

Kerdik glared up at me in frustration from his chair. "I asked you to do one simple thing for me. I fought a war for you, and you can't stay awake long enough to see if I'm missing a step in resurrecting your own father?"

My palms were sweaty as I took the letter from his hand again. "Sorry. You're right. I just… I…" I cleared my throat again, my hands trembling so badly, I'm not sure if I would've been able to read the letter even if I wasn't dyslexic.

"You okay, babe?" Bastien was eyeing me with caution, concerned that I was on the edge of a nervous breakdown over being asked to read a letter.

He was not far off.

I shook my head, but kept my eyes on the note. I could feel sweat breaking out on the nape of my neck. "One… An… Um, On. Yeah, On. On… l… l-buh… No, wait, that's a TH. On… th… these. Yeah, On these." I could feel moisture beading on my forehead now. "On these… quah-qu… On these qu-y?" I shook my head. "No, that's not right."

Reyn rubbed a circle in my back. "Are you alright, kiddo?"

Kerdik craned his neck to gape at me. "Are you trying to play stupid to get out of doing the one thing I asked you to do? This is actually your plan?"

My dad told Kerdik to mind his words, but no one heard the scolding except for me.

My dad will know now. He'll know his only daughter is a dummy. I'm That Stupid Girl. The Humpback Whale. Remedial Rosie. The Humpback of Notre Dame. Lazy-Eyed Susan. Baby Got Too Much Back. He'll know I repeated the third grade.

Bastien didn't seem to understand what was going on, but boyfriend that he was didn't need the whole story to stick up for me. "Hey, you don't need to be a jerk about it. Give her a minute. You sleep once every few decades. She needs to sleep every day, and she's long overdue. You have no idea what it is to feel exhaustion on a daily basis like she does."

My eyes were wet now. I couldn't help it; "stupid" was one of my trigger words. One of my favorite friends in Avalon had hit it dead on the nose – Kerdik had called me stupid, and I couldn't argue with his spot-on assessment. My third-grade teacher, my GPA and most of my classmates all agreed, as well. I leaned my back to the wall and tucked my chin to my chest so I could hide my forthcoming tears behind my hair and lashes. I held the paper out from my body so I didn't have to face any of them. "I, um, so the thing is… I, you know, um, I can't read. I h-h-have something c-c-called primary v-v-visual dyslexia, which makes reading something that I c-c-can't really do without a lot of help."

I could feel all the eyes on me, and I wished there was a space lower than the floor for me to crawl into. Of course that's when Lane came back with Remy and Draper. Of course there would be more witnesses to my eternal failure. Remy was one thing, but Draper? I wanted my brother to look at me like I was amazing and capable of anything, not like I was an idiot. I tried to hold tight to the memory of how he'd gazed at me like I was something special, not special needs.

"What'd I miss? Babe, what's wrong?" Lane leaned against the wall next to me. She didn't need the details to understand that I needed a hug, so she wrapped an arm around my shoulder. "Did something happen while I was out?"

I handed her the letter, whispering, "They know now. Everyone knows."

Lane's eyebrows pushed together as she scanned the letter. "They know what? They know how to get Urien back? Wouldn't that be good news?"

Kerdik looked over his shoulder at Lane in disgust. "How could you not teach your daughter how to read?"

Lane gasped and covered her mouth, revelation crashing down on her. She closed her eyes, feeling my pain, as she always seemed to be able to do. "Oh, baby. No, no." Her soothing words turned borderline frantic. "It's all fine. I'm sorry. I'm so sorry I wasn't here. I didn't mean to leave you exposed like that. No one thinks any less of you. You're so smart, baby."

Bastien's mouth was on the floor. "You truly can't read? Like, you can't read this small note? It's only one page."

Lane gaped at me. "You didn't tell Bastien?"

I shook my head and tried to suck in the tears that were a mixture of exhaustion and self-loathing, chewing on my nails so I could bite down on the tips of my fingers to punish myself for being a dummy. "I was hoping it wouldn't come up." I whispered to her, though the room was so quiet, I'm sure everyone heard me. "My dad knows. Now everyone I love knows I'm stupid."

"What could possibly... Maybe her brain is damaged?"

Though Remy was trying to be helpful and fix me, his words felt like a punch in the gut. Lane and I had been through so much with this thing; if it had been fixable, we would've found the cure by now. There was no cure for dyslexia. We could land a man on the moon, but there was no help for me, other than endless tutoring and "helpful tools" that did little in the way of actually getting me to be able to read anything more complicated than a picture book.

Lane didn't bother correcting my harsh words right away. She knew from years of experience that I couldn't absorb the comfort until I was in a better place. She hugged me tight, warning the guys with a sharp look to be cool. "Hey, I know who you are. I love you, and I know you're not stupid."

I pulled out of her embrace and waved my hand in the air to clear it of the dense emotional fog I was now mired in. "It's fine. I've got to get out of here, though. I'm going to bed, so if anyone needs me for anything but this, that's where I'll be."

"Rosie, wait. They're just surprised. No one thinks you're stupid."

Draper glanced around the room, confused. "Is this a joke or something? My sister can read. She's very smart. I've seen her..." He paused and then looked up at the ceiling, puzzling out if he'd ever seen me reading something.

I didn't bother to stick around and debate it. Instead I shoved my hands in my pockets and trotted out into the hallway. I did my best to keep a bland expression on my face, interacting as succinctly as possible with members of the staff who milled through the halls as I beelined for my bedroom and locked the door. I knew I was locking Bastien out, but I honestly couldn't face him. I couldn't handle the stunned looks, which were only slightly more palatable than the ones of pity, confirming that yes, no matter which world I was in, I would always be Remedial Rosie.

I changed into a lavender cotton nightgown, not even taking any pleasure in the spaghetti straps or the way it hugged my breasts and showed off my toned legs. I was stupid; it didn't matter if I was pretty. I crawled under the covers, too despondent to cry about all the respect I'd lost in a single conversation. I tried to let the soft comforter warm me, but I felt cold inside, bereft of the friendship and love I'd felt just an hour ago. My eyes closed, and as I waited for sleep to take me, I hoped with everything in my soul that when I woke, none of them would remember that they'd all bet their chips on the dumbest girl in Avalon.

BREATHING FIRE

*W*hen my lashes fluttered open, I was greeted by a pounding I tried to ignore. The sun wasn't up, but Bastien was determined to disturb the entire house. "Let me in, Rosie."

"I'm sleeping. I'll see you in the morning."

The knocking stopped, and I drifted back to sleep, grateful that the next time I woke, it was to the sun, and not to Bastien. I stretched under the covers, but the possibility of a new day didn't give me any sort of hope that life would have anything good in store. When I sat up, my eyes snapped to the spot of green in the room. Kerdik was sitting in a chair at the side of the bed, watching me sleep without a word.

My eyes darted away from him as I fiddled with the strap on my nightgown. "It's rude to watch people sleep, you know."

"You should know by now that I care nothing about rules of rudeness and manners. You wouldn't let Bastien in, so I wanted to make sure you slept safely."

I deflated slightly. "Oh. Well, then I guess I'm sorry I snapped at you. But you can go now. You can see I'm safe."

He was leaned back in his chair, his left ankle crossed over his right knee. His elbows perched on the armrests, while his hands were flat together in front of his face, so his lips could rest on his fingertips. It was his mulling things over body language, so I didn't pry. When he finally spoke, I wished he hadn't. "You don't know how to read."

I stiffened, not wanting to start out the day like this. "You know, I understand the grammar, mechanics and the rules better than anyone. I've studied them for years. But my brain doesn't see letters in the same way yours does. They scramble. So yes, I know how to read, but no, I can't actually do it. It's like having the blueprints for how to build a spaceship, but missing all the nuts and bolts, so you can't actually construct the thing." I sighed, leaning against the headboard and bringing my knees up under the covers so I could rest my elbows on them. There were angel wings engraved all over the wooden headboard, but the beauty of it felt grim this morning. "I was really hoping not to have it shoved in my face first thing today."

"Lane explained it to us last night, but I still don't understand. Dyslexia doesn't exist in Faîte."

"Well, it does now. Bonus points to me for bringing the median IQ down a few notches. It'll make everyone else feel smarter. 'Hey, I didn't pass my exam, but at least I can read. Thank God I'm not as dumb as that useless princess.' See? I'll make everyone feel much better about themselves. My gift to Province 9."

"Why didn't you tell me? And if not me, then why not Bastien?"

"Seriously? The most powerful being in Faîte is my BFF, and his trusty sidekick can't even read? And forgive me, but I'd rather my boyfriend not know how stupid I am." I stared out the window, wishing the rising sun brought any sort of life about in me. "Well, it was nice while it lasted."

"Does anyone know in your Common life?"

"My best friend does. Judah started out as my tutor, but we

stuck together even during the summers. He knew me before I was officially diagnosed, and never once called me stupid."

Kerdik winced. "No one thinks you're stupid."

I took him in with dead eyes. "Yes, you do. It's fine. Compared to you, everyone else probably is stupid."

"You say that word like you're stabbing yourself through the chest. Stop it."

I went back to staring out the window. "My dad heard it all. He just got his daughter back, and now he knows she's defective. Never thought I'd be glad he couldn't get out of that bed, but knowing he'd probably leave me if he could kind of shoots the day in the foot."

Kerdik scoffed, as if I was being ridiculous. "Urien wouldn't abandon his own daughter. He's a good man. If anything, he'd try to fix you."

It was my turn to scoff. I sank back down under the covers and rested my head on my pillow. "Oh, goody. Another tutor who'll eventually give up. More tests. More study sessions to take up my life, all so that Kindergarteners can run circles around me."

"What are you doing?"

"I'm going back to sleep. Maybe when I wake up again, last night won't have happened."

"I'm not sure that's how life works."

"That's how it works today. You can go do your thing. Enjoy your day. If anyone needs me, well, tell them to write down their requests in a letter. I'll read it as soon as I can." I let out a sarcastic one-noted laugh. "See what I did there? That was a little dyslexic humor."

His tone soured. "You're actually dismissing me? Am I some servant you don't want to be bothered with?"

I turned away from him and stared out the window. "I'm too depressed to spar with you today. You can win whatever argument you think we need to have."

Kerdik stood and moved to stand in my eye line. "This isn't you. What happened to your spark?"

I didn't bother shrugging, but simply stared unblinkingly at nothing.

I didn't expect Kerdik to stick around to deal with my funk. He was usually the one with the tantrums, but today it was my turn. When Kerdik ripped the covers off me, I shrieked, moving to cover myself as if I'd been naked beneath the sheets. I sat up, my face contorting into a glower as I tried to make my night-gown appear decent. "Get out!"

"Stop pushing me away, Rosie." He was just as angry as I was. "Bastien's been sitting outside your bedroom all night to make sure nothing got in here. Draper's been up with Remy, Reyn and Lane all night, trying to figure out a new plan to teach you how to read."

"I don't need anyone to fix me!" I raged, hopping out of the bed. My anger was big enough that Kerdik actually took a few steps back toward the window. "Lane's tried everything, and everyone just needs to accept that these are the cards I was dealt. I don't have it in me to keep trying new ways that everyone swears will work this time. I'm tired, Kerdik. I'm tired of all of it. I'm going back to bed because I'm useless now. No one needs an idiot princess to pretend she can keep up with things that children can do."

Kerdik straightened, looking down his nose at me. "You'll not hide in here simply because we didn't react the way you wanted when you threw us a curve out of nowhere. You're the princess of Province 9, and you'll make yourself useful."

"You want me to read something for the people? Give them all a good laugh? I could double up as both princess and court jester."

Kerdik marched over to my wardrobe and yanked out a dress at random, and then threw it on the bed. "Get dressed and then come downstairs. You're through feeling sorry for yourself. There's work to be done."

"I don't think so."

"The healers are downstairs, lined up to speak with the only one who can hear them. Now, I don't care all that much about these people, but it's my gift that allowed you to be able to hear them, and I won't have anyone questioning that my gifts are faulty. You'll go down and play nice with the locals."

"Fine!"

"Fine!" When I didn't move, Kerdik jabbed his finger at the simple green renaissance fair gown on the mattress. "You have two minutes to change, or I'm coming back and dressing you myself!"

"You'll do no such thing. Get out and go intimidate someone else. I'm maxed out on how worthless a girl can feel."

I expected him to go – I'd pushed him away enough to earn a little space – but instead Kerdik closed the distance between us. He cupped my face in his chartreuse hands, tipping my chin up to stare into his determined gaze. "You are not worthless, so it's time you start acting like it. You're their princess, but you're my queen. You're the daughter of the greatest king Avalon has ever seen."

I swallowed the lump in my throat, closing my eyes to fend off the sincerity Kerdik was beaming into me. "What if my dad doesn't want me anymore?"

"If he doesn't want you, it won't be due to your shortcomings, few though they are. It'll be because of you lying around in your pajamas, accepting defeat like a Commoner. That is not the girl I love."

My voice was quiet, uncertain and filled with all the things I was afraid might always be true about myself. "You still love me?"

Kerdik's stern expression was broken by half a smile tugging up the left corner of his mouth. He leaned in and kissed my lips gently, softly and with a promise that he didn't think I was beneath him, even now. "You're the sun in my sky. When you're gone from me, there's only rain and clouds." I inhaled at the sweetness of his grand declaration that was both metaphorical and literal, given how his mood swings sometimes swayed the elements. "You've got real warmth in your eyes, and it reminds me to not be so cold."

He kissed my lips again, only this time, it was different. There was a slow, steady intention to his movements. My heart picked up to a racing speed when his lips parted, and the sweet peck turned into a real kiss filled with delicious romance. We both indulged in the decadence of the breathtaking moment, ignoring the worlds as our lips made terrible decisions. He sucked on my lower lip, and my lashes fluttered through the utter high his kiss caressed me with deep down in my soul. Something swirled inside of me, starting from my mouth and zipping through my body like too much caffeine. It lasted only a handful of seconds, but when I pulled away in shock, both our cheeks were pink.

Kerdik touched his lower lip, as if testing to see if it felt any different now. "That was an accident," he clarified. "A beautiful accident."

I nodded, stunned. "An accident. We're... You're my friend."

"And I intend on keeping you as such. My apologies."

"I, um, it's cool. My fault, too." Of all things, I felt a belch building up in me. What can I say? I'm a sexy beast. I turned my head, expecting a small burp to slip out, but my eyes bulged when a blast of fire erupted from my lips. Hot and smoky, the flames rocketed a foot and a half out from my mouth, choking a cry from my shocked lips. I didn't know what to do. I mean, the firemen hadn't really covered the proper procedure for spontaneous fire burps. Stop, drop and roll didn't seem all that applicable here.

Kerdik's hand clamped my mouth shut, trapping the flames and my scream inside of me with no fear of the burn. "I'm sorry! I didn't mean for that to happen! Breathe through it and put it from your mind."

Panic shot through me, but his hand over my mouth kept my fear locked inside. When I was decently sure the flames were gone, I twisted in his arms, pretty well freaking out, and not caring that my nightgown was riding up in his iron grip.

"Breathe, darling. Nothing happened. You didn't... You're mistaken!" When that clearly didn't work, he repeated a desperate, "Put it out of your mind!"

Finally, I managed to jerk out of his hold. I patted my body down to make sure none of the rest of me had caught fire. "Put it from my mind? Are you kidding me? I just friggin' breathed fire!"

The walls started to tremble around me, and I knew that Kerdik was getting too worked up. "It didn't happen. I didn't... We didn't... It was an accident!"

I touched my forehead, stunned. "Has this sort of thing happened before?"

The guilt in Kerdik's eyes betrayed his quick, "No!"

I tried to calm myself down, since only one of us could freak out at a time, and Kerdik had taken that ticket. "Now would be the time for the truth, dude. Seriously. What just happened?" My tongue tested the inside of my teeth, which felt warmer than usual.

Kerdik shook his head, as if willing it all to be not true. Because, you know, it's easy to explain away an errant kiss from a friend, but not so simple to brush under the rug a fire-breathing girl without a clue. "It's something that'll never happen again. It was an accident, is all. The fire is nothing you need to talk about to anyone, understand?"

"Okay, now you're scaring me. What does it mean that I breathed fire? Like, will it happen again at random? Is it because we..." I blushed and looked away, unable to say the word "kissed."

Kerdik sank down onto my bed, leaning forward to rest his elbows on his knees. He stared at his fingers, as if they would solve all the problems he couldn't put words to. "It's happened before, yes. When I get carried away. I won't make that mistake again, so you needn't worry about the fire becoming permanent."

"Permanent?!" I exclaimed, my eyes wide and demanding answers.

He couldn't bring himself to look in my direction. "You don't need to be afraid of me." He closed his eyes. "Please don't be afraid of me. You're the one person who I couldn't bear to have shrink away in horror at the sight of my face."

My shoulders dropped the tense grip they had on my body, and sympathy moved my bare feet toward him. I placed my hand on the side of his face, stroking his cheek so he knew nothing had changed. "Why would me having a faulty valve that shoots out flames make me be afraid of you? You're still you. I'm still me. I'm just hotter now." I placed my palm on my belly and mimed a hearty laugh at my terrible joke. "Get it? Because fire's hot."

Kerdik covered my hand on his face with his, savoring the contact he'd been starved from for so long. "Always be you. Don't let me turn you into something less beautiful."

"Beautiful doesn't matter," I ruled, feeling like I was qualified to speak on the subject, since I'd grown up as the ugly girl.

"Very well, then don't let me turn you into something less you. I adore you."

My mouth curved at his lovely compliment. "Stop saying all the right things. Apparently if I get turned on, I light things on fire. Tread lightly."

Kerdik chuckled softly. "Thank you for making a joke."

My voice quieted. "Is this going to happen when I kiss Bastien next? Or is it just with you?"

"Just with me, and we won't be doing that again, so you don't need to worry. I am sorry, darling. I lost my mind for a moment. Your nightgown," he clarified with a guilty downward tilt to his head. "You shouldn't wear that around me. Burn it, or I might slip up again, and you'll light it on fire with your breath. Either way, it… I shouldn't see you like that. It does things to me that neither of us can handle."

I was stunned for a few beats, confused and embarrassed. Finally I leaned over and wrapped my arms around his neck, squeezing tight so he didn't crawl into his shell of self-loathing. "Never happened." I kissed his cheek before pulling away, reminding us both that we were solid, even when life shook us up. "I think I'm going to get dressed. I'll meet you downstairs."

Before we parted, Kerdik stood with a steady inhale, his chest puffing out, reminding me that he was tall, strong and leonine. He took a chance and brushed his lips to mine, pecking them for a quick taste. I tensed a little, but to be fair, I'd just turned full-on dragon when we slipped up not five minutes ago. Kerdik's shoulders relaxed that we hadn't forfeited our familiar rhythm. "For the record, that's what I meant to do."

"Me, too. I'll get dressed and go meet with the healers."

His hand alighted on my shoulder, fingering the spaghetti strap of my nightgown with something that looked akin to longing clouding his eyes. Goosebumps erupted, burning a line where his fingers brushed my skin. His next words came out barely above a whisper. "It's the nightgown," he ruled, as if trying to convince himself of the spell the simple material cast over both of us. He cleared his throat, straightening as he removed his hand from me and ran his palm down the front of his charcoal vest, his chin raised. "See if you can't figure out which of the healers are most loyal to Lane. I could use some help with Urien. Remy's hit a wall. Adding a spare healer to the household would be most prudent."

"Sounds good," I croaked.

Kerdik shot me a few more hesitant glances before he left, leaving me alone in the room with my shock and pink cheeks.

33

ROLAND'S TRUE COLORS

I heaved my relief when Kerdik left, and made quick work of getting dressed. I wanted to flee the scene of the crime, so I didn't even bother trying to tie up the laces in the back of my dress before I bolted out of the room and ran smack into Bastien. "Oh! Hey, I didn't see you there."

"I was just coming back up to see if you'd opened the door yet. I really didn't mean to call you stupid. It was a dumb thing to say. I thought you were playing around. Lane explained it all to us."

I banded my arms across my stomach, avoiding his penetrating gaze. "Can we not talk about it? I mean, I appreciate the apology, and we're cool. I just did the rehash with Kerdik, and I don't want to have to go over it all again."

Bastien held up his hands. "Fine by me. I've got questions, but they can wait until later. I'm out helping the men build a wall around the city. It'll take some doing, but we all need a project to unite the province, so this seemed like a good fit."

"Cool. I'm about to go kick it with the healers. See if someone can give my dad a fresh look." I made to give him a quick peck on the cheek, but he caught my lips instead, sealing our connection with a kiss that was as wonderful as it was comfortable. Plus, I didn't light his eyebrows on fire with a heated belch, so, you know, bonus. "You're the only one I want to be kissing," I whispered, reminding us both.

"Good. Remember that when the healers start throwing you a parade and declare you their queen." He kissed me once more before we parted. "See you for lunch?"

"It's a date."

Bastien paused and gripped my bicep, his brow furrowed. "Don't leave the mansion, alright? I've got a bad feeling about today. Something weird. I can't put my finger on it."

"Okay. I can stay inside." I gulped, hoping Bastien didn't catch wind of the non-kiss that had just happened.

I scurried down the hallway and stumbled down the steps ungracefully, still not totally used to wearing long dresses. This one was a dull green, simpler than the ornate ones Morgan had made me wear, and featured pink stitching to match the lace that poked out from underneath my elbow-length sleeves. I meandered through the empty kitchen, picking an apple from the fruit bowl and taking a crunchy bite.

"So, you decide to grace us with your presence."

The unwelcome voice wafted into the kitchen from behind me. My spine straightened, and I turned around only after I'd composed the worry from my face. "Go away, Roland. Bastien was pretty clear you're not to be alone with me. You don't live in the mansion. Your place is the house next door."

Roland held up his hands in surrender. "I'm not starting anything troublesome. I'm only making sure the princess has what she needs to start her day. Did you want some milk?"

Not if I was dying of dehydration would I take something you offered me. "No, thank you. I don't want anything you have to give me."

His mouth tightened. "Is that any way to speak to your cousin?"

"Oh, *now* we're family? I thought I was a witch who was only after the gems."

He pointed to my finger. "Well, you do wear that one quite often."

My fist tightened to make sure my ring stayed in place. "Did you want to wear it? It's a little girly to belong on your hand."

He sighed and leaned against the counter, his arms crossed over his chest. He wore beige pants and an emerald dress shirt with gold edges, in keeping with the royal colors of Lane's kingdom. He'd united what was left of his province with hers, and hadn't caused any problems since he'd moved in. "I'm trying to make amends, Rosie. I was wrong about you. I never got to say thank you for bringing back the gems you found in Morgan's castle. You handed them over like it was nothing. I guess I'm so used to Morgan and Avril that I didn't expect you to be any different."

Glad as I was that he could finally spot the obvious, I wasn't willing to be buddy-buddy with him. I nodded once, casting him a wary glance that told him I had no idea what to do with him showing humility. I studied his face, and the sideways tilt to his head that seemed to communicate sincerity. Lane's words of "know who you are" echoed in my head. I wasn't a vindictive brat, though I wanted to be one in that moment. I chewed on my bottom lip and tried to find grace in my heart for the man who'd tried to kill me. "Okay, Roland. Thank you."

I went to leave, but Roland stood in front of me, blocking my way. It didn't seem like he wanted a physical fight, but you never knew with this guy. "I've been watching you with Bastien." His face screwed up, his chin dimple deepening when I balked at him. "That came out wrong. I'm trying to tell you I see him changing. Some of it long overdue. Some might say it's a man in love, but I've seen the work of a witch before. If you weren't a woman, I could swear you were Gancanagh. I'm onto you," he warned.

I let out a labored sigh. *Of course we're back to this.* "Well spotted. The only way I can get a boyfriend is to cast some witchy spell on him." I wiggled my fingers around menacingly.

"He used to keep to the outskirts, hiding himself in the woods to avoid people. Now he's leading armies with me. I know it's because of you. Morgan's daughter, indeed. Be careful," he warned, snatching at my face. Apparently his lame stating of the obvious in lieu of an apology had run its course. He squeezed my jaw hard, making my pulse quicken. "Bastien is my best friend, and you've already turned him against me. I'll not tolerate your hooks sinking into him any deeper than they already are."

I yanked my head away from Roland, wound up and socked him hard across the face. I wasn't above forgiving my cousin, but I wouldn't tolerate anyone's hands on me like that. "You want to control me? You want to threaten me? Do it with your jaw wired shut next time, you tool!"

He held the side of his face, shocked that I wasn't afraid to fight back. I didn't have to play nice with Bastien's friend anymore. I spun on my heel and stomped away, furious that he would put his hands on me under my own roof. I made it a whole four steps before Roland flew at me from behind and slammed me against the wall with his lean musculature. His words came out like a knife, cutting through the fake niceness he'd tried to convince me was real. "Look, you. This kingdom will be mine once you and Lane leave it to go back to your life in Common. *I* fought for it. *I* kept my province afloat while Lane was gone after my mother died. I'm the one the people trust to stand up to Morgan. *I* hunted down Avril when we realized she was the one who'd stolen the jewels, and I tore them from her greedy hands."

I stomped down hard on his instep, but I was barefoot, and he was in boots, so it did little. I flung my elbow back into his gut, but despite his satisfying "oof!" he didn't release me. "What's your point, you jackwagon?"

He crushed his body to mine so I had no room at all to fight back. He pinned my arms above my head, securing them to the wall so high that my feet raised to stand on my tiptoes. His breath was hot in my ear, lighting my body with a fresh dose of fear. "My point is that I want you gone. The people are starting to get confused. They're saying Lane led them into battle, but it was me. Lane came out, sure, but *I* was directing Bastien and the rest of the Untouchables. Now they're singing your praises because you kept the children safe and got Kerdik to fight for them."

I hadn't been out of the castle since the battle, so I couldn't exactly speak to this. "I didn't ask them to do that! I wanted to be out there fighting with Bastien, but Kerdik locked me in the keep. Let me go!"

My voice picked up, so Roland cuffed my mouth. "I cared for this province when Lane abandoned it to look after you. And now Bastien's going to abandon his homeland to follow you to another world. Whatever. It's his choice. But once you're there, stay gone."

I shouted into his hand, hating him for making me feel helpless.

"When Urien wakes, I want your word that you'll ask him to stay here. They need him to rally around. If you take him to Common, the people will lose faith. They'll think he's abandoned us to Morgan's wrath."

I bit down hard on his finger, drawing blood. He ripped his hand away from my face, cursing at me before punching me hard in the kidney from behind. I saw stars when he grabbed my head and bashed it to the wall before I could reclaim my bearings. He moved back so I could stumble around, bracing myself on the wall. "Stop it! Dad will decide what he wants to do when he wakes up." I spun around and tried to take a swing at my cousin, but missed horribly when my vision blurred.

Roland slammed me down on the counter, spilling fruit from the overturned bowl out onto the floor. My chest was cold against the marble, but fire burned up in me like none other when Roland bent over me from behind, crushing my body to the hard surface so he could whisper in my ear, "King Urien will wake up once you decide to cooperate."

"What?"

"Give me your word that you'll leave for the Common *with* Lane and *without* Urien, and he'll wake up."

"What are you talking about?" I kicked wildly until Roland drew a dagger from his belt and used it to still my body so I didn't hurt him further. The flat end of the steel was smooth as it traveled down my side, freezing me in place so I didn't get gutted when I thrashed. "Roland, stop!"

"I need your word, Rosie. Give me what I want, and I'll let you go."

"Screw you!"

"Oh, Princess. That was not smart." He shoved an orange in my mouth so deep I almost choked. I bit down, so I could tear off a chunk and spit the rest out, but Roland held the fruit in place like a gag I couldn't escape. "People think Bastien's the one to be feared because he's Untouchable. But see, he has you now. He has the thing he wants. I don't. I want Province 9, and until I get it, I'm the one to be feared." The tip of the dagger quickly tore through the material of my dress, sinking itself into the back of my thigh. I gasped at the slice that felt like a gaping hole being torn through my leg. He left the blade sunk into my skin, so that every jolt I tried to move away from him caused me infinitely more agony. I screamed into the orange, but it was no use. "You don't like it here," Roland said, almost sympathetically. "Think of how miserable I'll make your life if you stay. Do you want a matching scar on the other thigh? You know, for all the talk about the Untouchables being this almighty force, they sure do leave you alone an awful lot."

He removed the knife, holding the orange in place while I panted like an animal. "I have followers, you know. Men who would do unspeakable things in my name. They'd even attack the princess if I wished it so." He gave a few thrusts with his pelvis into my backside, scaring me more than the knife had. "I personally don't see what all the fuss is about, but I don't need to." He leaned down just to crush the air and the will to live out of me. "Tell me what I want to hear. Nod for me like a good little girl."

Rage like none other roiled up inside of me. I thrashed, kicked and struggled, unwilling to go down without a fight – futile as my best efforts were.

Roland tsked me, as if this was all a game, and I was five years old. I could feel the blood running down my right leg as he ripped the steel from the back of my thigh and switched the blade to his left hand, still pinning me with his body. "Bastien's precious virgin princess. We'll see how long his infatuation lasts after my men have a go. See how difficult you are after they've torn your spirits from you." The fear spiked in time with the dagger that plunged into the outside of my left thigh, slicing through my dress and tearing a line down my flesh. "One way or another, you will be gone. Leave Uncle Urien to rule his new kingdom with me. It's all I ask of you." Then he sunk the blade down deep into an untorn section on the top of my thigh. He tugged me off the counter and lowered me down to the floor while I panted, focused only on removing the knife from my leg. Roland gave me the softest smile as he twisted the knife to dial up the pain to a level I was certain would make me insane. "Think it over."

And just like that, my cousin left me there to bleed all over the kitchen floor.

34

ON MY HONOR

I bit down on the orange with a trembling jaw, afraid I might faint and bleed out on the floor before I could call for help. I finally spat out the fruit and screamed with all my might for someone to help me. Of course no one was nearby. The house was a freakin' mansion. That was one point in favor of small apartments. If I sneezed twice from the opposite end of our place, Lane would already be getting out the cold medicine.

One piece of clarity finally hit me in my haze of torture. My hands were shaking too badly to remove the knife, but I managed to get my right hand to my chest, covering my heart with my ring and whispering three times the name I prayed would come when I called this time.

Errant thoughts swam through my agony-addled brain while I tried to get the knife out of my thigh. I wondered what Judah was up to, and if he'd acquired any scars while we'd been apart. I grasped the handle of the knife, but each time it slid out a fraction of an inch, I nearly passed out from the torture. I was losing blood too quickly for my heart to keep up. My grip weakened and my hand fell back onto the stone floor.

Kerdik took the long route and walked to me from where he'd

been discussing treatment with Remy in Urien's room. "Well, you finally decided to... Rosie!"

The walls of the mansion started to shake with his sudden rage. He ran to me, checking my eyes to see if I was alive and alert enough to answer whatever questions he was shouting in my face.

The knife, I wanted to say. *There's a knife in my thigh. Get it out!*

Kerdik's hand trembled when he finally was able to focus enough to locate the source of the problem. He called for help, afraid, as I was, to remove it and cause even more damage. He kissed my forehead, and I could feel the fear in his tremulous kiss. "I'll get you a healer. I can't... I just used too much magic on Urien!" His words came out in a panicked rush, unaccustomed to his magic failing him. "I'm not sure I could control myself enough to heal you without harming you. Wait here, darling. I'll be back in a blink."

I tried to think clearly enough not to freak out when he ran out of the kitchen, but if Roland came back, I was completely defenseless. I fought with my panic as my eyes started to close, the blood loss too much for my weary heart to keep up with.

I was completely alone when my mind left my body. Though Kerdik and consciousness left me, my panic never did.

* * *

I AWOKE to blinding pain lighting my leg on fire. Kerdik was holding me down while some dude I'd never met slowly removed the dagger from my thigh.

"I know it hurts, Princess. I assure you, this is the way that will cause the least amount of permanent damage." Then he clicked his fingers and motioned to my torso. *"Hold her still already!"*

I tried not to scream, to preserve what was left of my pride, but the bitten-off howl fooled nobody. I didn't exactly have much in the way of dignity, since my dress was hiked up to my waist, exposing my underwear and legs to the total stranger. Someone heavy was on top of my chest, crushing my shoulders to the stone of the kitchen floor.

"I need to knock her out, or all this movement's going to cause more tearing. Princess, can you hear me?"

"Yes! Do whatever you have to do!"

"Amazing! I hoped, but truly, you can hear me?"

"Yes, I can hear you! Knock me out! Bastien? Lane? Kerdik?" I didn't know who was with me, but I prayed it was someone safe.

Roland's voice rang out in my ears. "I'm here, Princess."

"No!" I screamed, thrashing anew. "Kerdik! Help!"

"I'm right here, darling." It was then I realized the heavy body crushing my chest was Kerdik. Roland must be at my feet.

"Don't leave me with Roland! Don't let me pass out if you're not with me!"

Kerdik shifted so I could see his face. His expression was that of a man being moved to greatness for the glory of battle. His eyes burned with intensity, boring into my soul with a permanence I was too deranged to fully appreciate. "Darling, I won't leave your side. On my honor."

"Promise me!"

He managed a small smile. "That's what 'on my honor' means. I promise to stay by your side until you wake. I'm here, Rosie."

Something that smelled like lemon and thyme was waved under my nose, and breath by breath, the pain and the world began to slip away from me. "Don't leave me," I begged over and over, until the darkness took me from Kerdik.

35

TAKING SIDES

I awoke to a groan and something smelly. I sneezed a few times, afraid of everything all at once. "Kerdik?!" I rasped, coughing until I was gingerly sat up, and a cup of water was brought to my lips.

"I'm right here, love." His green hand slipped into mine, and finally my breath found a steady rhythm. "I told you I wouldn't leave you, and I haven't."

The lantern light fell on three other bodies in the room, plus one in the bed next to me. Emotion rose in my throat at the sight of my still immobile father, looking as if he was merely taking a nap. "Is he any better?"

"I have feeling in my limbs, but I can't move them yet. Yet, sweet girl. Yet. Give me time, and I'll be the strong papa who never stopped adoring you."

I fished around for his hand and clung tight to it. "Can you feel that?"

"In my heart and in my hand, yes. Give me time, Rosalie. I'll come back to you."

I didn't want to cry, but being knocked out after so much blood loss tends to make a girl prone to emotional outbursts. I took a steadying breath as Kerdik held my head to rest against his chest. His long fingers combed through my hair to soothe me. I glanced down and realized my bloodied dress had been taken, and I was wearing one of Bastien's long flannel shirts that fit me like a short dress.

Bastien's voice broke through the darkness. "Are you going to tell me what happened?" He didn't sound pissed, but there was a cold calculation to his voice that made me cautious.

I clung to the hem of Kerdik's untucked shirt. He was never untucked, so I began to grasp how upset he'd actually gotten. "I was stabbed. Roland threatened me. Said he'd let his crew have a go at me if I didn't convince my dad to stay in Avalon when Lane and me went back to live in Common. If I didn't, he said he'd keep my dad frozen how he is now."

"I did what now?" Roland's voice sent a chill through me. One of the figures in the chairs leaned forward into the lantern's dim light to reveal his confused expression.

I let out a panicked shriek and clung to Kerdik. "He stabbed me! It was him! Bastien, he's not the friend you think he is."

Bastien stood, turning his head from me to Roland in confusion. "What is she talking about?"

Roland blew out a loud raspberry. "Do you think I know? I was out in the field all day, erecting the boundary fence with everyone else. You saw me out there."

Bastien pinched the bridge of his nose, and then crossed his arms over his chest. "Rosie, I was working with Roland out there. When did this happen?"

"Just before I called Kerdik. It was him, Bastien. Do you really think I'd confuse Roland with someone else?"

Roland scoffed. "This is for what I did when we were traveling from the Forgotten Forest. She's trying to get me hanged for not trusting her!"

I balked at him, horrified that this was the route he was taking. "If I was trying to do that, don't you think I would've spoken up a long time ago? What, do you think I stabbed myself?"

He stood next to Bastien, his arms crossed over his chest to mirror his friend's body language and unite himself with Bastien, as if they were on the same side. "My knife's been missing all day, so yeah, that's exactly what I think."

The healer whose name I still didn't know checked my eyes against the lantern light for pupil dilation. He had black skin darker than Reyn's, and a softness to his gaze that made for a decent perception of good bedside manner. *"There's no way she could've gotten an angle like this on herself. What an idiot. Do you think she could stab herself on the back of her thigh?"*

"Exactly!" I realized they hadn't heard a thing. "Sorry, would you mind writing that down for Bastien?" I met Bastien's pained eyes. "Do you really think I'd lie to you? Roland did this. He threatened me, somehow he's imprisoning my dad, and he stabbed me three times!"

"Do I think you'd lie to me?" Bastien sighed, and I saw how much this very conversation was aging him. I'd wanted to breathe play and life into my boyfriend, but the hard and hurt look on his face told me we were miles from either. "Before the whole reading thing? I wouldn't have thought you capable of lying."

I paled, horrified he was using that against me. "That's private, and it's not the same thing!"

The healer finished scribbling on the pad of paper he kept with him, and thrust it at Bastien. Bastien read it over, and then crumpled it in his palm before bringing his fist to his forehead. His words came out clipped and low. "He has information on how to wake King Urien?"

I nodded mutely, scared that it all might turn on a dime. When I finally spoke, my voice was quiet but firm. "Bastien, whether you believe me or not, I won't be under the same roof as someone who's attacked me this many times. I know he's your friend, and I'm not asking you to choose, but I'm telling you that I'm leaving. I'll take my chances with the doctors over in my world for my dad if you don't believe me. If Roland stays here, I'm out. I'm gone."

Kerdik pulled a handkerchief from his pocket, dabbing at the dots of moisture on my cheeks. "You won't have to do that, darling. Bastien knows what needs to be done."

Bastien closed his eyes. "I know." I jumped when he swore loudly, his fist sinking into Roland's stomach.

"Bastien, she's lying to you!" Roland choked out. "She wants the throne for herself! Can't you see that?"

"Damnit, Roland! Rosie hasn't wanted anything but her family and her life back in Common since she got here. Why'd you have to go there?" He picked up Roland's knife from the nightstand and slammed it into his thigh. Roland's howls echoed through the room, lighting my nerves with fresh fear. "Where were the stab wounds, Rosie? One on the left, two on the right?"

I scrambled to get to him, but I was weak from blood loss. "Bastien, wait! You don't want to do that."

Bastien was in a world unto himself, driven by rage and betrayal. "One on the left and two on the right?"

My healer nodded to Bastien, using his own legs to show exactly where they were. *"Gut the rat. Threatening King Urien and attacking the Avalon Rose? I'll heal him a thousand times just to watch Bastien stab him over and over."*

"Stop! Don't talk like that. Bastien, no! You don't want to be this person. You love Roland. Put him in jail, like the criminal he is, but don't stab him! You wouldn't survive that."

Bastien's rage flung wide, his eyes wild with grief and heartbreak. "No! I love *you*, and he knows that. He attacked you even though he knows I'm yours." He tugged Roland's hair up and stabbed down into his other thigh.

"Bastien, she's lying to you!" Roland collapsed on the floor while my father cried out for Roland's execution.

Kerdik was the only rational one in the room, if you can believe it. "You can't kill Roland, Bastien. If he's keeping Urien in this frozen state, I need to know how. I could get the information out of him, but my temper might not have the self-control it would need to keep him alive long enough."

Bastien was barely sane anymore, but he processed just enough of what Kerdik was saying. Blood dripped from the dagger he clutched, pooling next to where Roland lay howling on the floor. "Mad can do it. He's known for getting information out of prisoners in Éireland. It's what he did for his queen's army before he became Untouchable."

Kerdik clutched me, turning my head away from the sight of my cousin bleeding and cursing through his panic and rage. "Very good. Quick, now. My self-control's not known for lasting long."

36

SOMEONE TO WATCH OVER ME

The healer, whose name I learned was Jean-Luc, had given Roland something that made him pass out. Then Jean-Luc bound his hands behind his back while bandaging up Roland's stab wounds. He reasoned it would keep him alive longer, which would make for better sport when Mad got his hands on Roland.

I was a wreck, not used to torture scenes, and putting the hurt on people to get information. I clung to Kerdik until my fingers were numb and immobile, afraid to be without him while Roland was in the room. Honestly, after being sliced up like Swiss cheese, I was afraid to be alone, period. I was built for the soccer field, not bloodthirsty knife fights.

Link's head poked around the corner, his usual pep muted to match the grave ambiance. "Mad's all set up. Mind if I take out the trash for ye?" He took in my trepidation with actual compassion in his eyes. "Hey, it's alright, wee Rose. Mad's grand at this sort of thing. We'll have your Da dancing a jig with ye in no time."

"I don't like that Mad's torturing people." I croaked out, my fragile nerves palpable. "This isn't the kind of thing that should happen in our province."

Link squinted his eye at me, trying to figure out if I was joking. "How else do ye think we should make him sing for us?" He scratched his head, confused. "Didn't he stab ye over and over? Why are ye putting up a fuss over a little torture? I'd think you'd want front row seats for tha."

"I don't want any of this! I just want to wake up my dad and go home! Lane okayed this? Lane knows what's going on?"

Link nodded. "Of course. We couldn't very well use her dungeon without her knowing." His eyes traveled to my neck, and then he frowned. "I see ye haven't taken our mark yet. This useless lump might not've messed with ye if you'd been marked as Untouchable."

"Roland knows I'm Bastien's girlfriend, and it didn't stop him one bit."

Link met my scared gaze and crossed the room, eyeing Kerdik furtively before chucking my shoulder. "Take the mark, wee Rose. Bastien needs to know you're his. He needs to know you're safe. We all need tha. You're supposed to keep us lads in line." He shoved his hands in his pockets. "We already lost Meara. Don't ye know how rare it is for one of us blokes to settle down? T'wont do to lose ye just because ye aren't marked. Let us protect ye. Untouchables look after our own."

I looked up into Link's green eyes and saw the little lost boy there. I tried to slow my jumping heartrate and see his offer for what it was – need. "You're a convincing little leprechaun." I nodded. "I might just take you guys up on the offer. Thanks, Link."

Link bobbed his head in my direction, his eyes twinkling that he'd done a solid for Bastien by convincing me to be more permanently his. "Aye. Now, let's see what I can do about getting this lump downstairs. Get ready to watch me be amazing." Link slapped his hands together like a football coach, leaned down and hefted Roland up over his shoulders. "How much do ye want to bet that I can dance a jig with him like this on me?"

"I bet zero dollars. You're going to hurt yourself! Put him down."

"You're adorable when ye boss me around. Tell me to clean up my socks."

"I don't want Mad torturing anybody."

"Aw. Tha's sweet." Link started humming to himself, turned and made his way down the hallway with Roland slung around his shoulders.

I huffed. "Why doesn't anyone listen to me? This isn't the way to handle this." I relinquished my tight grip on Kerdik and swung my legs off the mattress, alighting them on the floor.

"What are you doing?" Kerdik asked me warily. "I wouldn't get up if I were you."

"This isn't right. No one's getting tortured under my roof. This is my house, too, and I say no." I hefted my body up, and immediately regretted it. My legs were nowhere near sturdy enough to hold me up. My body plummeted to the ground, my knees smashing into the wood and sending ripples of agony echoing up my bare legs. "Oh! Ow!" I swore and pounded my fist to the floor as my wounds reminded me just how fresh they were.

Kerdik huffed. "Well, I told you not to get up."

"Ow! Oh, yeah. That was a bad move. This is the last time I get stabbed. Man, that hurts. Did that healer guy give me something to numb my legs? They feel totally useless."

"Jean-Luc did, and yes, they are." Kerdik slid his arm behind my back, and his other under my knees, sweeping me up off the floor as if I was a child. "To bed with you. I want to take you upstairs, but I can't very well leave you unattended, and I need to monitor Urien. When Bastien comes up, he can take you to your room." Kerdik slid me back onto the mattress, giving my toe a playful tug before he covered up my legs with the comforter. "That's better. Let the Untouchables handle things the way they do. They have better self-control than I."

"Somehow I think there's a better use for self-control than this."

Kerdik moved his chair closer to the bedside and sat down in it, leaning forward to examine my fingers. He twisted my ring around and warmed my hand with his. "Whether you're marked or not, you're engaged to be married to one of them, and you're dating another of them. You belong to the Untouchables, and they don't take assaults on their own lightly."

An ominous chill ran up my spine. "I'm not sure how I feel about that. I don't even know all of them. I only know Bastien, Mad and Link."

Kerdik shrugged. "It's how they work. Luckily, it plays in our favor this time around. If Roland's really found a way to best me, I need to know what it is, so I can help Urien."

"You're a true friend."

"My dad appreciates the lengths you're going to for him."

Kerdik reached out and squeezed my dad's hand. "It's nothing either of you wouldn't do for me." He took in my tight smile and frowned. "You're in pain still. Shall I fetch you another healer? Jean-Luc is helping Madigan in the dungeon."

"Why would a healer be needed for torture?"

"To keep Roland barely alive while Madigan works."

I balked at Kerdik. "Don't say it like that! Like it's all so matter-of-fact and fine. This is wrong! Make them stop, Kerdik."

"You're getting cranky. I'll get you a healer so you're not uncomfortable. Remy's been out with the others building the wall. I'll have one of the servants fetch him for you."

At the thought of Kerdik leaving, panic drove me to reach out and clutch his shirt. "No! You can't leave us. I can't walk, and my dad's still frozen. On a normal day, I could probably defend him, but not if I can't even use my legs! You can't leave my dad unprotected. Please don't leave us."

Kerdik smiled at me, inching closer. His green face nearly glowed in the soft lamplight. He looked ethereal, like a mythical creature who'd been enchanted by the Queen Elf or something. "How I love when you beg me to stay near you. You'd rather be in pain than be without me for a few short minutes?"

I bit down on my lower lip as I nodded, not sure if I should be ashamed of that fact, or still more earnest so he didn't leave. "I don't care if I sound pathetic. I've been stabbed three times. I think that gives me the right to a little whining. Please don't go."

Kerdik stood, and for a second I thought my pathetic debasement would be for nothing. Relief flooded me when he scooped me up off the bed like a fairytale princess and sat back down in his chair, with me cradled on his lap.

Hamish scampered in, not wasting a moment before he crossed the room. He ran up Kerdik's leg and threw himself onto my stomach. His arms and legs were spread out like a starfish that clung to my torso. *"Don't make me go down there. I don't like the howling. Don't tell Abraham Lincoln I couldn't take it. Tell him you needed extra protection."*

"Aw, of course, baby. You can stay with us." I cuddled Hamish to me, letting him snuggle up and make himself at home. I yawned, turning my head and not bothering to cover my mouth as I lay back in Kerdik's arms. Though the bed was more comfortable, there was a certain kind of respite that could only be given by the strong arms that held me tight. Kerdik was terrifying, and that night, I knew there was nowhere safer than being curled up in his embrace. I didn't want to admit to him that I was scared for my own life, that part of me was asking him to stay not just to watch over my father, but also to guard me when I was down for the count.

Kerdik seemed to understand. Monster that everyone assumed him to be, part of him was capable of compassion and sweetness. Part of him was human, despite his inherent inhumanity. "Get some sleep, darling. I'll stay right here with you. You're in need of far more rest if your magic is going to help you heal in a timely fashion." He sifted through my messy curls with his long fingers, and tugged my head to his face, pressing a kiss to my temple that warmed me down to my toes.

"Rosalie, did Kerdik just... I heard a noise that sounded like a kiss." My dad's voice came to me confused, with a hint of sharpness to it.

"Kerdik's my friend," I answered, trying not to feel weird. It was hard to remember that my dad had front row tickets to our conversations. He was so still; it was easy to forget he was there.

"Indeed, I am." Kerdik lifted my tangles and draped them over his shoulder, burying his nose in the tresses. His deep inhale made me cuddle closer to him while I pet Hamish with clumsy fingers. "You smell a little like him."

"Him?"

"Bastien. You're wearing his shirt, so you smell a little like him. Except your hair. That's still purely you."

My eyelids felt weighted, and I knew Hamish's presence tipped the sleepiness I still felt from so much blood loss. "I like the way Bastien smells. Like cinnamon and Christmas."

Kerdik chuckled, and the deep sound vibrated his chest I was resting against. He played idly with my fingers, examining how the ring he'd given me sparkled in the lamplight. It needed precious little light to dance for my amusement. The stones were so clear and brilliant; it was hard to look away. "Do you like your ring?"

I nodded, transfixed by the light prisms trapped in the stones. "Not like. Love. It's the most beautiful thing that was ever mine."

I could feel Kerdik's gaze shift from the ring to my face, studying me while I enjoyed the sight of my gift that never stopped sparkling. He leaned in, his whisper tickling the shell of my ear to ramp up the intimacy that came natural to us. "Funny. I was just going to say the same thing about you."

I gave him a little smirk as if to say, "Oh, you."

He settled more comfortably in the chair, gearing up to hold me for however long I needed it – the mark of a good friend.

227

"Get some sleep, darling. Your body's burning through a lot of magic to heal you."

I yawned again, my forehead resting in the crook of his neck. "Alright, Kerdik. Love you."

"Rosalie," my dad said in warning, but I was too tired to address it.

I closed my heavy eyelids, my heart warming at Kerdik's tender whisper of, "I love you, too."

SWEPT OFF MY FEET

I was woken by Link, who had the look of being up all
night. Though I knew he didn't need sleep, it was clear
the torture Mad was up to had taken longer than expected. "Time
to wake, wee Rose. Mad needs ye downstairs."

I rubbed my eyes and tried to swing my legs from Kerdik's
grip, but he held me tighter. "Your healer would have your hide if
you tried to walk now. You're supposed to be in bed. Link, take
her just like this. See she doesn't try to walk at all." Kerdik handed
me over to Link's overly muscled and tattooed arms as if I was a
sleeping child – careful and steady. Link was thoughtful enough
to sweep Bastien's flannel down across the backs of my knees, so
my butt didn't hang out for all to see. Kerdik inspected the
bottoms of my feet. "Her feet shouldn't touch the floor. I'll know
if they have."

Though I had no reason not to trust Link, I didn't feel right
being parted from Kerdik. Mid-nap as I was, I voiced my bleat of
concern without a filter. "You're staying up here?" Hamish barely
roused, still sleeping on my stomach, holding his bushy tail while
he used my boobs like a squishy pillow.

Kerdik lifted my hand and pressed it to his cheek to savor the tenderness that was growing precious between us. I realized that I needed his strength and protection as much as he needed someone to be soft and kind to him. After infinite lifetimes of people recoiling, shrieking and running from him, it was the kindness he craved most of all. "You'll be safe with Link. I've no doubt Madigan's got Roland on his last breath. I need to try a few more rounds of waking your father, and I think he'd rather you not be here for it."

"Huh?" I was suddenly more alert.

"Go on, Rosalie. I'll try anything at this point. I don't care about the pain, if it gets me closer to being able to live again. You should go with your friend. I don't want you to hear me cry out."

"Stop this! I don't like you in pain!" My voice turned bossy as my spine stiffened. "Kerdik, don't you dare hurt my father. He can't tell you when it's too much if I'm not here. I'm serious. We can find a way without hurting him, I'm sure of it."

"Oh, sweet girl, it's alright. What a tender heart you still have. When I'm restored to myself, I'll need to thank Lane for seeing that your soul was spared the darkness that usually corrodes a person by your age. She did well, preserving the goodness in you."

I rolled my eyes and mimed talking with my hand. "Blah, blah, blah. Unless you're going to tell me you've come to your senses and won't let Kerdik hurt you, I don't want to hear it."

I huffed at my father's chortle, like he thought I was five and I told him monsters might get him if he checked under the bed. I knew now more than ever that monsters were real. I'd just been curled up in the most formidable one's lap.

Kerdik waved off Link, who, despite the bravado he wore around his neck like a Hawaiian lei, was wary to be around Kerdik for this long. "If this door is locked when you bring her back, then take her to Bastien, but see that her feet don't touch the floor."

"Aye. But Bastien's not here, Master Kerdik."

"Where is he?" Kerdik and I asked in unison.

Link looked uncomfortable ratting out his bro, causing an ominous warning to churn in my gut. "After Mad got Roland's confession tha Rosie was telling the truth, he took off for the local pub. Mad's still trying to work the remedy for King Urien out of the sodden lad. Bastien didn't need to be there for tha."

Kerdik's temper was hard to predict, but it waned in a sad understanding that felt something like progress between my BFF and my boyfriend. "Yes, well, I guess he's earned a night of drowning his sorrows. Take her to her brother's room, then, if this door's locked when you bring her back up. Then come straight to me with anything you work out of Roland that could cure Urien."

"Aye, sire." Link hiked me up in his arms, ready to get away from Kerdik. "Let's go, lass. Your strapping fiancé's got a gift for ye."

I swallowed my dread as I tried to psych myself up for whatever awaited me in the dungeon.

ROLAND'S FINGERS, AND KERDIK'S SECRET

or all his brash and bold behaviors, Link was careful with me as he walked down the stone steps I'd swept with Reyn. We'd worked on cleaning the basement so many days ago, that they piled into weeks. We'd painted the concrete dungeon walls a bright white to liven up the place for the children, since Lane didn't think she'd have much use for her dungeon in the traditional sense. Coming down into the long room that housed a row of cells on both walls running the length of it, my heart started to race when I heard moans of anguish.

This was supposed to be my playground.

Though I didn't really know Link enough to lean on him, my arms wrapped around his neck all the same. Link leaned his cheek to my forehead. "Aw, you're just a wee kitten. Best get this over quick, then."

I saw the pool of blood before I saw the cowering, naked man. Madigan was leaning against the bars inside a cell near the back, his arms crossed over his chest like he was standing outside a liquor store, trying to bum a smoke. He was taller than any man I'd ever seen in real life, but in the dungeon, he looked impossibly larger, startling me anew with his sheer girth. He idly twirled a knife in his hand as if it was a lighter, or something to play with to pass the time. Roland was at his feet with his back to me, writhing in a puddle of his own blood.

Jean-Luc had his doctor bag opened, and was fishing through it for a sharper razor. I could pick the thoughts out of his head easy enough. *"Something with a finer edge to make the cuts small but painful."*

I was frozen in Link's arms, ice traveling through my veins with lightning speed and deafening precision.

This is my home. This is my life now.

Link kicked his foot to the bars as we neared, drawing Mad's eyes so he knew we were there. "Oh, grand. I was worried his light would go out before she got here." Mad leaned down and grabbed a chunk of Roland's brown hair, forcing a low groan from the man who'd dominated me not too long ago. Mad's voice turned gravelly and harsh. "Your witch is here. Look at her, all terrifying and menacing. Look at all you threw away over this wee little kitten."

Link let out a laugh that felt totally inappropriate. "Ha! That's what I just called her."

Roland's back was still to me, so Mad dragged him around so I could see his face. Correction – what was left of his face. I shrieked in horror at the things that were missing. His left eye was the most terrifying, drawing my gaze like a magnet to the cavity that had blood spilling out of it in streaks like red tears. I clung to Link, afraid to get nearer. This wasn't the *Princess Bride*; this was a full-on snuff film I'd landed myself smack in the middle of. "Did you do this, Madigan? Did you... Did you cut off his ear?!" It seemed unendingly cruel for a man who had no hearing in his left ear to saw off the same appendage on a man.

Madigan looked down to confirm his conquest. "Aye. Of course. What, did ye want the right one?"

I gaped at Madigan, flabbergasted as the horror washed over

me in waves of terror. "Did I want the right one? What is the matter with you? You... and he... How could you do that?!"

Mad picked up the actual ear from the cell floor and thumbed it. "It's my signature. When I served in my queen's army, I got to keep one token from each lad I questioned. What I wouldn't give to have my jar of ears back again." He sighed at the missed opportunity.

I shook like a leaf in Link's arms. Link was a simple kind of dude, who I'm guessing didn't have much experience comforting women he wasn't trying to sleep with. "There, there," he offered awkwardly. "What did ye think we meant by 'torture'?"

"I never asked for this! I wanted Roland to get a fair trial and go to prison so he could change from being a total jackwagon! I didn't ask you to permanently mutilate him!"

"It's no trouble," Madigan offered, as if this was some great favor he was doing me. "What I need ye to do is see if ye can hear his mind. We've been keeping him lucid enough to speak and reason, but he's not telling us what we need to know."

"I'm not a mind-reader, Mad. I can't hear people's thoughts at random. I can hear the healers and the animals and my dad because their entire language is hidden. I shouldn't be here!" My fearful gaze fixed on my fake fiancé. "And neither should you."

"This is the only way, Princess. Even now, Duke Roland is stubborn. Even now, he would rather see your father be buried with him than restore King Urien to you."

Against my wishes, Link brought me closer. We were right next to the cell bars now. My body recoiled, but it had nowhere to go. I felt like a scared cat trying to climb up a tree to get away from a dog with the most vicious bite.

Link's voice chimed in where I chickened out. "Do ye see what's happened, Roland? Rosie's going to heal just fine. She's going to sit on Avalon's throne, if tha's what she wishes. We'll find a way to bring King Urien back, with or without ye. It's just a matter of how long ye want to suffer, or if you've finally had enough tha ye want Mad to put ye out of your misery."

Roland spat out a mixture of insult and blood on the floor. His voice was raspy, but still held the defiance and pride I'd come to expect. "I'd rather die than see that brat on Avalon's throne. I'll spare Uncle Urien the sight of his daughter causing the fall of the kingdom he loved."

My indignation brought me out of my fear a miniscule amount. "Dude, you are such a jag! Why would I sit on the throne, first off, and secondly, why would I be the fall of the kingdom? How dangerous could I possibly be that you're this afraid of me? I haven't done a single thing to hurt Avalon. I haven't challenged any policies or started any riots. I'm just a babysitter at this point!"

Roland had drool mingled with blood dripping from his chin. "You brought Province 9 home again. I didn't think that was possible."

"And you're punishing me for it? That was all Lane, anyway. All I did was not die in the well."

Roland sneered up at me from his place on his knees with a shaky upper lip. "Pity."

I gaped at him. "How are you this bullheaded?"

Mad motioned to Jean-Luc, who handed him a pair of heavy duty snippers. Though Mad wasn't given to smiling, the expression on his face was akin to peace. There was a calm that flitted over him like a thousand precious fairies when he was on the job he'd been trained to do. His fluid, unquestioning movements were well-rehearsed and done with confidence. I hated to think that this was Mad in his element, but as he picked up Roland's hand, I saw the sigh of relief that came from doing a task you enjoyed. For some it was playing the piano or learning a subject they excelled in at school. For Mad, it was torture. Pure, unfettered torture.

I scarcely understood what was going on when Madigan

brought the bloody fist up to the light. I whimpered when I noticed there were already three fingers missing from Roland's hand, and Mad was about to take the fourth.

"No! No! Don't do it!" I shouted, but no one listened to me. My howls matched Roland's when I heard the telltale snip that meant Roland was left with only his thumb. I whipped my head away from the macabre sight, burying my face in Link's neck so I could wail into the flesh. Of all the things I could have begged for in that moment, I needed my bestie there with me. Or more ideally, I needed to be out of this dungeon and in our apartment with him. "Judah!" I sobbed, knowing he would never make me watch something so terrible in real life. "Where are you, Judah?"

Link had no idea what to do with a crying woman, so he shifted uncomfortably a few times before swaying me back and forth like an oscillating fan. I felt cold inside, surrounded by monsters who enjoyed this sort of thing. "Mad, I don't think this was such a grand idea. Jays, I wasn't expecting tha. Wee kitten can't even look at Roland, and I don't think she can hear him."

Madigan sighed. "Give it a go, Rosie. Try and hear anything he's saying. Can ye pick out a word or two?"

"Roland? I'm so sorry this is happening! I just wanted my dad back, not to have you slowly killed like this. I'm sorry!" I scrambled around for any sort of reason I could give him to excuse my part in all of it. "I don't like violence like this. I'm a vegetarian! I just want to be able to pal around with my dad. Please don't keep him from his kingdom just to spite me. You hate me, sure, but you can't possibly hate him this much."

Roland was practically deranged from the pain, so I'm not sure how much he was hearing me. "Urien will sleep as long as I say!"

I swallowed, trying to find my bearings so we could get this over with as soon as possible. Despite all he'd done to me, I wanted the suffering to be over for Roland, so I tried to get the truth out of him as quick as I could. "Look, no matter what, my dad's coming back. Kerdik's working on him now. It's just a matter of time before he cracks whatever spell you've got on him."

"He's welcome to try for all of eternity!" Then Roland howled as a fresh dose of agony swept through him. I could tell his body was still in shock as it processed the pain in waves.

"Do you think Kerdik is a patient guy? Do you think he's a forgiving guy? He'll punish you for this way worse than Mad ever could."

Madigan seemed to take offense at this. "Hey, now. I'm doing a grand job here."

"I'll be dead soon anyways. What does Kerdik's wrath matter to me?"

Mad gave his naked thigh a kick. "Nah. Ye only think you're on the brink of death. You've got miles to go before tha. Not to fret. I won't let ye die before we've gotten every last bit of truth from your lying lips. If that takes months, I don't mind. I've got nothing but time. Time to let your good eye watch while Lane and Rosie clean up Province 9. Time to let ye see your throne taken over by a couple of women who do the job far better than ye ever did. Time to watch your best friend marry the lass ye hate. Oh, I wouldn't let ye miss tha. Why do ye think I left ye with one good eye?"

"How could you do this to Bastien?" I roared at Roland, my rage poking through the clouds of my fear. "He loved you, and you broke his heart with this."

It was hard to tell, but Roland actually appeared contrite at my scolding. "Bastien's head is twisted in your direction. He doesn't have to think about what's best for Avalon. He's not a duke. He's a fool in love. I can't fault him for that, but I also can't let him walk headfirst into a witch's arms."

"I'm not a witch, you tool! Don't you think that if I had super-powers, I'd use them to, I don't know, heal myself?"

Roland was beyond seeing reason. "I had to protect Bastien

from you! I'm the Duke of Province 4! I'm doing what I have to do to protect my people. You're a danger to them, no matter how many powerful men you take into your bed. Bewitching them with what magic lies between your thighs, no doubt."

I gasped, scandalized that he'd go there. Though really, nothing was off-limits at this point.

Link growled and moved over to Jean-Luc. "Hold onto her a minute. Let me have a go at him, Mad. No one talks about an Untouchable's lady like tha."

Madigan shook his head. "No. You'll lose your temper, just like ye did with the last one in Éireland. We need this lad alive so we can get Urien back."

Roland seethed at me. "I'll hold out long enough to watch Master Kerdik turn fool for you more than he already has. It'll be my pleasure to watch him mutate you into a monster, just like he did with Tara."

My nose crinkled. "I don't know what you're talking about."

"I keep waiting for Master Kerdik to kiss you. It's only a matter of time. I see the way that monster looks at you. I only hope I live long enough to watch him turn you into a dragon."

Link reared back in confusion. "What are ye talking about?"

Roland laughed like the madman the pain had pushed him to being. "Such a well-kept secret. Dear Aunt Avril isn't so tight-lipped. She told me what came of the last woman Master Kerdik fell for. Why do you think he stays away for so long?"

Link frowned. "Mad, he's not making any sense. Cut off his thumb and see if tha clears his head."

Roland clutched his bloody stump to his chest while he cackled, blood spilling out from his teeth. "You really don't know. Maybe Lane doesn't know, either. Ask your precious father about Tarasque."

Jean-Luc chimed in with, *"The reclusive dragon who lived in the ocean? What of her? She's long dead."*

"There's a reason Master Kerdik's alone. It's not by choice; it's by destiny. He loves you; we've all seen it. It's only a matter of time before he tries to steal you away from Bastien. When he does, we'll all see the evil in you." A cloud passed over his face. "I only hope you don't destroy Avalon when his kiss transforms you."

"Destroy Avalon? What are you talking about? Kerdik's kiss won't transform me into a… whatever you're thinking is going to happen." *Because we've already kissed, and aside from burping fire, I'm still me.*

Puzzle pieces slowly started to reveal themselves.

The reason Kerdik lived away from everyone.

The flames that erupted from me seconds after our misplaced kiss.

A female dragon who'd needed slaying.

39

MAD'S MADNESS, AND MEARA'S MAGIC

*R*oland cackled as he watched realization dawn on me. I shook my head with a stubborn frown. "You're lying. You're just trying to screw with my head."

"Why bother making up a lie, when the truth is so much more compelling? Ask your dear lover about Tarasque. A monster, half dragon and half sea monster who appeared out of nowhere. Tame as a person, but mutated beyond recognition." His smile turned evil. "Your father knew her when she was a handmaiden in his castle. Urien's legendary friendship with the daunting Master Kerdik brought the two together. It wasn't long, probably no more than a few nights of passion before Tara was mutated into a foe no one could defeat." Roland caught himself. "Oh, Master Kerdik could, of course, but he loved Tara too much, so she rested by herself in the ocean, mourning the life she had before Kerdik fell in love with her."

I cried out with heartbreak and revulsion. "How could you make up such a terrible lie about Kerdik? He's got goodness in him, and you're just trying to tear him down because he's my friend. You're so petty, it's disgusting!"

Roland laughed again, the cocky bastard. "I see it won't be

long before you fall for him. In one man's arms now, engaged to my tormenter, in Bastien's bed tonight, with Kerdik in your heart. My, one doesn't even need witch abilities to ruin lives the way you will."

I struggled against Link to get down, but Link took Kerdik's command not to let my feet touch the ground quite literally. "Don't let him get to ye, kitten. He's just trying to rile ye up. He's trying to provoke Mad so he'll end it quick. It's desperation, not truth. End of the rope talk, for sure."

I didn't care what the motivation was; it was cruel. "How could you hate Bastien this much? I'm only in Avalon because of you, you know. He and Reyn scoured earth to find me so I could bring you back to Avalon. I wouldn't even be here if you hadn't given up on your province!" Okay, maybe that wasn't fair, but if he was going to play dirty, I could sling a little mud, too. "Give me back my father, and I'll leave Avalon. If you don't help me, then I'll stay here forever. I'll sit on *your* throne and rule *your* people. I'll dismantle the army and make them plant pink flowers and play with puppies all the livelong day! I'll destroy everything you've dreamt of for Province 4 and Province 9. Lane and I will turn this into a town of rainbows and unicorns and just hope Morgan doesn't try and take our land again." I watched his cocky smile twist into a grimace. "If you don't give me back my father, you'll be abandoning Province 4 again. Typical spoiled prince. Things don't go his way, so he skips off into the Forgotten Forest, leaving everyone else to do the dirty work. Now you'll abandon your people, knowing I don't know how to rule. Knowing I'll be a terrible fit for your people. But still you only care about revenge. Still you only care about your pride. Still you care not even a little bit about your people."

His voice was furious and loud, despite his blood loss and torment. "Don't tell me what I care about! I gave up everything for Avalon! It was taken from me, and there was no way to get it back."

"So you left them," I said, disgusted. It was hard to be domineering in Link's arms, but I managed. "You left your people to flock to Morgan."

"She made me! I gave myself up so that my people could at least have food on their tables. You know one of the conditions of her sparing the lives of Province 4 was that the ruler had to go to the Forgotten Forest. Aunt Avril went through the same punishment!"

"You gave up!" I raged. "You gave up on a great province. I'm not like you, Roland. I won't give up on my father, even if it means I live in Avalon forever! Suck on that while you wait out the darkness down here. Think about me with my scarred thighs sitting on your throne for years, making calls that would make your skin crawl. For once in your life, think about what's best for your province! If I get my father back, Lane, Draper and I will go to Common with him, if that's what he wants. That leaves Damond in line next to rule once Lane adopts him, if he decides to stay behind in Avalon. Wouldn't you rather have Damond than me? I don't want to sit on that throne any more than you want me to. Play the right game, you tool!"

Roland stared up at me with his one eye, sifting through my words to test their veracity and poke holes where he could. "You'll really leave the throne to Damond?"

My breath caught in my throat that we were actually making progress. "Absolutely. I won't be here any longer than I have to."

He seemed hopeful, but then his expression fell into a snarl. "Morgan won't let you rest in Common."

"She won't let me rest in Avalon, either. At least I have the advantage in my home turf. She can't use magic there. Plus, I hid myself well enough for twenty-one years. Best of luck to Mom of the Year."

"You'd really go back to the concealment charm Lane put on you to alter your appearance? I'm told you were quite off-putting."

I kept my chin steady as I debated keeping the face and body I had now, or being able to return to my regular life, even if it meant I was the ugly girl again. "In a heartbeat, I'd trade it all if it meant the people I loved were safe." In that moment, I knew who I was. I was Rosie Avalon, no matter what my face looked like.

"You'll really leave Avalon if I give you Urien?"

"In a heartbeat. It's only what I've been telling you this whole time. I help Avalon get back on her feet, then I'm out."

"But you'll take Uncle Urien with you."

"My dad can decide for himself where he wants to be. You should want him to have a choice in how he lives his life, after he's spent so much time with all of his choices taken away. To control him like you're doing? It's what Morgan would do." I met his eye with disappointment. "It's what she did."

Roland paused for so long, it felt like the world stood still. I waited for his lips to part, to give me the life back that I'd been missing. Finally, the truth tumbled out of him. "Fool's Parsley. I prolonged the paralysis with Fool's Parsley. It's beneath Kerdik. He's looking for loftier, more complicated magic, so I knew he'd overlook something so simple."

Link gasped and kicked at the bars with his boot. "Fool's Parsley can do serious damage! If King Urien doesn't come out of this in one piece, I'll see ye live a long and miserable life in the public eye, a slave to whatever whim Mad has for ye. Jays, Roland!"

Roland scoffed. "I'm already at rock bottom. Do what you like."

Mad chuckled, and the deep sound dragged a chill up my spine. "Oh, no. Ye've got miles to go before ye hit the bottom. Ye made me wait, little pig. Ye made me wait for the information. I don't like to wait." He threw an "aw shucks" look at Link. "Think we can get Antonio in here?"

Link blew out a low whistle. "I don't know. He usually likes his sex slaves in one piece, and you've already made pieces of this one."

I gripped the back of Link's neck hard, digging my fingernails into the skin and hoping I drew blood. "Until I leave, this kingdom belongs to Lane, Draper, Urien and me. You won't do any such thing on our soil. If I see this Antonio guy, he's getting sent straight home with a note from the principal."

Mad made a show of taking off his belt, and Roland whimpered, cowering away from the leather and rolling himself into a ball to protect what was left of his body. "Alright, let's see if there's more truth to beat out of ye."

"No, Mad! Please! Don't hurt him!" I struggled to get to Madigan, but Link was just plain stronger.

I screamed louder than Roland when the crack of the belt whipped down on his back. "He's got to learn, Rosie. Ye don't lay a hand on an Untouchable's lady. Ye belong with us now, and we don't tolerate tha."

"Stop it! This doesn't help anything! You don't want to be this person!"

Madigan stopped and glared at me. "This is who I am, Rosie! This is who they trained me to be. I was the only one with the stomach to carry out what needed doing for the queen. It's not my fault they couldn't hold me in Éireland's army. They unleashed me on Faîte, so they'll take the monster they made!" Fury built up in Madigan, transforming him from the calm dungeon master to a rage-filled man on a tear. Over and over, he belted Roland, each lash cracking louder than the last.

Jean-Luc's mind was a stream of nervous cussing and *please don't let him turn on me* pleading. I screamed for Mad to stop, to come back from the life he'd gone to in his mind. That life held no compassion, no humanity and no way out.

Link practically shoved me into Jean-Luc's surprised arms and bolted for Madigan, taking a belt to the chest before Mad slowed Roland's punishment. He wrapped his arms around

Madigan and shoved him into the bars so hard, the metal protested the assault from the two large men. Link squeezed tight, fighting Madigan's desire to go at Roland with all the rage in his sordid past. I was terrified, but Link's voice was gentle. "Easy, brother. Easy now. Ye don't want to kill him yet. If he's lying, you'll need to take your time. Ye can't lose your temper. What would Meara say to tha? She believed ye were more than what they made ye to be."

Madigan's short breaths and dilated pupils began to level off. It was as if he had gone somewhere else in his mind, and Link's voice had been the thing that brought him back. "Meara," he murmured.

"Aye, Meara. She would've wanted better for ye than this. She knew ye could be more than the killer they warped ye to be. I knew it, too. Tha's why we're brothers. Do what ye need to with this one, but don't lose yourself in it."

Mad was silent, opening his mouth and closing it a few times before the fight in him finally settled. "Aye. I'm okay now." He glanced over at my tearstained face when Link finally loosened his grip and stepped back to take me from Jean-Luc. Madigan cleared his throat and rolled his shoulders back. "Don't worry, Rosie. Avalon will be safe for ye by the time I'm done with him. Untouchables protect what's theirs."

Jean-Luc motioned for Link to go. *"Get her out of here. She's delicate, and she's already seen more than she needs to."*

Link shifted me in his arms. "Alright, wee kitten. Let's see if Roland's telling us a lie. There'll be no holding Mad back if this doesn't work."

I clung to Link because I had no other choice. There was no beacon of kindness or goodness to hold onto, so I let him carry me up the stairs into the light. But after all I'd seen, the light didn't feel much better than the darkness.

40

THE PSYCHOPATH AND THE PRINCESS

*L*ink laid me in my bed, grateful for the excuse to distance himself from the sobbing mess that I was. I wasn't a huge torture movie fan, so I hadn't been exposed to much of that. I liked the *Princess Bride*, and had gladly skipped out on the *Saw* series. My sweet Wesley would never have resorted to such violence. Though he'd threatened such things, he would never really do it. Wesley was a lover.

Mad was a psychopath. A psychopath I was engaged to.

Link ran his hands through his honey-colored hair several times before speaking, messing the tresses more than their usual chaos. "Yeah, so I'm going to go down and tell Kerdik what we found. Do ye want me to try and find Bastien?"

I shook my head. "Bastien knew what Mad was doing down there, and he just let him! How could he let Mad do that?"

Link's eyes looked anywhere but at me, the typical guy who was allergic to female emotion. Or you know, a man who couldn't handle the normal human response to unthinkable torture. "Bastien let Mad do what he does because he loves ye. He gave up his mate so ye would be safe, and ye could have your Da back." He crossed his arms over his broad chest. "This is what it means to be one of ours. You're an Untouchable's lady. We don't tolerate our women being stalked and stabbed. So while you're crying over the state of the world, remember tha Bastien and Mad are just protecting ye. Remember tha ye wouldn't have been safe if they'd let Roland get off with a slap. Now his followers know that you're Untouchable, too. It's a necessary message, especially after ye said he was going to let his lads have a go at ye. Jays, Rosie. How can ye not see tha this is the best way?"

"Stop it! Don't tell me that Roland's violence is a good excuse for more violence. Don't try and convince me this is a way to win a war."

"Ye need to get our mark today." Link tugged on his shirt collar with his tattooed wrist to display the permanent blight that declared his royalty-adjacent status to the world. "An engagement can be broken, but ink is forever. I'll send for the artist, and tha will add another layer of protection for ye."

I chewed on my lower lip, making the decision I still wasn't sure about on the fly, and under duress. "Fine."

"Good." Link blew out a loud breath. "I don't feel right leaving ye up here without protection. I'll send your brother up."

"Draper would never let you do this. He'll freak out when I tell him what you've done."

Of all things, Link patted me on the head. "There, there. I'll go see about waking your Da." He backed toward the door when more of my tears came rolling down my cheeks. "I don't know what to do when ye cry like tha, so knock it off."

I guffawed at him. "You are such a jerk! Here's a page from Being a Nice Guy 101: When someone's traumatized, let them feel sad about it. A hug is different than patting someone on the head – which, incidentally, is going to get you punched the next time you do that to me."

Link sniggered. "Alright. Tha's a good tip. Anything else I should know, since you're our lady?"

I groaned. "The possessiveness of your language is gross." I thought through his question, knowing I wouldn't get a better invitation than that one for some good old course-correction. "Stop acting like I'm the house pet."

"Ah, but ye do belong to us. Just as we belong to ye. Tha's how the Brotherhood works. Did ye see how I calmed Mad down when he lost it?"

I shivered. "Yeah. That was intense."

Link nodded with the air of a professor. "Mad belongs to ye too, now, so if tha happens again, do what I did. Ye need to know how to handle us, just like we need to know how to handle ye. We only have each other."

"I don't know what to say to that. How do you need to be 'handled'?"

"Do ye want the real answer, or a joke about how Link Jr. likes to be handled?" He looked down pointedly at his crotch.

I harrumphed. "What do you think?"

He leaned on the doorjamb, his face pensive. "You'll have to ask Bastien tha. Off the top of my head, I'd say don't split on me in the middle of the night. I lost Mad tha way when he disappeared into the Forgotten Forest. Damn near drove me over the edge. So when ye go back to Common, give me plenty of fair warning. Don't just run out on me."

I mulled over his words, surprised something so thoughtful came from the goofball. "I can do that. You really care if I'm here or not?"

"Aye. You're the closest thing I'll ever have to a wife." Before I could rein in my reaction, his face broke out in a grin. "See tha? I didn't even make a joke about ye handling my beefy cock, which is what I would've done if ye weren't ours. Because I'm learning how to handle ye. Ye like sweetness, my smile, and daisies."

I balked at him. "I don't need to be handled!"

He caught my eye as he fisted the door's handle. His look suddenly seemed of a person far older and wiser than me. "Aye.

We all do. And gently, at tha. Stay in bed, now. Let us take care of the rest."

I narrowed my eyes at him. "You don't get to be wiser than me. It throws off our balance."

Link tossed me a charming grin, blowing me a kiss before he left.

I was alone with my confusion and my fear, reliving the horror of Roland's disfigurement for a solid five minutes before there was a polite knock on my door. "C-Come in."

Draper let himself inside, his business face melting when he took in my expression. I was in the throes of an ugly cry, but Draper didn't look away from my pain. He crossed the room, letting Abraham Lincoln in behind me. My bear shut the door with his round rump and moseyed on over, climbing onto the bed after Draper, so I was surrounded by strength and kindness on both sides. Draper wrapped his arms around me and pulled out a handkerchief from his back pocket, dabbing at my eyes. "Link tells me you discovered the real use for the dungeon."

I nodded. "How... How... How could Madigan d-do that? Clipped off Roland's fingers, Drape! Tore out his eye!"

Draper was unperturbed by the violence. His only concern seemed to be my upset over it all. "He shouldn't have let you see that. It's alright."

"It's not alright! I'm living in the s-same house as that! This is our kingdom, right? We shouldn't allow crap like that to go on. Is this the kind of ruler you want to be?"

Draper shifted against the pillows and brought my head to his chest, so I had a safe place to rest while I sobbed. "You forget that I don't want to rule at all. I'm here because you and Lane are in Province 9. When we go, I'll leave all of it behind."

"We're leaving this world broken if stuff like this is going on. We're supposed to be the good guys. Where is Lane, anyway? Shouldn't she be here?"

"She, Reyn, Remy and Damond left for Province 5 to see if

Lot's people wanted to align themselves with us. Keep their land and independence and whatnot, but come when we need reinforcements, and the other way around. We need all the allies we can get if Morgan attacks again. And frankly, we have more resources than they do, since we have more jewels. We can offer them aid."

"Lane would flip out if she knew what Mad was up to. Can't you order him to stop or something?"

"I could try, but I won't. Roland stabbed my sister three times. Do you really think I'll spare his life or his comfort after that?" He scoffed. "I'm just sorry I don't have the stomach for it. I'd heard of Madigan's methods, but man. Seeing him at work is a whole other story." He kissed my forehead while Abraham Lincoln burrowed his muzzle under my chin. "But Link shouldn't have taken you down there. You didn't need to see that."

"*Mommy*," Abraham Lincoln cooed. *"I don't like it when Mommy's sad."*

"I can't believe you're okay with this!"

Draper was unapologetic. "More than okay. He snowed Bastien for a while, but I'm glad your guy came around. I never trusted Roland after the first time he tried to kill you. Why do you think I'm always hovering?" He hugged me tighter. "Let it all out with me, but maybe don't bother Bastien with this stuff. He's not doing so hot."

"What do you mean?"

"I was just at the pub with him, making sure he didn't drink himself into the grave. He loved Roland like a brother. To have your brother stab the woman you love? To have your brother threaten to have men do unthinkable things to the woman you swore to protect? Cry to me, pumpkin. Bastien might be broken for a while after this."

I wanted to yell at him, but I was too distraught. I sobbed in Draper's arms for I don't know how long, hoping he'd find a way to undo all the wrong that had been done under our roof.

41

HEART TO HEART

I wanted to cry myself to sleep, but I was too haunted to rest. "We need a plan," I said quietly to Draper. "Whenever I got stuck, Lane would always stop the madness, and we'd sit down and make a plan. She's gone now, and so is Damond. With Dad still down and out, and Roland... indisposed, it's you and me, right?"

"I suppose it is. I've been out on the wall as much as I can, but soon I'll need to go downstairs and hold court."

"What can I help with?"

"Nothing. You can rest. You were just stabbed, Rosie."

"I wasn't just stabbed. I've been patched up, and I'm fine. I need something to distract me, actually. How can I be helpful? I don't want Lane to come back to her province and find me lounging around, eating macarons all day." I stared at the ceiling wistfully. "Actually, that's exactly what I'd like to be doing right now."

Draper smirked at me. "I'll send down to the kitchen for more macarons. The three sisters love your reactions. I swear, sometimes I think they come up with new cookie flavors just to hear you gush about how creative and cool they are."

"Well, they are creative and cool. Hazelnut and coconut? Blew my mind." I swung my legs off the bed and tested my feet on the floor, grateful the numbing medicine had worn off. Everything was just a dull pain now, but I could deal with that. What I couldn't tolerate was being useless. "Morgan locked me in my bedroom for days on end. I'm not going to be the useless princess here, Draper."

"No one thinks you're useless. What I do think is that you're new. I'm not sure what you can help with, because you're unfamiliar with the customs and laws."

"Then can I shadow you? While you hold court, can I listen in and learn?"

Draper's small smile touched his eyes and made him look like the kind of boy who got his kicks raking leaves for the elderly neighbors. "I'm constantly amazed at how much like Lane you are. Of course, Ro. You can be my shadow. I'd love nothing more." He moved to my wardrobe and fished out a dress, laying it out on the bed for me. "Change into this, and I'll wait in the hall to help you down the stairs."

I touched the light green material. It had white embellishments and swirls on the bodice, and a skirt that wasn't too intimidating. I dressed quickly behind the partition, and joined my brother standing as straight as I could, so he didn't send me back to my room to rest.

Draper offered me his elbow, but Abraham Lincoln had other plans. *"Let me carry you. I can be a good horse,"* he promised.

"I'm not sure I'll ever get used to that," Draper commented as I carefully straddled my huge bear. On two legs, he was as tall as my brother. On four, he was a perfect mount to ride down the stairs.

"Thanks, baby. That actually is very helpful."

We moseyed down to the main floor and into a long, narrow room, where a late-fifties man in green uniform stood with a piece of parchment. He gasped when he saw me, more shocked at my appearance than the bear, whom everyone had pretty much gotten used to. "Your majesty! I didn't expect to be seeing you in the court room. It's my greatest honor to serve you."

"Aw. Thanks, man. What's your name?" I winced when Abraham Lincoln stopped in front of Lane's throne (it had her name on it), and ungracefully plopped myself into the chair.

"Herald," he replied, his blond head of hair still bowed to me.

"Nice to meet you. I've never done this before. Any tips?"

Herald gaped at me, as if confused to be asked his opinion. "I'm not sure I understand. You want my advice on how to hold court?"

"Um, yes?" I shrugged, wondering if I wasn't supposed to ask that. "I'm guessing you've got the front row seat to the hoopla. Any suggestions?"

He spluttered a few times, caught by surprise. "Well, I'm from Province 3 originally. I serve the Ninth Province now, and Duchess Lane runs things quite different. Less formal than I'm used to. If I may be so bold as to suggest limiting court sessions to only one hour per day? That might make the people more succinct with their complaints, and would make them think twice to see if they can't sort out their problems without involving the throne. The way it was done in Province 3 under Duchess Gliten and Ferdinand the Grave's rule was that court lasted four hours. It was most difficult for the duke and duchess to remain objective after the third hour."

I nodded. "That's great advice. Thank you, Herald." I turned my chin to Draper, who was petting Abraham Lincoln. "Would that work here? Limiting it all to one hour?"

"I say it's worth a try. We have so many other things to take care of. It would be a relief to only hold court for one hour each night."

"Done." I extended my hand to Herald, smiling when he broke through his upright demeanor and handed me a high-five. "Anything else you think of, I don't want you to be afraid to tell me. You've got more experience, and I appreciate any help I can get."

I didn't expect Herald to drop to his knees and kiss the toe of my slipper. "You are most fair, my Princess. Thank you."

I grimaced, and then affixed a patient smile on my face when he rose. "It's nothing, dude. I appreciate you being good at your job."

Herald's chest puffed as he rose. "There is nothing I wouldn't do for the Lost Duchess, or the Avalon Rose."

Draper took the seat next to me, grinning at the sight of me fidgeting on the throne. "That will do, Herald. My sister and I are ready. Do open the doors and let the first citizen in."

I jumped when Herald shouted, "Jean Franco of Province 4!" He wasn't calling the man to attention, but announcing his name and affiliation to us, so we were prepped.

The first man came in, bald and thin, balking at the sight of me in Lane's seat. He was so stunned that he forgot his complaint and spent the entire three minutes bowing and singing the throne of Province 9's praises.

Like, dude actually sang. Rhymed my name with "cozy".

Abraham Lincoln eventually dozed off, snoring next to me and providing a barrier between myself and the strangers as they came in with problems, and went out with hopefully less to burden them. My bear's fur was warm and soft, reminding me that I used to be both of those things, as well.

"The home we were assigned isn't the one we had when we left Province 9 years ago. We'd like permission to ask the people living there now to leave, so we can have it back," a round-faced, harried woman pleaded with me.

Draper had been handling the complaints for a solid half hour, but this time, he turned his chin, deferring to me. "What do you think, Rosie?"

My mouth went dry at having to make an actual decision that affected where people lived. It seemed too much responsibility for me to shoulder, but if Draper thought I was ready, then I decided I should give it a try. "I'm so sorry, but when you left Province 9 years ago, you forfeited your land. This isn't the same province as when you left. You're not the same person, either. We've all changed since then. I think your new home will be a good start for the new you. Who do you want to be in your new life in the new Province 9?"

The woman deflated, but then pursed her lips in actual thought. "I want to be a butcher. My husband and I had a small shop in Province 1, but we were taxed so high, eventually we had to close it. Might we petition for space to open a butcher shop here?"

"I don't see why not. Lane's set the taxes at a reasonable rate. Speak to the Homeland Planner – that's Girard. He'll let you start paying for the storefront one month after you open, to give everyone a chance to start fresh." I smiled at her. "See what you're doing? By being one of the few people who can look forward to what your life might look like, instead of wishing for the good old days, you'll be the first butcher in your area. Congratulations."

"Thank you, Princess!"

The hour passed much like that, with a few actual complaints and requests that Draper fielded so I could learn more about what resources were available to us, and how to handle the troubles of the people. The others were given tickets by Herald, guaranteeing them first spot tomorrow night. It was actually a pretty great system, for which Herald earned himself another high five.

When we finished, Abraham Lincoln escorted Draper and me to the kitchen, where we ate our fill of a goat cheese and shallots quiche. I was sort of in love with the three sisters who kept me in good quiche.

Bastien didn't come home, even as twilight crept off into the black of night. While Kerdik and Jean-Luc worked on my dad, Draper and Abraham Lincoln tried to distract me with conversation and plans for the future while we sipped tea like royals, and devoured multicolored macarons like children.

"Draper, you can't keep this up all night."

"Keep what up? I'm just talking to my sister."

"Yeah, but you're also trying to distract me from figuring out that it's late, and Bastien hasn't come home yet."

Draper rubbed the nape of his neck and looked sheepishly over at me. "Was I that obvious?"

"Can you take me to the pub he was at?"

"I can't imagine he's still there now. Probably just out with friends, or helping the men build the wall."

"In the dark?"

Draper grimaced. "Yeah, I didn't think you'd buy that. I can send Link out to bring him back."

I patted my gut. "I can find Bastien with my Compass easy enough." I was careful as I put a small amount of weight on my legs. I hadn't used my thigh muscles much since I'd been stabbed. *I've been stabbed*, I repeated to myself, wondering when life had gone so far south that it was barely recognizable as mine anymore. When I let go of the table I was bracing myself on, my thighs groaned, and I felt the slices afresh.

"You should go lie down. Jean-Luc would want you in bed, kiddo." Draper's hand came under my elbow to steady me. I hated that I actually needed the help.

"I'm fine. Just a little sore. I'm sure this is good for me. I need to stretch my legs a little bit."

"That's the exact opposite of what Jean-Luc told you to do, and you know it. You're not supposed to use your legs at all for another day or two. You might tear the muscles more or rip your stitches."

"Crap. I hate that he wrote it down for you."

Draper sniggered as he steered me back to the chair. "Lying to your old brother? Such treachery. Link can bring Bastien home when he's ready to come back. I wouldn't worry about it."

I slumped at the blond wood of the table, examining my bare knees as if they held all the secrets of the universe. "This is neither here nor there at this point, but I used to have actually decent legs. Now they're all carved up. I was hoping to leave Avalon behind when we go home, but my scars are going to be a solid reminder. I wear shorts to play sports most of the time. Now everyone's going to see what Roland did to me."

"That's the thing about scars. And you can ask your boyfriend his opinion on your legs. I'm sure he won't have anything bad to say about them."

I let out a humorless chuckle before I looked up and met his eyes. "Tell me it all gets better, Drape."

I don't know how Draper found the strength to smile, but the slow sweep of contentment brushed over his face, coloring him with life and light. "For me, it's already loads better. I found you and Lane. What more could a boy ask for?"

I studied the honesty in his eyes under black lashes, the kindness in his smile and the sweetness in his expression. "Man, how did I get so lucky?"

He chuckled at me. "You've been stabbed three times in the past forty-eight hours, and walked in on a torture carried out on your cousin by an Untouchable, yet you have the grace to call yourself lucky. That's how, Ro. It's you. If you can keep that optimism about you, then you'll always be lucky." He patted Abraham Lincoln on the back. "Up to bed with you."

"I can still help you. There's so much I need to learn. It's not fair of me to dump an entire kingdom on your shoulders."

Draper shook his head. "Help me plenty when you're better. Let's go." He remained by my side as the three of us made our way up the steps, me on my trusty steed. Draper helped me to the bed and pulled the sheet up over my lap. "I'll lock you in with Abraham Lincoln, okay? He'll watch over you while you rest. Let me check on Uncle Urien and send Link out for Bastien. I can bring you up more tea, too. What do you want?"

I shook my head. "I'm not thirsty. Thanks, though."

Draper gave me another glance over his shoulder before he left, as if to confirm that I wouldn't be dancing jigs or something. "Goodnight, pumpkin." We shared a smile before he turned off the lantern and left me in the dark.

Abraham Lincoln was sleepy, and wanted nothing more than to zonk out flat in the middle of the bed, taking up most of the space. I didn't like the dark ever since the well, but there were certain dangers in leaving an oil lantern burning all night long. I swung my legs off the bed and padded slowly to the window, ignoring my bear's protests as I popped open the pane to let a little of the blue moonlight in. The soft color painted my skin as I rested my hands on the sill, leaning out a little to gather up a deep inhale of the fresh air. Though the city didn't sleep, most of the activities were taken indoors at night. I watched people through windows in the distance as they sat at tables, several families socializing and chatting to pass the dark hours.

I missed Judah like I missed the ability to run. I wondered if he was happy, if he'd worked things out with Jill, and if he'd returned to his regularly scheduled program of school and adorable geekdom. I wondered if he would even recognize me anymore. I barely recognized myself. While he was LARPing with his buddies, dressing up like magical creatures and playing along with well-constructed plots, I was hoping my new BFF's accidental kiss didn't mutate me into a dragon. I glanced down at my hands, not for the first time that night, to check for scales. I would've dismissed Roland's warning entirely, if not for the fire-breathing belch.

I didn't want to go back down into the dungeon, but if Madigan got carried away, it would be too late to get my questions answered. I wanted to ask Kerdik about Tarasque, but when I'd asked him if he'd had parents, he'd frozen my body in a block of ice. Something told me that if his kiss really had turned a woman into a sea dragon of sorts, he wouldn't be all that cool and collected about it.

Roland was my best option, and I didn't have much time, if I had time left at all.

I brushed off Abraham Lincoln's worrying as I padded across to the wardrobe and slid on a pair of jeans. I probably should've chosen a dress, so the stiff material of the pants wouldn't rub up against my bandages, but whatever. Shoes were harder, but I managed. I opted for a simple white V-neck t-shirt that hugged my curves. I breathed anew at the clothes that fit and made me feel like a person, instead of a bedraggled mess of limbs, or dress-up Princess Barbie.

Abraham Lincoln whined at me when I moved toward the door. He was worried that I would fall down the stairs and die. His exact words.

"You're being dramatic. You can always help me, you know."

My bear decided to plop down right in front of the door, judging that as the best way to help. *There. I'm helping your legs stay healed. And I'm keeping you away from the bad one.*

"You could always come with me to go see Roland, you know. What could possibly hurt me if you're around?"

He gave a tired yawn and didn't move. *You should stay up here.*

"Look, sweetie. I have a limited window to get information that might be very important to me." Why it would be important, I couldn't totally tell you. It's not like I was ever going to kiss Kerdik again. Still, the unsolved puzzle nagged at me. Would I turn into a dragon eventually? "I need to go, hun. Will you help me down the stairs?"

After a few more back and forths, Abraham Lincoln consented to take me down the steps. I sat on his back as if he was a horse, gripping handfuls of his fur as he made his way through the hall and down the stairs. The stone steps were narrow for a bear, but we made it without me flying headfirst over his shoulders and bashing my head on the floor. So you know, bonus.

I didn't look forward to seeing what was left of Roland's face, but I braved the grotesque sight as best I could. Jean-Luc gave me a curious look, and Madigan glanced up from his work upon our arrival. *"You're supposed to be in bed. You're going to rip your stitches, Princess."*

"Aren't ye supposed to be in bed?" Mad groused. Though he'd been torturing Roland for far too long, his short, light brown hair was still combed, and neatly parted on the side.

"Sheesh, with the two of you. I'm alright. Just a little sore. Plus, I rode on Abraham Lincoln the whole way, which is pretty much bedrest."

I could tell Jean-Luc was getting comfortable around me because he shot me a dubious look. *"Riding a bear is hardly bedrest. Go back to your room. You've no need to see more of this. Even my stomach's starting to turn. I've never seen an Untouchable at work before. So meticulous. So gruesome. Incredible."*

"I'm not here to see more torture."

Madigan straightened, raising a thick eyebrow at me. "I'm not going to stop what I'm doing. I'm keeping him alive until your Da's all better, but this little piggy's going to regret crossing an Untouchable by messing up his lady."

"I know, though I wish you'd stop this. It's horrible, Mad. I mean, truly awful. I came down here to ask Roland a few things before his time's up." It was my nice way of saying "die."

"I'm sleepy, Momma. I'm going back to bed. The bad one won't let the mean one out."

I was tired, too. I kissed the top of Abraham Lincoln's head and toddled closer to the cell, the dank air filling my lungs and making me question everything.

"By all means, Princess," Roland croaked out. "How can I make *your* life better?" The sarcasm was thick, and to be honest, I was shocked he had the presence of mind to speak, let alone allow his acerbic personality to register.

I glanced up at Madigan and Jean-Luc. "Could you guys give me a minute?"

Madigan scoffed while Jean-Luc's shoulders shook with silent laughter. "Ye must be joking."

"What? He's locked up and barely alive. He's not going to hurt me."

"It's not tha I'm worried about. You've got tha bleeding conscience tha drives people to insanity. You're going to try and sneak him out the second I leave ye be."

I sighed. "Fine. I wasn't going to jailbreak him. I just wanted to have a private conversation."

"Come to have a little family picnic?" Roland snarled at me, his gaping eye cavity staring at me like it was its own entity.

My legs were stiff as I moved to touch the cell. Mad stopped me before I could enter. "Not a chance. Ye stay right on the other side of the bars. He can still hear ye with his one ear from there."

Roland let out a pained noise of agony, his hand moving up to touch the phantom ear that was now a hole on the side of his head.

I gripped the cell's bars to keep me from wobbling. "Not a picnic. More like story time. I was hoping you could tell me the one about the dragon."

"Tarasque?" Roland squinted his remaining eye at me. "Everyone knows there was a sea dragon in Avalon years ago. Ask your precious boyfriend. I bet you won't even have to bewitch the information out of him."

"I'm asking you. Only you seem to know Kerdik created her with a kiss."

"That part's a more guarded secret. Urien knows all about it, but not many others do. Tara was a handmaiden in Morgan's castle, back when Urien was alive, way before you were born. Master Kerdik was a more frequent visitor back then, and he spent most of his time with Urien." He said this bitterly, as if he'd wanted to be the special birthday boy who got to be the line leader. "Story goes that Master Kerdik fell for Tara, slept with her, and she transformed into Tarasque – part dragon and part sea creature. She was a gentle girl in her life, though, so even though she was a monster, she didn't kill anyone. She disappeared to the sea, and eventually impaled herself to end her life."

I covered my mouth with my hand. "Why did she kill herself?"

Roland shrugged, but then let out a loud whimper as the small movement caused ripples of pain to echo through his cowering naked body. "How should I know? I'd say she probably didn't like who she was anymore. She was feared, even though she never hurt a soul. Probably killed herself to save Avalon the trouble. There was already a brigade forming to take her down."

"Did she transform right away, or did the dragon mojo happen over time?"

"Oh, right away. The first time they coupled. She broke through a wall in the castle. You probably saw the newer stone put in on the east wing of Morgan's castle?"

I nodded, vaguely recalling the discoloration. "I didn't think to ask about it. She really was so big that she broke through stone?"

"Everyone knows that story. They just don't know how she became the monster she was when she died. They think Kerdik did it to her on purpose because she angered him. Only a few knew that they'd been entertaining a secret affair."

I bit down on my lower lip. "So Kerdik can't have sex with anyone, or he turns them into a dragon?"

"That's the way of it, yes. Why do you care?" A wicked smile swept over his face. "You fancy him, no?"

My mouth popped open, and Mad rolled his eyes. "No! Of course not. I love Bastien. Kerdik's my friend. He's just very secretive, and since he hangs out at the mansion a lot, I need to know things, like if he's going to go screwing the help and accidentally turn one of them into a dragon! That's maybe something you could've told us, since he's staying under our roof."

Roland chuckled, and I admit, I didn't think he had any levity left in him to risk what was left of his life. "You're pink for the green monster. And I worried I'd wounded Bastien beyond recovery, but it appears that spot's reserved for you. Promising to marry his Untouchable friend wasn't enough of a dagger in the back?"

Madigan held up his hand to stave off my stammering response. "He's trying to provoke us into cutting his miserable life short. Ignore him. I know ye don't fancy Kerdik or me. It was Bastien's idea I marry ye to begin with. He couldn't stand the thought of ye with someone who would want to get ye into bed. None of tha was your idea." He didn't say this with sadness, but rather stating an obvious fact. Mad didn't let the lines get blurred, which was one of the things I respected about him. "Don't let him mess with your head."

I lowered my chin and let my hair fall forward to cover the heat from my cheeks. "I know you love Avalon, and you fought hard for your province before it was taken from you. I know you hate me, but I never hated you. I didn't ask Mad to do this to you."

Roland spat on the floor at my feet. I guess his continued loathing wasn't a huge surprise, but it stung nonetheless.

I cleared my throat. "So if there's something you want done for Avalon, or a rule or policy you think might be helpful for Province 9, let me know. I'll tell Lane when she gets back."

Roland's intake of breath was barely audible, but his shock was plain on his torn face. "I don't understand."

"If you want something done for your people, tell me what. I'll do my best to make sure it happens." I sighed heavily. "The only regret I want you to die with is how terribly you treated your family."

Roland's snarl came back. "I was a good son, a good nephew."

I tipped up my chin to meet his eyes. "But *I* was your family, too. I wanted a cousin so badly. I would've done anything for you. So now that you can't keep trying to kill me, I'll help you look after the one thing you love. Let me know how you want things to be run, and I'll do my best to see your life's work wasn't for nothing."

There was an elongated silence between us that seemed to stretch on forever. Madigan's mouth was dropped open in astonishment, and Jean-Luc was actually speechless. Roland watched my face in the dim lantern light for signs that I really was the witch he'd pegged me as. I wasn't sure what was going to come hurtling out of his mouth when he spoke, but to see him cooperate was a bit of a surprise. He slowly stood, moving in all of his naked glory forward to grip the bars with the one hand that still had fingers. He cried out at the slight movements, breaking my heart all over again. I kept my eyes fixed on his bloodied and bruised face so I didn't catch a glimpse of the nude parts of him no cousin should ever have to see.

Roland studied my face for signs of a lie. "If bounty hunters set up in the province, they have to register, and they can only carry out business in the other provinces. For some reason, the more of them that do business close to home, the worse our land gets."

I nodded, glad we were making such leaps. "Okay. I can do that."

Roland's blue eyes burned with a fire that told me I'd touched on his sweet spot. He didn't know how to be a good friend or a cousin, but he loved Avalon, so I tried to pick out the noble attributes, so I could look back and remember the good parts of my cousin. I couldn't stand his whole life being remembered by his murder attempts on my life. A man had to be more than his worst moments, and I would find that light, so help me.

Roland's voice rasped as his body trembled with the draft all basements seemed to come with. "Let the shepherds handle their own territory disputes. The more government tries to get involved in their squabbles, the worse it all gets. Unless a life is taken in the feuding, don't bother with it. It makes us look weak, and no one's happy in the end. They just want to fight, so let them fight each other, not you."

"That's good advice. Keep it coming. I'm listening."

"Don't give Morgan an inch!" His voice took on a passion that showed just how deeply he'd been wounded by my mother. "I promise to haunt you for all of my days if you give any of my people back to Morgan. It's how I landed myself in the Forgotten Forest. Those of us who gave up plots of land bit by bit? It's a slow death." He swallowed hard and glanced at Mad, who leaned against the bars next to him, unperturbed but ready to pounce if Roland made any false moves. "Trust me on this; a slow death is one that crushes everyone's spirit. Province 9 is filled with tough, resilient people who want to live out their lives in peace, free from Morgan's rule. They left comfort to risk a new start because they believe we can be more than what Morgan allows. Do not move the boundaries I was helping the men set up, no matter what Morgan offers or threatens. I would not forgive you for that."

I nodded, tucking my hair behind my ear. "I wasn't planning on letting her anywhere near us."

Roland scoffed. "She's your mother. You'll crack, and Province 9 will fall."

It was hard to look at Roland's face, the dark cavity where his eye should have been gaped at me with all of its blackness. "My mother threw me down a well. She hurt my dad." I reached out and touched the remainder of Roland's fingers that were holding tight to the bar. "I so wanted us to be a family. I was scared to meet you, worried you'd hate me or think I was stupid."

"*You are not stupid, Princess. The duchess explained your learning errors to us. Stupid is not the right word at all.*"

"Thanks, Jean-Luc." I turned back to Roland, surprised he was letting me touch his fingers. "I want you to know that I forgive you for trying to kill me. I forgive you for threatening me and stabbing me. I didn't ask Mad to do this to you."

Madigan looked at me as if in disappointment. "Your forgiveness changes nothing. He's still going to die slowly for harming the lady of an Untouchable."

Roland's expression hardened. "I don't need your forgiveness."

I swallowed hard and dipped my chin, trying to remember all that Lane had instilled in me. When the kids at school ostracized me, picked on me and made every day worse than the one before, Lane encouraged me to forgive them. They were young, and thanks to them, I'd always been far older. If I didn't release them from my anger, I would become them, hating what I didn't understand.

Now that I was staring down my own personal tormenter, I finally understood the lesson she'd been trying to teach me. "Forgiveness isn't for you; it's for me. I won't carry resentment around. When you die today, all of you dies. You won't live on through my anger. You'll affect nothing, and I won't lose a night of sleep over the terror you tried to scare into me. I'll take care of your province, because the only parts of you that affect me are the honorable ones. Your evil will be buried with your bones. Only your kindness will be allowed to live in Avalon." Roland spluttered, but I ignored him. "You only saw the witch in me, no matter how much I tried to be your family." I shook my head sadly. "I want to be the kind of person who sees what good there is inside of you, and isn't haunted by your wickedness. So that's how this is going to end. You don't have power to decide any of it; I do."

I could hear Jean-Luc's reverence for Lane's words that spilled out of my mouth, and Mad's curious glances that told me he didn't quite understand, but he respected me all the same. "Run along now, wee Rose. Go quickly and I won't tell Bastien you've been skipping about the castle when ye should be in bed."

"Bastien's not home," I informed him. I let a weight settle on my simple words, telling Mad that Bastien wasn't doing so hot.

"Aye." Mad's blue eyes met mine, letting me know that he heard me, and he would deal with Bastien's bout of drinking when he finished up in the dungeon. "He'll be grand before ye know it. Just give him time. He loved this piece of shite."

I nodded, limping back from the bars with as serene an expression as I could muster on my composed features. "No more torture," I ruled, sounding more sure of my new royal role than usual. "The pain will only distract him from the misery he should be feeling. He broke Bastien's heart. He deserves to feel nothing but that for a while."

I could tell Mad didn't love this idea, but eventually he consented. "Aye. Up the stairs with ye now."

I hobbled to the stairs, wishing I had my bear to hike me up the stone steps. My room was on the third floor, and I was in the basement. I kept my chin up and limped up the first step, keeping my face neutral so no one could see how painful this was.

"Jays, I can't watch this. Ye shouldn't have come down here." Mad stepped out of the cell and locked Roland inside. He didn't even debate giving Jean-Luc the keys. I knew that as solid as Jean-Luc was turning out to be, Mad trusted only the Untouchables. "Up ye go, wee wife."

In the next second, I was scooped up into Mad's thick arms, cradled to the dirty shirt that covered his broad chest. He was careful not to touch the wounds on the back of my thigh, and carried me up all the flights of stairs until I was at my bedroom. He kicked open the door, startling Abraham Lincoln. He frowned, holding me in the doorway instead of putting me down on my bed. "Where's Link? I don't like the idea of ye being alone in here."

"*Pfft. Like I wouldn't watch my own mother,*" Abraham Lincoln huffed with a yawn.

"Abraham Lincoln will stay with me. Link's out bringing Bastien home."

Mad's eyebrows pushed together. "I still don't like it. Roland's got at least eleven men who might want to avenge their duke. Everyone knows ye sleep. It would be the perfect place to run a blade through ye."

I glowered up at him. "Your bedtime stories are severely grim. I'll be fine."

His jaw tightened as he took a step back. "No. I'll take ye to your Da. Master Kerdik is with him. Where's your brother?"

"I dunno. Probably helping with dad. Really, Mad. It's fine."

Madigan didn't even act like carrying me down two more flights of stairs to the main floor where my dad was being kept was an inconvenience. I don't know how these guys did all they accomplished, and without sleep, no less. Mad tapped on the door with his foot, waiting patiently for Draper to open it. "She shouldn't be unguarded," Mad offered, shoving me at my brother.

Draper fumbled to get his arms into position, holding me with tight hands and worry on his features. "Okay. You can't be here for this, Rosie. I'll take you back upstairs."

My spine stiffened when I heard my dad howling his pain. "Wait! Dad, what's wrong? Help him! He's hurting, Drape!"

"I know, pumpkin. We're trying to draw the Fool's Parsley out of him. It just takes time."

When Kerdik shouted, "Get her out of here!" it shook the walls with his frustration. "She shouldn't be here for this."

I tried to hoist myself up so I could look over Draper's shoulder, but Draper slid quickly out of the room and shut the door behind us. "Why were you even out of bed in the first place? I thought you were sleeping."

"Dad! I won't leave you! I'll help! I'm here!"

Mad watched me struggle to get at my dad, thrashing in Draper's arms to no avail. He huffed at my effort and wrapped an arm around my ankles to band them together. "Hush now.

T'won't do for the king to hear ye crying for him." He shook his head. "And ye ripped your stitches. Your leg's bleeding through your jeans."

"I don't care about my leg! My dad's hurting!"

"Well, it's painful to draw out poison, but the only other option is to let it stay in him. Is that what you want?" Draper was frustrated that he hadn't been able to contain me without help.

Kerdik poked his head out, his eyes falling on me. "Perfect. Bring her in here. We need a magic transfusion for Urien, and she doesn't use hers. I would give him some of mine, but I need it to be able to bring him back after he's been reinfused with fresh magic."

Draper and Mad both shook their heads. "No," Mad said, "She's already ripped her stitches open, and she lost a lot of blood yesterday. Ye can't go taking more from her."

"I'll do it!" I shouted, making Draper grimace. "Whatever it takes, he can have my magic."

"Perfect. In you get. Fetch me Jean-Luc. He can help you do it right in here. The fresher the better. Quick, now."

Draper and Mad exchanged a look of frustration before Draper carried me into the room where my dad was still crying out in agony.

ALL I HAVE TO GIVE

"Just a little longer," Kerdik said more to himself than to me. "Does she have more?"

Jean-Luc glanced up at my pale and sweating face dubiously. He was saying something to me, judging by the intention in his eyes, but I couldn't hear it. I couldn't hear much besides my dad howling his pain, and even that was starting to fade from my psychic ear. It felt positively claustrophobic with Jean-Luc, Madigan, Kerdik, Draper and me stuffed in the small room with my dad. I was sitting in the only chair, my abdomen crumpling in on itself as the tube going from my arm to my dad's took more and more blood from me.

I couldn't feel my arm anymore, but that hardly mattered. I couldn't feel my feet or my face, actually, but if it brought my dad back, I would give him all the blood in my body. I needed him to be alive. I needed him to smile at me and give me more than what I'd been dealt. I needed him to call me Rosie and tell me he loved me because we'd been spending so much time getting to know each other, and he genuinely liked me as a person. I needed...

I needed...

Draper caught me when I couldn't support my weight

anymore. I nearly face-planted on the floor, but he steadied me with his shoulder, his arms wrapped around my middle. I wished I could communicate. I wanted to tell him anything that might help get us out of this dark place that never seemed to give us many breaks, but my lips were fuzzy and my jaw went slack.

"This is too much, Kerdik!" Draper shouted. I couldn't tell if he was far away or right in my ear. Everything sounded like it was underwater, echoing into me, but not making much sense. I felt disconnected from the reality I'd fought to involve myself in. Maybe I should've listened to Mad and gone up to my room before Kerdik could grab me.

No. I knew that no matter how inconvenient it all was, I would do it all over again, giving my dad whatever he needed to survive. I'd lived too long without a father. That shiz ended tonight. I wasn't even aware that I was closing my eyes until drool dribbled out of my parted lips onto Draper's shoulder.

The last thing I felt was the tube being ripped from my arm, and Jean-Luc's fingers digging into my skin while Draper yelled my name. Madigan was shouting something, but I had a hard time understanding him on a good day, which this was not.

The darkness took over, plunging me into the black that never stopped scaring me after my time in the well. I'd been sleeping with the lantern on most nights, or at least the curtains open, so the moon could light the room. I hoped that when I closed my eyes, the small light I insisted upon would still be shining on my grim parts, giving hope to my despair. I was gone from myself, from it all, actually. The well surrounded me, encasing me on all sides. The walls of my father's room were replaced with the slick stones that had been too smooth and shallow to climb up. As much as I wanted to be free, I was stuck in the well, in the black that felt like it ate at my thinned skin.

Demi shivered next to me in my mind, but I had nothing to warm him with. We huddled together, two petrified children who'd been ravaged by Avalon.

I'm not sure how long I was out for, but it was no exaggeration to say that an eternity was a good guess. I hoped and waited for Bastien to find me, to take the lid off the well and hoist me up from the pit, but he didn't save the day this time. I prayed that Lane would find me, using that instinctual mother-daughter bond that served us so well on many occasions. I needed someone to find me, to know that even though I was gone from the earth, I was still there, waiting and calling for anyone to rescue me from all that threatened to hold me down.

I wanted to superhero myself out of the hole I'd been shoved into, but I couldn't so much as lift my arm to save myself. When Lane didn't come, and Bastien didn't show his face, I decided to stay down for as long as the darkness would have me. The darkness was quiet. Demi was with me in the dark.

43

LINK'S ANACONDA

*W*hen the light entered my room, I felt it before I saw it. The warm patch on my arm made me want to shift closer so I could be nearer the purity that soaked into my skin.

I heard giggling that had the hint of innuendo to it, accompanied by a low, throaty chuckle I recognized as Link's. The distinct sound of spit being swapped stung my ears. I remained immobile so I didn't have to let them know I was awake through the make-out. Link had been a good friend to Bastien, and had even taken Province 9's problems to heart, rebuilding and helping where he was needed. He was loyal to the Untouchables, and to me by extension. He'd been mired in work lately; I couldn't begrudge him a little teenaged fun.

"Oh, Link, right there," the woman groaned.

Internally I rolled my eyes. At least they weren't on the bed next to me. That would be awkward.

"Ye like tha?"

You wouldn't think the word "yes" would give me the urge to bathe the filth off my skin, but the way she moaned it sure did. The two of them carried on until I heard the telltale click of a belt buckle, and the downward slide of Link's zipper. I raised my hand but kept my eyes shut. "Third party in the room, peeps. Pants stay on."

The woman squealed her embarrassment, and then I heard her swat indignantly at Link. "You said the princess wouldn't wake! You said she'd been out for days!" I heard her standing and scampering toward the door. "A thousand apologies, your majesty. A thousand will never be enough. I'm so ashamed!"

"It's cool." I motioned to my lashes. "I've kept my eyes closed, so I don't know who you are. Might want to keep it that way, yeah? Then you don't have to feel embarrassed, because I'm still in the dark about it all."

"Of course, your highness. Never has there been a ruler more gracious." She stammered another apology before she fled the room, I'm guessing red-faced and in a tizzy.

"So, whatcha been doing?" I asked nonchalantly, opening my eyes to take in the noonday light. "Don't tell me *who* you've been doing; I don't think she could take it if I knew."

Link snorted, doing his belt back up and straightening his black t-shirt. "How much of tha did ye catch?"

I rubbed the sleep from my eyes, noticing for the first time that I was wearing one of the cotton strappy nightgowns I liked. "Enough for her to complain you were only packing three inches. Not so much that I had to witness your inchworm in action."

Link stared at me, dumbfounded, and then threw his head back with a loud belly laugh. "Ho! I didn't know Bastien found himself such a firecracker. Inchworm! Tha's funny." He looked pointedly down at his crotch, frowning in dismay. "But it's not a wee worm. I've got a solid Anaconda."

Of course, this spiraled me into a rendition of Sir Mix-a-Lot's greatest hit. I mean, how was I expected not to rap the best song in the world after he threw me a bone like that? "'My anaconda don't want none unless you've got buns, hun.'" I rapped a few more lines until they got too filthy for me to say in front of a dude who had no idea where I was pulling this from.

Link was howling on his knees by the time I trailed off, clutching his stomach while he laughed. "Please tell me ye made tha up just now. Grand tha was, Rosie!"

I tried to scoot my way up the bed so I could sit up, but my muscles protested being put to such arduous use. Being able to rap made me foolhardy, I guess. I ended up just lying there like a dead fish. "Nah, I didn't make it up. Wish I did. Best song ever." I tried again to sit up, but couldn't manage more than staring up at the ceiling and moving my arms a little. "Is Lane back yet?"

Link finally stood, wiping the tears from his eyes. Link was great at smiling when it wasn't done with a psychotic flair to it. "No. She's still visiting Duke Lot with Reyn, Remy and Damond."

"Where's Abraham Lincoln and Hamish?" I'd missed my constant companions.

"Ah. Well, since your magic was drained, Draper was worried the animals might get frustrated when ye couldn't hear them. Not many things worse to lock ye in a room with than a surly bear, so they're making themselves useful outside. Plus, they'd only keep yapping to ye, and ye'd never wake up because they'd be constantly draining ye. Outside's where they belong anyways."

"Where's Bastien? How about Kerdik? Did my dad wake up yet?"

Link's guarded expression told me something wasn't quite as peachy as the forced lightness of his tone made it all sound. "Most everyone's helping your Da. He's awake, and all's well, but it's taking time for his muscles to be of any use."

"I guess that makes sense. He's awake, though? It actually worked?" Joy danced in my eyes at the prospect of being able to hang out with Superman.

"Aye. T'almost didn't. Almost killed ye both. Mad had quite a few words with Master Kerdik over tha. Then when your Da came to, he started in on Master Kerdik all over again. Never thought I'd see the warlock show actual contrition, but Master Kerdik's barely left your side, other than to go see to King Urien."

I mulled this over and tried to put my thoughts in proper working order. "Do a girl a solid and help me up? I need to go see him."

Link shook his head. "You're supposed to be resting."

"Um, you just told your little hottie that I'd been out for days. I think I've had enough rest."

"Okay, then. Get on outta tha bed and dance me a jig. Ye should be able to if ye've had enough rest."

I glared at him and clenched my fists at my sides. "Come on, Link. Be serious. How am I supposed to get anything done if I'm stuck here?"

"Ye aren't supposed to get anything done. Tha's the point of bedrest."

"Oh, you're hopeless." I thumbed the comforter that was draped around my waist. "Could you at least help me to sit up? I feel ridiculous like this. My brain's working, but the rest of my body is being a wuss."

Link's arms around my shoulders were steady, moving me to sit up against the pillow he propped up to the headboard. "There ye are." He winced when his hand palmed my back as he stood, bent over at my bedside. "You're too thin. King Urien had a freezing charm to preserve him while he was out, so he has muscle still and weight to his face. Ye can't go sleeping for days on end. You're just a wee thing."

"Well, I didn't do it on purpose." I studied my wrists, grimacing at the thinness that had come from being starved in the well, and then passing out for days on end. I was starting to get too skinny to be a serious threat on the soccer field, which didn't sit well with me. "Can I go get some food?"

"Aye. I'll have some sent up for ye." He grinned at me. "How did ye put it? We like our ladies with back?"

I smirked at him, glad that in my first few minutes awake, I'd managed to make someone smile. The Untouchables were a strange bunch, but I was starting to feel at home with them. I looked up at Link, grateful that he'd always been good to Bastien, and thus, nice to me. "While you're putting in requests, how hard would it be to get someone up here to put Bastien's mark on me?"

Link froze, his eyes wide, and neck shrinking. The suddenly stooped posture of his shoulders made him look... guilty? "Um, tha can be arranged. Might want to wait until you're on your feet."

My nose wrinkled. "Why? You three were all about me getting it right away. I've been thinking that maybe I'd get stabbed less with the mark." I shrugged, trying to make a joke, though Link had suddenly grown serious. "Sure, some stabbing, but definitely less."

Link offered up a one-noted perfunctory laugh, and then rubbed the nape of his neck like he was trying to hide something. "I'll go get ye some food. No getting stabbed while I'm gone, ye hear?"

"Well, there goes my plans for the afternoon. You're no fun." I waited until he was gone to try my hand at getting dressed, so I could go down and see my dad. My clothes were all the way in the wardrobe, which was on the other side of the long room. I flopped my legs over the edge of the bed, giving myself a pep talk before attempting to put weight on my feet. I'd been injured lots of times in the various sports I'd played. Each time back on my feet brought about the same mentality, no matter the injury: deal with it.

My toes wiggled before they tapped on the floor, but the second I stood, my legs crumpled like a Jenga tower. I wasn't expecting total defeat, nor was I expecting to bang my head so hard on the nightstand on the way down that I passed clean out on the floor.

44

TRICKS AND TATTS

"*I* was gone for two minutes!" I heard Link yell. He was slapping my cheeks and flicking water droplets onto my face until I finally came to. The world swam in my vision, and if there was anything in my stomach, I would've puked it out right then and there. "I'm about to tie ye to this bed to make sure ye don't hurt yourself. Let me guess, ye were trying to walk to your Da? Jays, you're predictable."

I moaned through my headache that seemed to split my cranium when I pried open my eyes. "Ouch."

"'Ouch,'" Link scoffed as he lifted me off the floor and put me back in the bed. He grumbled as he flopped onto the mattress next to me on his belly, grabbing a bowl of oatmeal off the tray. "Here. See if this will put some meat on your bones."

I wanted to make a vegetarian joke, but my brain was too fuzzy after the fall. "Can I at least have some clothes? It's the middle of the day, and I'm wearing my nightgown."

"Aye. Eat tha, and I'll send in a handmaiden to help ye change."

I hated that I needed help. "Lane's not back yet?"

"In the two minutes since ye last saw me? No, I can't say Lane's back yet."

My hand was feeble and uncoordinated, but I managed to get the spoon to my mouth without dropping the warm groats all over myself. Bonus. If I could feed myself, dressing myself wouldn't be too far behind. "Did Roland..." I couldn't bring myself to ask if he'd died, but part of me needed to know. Maybe it was all a bad dream, and Roland was in the next room, not hating me by some miracle. Maybe he had a heart after all, along with two functioning eyes and all ten fingers.

Link didn't bother sugarcoating it for the viewers. "Roland died a couple days ago. About a minute after your Da woke up, Mad slit his throat." He drew a line across his own neck with his thumb, in case I was so slow that I didn't understand the mechanics of slitting someone's throat. "Gone and buried already. No ceremony because he attacked the throne, so he died a prisoner, and they don't get big funerals."

"Oh. I guess that makes sense." I swallowed my oatmeal, though it felt like a brick sliding down my esophagus. "How's Bastien taking it all?"

Again, that evasive look. "He'll be alright. Tell me about your life in Common."

I stuck the spoon in my mouth, giving Link a look that lasted well beyond what normal eye contact was supposed to. "What aren't you telling me? Is Bastien okay?" When Link didn't immediately answer, I shoved the bowl at him and ripped the covers off my legs. "Is he hurt somewhere? He wouldn't stay away this long if he knew I was awake. Something's wrong! You let me just lie around up here while he's hurt? He's going to think no one's coming for him. We have to go, Link!"

When I tried to get out of the bed, Link steadied me with his hand on my arm. "Easy, wee Rose. He's not injured. Just a little lost." He let out a whistle. "Wow. Ye really do love him. I didn't think you'd up and go after him; ye can't even walk yet."

"Of course I love him. Where is he?"

When a knock interrupted just when Link hesitantly opened

his mouth, he blew out a gust of relief and popped up from the bed. "I'll get it!" He flung open the door, letting Kerdik in with more gusto than usual. "You're good with Master Kerdik, then?" He didn't wait for my response. "Grand. I'll go downstairs and check on... your surprise." It was as if the idea just occurred to him. "Yeah! Bastien's working on a surprise for ye, and tha's why he's not up here. I'll go help him so he can come back up when he's finished. With the surprise. The surprise for ye." He banged the door shut, leaving me alone with Kerdik before I could throw another question at him. I wanted to say that I didn't need a surprise; I just wanted Bastien.

My eyes fell on Kerdik, who looked ruffled and untucked. "Hey, Kerdik. How's tricks?"

"Tricks are slow, but steady. Urien's able to speak now, but just barely. Healing him is taking a fair amount of magic." He glanced at me with guilty eyes. "I shouldn't have taken so much from you. I needed the help, but I should've been more careful. Draper, Madigan and Jean-Luc were... not pleased."

I quirked my eyebrow at him. "Not used to feeling remorse, huh." I waved my hand to clear the air, like it was no big deal. "It's cool. I lived."

"Now I feel even worse. You're pale as a sheet. You're confined to your bed!"

I blew out a loud raspberry. "I'm totally good as new. I was just getting up." It was pride that led me to try standing again, and foolishness that pushed me to take a wobbly step. I'm not sure why I assumed a few minutes would make a world of difference, but if you can believe it, I wasn't up for tap dancing just yet. I plummeted to the floor, banging my knees on the wood, yet again.

Kerdik was at my side, hoisting me up in his arms that were sweaty, but more than capable. "Well, that was a mistake. Clearly you're not healed yet. I took far too much magic from you."

"Magic and blood," I amended. "It's fine. I think maybe I've just lost a little too much blood recently. I mean, the stabbing and then the blood and magic donation. Sorry my body's being a wuss. Totally embarrassing." He set me down in the bed and covered my lap with the comforter. I shifted my nightgown around me so it wasn't so twisted, and then blinked up at him. "Could you not tell anyone I fell? I already feel like the weakest link. I still can't believe I let Roland get the jump on me."

"Roland was armed, and twice your size. He's dead now anyway. You don't have to worry about him."

I fiddled with the edge of the comforter, wishing I could make the world spin the right way again. Everything had felt so wonky for too long. "When can I take my dad home?"

Kerdik watched my small movements carefully before sitting on the edge of the bed. "Urien's not going back to Province 1, if that's what you're asking."

"I meant my home in Common. I wanted to take him there, so he can live with Lane, Reyn, Draper, Bastien and me."

Kerdik's gaze hardened, but he didn't speak right away. I could tell he was choosing his words carefully. "I'm not sure it's as simple as you're thinking. For one, Urien might want to stay here. Redeem Avalon, if he can. You might not love it here, but this is his home. I don't think he'll be satisfied letting Morgan roam free after what she did to him. Urien coming back is going to cause a lot of waves throughout Avalon, especially when they find out Morgan was behind it all. What's left of her province might split off from her, and she doesn't lose gracefully."

I swallowed the lump in my throat, somehow knowing it wouldn't be as easy as I needed it to be. "How long do I have to stay here?"

"'Have to'? You don't *have* to stay, but I hope you do. For selfish reasons, of course, but also because Morgan will have her soldiers hunt you down if she learns you're unprotected."

"Bastien's my *Guardien*. He can keep me safe, right?"

Kerdik looked toward the window, saying nothing for a long

time. The silence grew uncomfortable, and then settled between us until he decided on the right words. "He's your *Guardien* for as long as you'd like him to be. If you someday decide to move on, you have that right. You can dismiss him, you know."

My nose crinkled. "Why would I do that? It's not his fault I got stabbed. No one was expecting Roland to go off the deep end like that."

Kerdik cleared his throat. "Yes, well. Should you move on from him for any reason, I want you to tell me first thing. It's too dangerous for you to be unprotected, no matter which world you're in."

"You don't have to worry about that. Bastien and I are together. He asked me to take his Untouchables mark, and I accepted."

Kerdik's eyebrows raised, and he turned his chin toward me. "You did? Does he know you said yes?"

"Not yet. I haven't seen him since Roland was taken to the dungeon."

Kerdik stood, and then kissed my forehead. "I'll bring up a tattoo artist who has the necessary tools. If you want to be marked as Untouchable, then we can get that done straightaway."

"Oh, cool. Thanks." My eyes darted toward the door. "Shouldn't Bastien be here for it? I mean, it was his idea."

"Oh, I'm sure he'll turn up. And what a lovely surprise you'll have for him."

Before I could reply, Kerdik spun on his heel and exited, leaving me to examine the unsettled feeling that was churning in my gut.

45

MARKED

The stooped sixty-year-old artist was nothing like the tattoo professionals in Common. I expected him to wear tons of ink himself, but he was clean, all except a black X on his forehead. I tried not to be put off by it, but it had an ominous vibe of "stay away" to it. "You're sure this is safe?" I asked, chewing on my lower lip. Kerdik had helped me slide on a shirt over my nightgown, so I was somewhat less exposed for the stranger.

Kerdik held my hand as we sat on the bed, our legs over the side as I examined the tattoo guy with wary eyes. "Of course it's safe. Bastien already spoke to Bellamy over a week ago, so he'd be ready to mark you as soon as you said yes. Madigan told me as much."

Bellamy's hands trembled as he took out a heavy steel quill, complete with a steel feather on the end. It did not bode well with me that the dude doing my tattoo had the shakes. "If you're ready, your majesty."

"What's that?" I asked of the small black pot he unscrewed.

Bellamy was patient with me, though he didn't need to be. That was my thirtieth question so far. I knew I was being annoying, but I was so nervous. "It's the ink. Since this isn't an average tattoo, but the mark of an Untouchable, a little of Bastien the Bold's blood was mixed in with the ink. It imbibes the wearer with magic that connects the two of you."

"Huh. Anything crazy? Like, will I be able to shoot hummus out my fingertips if I get hungry?"

Bellamy managed a small smile, his bald head wrinkling. "It's more an indicator if something's wrong."

Kerdik unbuttoned the cuff on his white dress shirt and rolled up his sleeve. "Mix a little of my blood in there, too."

Bellamy's mouth fell open. "Surely you don't think me worthy to touch your blood, Master Kerdik."

Kerdik's chin lifted, and his voice came out snippy. "Of course you're not, but it must be done anyway. The princess belongs to me; I won't leave her unprotected. Mark her with Bastien's blood, and also with mine."

I bumped my shoulder to his, leaning into him easily, like how good friends were meant to do. "You don't have to do that."

His eyes sharpened. "You don't want to wear my blood? You don't wish for my protection?"

Bellamy took a step back, wary of Kerdik's childish temper. I rolled my eyes. "Of course I think it's the sweetest thing, but there's nothing I can do that's the equivalent. I mean, your protection comes with some clout. I can barely get out of bed to help if you needed something. Say some old lady comes into the castle and whacks you over the head with her purse, and you needed backup. What could I do from my bed to save you from her elderly wrath?" Kerdik's chuckle did my heart a world of good. "I don't feel right taking something big from you, and giving you nothing. That's not a friendship."

Kerdik reached up and touched his fingers under my chin, feathering them along the sensitive flesh. "But darling, don't you know? You love me, and that's given me everything I need. Your love is my protection, and I wear it proudly everywhere I go.

Using my blood with the ink is mostly selfish on my part. I need you whole and well. This ensures that you stay mine, and I always remain yours."

I leaned my chin on his shoulder, sighing contentedly at the sweetness he never seemed to run short on these days. "How'd I get so lucky?"

I could feel his cheek lifting in a bashful smile. Then his tone sharpened as he addressed the stunned Bellamy. "I'll give you my blood, and then you'll mark her. I'll burn the rest of your ink that has my blood and Bastien's, so it doesn't get used for anything else."

"Yes, your grace."

After Kerdik cut a small slice across his finger and dribbled a few drops into the ink pot, Bellamy started in on his work. I'd never had a tattoo before, and wasn't sure how much this one lined up with the more traditional ones in Common. The quill scratched deep into my skin, feeling like an acidic claw from a cat, raking in slow motion over the thin flesh of my left wrist. Kerdik held my arm still so I didn't rip my hand away when the slices grew too hot for comfort. He turned my forehead into his neck, cradling my head to his shoulder so I didn't see the blood dripping down my skin, or the angry red that burned me like a blush rising from my wrist.

The tattoo on my neck took longer, was awful to grit my teeth through, and I don't feel like describing the pain of it. It was so bad that I almost cried right there on Kerdik's shoulder. Luckily, I'm never doing it again. End of story.

When it was finally over, Bellamy was visibly sweating. He kept shooting Kerdik furtive glances, but said nothing. No doubt this was the most stressful tattoo he'd ever done, but in the end, it looked exactly as I expected it to. It perfectly matched Bastien's, Link's and Mad's, and I couldn't wait to show them. It felt like a rite of passage into the cool kids' club, and finally, *finally* I was ready to make that leap. I was cleaned up and bandaged, grinning from the high of getting my very first tattoos.

Bellamy packed up and nearly ran for the door. I caught him before he vanished and said, "Thanks, man. I'll be sure to tell Bastien what a great job you did. I appreciate you making a house call like this."

Bellamy shook his head. "No. Don't tell Bastien it was me who marked you. I was never here." He winced. "But he'll know because he gave me his blood last week to use for it. He'll know it was me!"

I was so confused that I didn't find the words to ask him what he meant before he ran out of the room. "Well, what was that about?"

Kerdik moved my feet back onto the mattress. "Bastien's been in a state since Roland was executed. Causing trouble in the village." He picked up a bowl of cut up fruit from the nightstand and fed me a piece. The strawberry was sumptuous, and tasted like tart sunshine on my tongue. He filled me in on my dad's slow progress while feeding me bite after bite as I reclined against the pillows that were propped up against my headboard. "I'm hoping to have Urien walking in a few hours. I've been giving him small transfusions of my own magic, which works far quicker than anything else."

"You love him," I stated, seeing clearly what it looked like when Kerdik truly cared.

"I do. Urien's one of my few true friends."

When he pressed another berry to my lips, I pulled back with a grimace. "Whoa. I just realized you're feeding me. Sorry. I can do that."

"I don't mind."

"But I do. I don't want you to always be taking care of me. I promise I'll try to get stabbed less from here on out." I arrested the bowl from his hands and set it on my lap. I popped another berry in my mouth and chewed thoughtfully. "Should I be worried that Bastien's not back yet?"

"Do you want to spend your time worrying?"

"I guess not. It feels weird that he wasn't here when I got my tattoo, you know? It was such a big deal to him. He'll be happy about the surprise, right?" I munched on some more fruit while I thought aloud. "Link said he was working on a surprise for me. This is a good one for him, right?"

Kerdik studied my face, a sharpness glinting on his features. "I simply can't wait to see his face when he finds out you've been marked as his."

46

MY BIG SPEECH

"*O*kay, he can't lean on you, Rosie. You're barely stable yourself. Here, Uncle. Use my arm." Draper offered his elbow to my dad. My brother's calm authority made both of us feel a little more at ease with our limited progress.

"I remember when Roland was born. He knew you when you were just a baby. I can't believe he would attack you like that, sweetheart."

I beamed up at Urien as Kerdik helped me to sit in a chair in the corner of my dad's room. "I know I'm supposed to be paying attention to what you're saying, but all I can think is, 'I have a dad!'"

Urien chuckled, which he did often. He had a soft lightness to his features I hadn't noticed when his body had been asleep. His hair went down to the middle of his neck, curling on the ends after he'd been bathed and dressed for the day. Richard the Lion-hearted, in the flesh. "Indeed, you have a father, and I intend to be the best one Avalon has ever seen."

I grinned like a goofball up at him. Since I'd come to his room to offer what limited help I could, my eyes saw only his. He was broad-chested and wore his button-up dress shirt like a king. He was tall, had a strong chin, and hands that could build a medieval castle complete with a kingdom of loyal subjects out of rocks and mud. His blue eyes stood out from his caramel-colored hair, twinkling each time he looked at me. My dad was utterly and completely magic.

My dad. Like, a dad who belongs to me. I started daydreaming about the fun adventures we could have together. Maybe he could teach me how to use a bow and arrow. Maybe we could play catch together.

Draper had been talking to me, but I only caught the tail end of whatever he'd been saying. I turned my gaze to him, my brow wrinkled. "I'm sorry, what? I missed it."

Draper sniggered at my inability to focus on anything other than my dad. "I was asking if you were in pain still. Your legs. Your wrist. Your neck."

I glanced down at my jeans, shifting to feel the bandages beneath. "I couldn't feel pain if you knocked me over the head with a brick. I'm too happy."

"You're going to have to go out soon," my dad reminded me. *My dad.*

"I know. Just soaking it all in. I don't want to leave you. I feel like the second I turn my head, you'll be back in that bed all over again."

Urien smiled, looking regal, even though he was walking like a zombie with arthritis. "I feel the same way about you, dear. But this is the crown. The people will grow restless if they don't hear from us. Roland's death was hard on them, and many still don't understand it. It's good for them to see your lovely face, hear your voice. Reassure them that our kingdom still stands, and that they didn't leave their homes in Province 1 for nothing."

Draper squeezed my father's hand. "Not to worry. I'll be with her the entire time."

"I'm not really one for public speeches, Dad." I giggled, covering my mouth. "I called you 'Dad'. Too funny."

"Too perfect." Urien straightened his spine, trying to appear regal instead of sickly. "You can read the speech Draper and I worked out for you, then come right back to me."

"Wouldn't it be more moving if you did it? I mean, 'King Urien: Back in Action' has a nice ring to it."

"Indeed, but I'm not at my best yet, and the people deserve my best. You'll have your brother with you, plus your fiancé and your *Guardien*." Almost to himself, he added, "You'll be safe."

I nodded, not wanting to tell him that I hadn't seen Bastien in over a week, and Mad and I weren't really super engaged. Link and Mad had given me a wide berth, eating in the kitchen and leaving early in the morning to lend a hand to the men and women who were rebuilding the city. I was itching to help out, but my dad and Jean-Luc were pretty strict.

"I can go with her," Kerdik offered. "They would listen if I was by her side."

Urien narrowed his eyes at his old friend. "You're publicly allying yourself with Province 9? You're willing to fight for our kingdom? Because if you stand with Rosalie, that's what you're telling the people."

Kerdik frowned, looking uncomfortably to the side. "I guess you're right. No, I'm not going to stick around and fight wars that aren't mine. I just don't like the idea of her being unprotected out there."

"Unprotected from what? Who's going to attack me?"

"No one," all three men answered in unison.

"Okay, guys. That's not suspicious at all. Seriously. What've I missed out on while I've been on bedrest? Who hates my guts now?"

Draper spoke in a light voice I could tell was forced. "Nothing. Just a few of Roland's followers are upset that he was put down without ceremony. They don't understand all that he did to you because we didn't want it to seem like there was feuding in the royal family."

"But there was feuding. Big time family feud."

"I know, but admitting that shows the kingdom's rulers are weak. Unity is what they need to see from us." Draper jerked his chin toward the door. "Don't worry about it. Go on up and change, and I'll grab Madigan and Bastien."

"You know where Bastien is? I thought he was too busy building the wall with the guys to come home." I tried not to let the hurt linger in my voice, but it was no use. I tried to pretend like it was all fine. I mean, who was I to make demands on my boyfriend's schedule? I didn't want to be the girl who forced her guy to check in, but at this point, it felt like he was dodging me, and I couldn't understand why. I mean, if he'd been stabbed three times, no way would anything keep me from him. Link kept telling me when I woke in the morning that I'd "just missed Bastien," but I had the feeling that wasn't really what was going on.

Draper's voice had the edge of avoidance to it. "Don't worry, kiddo. I'll have him back before your big speech."

I nodded, none too confident that was the case. Abraham Lincoln hadn't seen Bastien with the men at the wall. I would've been worried, but Link assured me he'd just seen Bastien, and that all was just fine.

Kerdik didn't like it when I refused his help getting up the stairs, but he respected it all the same. My legs burned still with the slight exercise, but I gritted my teeth through the tearing feeling I couldn't shake. When I reached my room, I undressed, tossed my gown over my head and tied back my curls, hoping I looked the part of the princess I was pretending to be.

Kerdik met me at my door, waiting to escort me down like a gentleman. His eyes were guilty, staying on mine for only a second. "You look lovely, as always."

I fought the urge to roll my eyes. I looked ridiculous in the pink dress with maroon and gold edges on the capped sleeves. "What's wrong, K?"

He took my hand and tucked it into the crook of his elbow. "I'm sorry I'm not going out there with you. Urien's right. If I stand with you, the people will expect me to fight all their battles for them, and I'm not willing to seal my allegiance like that. The second I don't show, they'll blame you for my absence, and you'll be in the line of fire."

I snuggled into him, cherishing the friendship that had bloomed between us. "You don't have to be sorry for that. I totally get it. I won't be alone up there. Just make sure my dad is safe, okay? I don't like being so far away from him."

"You're only going to the town's square. It's not more than a mile into the city. Then you'll come straight home to me."

"Of course." I sighed. "It'll be good to see Bastien again. I know he's been working hard, but man. I miss seeing my boyfriend, you know?" I'd mostly healed from being stabbed, and he'd been nowhere around for most of the whole ordeal.

Kerdik gave me a curt nod, but nothing more until we reached the kitchen door that led out back to the stables. He was hiding something.

They all were.

47

FRIENDLY CHAT WITH BENOIT

*T*he coach with two horses made me feel like Cinderella, and the coachman bowed to me when I approached. He wore an emerald-colored dress jacket, and had focused eyes that seemed to be seeing and sifting through everything in his periphery. I'd still not grown accustomed to all the formalities, and insisted on shaking his hand instead of merely accepting that yes, I'm above him, and yes, he should totally bow down. A simple handshake felt like a much better way to seal things, even if it confused the poor guy.

Draper trotted down the trail to the stables with Abraham Lincoln and Hamish by his side, waving for us to wait for him. "It's just you and me, I guess," he said, offering his hand for me to use to hoist myself up into the green painted coach. "Up you get, Ro."

I sat back in the coach, thumbing my skirt that draped like a waterfall down my legs. It wasn't a poofy dress, like the ones Morgan preferred me to wear. This one cut just below my bust, and fell steadily to the floor, dusting my gold sandals when I moved. "Um, where's Mad and Bastien? I thought you sent word to them that this was a big deal."

Draper nodded, motioning for the coach to get going. Kerdik kissed his fingers and waved them in the air at me when we took off, a sadness in his eyes that I couldn't quite place. "I did. They couldn't make it."

I chewed on my bottom lip to keep the selfish words from spilling out of me. "I guess that's fair. I mean, they're working hard to build that wall to keep Morgan's soldiers out. Can't really complain about that. I guess there are worse things than your boyfriend being a workaholic, especially when his work keeps hundreds of thousands of families safe." I glanced out the window at the trees that rushed by us. I could hear Abraham Lincoln running beside the coach and saw he had Hamish clinging to his fur. Just that little assurance helped me to relax. "It's kind of heroic, if you think about it."

"Bastien doesn't deserve you. I can't believe after this many days, that you're not mad at him for ditching."

"But he's not ditching. He's rebuilding Lane's kingdom. As much as I wish he was here, I can't be selfish. Not now that I've got a whole province to think about." I tried to be the adult, but the childish insecurity in me flared up.

Draper pulled the golden drapes of the coach closed, and tucked me into his side. "Careful, now."

"Careful of what?"

"Nothing. Just sit back with your old brother and relax a little before we get there. You want to go over your speech again?"

"No, I've got it locked in." I tapped my temple. "Thanks for helping me memorize it. That's a job that usually falls to Lane or Judah."

"Well, I'm family now, so it's my pleasure to help where I can."

The coach wobbled, making me slightly car sick by the time we got to the Town Square. A crier had been there, gathering the people and ringing the giant gong of a bell so that everyone would be around for the grand speech I was pretty sure I would screw up. Draper got out first, and I noticed his palm teasing the hilt of his sword when he offered his other hand to help me out of the coach. He was worried, and that gave me no uncertain amount of discomfort. I wished Lane, Reyn, Remy and Damond were back already. Politics wasn't really my thing.

I kept my chin high and a pleasant smile on my face as the crowd shouted their greetings to us. I waved like the celebrity I pretended to be as Draper walked with me to the platform in the middle of the square. The crowd parted for us, most with reverent bows, but a few, I realized, wore angry sneers. I tried not to let my fear show, but kept my smile as steady as I could when Draper led me up the steps onto the open platform that had a 360-degree audience I couldn't escape.

I was supposed to give a speech, but everyone was talking and shouting – some happy greetings, and others that were angry and violent. "String her up! She's no better than her mother!"

I held tight to Draper's hand, unsure what I should do. Going with the prepared speech didn't seem quite right anymore, not that anyone could hear me if I did. The shouting was directed at me, but eventually the people started arguing with each other, throwing down gauntlets over whether I was innocent or not. The din grew to an unsettling volume, and I was scared at what chaos might go down if I didn't get ahold of the madness right quick. Even the trees that fanned out in a perfect circle to encompass the Town Square seemed to be warning me with their swaying branches, saying, "Oh, girl, we could've told you this would go badly."

My eyes scanned the crowd for an angry face, landing on a nearby one who held up a sign he painted. It had some words written across it under a picture of me with a dagger in my bloody hands. The art was actually pretty impressive, though I knew my boobs weren't *that* big. "You there! Come up here so I can talk to you."

The man, content to boil in his own disgruntled fury, tried to suppress a shock of worry at being called out. I learned from the social media life in Common that everyone could be super brave behind the anonymity of a computer or a crowd, but face-to-face? People tend to recall their humanity when they remember the one they're jeering at is an actual person with flaws not too different from their own. The dude obeyed after a grimace of nerves, coming up onto the stage, much to the uproar of the crowd. Draper was in my ear with a fretful, "What are you doing?"

I tried to ignore everyone, and stuck my hand out to the stranger. "Hi. I'm Rosie. Can you speak for the people who're pissed at me?"

His sweaty face was pink, but he didn't shrink away from the mission of the protestors. He was there to make sure I knew he was upset, so I made certain he got his audience with me in front of Province 9. There were easily fifty thousand people fanned out from the stage, and I felt the pangs of Britney Spears being on trial for cutting her bangs. "I sure can," he spouted, as if I'd asked him something offensive. "There are many of us who demand you see the gallows for what you did to Duke Roland!" His voice boomed out far louder than mine, so I knew I'd chosen the right jag. Everyone fell quiet finally, wanting to hear the sparring that would add clarity to the province-wide argument over my guilt.

"Cool. What's your name?"

"Benoit of Province 4," he answered with a sneer, as if his name was supposed to mean something to me.

It friggin' didn't, so I refused to cower. "Nice to meet you." Then I turned to the crowd, most of whom were afraid to have me so near Benoit, but many who were ravenous that he tear me apart. I chose to have faith in the basic rules of society that most dark deeds were done in secret, and that with it being midday, I didn't have to worry about Benoit trying to gut me in public. I tried to speak as loud as I could, and thankfully, the crowd fell silent to accommodate me. "There seems to be a problem with how Duke Roland's death was handled. I've got loads of things to talk to you all about today, but if you'd rather start out with that, I've got nothing to hide. Benoit and I are going to hash this out, so I suggest everyone get good and comfortable, so you all hear what went down and why." Then I took a chance and sat down on the floor of the wooden platform, spreading my skirt out around me so my crossed legs were covered. I motioned to Benoit. "If you want to have a heated conversation with me, you'll sit down and talk like a gentleman."

"I'll speak how I wish," he spouted, ignoring the fact that most of the crowd shifted to sit in the dust to follow my lead of peacefully resolving the upset in the land.

I looked up at him, trying to appear unruffled, and like I had all the time in the world. "Fine, then mouth off to someone else. Don't tell me you're so bull-headed that when a princess offers you an exclusive interview, you waste it by being prideful. If you want answers, play by the rules. Sit down and set a good example. Honor Duke Roland's life by getting to the truth, instead of flying off the handle and causing chaos in the land he loved." I frowned up at him. "I won't stand for you disrespecting Duke Roland like this, stirring up chaos when actual answers are right in front of you."

I held Benoit's gaze until he sat down. He appeared sullen that his brutish protest and anger wouldn't triumph in one fell swoop. "Fine. But we demand you answer for Duke Roland's death."

That's what I just friggin' said I would do, jag. I sat up with my spine erect on the platform, keeping my voice loud enough to carry when everyone was leaning in to listen. Draper stood between us, his arms crossed over his chest to moderate. "I'll tell you anything you want to know. Let's start with the blunt truth. Duke Roland was upset that I came back to Avalon. He saw that I was friends with Kerdik, and that I was trying to get my hands on the gems. My goal this entire time has been to return the jewels to the provinces they came from, which is what I've done. Duke

Roland misunderstood, and thought I wanted to keep them for myself."

This brought about a lot of murmuring, which was hard to talk over. Draper's hand went up, and the crowd stilled at his silent command.

"I thought that anger would've died down after the rulers who were still alive got their jewels back, but Duke Roland didn't want me anywhere near the throne."

"Neither do we!" Benoit shouted, his fist in the air. His loyalists pumped their fists in the air alongside him.

"Then why are you here? If you hate the way things are this much, then why not go back to Morgan?"

"Because this is our land, too. We won't have you chasing us out of it."

"I welcomed you here." I quirked my eyebrow at him, my thumbs playing with a thread on my skirt. "You're really that afraid of me? I've never chased anyone out of here. Lane, Draper, Damond and I opened our gates to anyone who wanted to escape from Morgan. Is there something more I'm supposed to be doing here that you're all pissed at me for?"

"Duchess Elaine left her people to look after you. *We* belong to this land more than you do, and certainly more than she does."

"Hello, King Urien told her to take me and go. At what point do you think you're so awesome that you'd flat out disobey the King of Avalon? What makes you think Duchess Elaine would tell King Urien to go screw himself? If my dad was standing here right now, and he gave you a direct command, I'd like to hear you say, 'Screw you, Urien.'" I paused for the collective gasp of the masses at the mere suggestion of such disrespect toward their beloved king. "Lane obeyed the law of the land, and you're punishing her for it. That's subjective obedience to the throne you're screaming should be protected. Is that the kind of man you want to be?"

That shut Benoit up temporarily until he found another argument he no doubt felt confident he could win. "Why was Duke Roland put to death without ceremony?" This brought about a few murmurs from the crowd.

"Because Duke Roland stabbed me three times. I'm pretty sure you all know the basic rules of the kingdom. I'm only just learning them myself, so you tell me what happens to someone who attacks the throne. Tell me what your rules state, and how we violated them."

Benoit's jaw was clenched, and he didn't speak.

Draper was standing between us with his arms crossed. I could hear the steel in his voice when he opened his mouth. "You'll answer your princess when she asks you a direct question."

Benoit's reply was grudging. He clenched his fists, and I could tell he hated that we were sitting. There was so much that could happen in the throngs of chaos, so much he could get away with. He was bigger than me when we were standing. Sitting, we were pretty much on a level playing field. "They're stripped of their title and put to death without a funeral, then buried in an unmarked grave."

I nodded. "Sucks, huh. I didn't want that for Roland. In fact, I saw to it his body was shipped off and buried with his mother and father in his family's crypt in the old Province 4." That had been a long back and forth with Draper, which thankfully, I'd won in the end. "It's not much, but no one's trying to piss you all off. The rules exist for a reason. As much as you might hate me for reasons I don't understand and can't control, we can't have people going around attacking the throne at random. Duke Roland stabbed me three times, and I'm still not sure why. He seemed angry that Duchess Lane and I came back, and even though he wanted us to restore Province 9 and unite the flailing provinces, he didn't want me on the throne." I shrugged. "I can understand that."

"We don't want you on the throne, either." He spat in my

direction, causing Abraham Lincoln to roar, and Hamish to raise his fist in anger. Several nearby villagers cursed Benoit for such a display.

I nodded, petting my bear who sat almost as tall as I was when I was standing. He'd been circling the stage, letting out chuffs of warning that he was no tame bear. My baby was getting to be such a big boy. "I'm sorry you have to deal with that, then. It's hard to live in a place where you don't like the person in charge. That happens on occasion in Common, too. I really am sorry I'm disappointing you all so much. I don't know enough about Avalon to get it all perfect." Then an idea sparked in my mind. "Could you write me a list?"

Benoit's mouth fell open. "Excuse me?"

"A list. Could you write down all the complaints about how things are being run that are upsetting to you? I can't promise I'll be able to fix them all, but I can at least listen and talk with Duchess Lane and Prince Draper and Damond about them."

Benoit was red-faced, and he spluttered several times before his words came out. "You... You're trying to turn things around! You're trying to prey on our emotions."

My nose crunched. "By listening to you? Would you rather I ignored you completely?" I harrumphed, on the edge of my waning patience. "Look, if you don't want to try and make Avalon better, then don't. But you should probably stop complaining if you're not willing to help out by at least talking about what's wrong, like a grownup. It's easy to throw a fit. Any baby can do it. Are you a baby?"

"No," Benoit spouted, his frown comically petulant.

"Actually help your country, is all I'm asking."

"We have no proof of these supposed stabbings," he argued.

I'm not sure what he was expecting, but when I stood and flipped my skirt up to reveal the knife wounds that were still on the road to healing, the entire crowd gasped. I'm not sure which was the bigger scandal – that I'd been stabbed three times by a duke, or that my thighs were on display. I empathized greatly with Britney Spears, having to prove so much of herself just because jackholes with a Twitter account demanded it. "That proof enough?" I asked Benoit with a pleasant smile on my face.

Draper lowered his chin and covered his eyes in chagrin. "That'll do, Rosie."

"How did Duke Roland die?" Benoit roared, cutting to the chase the moment I sat back down on the platform. "How terrible was his death? How gruesome? By whose hand did he breathe his last? Was there even a trial?"

Even though Mad hadn't shown up to come with me and play the dutiful fiancé, I couldn't rat him out to the angry crowd. "I did. I killed Roland." I held up my hand to stifle the shock of the crowd, and silence Draper's angry protest at my lie. My arm trembled as my nerves built, but I held my ground. The Untouchables protected me, and now it was my turn to guard them.

I heard a ripple of shock and awe as one by one, people pointed to my tattooed hand. I tried to ignore the whispers, grateful that the curls brushing my neck covered over the more noticeable tattoo. I refastened the waves that had come loose, so both tattoos were on display to the people, declaring that I was Untouchable. "You all know that my father's been in a deep sleep for twenty-one years, right?" I waited for the bobs of the heads before continuing. "Well, I don't think it's all that big a shock to tell you that Morgan poisoned him, and imprisoned him in his own body." I cleared my throat at the murmurs of sadness that held fewer gasps of surprise than I'd been expecting. "Well, Master Kerdik's been working around the clock to try and break through the spells Morgan locked King Urien with, but he couldn't. Come to find out, Roland put an extra layer of the curse on my father to keep him asleep. That's why he stabbed me; because I wouldn't go along with his threats. So he kept my father asleep – your king – as a way to make me obey."

I'd hoped a soft "Oh, snap" would break out over the crowd as realization dawned on them that Roland had many layers of deception they'd not been exposed to. However, the roars of the crowd only grew in number and in volume as outrage poured in from every angle. "No, Duke Roland would never!" was put up against, "They should've hung Roland's body from the highest tree for hurting King Urien!"

I held up my hands, and eventually the crowd calmed back down. "None of you have to take my word for it. I'm hoping my dad will be able to tell you all of this himself in another few days. He's doing his best to come back to you. I know the story sounds off, and you all don't know me well enough to just take my word for it. So don't. Wait until my dad can tell you all that Morgan was behind it. He can tell you about Duke Roland's additional poisoning, too."

Benoit glared at me. "What do you expect us to say to that?"

"Well, you can say whatever you like. I'm not Morgan. I'm not going to shut you up just because you're mean. However, I hope that Province 9 is a people that thinks with their brains, rather than follows their anger to their deaths. I'm sad Duke Roland died, too. I didn't want that for him. I just wanted to pal around with my cousin. I guess I could rage, like you and your boys all are. Make threatening signs and let my temper do the talking instead of my brain, but instead I'm trying to honor the great Province 9 that I'm trying to serve, and behave like a princess you might someday want on your throne."

"You murdered our ruler!" he shouted, as if he was upset the yelling had died down. This time, fewer shouts echoed Benoit's fury, giving him less and less fuel for his side of the discussion. I refused to call this a fight. Benoit and I were having a simple discussion, and I wouldn't let there be more to it.

I nodded, ignoring Draper's hiss that let me know he was pissed I was taking the heat. "I did. Duke Roland broke the law, so he died, exactly like the law you live under says. If you don't want to live under a law, I get that, but you can't stay here. If you let him get away with all he did behind closed doors, you'll let him destroy all Province 9 stands for."

Benoit shook his head. "You're twisting words and making it all sound like murdering Duke Roland was okay."

I let out a nervous laugh. "Believe me, there's nothing about Roland's death that was okay. You think you're unhappy about it? You lost a friend, but I lost my blood – a member of my family. I'm doing my best, here, Benny. I know you don't give two rips about me. That's fine. But I thought you would've at least cared about King Urien. He didn't deserve what Roland did to him."

Benoit's voice was less antagonistic now, seeing reason and playing the card that made sense, rather than chucking random bullets at me. "We would die for our king, but you have no proof Duke Roland was involved in his slumber."

I nodded. "And I don't expect you to blindly trust me. But I hope you'll give me just a few days, so my dad can speak for himself and tell you the truth. Can you do that for me? Listen instead of rage?"

Benoit looked out at the thousands of faces who were glaring at him, each with solid reasons that were finally starting to unite into a cohesive nation. Benoit swallowed hard before his gaze landed on me. "We can wait for King Urien to speak."

"Thanks, Benny." I took a chance, my hands shaking, and stood to my feet. I closed the gap between us and offered my hand to him, hoisting him up and wrapping him in a quick hug that shocked him too much to be able to pull out of it. It wasn't the perfect ending, but no blood had been shed, so it had to be good enough for now.

48

IF THE NOISE RISES

I didn't notice the grumbling, nor the men stalking toward us until Madigan's brogue reached my ears. "Ye don't need to lie for me, Rosie," Madigan huffed when he reached the platform with Bastien in tow. Murmurs and gasps broke out all through the peace I'd worked hard to instill in the crowd. People fell back from the revered Untouchables by the dozens. "I've got nothing to be ashamed of." Mad moved up the steps and stood in front of me, blocking my body like a wall. His rough voice shot out across the Town Square, shutting everybody up way better than I had, but with unease instead of reason.

Bastien stood behind me, his movements sluggish, his pallor grayish-green and his eyes vacant when they passed over me. He stank of cheap beer, enough to sting my nose from a few feet away. He was unshaven, rumpled and dirty, and though I'd been longing to see him, my heart sank that he clearly hadn't been rebuilding the wall, but rather tearing down his life, one drink at a time.

I put my angst on hold and decided to deal with the situation at hand. "Mad, it's fine. I handled it."

It was as if I hadn't spoken. Mad clenched his fists, and I could tell he was hungry. He always got crabby when he hadn't eaten enough. "Listen to me, ye sorry lot. I don't know why ye think your princess is someone ye can protest and complain about. I killed your precious Roland, and I took my sweet time with it. He attacked the throne of Province 9. Do ye stand for tha?"

"No!" they answered in a voice far more unified than I'd been able to draw out.

"He imprisoned King Urien. I trust ye would avenge your king if ye knew the man holding him down?"

"Yes!" they cried as one.

"Princess Rosie begged me to spare him. She's only taking the heat for me because she's a good person who thinks I need protecting." He glared over his shoulder at me, as if I'd offended him. "I don't."

I sealed my lips together to keep from getting into it with him in public. I wasn't sure what to do or say, but that mattered little when someone deep in the crowd called out *"Ionsaí!"* The war cry made no sense to me, but I stiffened all the same.

Madigan's eyes slid out of focus, and he mumbled in response what sounded like a rehearsed mantra. "If the noise rises against the Breithiúnas, the Breithiúnas silences the noise." As if suddenly not himself, Mad's spine straightened, like someone else was pulling his strings, his muscles all at once tensed to strike from neck to foot. His heels slid in and his shoulders tightened – a soldier being called to attention.

"Madigan?" I tried to call him out of his intense focus, but it was no use. Mad wasn't present anymore. In his stead trembled with rage the fearsome Madigan the Formidable, his muscles tensed with an ominous message of rip, tear, kill. "Mad? Honey, are you alright?"

"If the noise rises against the Breithiúnas, the Breithiúnas silences the noise," he repeated, this time with more fervor. It was as if my words were ricocheting off of him. His only response was the recited mantra that had made him the soldier he was.

Benoit cocked his eyebrow in confusion, as if the whole thing was one big, awkward joke. "Your Untouchable's cracked, your majesty. One too many hits to the head, I guess." Benoit spoke as if everything Mad had gone through to keep his own life and escape his country's army was a joke – as if Madigan himself was a joke.

Mad turned to Benoit and gripped the man's face in his giant hand. His long fingers had seen too many dungeons and carried out too many dark deeds. "If the noise rises against the Breithiú-nas, the Breithiúnas silences the noise."

Benoit cried out in fear that was coupled with sudden pain. His hands scrambled to remove Mad's grip from his face, but there was no stopping the Mack truck that was Madigan. "Ah!" Benoit choked out. "Help!"

But of course, no one came to Benoit's aid. The reverence for the Untouchable was the highest law, so no matter how many came out to side with Benoit's cause, they were mute now, stuck under the rule they adhered to above all else.

"Bastien, do something!" I whispered, but Bastien didn't respond. Instead he turned around and vomited right over the side of the stage, splattering a few gray chunks on the hem of my dress. It wasn't the puke of a man with the flu, but that of a frat guy at the punishing end of a drinking binge. Draper was confused at the turn the speech had taken, unsure how to step in and help.

I knew Madigan wouldn't hurt me, so I took my chance and stood up to him, moving next to Benoit's struggling form so that Mad could see my distress. "Stop, Mad! This isn't you!"

Or maybe it very much was him. He'd been a monster to Roland, but there was always the note of control behind it, his emotions never touched. This was different. Someone else was in control this time.

"If the noise rises against the Breithiúnas, the Breithiúnas silences the noise," Mad chanted, stuck on repeat, his eyes locked on Benoit's, which were bulged as he struggled fruitlessly against the brick wall that was my fake fiancé.

My hand on Mad's was a risk, but I knew this could end in a bloodbath if I didn't at least try. Mad stiffened and jerked at the light touch, his nostrils flaring that I would intrude on his personal space so publicly. "If the noise rises against the Breithiúnas, the Breithiúnas silences the noise," he warned. Then I heard a note of panic as the Madigan I knew tried to break through the command that would see him turned into an angel of death. "I can't control it, Rosie! He... He has to die. I don't know why!"

I tried to keep my voice steady, rallying when I felt Draper at my side. Abraham Lincoln meandered around the stage with his menacing stare, grunting and growling, confused that Mad and I were at odds. Hamish was on his back, chittering his opinions that Mad was in the wrong. "If you hurt Benoit, it won't solve anything."

Mad snarled at me, spittle flinging out between clenched teeth, his rage-filled eyes warning me away, lest his wrath turn on me. "If the noise rises against the Breithiúnas, the Breithiúnas silences the noise!"

His words felt like they were meant to be a slap, and I flinched accordingly. I swallowed, removing my hand from his arm, but staying close to let him know I wouldn't be bullied away. "You're hurting me with this, Mad. Please. What's going on? What's cracked you so badly?" I closed my eyes and covered my mouth when Benoit cried out after Mad's unforgiving grip gave his jaw a scary-sounding crack.

Bastien was on all fours, still uselessly puking over the side of the stage. Abraham Lincoln was worried at the state of his daddy, and galloped to Bastien's side to rest his maw on Bastien's shoulder while he puked. Hamish pounded on Bastien's butt, scolding him to pull it together already.

Draper started quickly directing the crowd to go on home and wait to hear from the king, now that an agreement had been reached. Abraham Lincoln turned from Bastien and moved to my side, howling at Mad to get away from his mommy.

There was no one else to save Benoit. Even his buddies who protested me alongside him were fleeing in the crowd to escape being associated with him and incurring more of Mad's wrath. I threw what little caution I had left in me to the wind and ducked under Madigan's outstretched arm, pushing my back to Benoit, so I could get in between them. I stared Madigan down as calmly as I could. "Sweetheart, you have to stop this. Let him go."

Madigan only squeezed harder, angry that I was trying to sway him otherwise. "If the noise rises against the Breithiúnas, the Breithiúnas silences the noise."

I shook my head, begging him with my eyes to see reason. "You do this, and the people will never trust me. Please, Mad! I don't understand what snapped! The man who shouted at you, what did he say to you that set you off? What did that word mean? This isn't you!" Though, part of me wondered how true that statement was, and how much of it was wishful thinking.

The voice in the crowd that had started all the chaos boomed out again in a sinister voice that had the grating edge of something metallic to it, "*Ionsaí*, soldier! Kill the princess, Madigan!"

I tried to locate the source of the command, but the people were in a frenzied state of get-me-the-crap-outta-here, so it was hard to make heads or tails of anything. All I saw was a person in a black hood, face hidden, but nothing more descriptive or specific than that.

I screamed when Benoit's neck snapped, turning his head forcefully to the side to stare and gape at me with his last exhale. His body fell limply to the wood floor of the stage with no protest to it, and no life, either. I had no words, no plan, and no fiancé that I recognized.

Mad's eyes narrowed on me, torn between attacking and issuing me a fear-laced warning. "If the noise rises against the... Run, Rosie!" Mad bellowed, warning me that he was the danger, and there was no protecting me against a force like him. He was no longer an island of a man who was under his own control, but rather a lost soldier – dancing while someone else pulled the strings.

"Draper, take out that guy!" I pointed my finger into the crowd, hoping dude was wearing a neon t-shirt that said "I'm the bad guy." I knew I couldn't win a fistfight with Mad, so I did what came natural to me. I flung myself into his arms, hoping my hug would soften him. Somewhere inside of me, I believed my love was stronger than what I was guessing must be the deeply engrained mind control of a soldier who'd been twisted, perhaps beyond repair. "Please, Mad!"

He held tight to me for a few panicked seconds, but then shoved me so he could deliver the heaviest backhand of my life. My body dropped on all fours, my cheekbone throbbing in time with my heartbeat. I heard the people screaming around me, and knew I couldn't allow myself to feel the pain until the insanity was over.

I thought I knew what fear was, but until Mad grabbed me by the back of the neck, I'd severely underestimated what I'd thought was the peak of that particular emotion. His grip was so steely, I couldn't move my head, but stared up at him blankly with my mouth open in shock. He pulled me back so I could take in the full breadth of his roar. "If the noise rises against the Breithiúnas, the Breithiúnas silences the noise!"

"Madigan, stop!" I choked out, my trembling hands clawing at my fiancé's arm. People were fleeing now, and I could hear women crying their fear in the streets.

Mad wouldn't hurt me. I just knew he couldn't once he calmed down and saw reason again. Both of Mad's hands curled around my throat, covering the raw tattoo that matched his own. My engagement ring hung on a chain around my neck, the gold shining out at him and meaning absolutely nothing. A brand new terror engulfed me when his thumbs closed around my windpipe. His eyes closed in dread and fear as he whispered a scared, "If the noise rises against the Breithiúnas, the Breithiúnas silences the noise."

I heard Draper shouting into the crowd, trying to get to the mystery man who was calling the shots. He no doubt figured, as I had, that Madigan wasn't in control of himself, but rather someone else was calling the shots. If we wanted Mad to stop, the ghost who'd started the chaos would have to be located.

My eyes bulged when Mad squeezed tighter. My hands scrambled to find purchase on his beefy arms. I wouldn't let my last moments be spent accepting the inevitable, but I would fight for my life – the life I hardly recognized anymore.

"She's wearing your mark!" Draper cried, frantic when my eyelids started to droop. My brother shouted toward the stage from his spot in the crowd, torn as to where he would be most useful. "Bastien, get up and tell him!" But Bastien didn't come to my aid. He was passed out on the stage in a puddle of his own puke. I barely recognized how he could be the man I loved. If this would be my last image of my boyfriend, it was a crushing one, for sure.

I pulled an image of Judah into my brain, on one of our road trips back to home on break from school, singing our favorite songs from Lost and Forgotten's extensive music catalog at the top of our lungs.

I planted a mental picture of Lane painting my toenails as I painted hers. I must've told a funny joke, because she laughed so hard, she snorted. I loved it when I made her do that. If this would be my final moment, that was a perfect note to go out on – the sound of Lane's happy snort.

Abraham Lincoln decided he understood enough of the situation to choose sides, once he ruled out the possibility that we were just playing with each other. He roared out a cry of *"Don't touch my momma!"* before Hamish leapt off of Abraham Lincoln's back to attack Madigan.

As if in slow motion, I watched as Mad caught my brave squirrel, shook him like a rag doll, tossed him onto the platform and stomped his boot down on my Hamish's head.

I couldn't scream – my throat was too damaged, but Abraham Lincoln's roar more than made up for my muted howl. It was then that my bear turned truly animal, sinking his teeth into Mad's calf muscle. Madigan howled, dropping me to the wooden platform like a sack of potatoes. I sucked down air and tried not to drown myself in my own tears, which fell freely down my face.

Draper fought his way back to me, scooped me up and ran me to the coach while Madigan palmed the wooden floor of the platform. He heaved like a beast, trying to decide if he was going to fight or stand down. My heartbeat stuttered when I looked over Draper's shoulder and saw the brawl that turned from man-on-man, to man-on-woman, to man-on-beast as Madigan surrendered to the ghost in the crowd's command. I tried to call out for Abraham Lincoln to run away, now that I was breathing, but I couldn't manage more than a rasp.

The sound of my bear's howl through the air lit my spine on fire. I fought with everything in me to get out of the coach Draper wrestled me into, and run to Abraham Lincoln. The curtain swished as we jolted down the path past the fleeing citizens.

I screamed mutely when my eyes took in the horror I could not comprehend.

Madigan's long, arched blade sunk deep into Abraham Lincoln's side. My baby swung his massive paws through the air, but they didn't hit with the precision they needed to. My silent scream ripped through my injured throat when my precious protector fell with a final chilling roar, lifeless next to my squirrel at Madigan's feet.

49

THUMBPRINTS ON MY THROAT

*T*he coachman wasted no time driving the horses back to the mansion. So deep was the mind control, that Madigan ran after us, as if willing his muscles to be stronger than two horses. It gave us enough time to get into the castle and bolt the doors. I tried screaming for Link, but my throat was still hoarse. Draper picked up the slack and barked "Link!" through the overlarge house.

Link trotted down the hallway, as if he had nothing but time to kill. His laid-back shoulders stiffened when he saw my bedraggled state and the no doubt red marks around my throat. "What happened, wee Rose?"

I pointed to the front door. Though we had a good distance on Mad, he was determined to end me, so I wasted no time, but whispered the story as loudly as I could. "Mad hulked out and turned super soldier! Someone in the crowd shouted out a weird word, and he turned into this maniac who couldn't stop saying this 'If the noise rises, blah, blah, blah' mantra. Then he killed a man in front of the whole province, and tried to choke me out!"

Draper's fingers feathered on my neck, checking me for the third time since we'd escaped. "You're alive," he breathed, and then repeated the nervous declaration a few more times to reassure himself.

Link was on high alert, his shoulders tensed, and no trace of the smile I loved anywhere in sight. "Someone triggered Mad? And they told him to kill ye? How did ye escape?"

"Barely, that's how. Hamish and Abraham Lincoln threw themselves into the fight, and Mad murdered them! Mad murdered my baby and my friend!" I croaked out in a mournful bleat of agony. "He's trying to fight it, I can tell, but he can't! He's running here now to kill me."

Link took in the tears on my face and cleared the distance between us so he could press a kiss to my forehead. "It's alright, sweet lass. I'll handle it from here."

I clung to Link's shirt, afraid to let him go. "Don't hurt him! It's not him who tried to kill me. I saw the switch. Mad didn't know what he was doing."

"I know. Shh. You'll stay tucked in here. Maybe go wait with Master Kerdik and your Da." He patted my back twice. "Ye might want to lock yourself in the room with them, just to be safe. I can talk Mad down, but sometimes there are flare-ups." He turned to Draper. "Alert the staff to lock themselves in rooms until I come around with the 'all clear'. Then lock yourself up, too."

Draper wasted no time with questions. He ran to the kitchen, shouting the command as he went. I limped to my dad's bedroom, startling Jean-Luc, my dad and Kerdik with my disheveled state as I ambled into the room, followed by the slammed door. When Draper joined us, I bolted the door and sank to the floor, my back to the wood. I tried to tell myself I was safe, and everything would be okay.

The three men wanted answers, but I could barely work out how it all went so far south. It took a few tries before the whole story came out. I hugged my knees to my chest and tried not to fall apart.

"And he's on his way here now?" Kerdik questioned, with no room in his tone for mercy.

"You can't hurt him, Kerdik. Mad didn't know what he was doing. Someone else was controlling him."

"I realize that, but until Link can break through the barrier in his mind, you're at risk." Kerdik knelt in front of me, examining my face as he tucked a few strands of hair behind my ear. He leaned in and kissed the sore spot on my tearstained cheek. "I'll take care of it."

I didn't want to voice how frightening the whole thing was, so I simply clung to Kerdik's shirt collar, bringing him closer so I could wrap my quaking arms around his neck.

"Get my sword," my dad commanded in a tone that was every bit as regal as it was brutal.

"No! You'll hurt him, and that's not what I want. Or worse, he'll hurt you. He's huge, Dad."

Kerdik remained in control of his temper and the whole situation, which surprised me. "I won't hurt your little friend, but I'll contain him until Link can calm him down." He fingered my chin and lifted it to expose my throat, his gaze hardening when he saw the deep thumbprint impressions Mad's hands had left on my tender skin. "No, no. That won't do." Then he stood, bent over and scooped me up off the floor like I was a legit princess. Kerdik was strong, and in that moment, I felt weak, and so very, very small.

Being small requires a fair amount of trust in the people you let into your heart. With that small gesture of carrying me in his arms, I realized that I trusted Kerdik more than I'd ever meant to. When life grew unrecognizable, Kerdik let me hold tight to him. What's more remarkable is that *I* allowed *myself* the freedom to cling to the person I needed.

"Jean-Luc, see to her injuries," Kerdik instructed as he sat me on the bed. "I'll be right back."

"I'm coming with you," my dad said, his gait sturdier than it had been before I left.

Kerdik and I were of the same mind. "No, you'll stay here."

My dad's chest puffed, indignant. "You're not the king, Kerdik. You don't tell me what to do."

Kerdik managed a smile. "See, that's the thing about you being you, and me being me. You'll stay where I put you, and be grateful you're not going to risk your life against an Untouchable who's come unhinged." With that, Kerdik exited. The second he shut the door, the space between the door and the jamb immediately filled with concrete that hardened in seconds. I heaved a sigh of relief that he'd sealed us inside.

My dad whirled around, livid. "I am not useless! I can fight for my own daughter when she's attacked."

"Kerdik loves you," I explained, unapologetic.

My dad's eyes fell on me as Jean-Luc started prying at my neck with gentle fingers. "No, darling. Kerdik loves you."

* * *

We waited in suspended silence for too many minutes before Kerdik finally disintegrated the concrete that held us in place. My voice was a little raspy, but I managed to make myself heard over the din of voices that demanded explanations. "Is everyone okay?"

Kerdik nodded, walking past Jean-Luc and my dad to take my hand. He pulled me up to stand before him, again tipping my chin back so he could examine my throat. "Apparently there's a safe word that works, but not fast enough for an immediate switch. Madigan's still coming down from the frenzy he's worked himself up into. We moved him to the dungeon, though, so it's safe for everyone to move about the house."

My mouth formed a tight line. "Is anyone with him?"

"No. He's locked securely. He doesn't need a warden. I'll go get him out in an hour or so, once we're absolutely sure he's himself again."

"Okay. I'm going down to wait it out with him."

Urien, Draper, Kerdik and Jean-Luc all shook their heads. "No," my father ruled. "He tried to kill you. You'll stay on this floor. I don't want you venturing near the basement."

"I wasn't actually asking for permission to move around my own house, guys."

My father frowned imperiously. "I wasn't giving you any."

I sighed heavily. "He's my fake fiancé. I'm not going to leave him in a dungeon by himself. He's probably scared out of his mind down there."

Urien pinched the bridge of his nose, no doubt wondering if it was too soon to lay down the law with me. "Take someone with you, then. If this is how your heart bends, I accept it."

I'd been working my way up to hugging my dad. Morgan had been so adverse to physical affection. I was afraid to step on the wrong landmine and set him off, hurtling my father farther away from me than I could ever bring him back. But when he made it clear that I could be who I was, just with a little added protection, I found I couldn't hold back any longer. My arms wrapped around his waist, my ear pressing to his chest so I could hear the steady thrum of his heart. It didn't seem to beat with any ill will toward me.

Oh, that I could explain the wonder that it is to be held together by your father. He was strong when I was frazzled, protective when I had no sense of self-preservation. He was loving when I'd been throttled by the man I was supposed to be in love with. Urien was my father, and one single, solid inhale in his arms spackled together the cracks my heart had been operating with since I'd been a child.

"Thank you for letting me be myself. This really is important to me."

His hands remained out from his body for a solid three

seconds, letting me know he was a little stunned at the outburst of physical affection. Slowly his arms found their way around me, tightening and holding me to him with more emotion than even I put forth. When I moved to pull away, he held me in place. "Just a few seconds longer. You have no idea… I never dreamed that I'd get you back, and that when I did, that you'd be as loving and warmhearted as the woman standing before me now. I am the luckiest of all the fathers in all the worlds."

I let out a toneless chuckle. "You've been frozen for two decades, and you still see yourself as lucky?"

"Of course I do. I have you. What further luck could any father need?"

I beamed up at him. He was suddenly the kindness I knew my world would refuse to spin without, now that I knew the draw he had on my heart. "I'll be back up, once I'm sure Mad's okay."

"Be safe, darling. Take one of the guys with you."

I didn't want to argue with him and tell him I was twenty-two now. I was capable of defending my own honor, and throwing my own punches. Instead I smiled at my dad for being overprotective. I let him shelter me and do what good fathers are supposed to do. If he was going to allow me to be myself, then I should allow him to be himself. "Okay, Dad."

Urien placed his hand over his heart, like the simple act of naming him his rightful role had thrown a dagger of permanence through his heart.

Yes, I could get used to having a dad.

50

CHILDHOOD TRIGGERS

$\mathcal{T}$he dungeon was dank, despite mine and Reyn's best efforts to make the place an area children would want to be. After Roland's blood had been spilled there, it didn't have the same possibility I'd seen in it before. I wondered if the dungeon had changed, or if it had been me who'd lost the function of play.

My gimpy footsteps echoed down the long aisle that rested between the two rows of cells. My gold sandals had been traded in for sturdy black work boots, and my dress was exchanged for my usual jeans and a fitted white t-shirt. My hair was twisted in a knot on the top of my head, and I was careful none of the wayward curls dripped down into the bowl of stew I was carrying on a tray for Madigan.

"Go away," I heard him growl from his cell at the end of the row.

I nodded to Link, who gave me a sullen wave with only half a smile. It was a sad day that muted an entire half of Link's charming grin. "I'll go away after I see you eat a few bites."

As I neared the lantern that was set on a hook on the wall at the end of the aisle, I saw Madigan sitting in a cell in the far corner, his back to Link and his eyes trained on the concrete wall at the back of the cell. His knees were hugged to his chest, and for all the enormous The Rock-ness I'd always attributed to Madigan, in that moment, he looked like a sullen child, sent to the corner for bad behavior. "Take your tray and go."

My eyes cut to Link, who shrugged as if to say this was par for the course. "I don't think you want to turn up your nose at stew this good. I usually don't feed the prisoners anything more than spider webs and gruel sandwiches."

"Gruel sandwiches?" Link inquired, perking up. His arms were still folded over his chest, but he sat a little straighter on his stool that was positioned against the locked cell. "Got anything for me on that tray?"

"Not a bite. My fiancé eats first. I'm old-fashioned like that. In fact, I'm so set in my oppressed female ways that I'm not going to eat anything until my future husband has the first bite. As my official monkey, you don't eat until Mad tries his stew, either."

"Shut your gob, Rosie. Link can do what he likes."

Link put on a show of pouting. "I should've opted to be the one to fake marry ye. Then I could be eating stew by the bucket."

"Quiet, monkey," I admonished him with a wink. The small motion was slightly painful from Mad's sturdy backhand. I hoped I wouldn't have a shiner in the morning. "How under the influence are you, Mad? Like, you're yourself again?"

Mad didn't turn to us – I doubt he even blinked when he answered with a toneless, "Aye."

"Then I'm coming inside. Set your Tasers on stun."

"I told ye to go away."

I looked around for the keys, and found them dangling from Link's fingers, a wicked gleam on his face. "*Now* who's the monkey?" he asked, jangling the keys. "A bite of stew as payment for your entry, lass."

"You can get your own stew. Mercy's making a giant pot in the kitchen. Give me a minute with my fake fiancé."

Link sniffed the beefy broth with a gluttonous sigh. "I don't think your Da would want ye down here without protection."

I quirked an eyebrow with probably too much attitude laced in. "You protect each other, not me. If you cared about me, you would've told me my boyfriend was off on a week-long bender. Instead you covered for him while I limped around the mansion, pining after him like a chump." I cocked my eyebrow at him, my lips tightening. "In case you didn't realize it, you and I are fighting."

Link blew out a loud gust of air that I'd finally cottoned on to what they'd all been hiding from me. "I was hoping ye wouldn't find out. Bastien's not used to living with other people. He's used to being able to go on a drunk for as long as he pleases without it affecting anyone. He doesn't often do it unless life gets as grim as it is now. He's been doing so much better since he met ye. He'll come back around. He just lost his mate in the worst way."

"I'm not talking about him; I'm talking about you. You protected Bastien, not me. I can handle myself around Mad. I know he would never really hurt me."

Link hung his head, but Madigan scoffed. "How can ye say tha? I nearly killed ye, Rosie. Ye have hardly any friends, and I snuffed out two of them right in front of ye." The muscles in Madigan's neck tightened. "Abraham Lincoln was a useful bear, too. I didn't want to hurt them, but I saw myself put out their lights. The whole thing makes me... Just go away."

Balancing the tray in one hand, I snatched the key from Link's deflated grip and jammed it into the lock. "I'm in this, okay? You can't flip a switch like that and then expect me to just take it and skulk off with my shame. If I'm going to stand by you through all of this, you can't treat me like an outsider."

"Ye are an outsider. Ye can't possibly know what it's like to be Untouchable."

I slid into the cell, setting the tray down in the far corner before I moved over to him and sat by his side, facing the concrete wall. "Then tell me. Tell me how I almost died because of a word. Tell me what we're up against."

"'We' aren't up against anything. It's me and Link, and sometimes Bastien when we're in Avalon."

I held up my hand to show him my tattoo, and then fingered the tender spot on my neck. "Think again, chief. Be as Untouchable as you want, but whoever sprung you into action out there today knew he couldn't get you to kill me without triggering you. He knows I'm in this. Tell me why I almost died, Mad. I think that, of all the ways I could be a pain to you right now, I deserve to know that small detail, at least."

I let my words settle between us, not speaking anything further, so Mad would know the ball was still in his court, and I was going to just friggin' leave it there for him to puzzle with. Link moved into the cell and sat down on my other side, facing the wall with us, and waiting.

I couldn't tell you how many minutes I waited, staring at the wall between Mad and Link before Madigan finally broke. "I was taken from my mammy when I was too young to remember her. I like to pretend her name was Sheila, but it could well be Bertha, and I wouldn't know."

I turned over his words before speaking softly. "Sheila's a nice name. Who took you from her?"

"Éireland's army had a radical faction not many know about. They wanted to create soldiers who would be worth more to the queen. They decided we should be groomed from childhood, instead of volunteering when we came of age. I was raised in a commune with a bunch of other lads who didn't know their mammies."

I didn't want to speak, for fear of saying the wrong thing and making the wounded animal retreat back into his hole of solitude. Link was stock-still, looking straight ahead at the wall, his eyes wide at the rarity that was Madigan opening up. Finally, I managed a gentle, "That sounds awful."

"Aye. We didn't know it could be any different, though." He looked at his hands, turning his palm up so I could see it. "The woman who fed us wore mittens with briars on them. When she'd pat us on the heads, it would scrape us and draw blood. Taught us to hate touch from a young age. Smart."

My heart clinched in my chest. "Do you still hate it, or do you just think it's going to hurt each time? Do you still feel the briars?"

He squeezed his hand a few times. "I don't know. It didn't hurt when Meara touched me. Sometimes Link or Bastien or the other lads bump my shoulder, hug me, or slap my hand. Tha doesn't hurt. Everything else feels wrong, though."

I nodded. "That makes sense. So the woman who fed you, did she have a name?"

Mad shook his head, not seeing the shadows on the wall in front of him, but more plagued by the flickers of a life that never seemed to leave his mind. "No. She wasn't allowed to get too close to us. The soldiers were afraid she'd soften us, turn us weak. The weak ones were killed off, so I didn't get close to her." When I didn't chime in with a question or anything to say, Mad continued. "They didn't tolerate flaws. They didn't allow emotions. If one of us failed a task, we were given one more chance. If we failed then, one of us had to kill the failure. 'Failures don't fly to greatness,'" he said in monotone, and I could tell he was quoting some mantra or something that was too deeply engrained to iron itself out over time. "The other lads didn't have the stomachs for killing, so I usually did it. When I escaped the compound, and offered myself to Éireland's army with Link, the commander noticed my unique talents."

When Madigan stopped talking, Link picked up the trail. "They made him carry out the torture he'd tried to run away from. At first it was one insurgent who needed a reckoning. Then a few more. Before long, Mad was being used exactly as the compound he'd left had intended. He was a killing machine, and nothing more. So we fought our way out together and never looked back." His eyes darted to mine. "I think tha earns me a fair bit of his stew. He's not going to touch it."

When Link reached for the tray, I slapped his hand. "Not on your life, monkey. His story's worse. Mad gets the stew."

Link harrumphed dramatically. "I was sometimes sent to bed without sweets when I was a wee lad. Tha has to get me at least a bite."

"You let me be afraid for Bastien while he was out drinking himself into the toilet. You can go hungry tonight."

Link slumped next to me, dejected that I wasn't about to let him off the hook, simply because he was adorable and impish. "You're still sore about tha?"

"We're not talking about Bastien or you." I turned my attention back to Madigan. "I didn't realize touch actually hurt you. I'm sorry I hugged you so tight at my coronation. I know I said so before, but I didn't realize all that went into it. I shouldn't have been so inconsiderate."

Mad shook his head. "And I told ye before, you've no need to apologize for tha." He glanced at my hand. "After tha day, it didn't hurt when ye touched me anymore."

I stared at him, confused at the rules I didn't fully understand. "Oh, well that's good to know. Can I... Can I hold your hand then?"

Mad glanced at me sideways, wary of my offer. "Why?"

"Because you've had a hard day. I want to be your friend, and this is what friends do for each other. If I had a hard day, I'd want someone to care about me enough to sit in a dank cell and hold my hand until it didn't hurt so much." I extended my hand, palm up, in case he wanted to take me up on my offer. I knew that if I just reached out and took his hand, Mad would withdraw. It had to be his choice to let me be there for him, or all of this progress would be for nothing.

It took another minute of me holding my breath, but after a

few false starts, Madigan reached out and closed the gap between us. His larger mitt swallowed my hand in his, but for some reason, it finally felt like we were equals. No matter what he'd been through, and what darkness was certain to lie ahead, it was a comfort to both of us that he knew he had me to lean on. I vowed that I would be strong enough and gentle enough to be there for a man as formidable as Madigan.

My fake fiancé examined my hand in his, turning it over like he was searching for hidden truths in my knuckles. "I don't know who it was out there who triggered me, or why he'd want me to kill ye. But you're not safe around me anymore."

I bristled at the insinuation that I couldn't handle myself, or that Madigan was a monster who couldn't be calmed. "I'm no less safe with you than I am with Kerdik or Bastien or any of the other magical creatures. I'm fine. You barely even hurt me."

This brought life to Mad's stony features. "Pfft. Ye have to know how much shite tha is. I nearly killed ye. As soon as I get myself together, I'll be leaving Province 9."

Our gentle handholding turned into a hard grip from me. "I've got the feeling that if Mr. Black Hood wants me dead, proximity isn't a huge issue. Can't he just control you wherever you go, send you after me, and that's that? I don't think being away from people who care about you is the solution."

Link wrapped his arm around my waist and scooted closer. "Listen to the wee lass. Running's no way to handle this. We can't hide forever, Mad."

Madigan moved his eyes back to the wall. "*We* wouldn't be going, Link. Ye would stay here while I go sort out what's left of the compound. I thought we killed them all, but if someone out there knows my trigger word, I must've missed someone. I'm not safe to be around."

Link stiffened. "You're daft if ye think I'm letting ye go off on a spree without me. We're brothers. Your fight is my fight." He looked over me to Mad and nodded. "To the death."

"If someone survived from the compound, then it just might be your death." Mad traced his thumb over mine, examining how it felt to be touched and to touch without agenda or pain. "When we became Untouchable, Link and I went back to the compound. We pulled out the wee lads, sent them off with a healer, bolted the doors and burned the rest." He shook his head. "We should've done a count. I assumed they'd all be there because it was the third day of the harvest moon. I shoulda counted the men."

Link moved his grip from my hip to latch onto Mad's tricep. "We'll find him, brother. One gnat's nothing to stomp out. But going it alone isn't the way. If they get ahold of ye, you'll be the weapon they always dreamed ye would be." His hand migrated back to my hip and squeezed. "If tha should happen again, the safe word is 'Meara'. Say her name over and over, and he comes back to himself."

I looked from Link to Mad and back again. "At what point am I allowed to ask about Meara? Like, who she is and what ever happened to her?"

"Never," Mad ruled. "Ye don't need another reason to be afraid."

325

51

RETURNING BASTIEN

*W*e'd progressed to Madigan finally taking a bite from the stew, though I'm pretty sure he only did this to shut Link up. Link grinned when Mad started to eat, and I gathered that Link hadn't really been after the stew for himself, only to goad Mad into eating. They had a strange friendship, but after all they'd been through, I couldn't begrudge them a little weirdness. Heck, Judah and I used to do rap battles in our PJs, so no judgement from me.

When I was satisfied that Mad was enough on the mend that I could take care of business elsewhere, I stood. "Link, if you've got things from here, I'm going back out."

"Back out where? The only place you're safe is the mansion, so I'd keep your adventures indoors."

"I believe I left my former boyfriend in a puddle of his own puke. Not sure that's the best place for him."

Link hung his head. "Don't go ending things because he's had a rough go of it."

"There's nothing left to end. He bailed. He's told me over and over how much he doesn't know how to do relationships, and I think I finally heard him."

"His mate died after trying to kill his lady. Cut him some slack."

I don't know why this, of all things, made me bristle. As I rolled my shoulders back, I looked down on Link with an unemotional glare that kept my broken heart far from view. "Not to be all dramatic, but I almost died today, and my knight in shining armor was too drunk to give a crap. I don't need him to save every day, but today? I needed him to save the day today. He knows Mad's safe word, I'm guessing?"

Link nodded, while Mad hung his head. "Aye. All the Untouchables know it. We're the ones who helped train him to respond to it."

I shoved my hands in my pockets. "All Bastien had to do was say a word, and he wasn't sober enough for even that. He's the one who left me. I'm the idiot girlfriend who's picking his sorry butt up and dragging him home. I'll get him sober, and then he can go back to the glorious hermit life he's been missing so much. I'm guessing no one nags him to stay sober there. Dream come true for all involved." I held up my hand to stave off Link's protest. "It's done. I could barely walk after being stabbed, and he didn't give a crap. I was so stupid, thinking how selfish I was being that I wanted him home with me instead of rebuilding the wall."

Link shook his head. "Rosie, you're being rash. Ye have no idea what it's like to be Untouchable."

I bit down on my lower lip, but the venom bubbled out of me nonetheless. "You're right. I wasn't a child soldier, and I didn't fight in a corrupt queen's army. I was only ripped from my parents the second I was old enough to walk, and then taken from my home again to come deal with the mess in Avalon. I was only stripped down and thrown into a well by my mother. I was only stabbed by my cousin after the first time he'd tried killing me on the Cheval Mallet didn't work. I was only..." I inhaled through my nose, frustrated with myself that I was getting

327

worked up into a tirade. "Everyone's got a reason to drink themselves stupid! I'm not going to begrudge Bastien his reasons or his choices. But I think I'm worth a guy who can bring himself to utter a single word if it'll save my life. Not to oversell myself, but I'm worth a man who'll stick around after I've been stabbed!" I started talking with my hands – a sure sign I was too upset. "I shouldn't have to even say that! Neither of you are Judah! Neither of you are Lane. I wouldn't have to explain anything so obvious to anyone who actually gave a crap about me."

"Ye don't understand," Mad said quietly, towering over me with no sign of his usual intimidation scowl. He looked a mixture of sick and frantic to undo Bastien's crimes. The Brotherhood loved each other, that was for certain.

Link opened his mouth to add his two cents, but I held up my hands to stop him. "I don't need to hear it. It's fine. Bros before hos. I get it completely. The Brotherhood's been through a lot. I'm not asking for anything from you two. You can have Bastien back."

Link watched me with sad eyes. "Bastien loves ye, Rosie."

I managed a shrug I didn't feel. "Yeah? Then where is he? I almost died today, and where is this almighty prince charming? Is he out picking me flowers so I'll have something pretty to look at while I heal up? Is he slaying dragons in my name? Is he... Is he laying in a pile of his own puke in the middle of Town Square, mere feet away from where I almost died?" I wrapped myself in a hug I didn't feel, but knew I needed. "Even before I was a princess, I knew I deserved better than that. And shame on both of you for trying to make me believe I don't. I love Bastien, but if he loved me, he'd be here."

Before Link could convince me otherwise, I spun on my heel and walked out of the cell and down the aisle. I was unwilling to listen to an argument that would only make me feel worse, and somehow leave me even more alone.

I limped up the steps from the dungeon and ran smack into

Kerdik, who had the look of an eavesdropper about him. His arms secured themselves around me, squeezing me tight. "I'll go out and bring him home," he said with an air of darkness to him.

"No. He should be where he wants to be. He wants to be lying in a puddle of his own puke, so that's where he should be. He's my responsibility, not yours." I held my chin up, unwilling to break down. After everything, I wouldn't let this be the thing that dissolved me into a crying mess. "I swear, I'm fine. I just feel stupid because I thought he was out rebuilding the wall and being all selfless and altruistic. How did I not see this sooner? Am I really that stupid?" My buzz word hit me hard, sinking into my chest where I knew it would truly smart.

"No, darling. You believe the best in people. That's admirable, not stupid."

I gave a light "pfft." "Feels about the same on this end. Did you know?" My gaze up at him turned penetrating when I saw the hesitation in his eyes. "You knew?"

"I didn't know the extent of it, but yes, I knew he wasn't out rebuilding the wall."

"Where was he? How is the city barely rebuilt, but there's already a functioning pub?"

"The people know what they need. They've been through a lot. They want a place to drown their troubles in booze and women."

For a brief moment, my world stopped turning. "'Booze and women'? This pub, there's women there? Like Draper's kind of women?"

My brother's voice sounded from down the hall where he'd come from the kitchen. He chomped down on an apple with a disapproving squint. "Hey, now. I've got nothing to do with the tavern in Province 9. They set that up entirely on their own with no help from me. My girls were top shelf in the Lost Village. A lot of the women they have for rent here aren't the type you'd go visiting twice." He shook his head. "Rookie mistake. Repeat business was my bread and butter." He took in my gaping mouth and guessed he'd missed the more important part of the conversation. "Why are you looking at me like that?"

Kerdik closed his eyes as if Draper's presence pained him. "I'm sure Bastien was only drinking there. I'm sure he wasn't sleeping around."

"Does Lane know there's a brothel in her province?"

Draper shook his head. "Of course not. It only just opened its doors earlier this week. Shutting it down is on my list of things to do, but waking Uncle Urien up took top precedence, don't you think? I was getting around to it, Ro."

My fists clenched at my sides, and I was surprised the earth wasn't trembling beneath my feet with all the rage that swirled up inside of me. So much for feigning indifference. "Take me to the tavern, so I can see who my boyfriend's been spending his time in bed with."

Draper swallowed a partially chewed bite of his apple, the color draining from his face. "Oh, man. I didn't realize." He rolled his shoulders back and lifted his chin. "I'll go get Bastien, Rosie. I'll bring him home."

"Don't bother. I'm going. I want to see this thriving enterprise. This is my province, too, right? I should know what's going on in my own country."

Kerdik's hand on my shoulder only infuriated me. "I'll go."

I shook off his touch, bristling that *now* he was offering his help. *Now* he would step up, after everything I'd been going through, being worried about my poor boyfriend overworking himself. "No! You were supposed to be my best friend here. You knew that Bastien was screwing around behind my back, and you said nothing?"

Kerdik held up his hands in surrender to my swinging temper. "I only knew he'd been out drinking instead of working. You told me I wasn't allowed to hurt anyone anymore, so I stayed out of it."

My glare did its best to cut him at the flimsy logic he offered. I flipped my hair over my shoulder and tried to keep my voice even. "Fine. Come on, Draper. Let's go see all that Bastien's been up to."

Draper and Kerdik exchanged a wary look, but I was already halfway to the back door.

52

A SPANKING FROM DRAPER

*D*raper kept me tight to his side as we stalked through the night in our hooded black cloaks. The lantern in his fist shed the bare amount of light on our path, but luckily, I didn't trip and injure my janky legs even more. "I think it's this way," he suggested, motioning to the left.

My gut tugged me in the opposite direction. "I think you're leading us in circles. I think you know exactly where it is, but you're stalling."

Draper let out a deep sigh. "Man, I don't know how you get me this easily. So much for being a creature of mystery."

"I've got enough mystery in my life. Time to solve the case of the missing boyfriend."

As I suspected, Draper knew exactly where the tavern was. The building had been quickly erected, and lacked a few creature comforts that I'm sure would be added in later. The roughly hewn wood structure looked more like a two-story barn with a bar on the first floor, and stall-like rooms on the second story. Most of the rooms had only three walls, so when you looked up from the main floor, you could see directly into the bedrooms to get yourself a good show while you drank. I gaped at the sight of

HBO unplugged going on in four of the eight stalls above me. As if he thought I was six years old, Draper cuffed his hand over my eyes and pressed my nose to his chest to shield me from the rated-R sights.

I limped over to the bartender and placed my hands on the bar, my hood shrouding most of my face. He had a busted lip, and dark greasy hair pulled back in a ponytail. His mustache was waxed, and looked ripe for twirling, like a true comic book villain. Maybe I was projecting a little, but of all the dudes I'd met thus far, this one looked fit to run a whorehouse. He looked right past me and up at Draper. "Prince Draper, at last." He motioned to himself before reaching out and shaking Draper's hand. "I'm Gustav. I was wondering when you'd stop by. You looking for a drink or a girl?"

Draper didn't miss a beat. "I'll take whatever girl Bastien the Bold had last. Can't go wrong with a girl who's serviced a warrior."

The bartender gave him an evil laugh. "That'll be Ruby. She just finished with him a few minutes ago, actually, but after she cleans up, I'll send her down to you. What can I get you and your servant to drink while you wait?" His eyes finally fell to me, but he couldn't see me seething beneath the black hood that cast a shadow over half my face.

Draper chuckled, his hand on my shoulder to steady me. "Bastien the Bold is here, then?"

Gustav pointed up to one of the stalls that appeared empty. "Came straight here after the upset in Town Square. Had a few drinks, some time with Ruby, and now he's sleeping it off in one of my beds up there. Not the quietest place in the province, but he seems to need the bed more than most." He bowed his head to Draper with a smile that made my skin crawl. "We do what we can to keep the Untouchables and royals happy."

"Thanks, Gustav. I think I'll just wait here for a word with the war hero when he wakes."

Gustav eyed me, though he could only see my fingers, a sliver of my body where the draping of the cloak gapped, and my chin. "If your servant's looking for a job while you're occupied with Ruby, I can set her up with a line of men who'd pay handsomely for a girl who's not so... seasoned."

I'm not sure why that was it, but that little comment crossed my threshold of tolerance. With hands that shook with rage, I tore back my black hood and let my stray curls fall like autumn leaves around my face. My determined eyes met Gustav's, and I watched with satisfaction as all the color drained from his face. "Say that again. Tell me exactly who you'd like to sell me off to."

A drunk guy at the end of the bar held up two fingers. "I'd pay a fair amount for an hour with that." He got up and ambled past me with all the grace of a toddler, drink in hand while he smacked my butt with the other. He leered down at my breasts, and I saw the glaze of I-won't-remember-this-night about him. "Nice and bouncy, just how I like them."

I didn't have much patience for being grabbed at. The guys on the teams I played on all understood that. I reached for my quick and anchored left hook, which rarely ever failed me in situations such as these. I swung with too much rage, decking the dude so hard, he dropped his drink.

Draper was usually a man with total control over his temper, but perhaps that was because I compared most tempers to Kerdik's, which swung hard and fast in whatever direction it pleased. In a move so quick, I barely saw where it began, Draper had the dude's head pinned to the bar with a loud crack. The bartender backed up with his hands raised, as if to drop any pretense of ownership over the whole establishment. Draper seethed in the stranger's ear, "You like my sister's breasts, do you? You think it's a good idea to go around smacking young girls wherever you feel like?"

I jumped with a frightened squeak when Draper pulled his hand back and gave the man's butt a hard whack. A few men at nearby tables got up and ran out the door, afraid of being caught in the prince's and princess' ill graces. The bartender was stuck, and the scared look on his face told us he knew it. "Look, no one knew the Avalon Rose was in the bar. Why would you bring your sister to a place like this?"

"She's come to collect her *Guardien*, and I've come to shut you down. Places like these belong in the Lost Village. If you want to open one, that's the place you should go. A bar is one thing, but a brothel? You waited until Duchess Lane left, and then you turned that top floor into beds for rent."

I could tell by the prolonged silence before his response that Gustav was weighing out his limited options. "Is it a tax you want? Because I'm not above paying handsomely whatever the throne requires. You're welcome to any of my girls, your grace. No charge."

Draper's eyes turned evil with anticipation that was altogether sinister, and made the hairs on my arms stand up in alarm. I could tell he was well-versed in dealing with scumbags. "Offer my sister a job as one of your whores again."

Gustav's eyes fell to me in horror. "I meant no disrespect, your grace. How was I supposed to know it was the Avalon Rose behind that hood?"

"You weren't supposed to offer a girl fresh off the street a job hooking, that's for sure. We don't need people like you in Province 9. I'm sure Morgan's got tons of room for you."

Gustav's face paled yet further. "No, your highness! Please don't send me back there. The soldiers were too rough. The girls barely lasted a few weeks before they either killed themselves to escape the rough way of the soldiers, or before they were murdered in the throes."

I used my hands on the bar to hoist myself up, shocking him when I threw my legs over the bar and landed with a wince in the small space with him. I recovered my stumble as my thighs groaned; they really weren't up for this kind of abuse. I grabbed a fistful of Gustav's shirt and yanked him down so he was on my level. "Tell me what I should do with you. Tell me how you're making this new province better. Tell me how you're not trying to tear down the new start we're building for Avalon."

Gustav swallowed, as if my slight stature and less than impressive musculature was Andre the Giant level of spectacular. "I'm... I'm going to send the girls back to their families. I'm... This is going to be a pub only."

I growled at him. "I think we're way past that. You can do better, Gustav. I think you *have* to do better, or you don't want to know the fury I'm bringing down on your head." I kept my back to Draper, who was setting down a series of hard spanks on the drunk dude's saggy britches, no doubt taking out a lot of his pent-up aggression on the man's hindquarters.

"A pub that gives out free bread to anyone who has need of it!" Gustav declared, coming up with a plan on the fly.

I considered his offer. "And if you're caught renting out girls to the highest bidder?"

"I'll be hanged," he said, his chin lowering in defeat.

"I think that's fitting. I think that's exactly perfect. In fact, I think I'll post a little sign out front so that everyone knows where the free bread is, and where the girls for rent are not."

His head hung lower. "Yes, your majesty. As you see fit."

"Now please go get me my *Guardien*. And I want a little pep in your step, now that you get to keep your head on loan. That is, until you see to screwing up this province again." I shook my head at him as he all but ran toward the steps that climbed up the side wall. My voice carried to the johns and the girls who were finishing up and dressing when they'd each taken in my shouts of indignation. "To think, we went through all this trouble, marching out of Morgan's province to build our own nation, and this is what you all do with the freedom you've been given. This is the toilet you want to stick your head into. Lane's gift was wasted on you!"

Draper finally finished spanking the drunken man for the bad boy he was. Then my brother dragged him sobbing like a baby and threw him out the door, not caring where he landed. Draper sneered at the other men who came stumbling down the steps. "Does anyone else want a go at my sister? Does anyone else want to pay two coins for an evening with your princess?"

The humble "No, your grace" replies, coupled with frightened bows, showed me just how much they were scared of the throne. It was a good thing, really. My legs weren't all that steady, and Draper was my only backup. If they'd revolted, there wasn't much I could do about it.

I moved to the door and spread my body like an X to block the way. "Tomorrow morning after you've slept all this off and bathed until your skin is sparkling clean, you'll come to the mansion and present yourselves to me in the daylight. Since all of you clearly have too much time on your hands and nothing productive to do with it, you'll be given new jobs. You'll work so much that you'll look fondly on these days of screwing your-selves into uselessness." I met each of their guilty gazes, letting them know I would see if any of them weren't there tomorrow.

They each dropped to their knees and bowed, I guess grateful I hadn't chopped off their heads or something. I let them go, watching them scramble out into the night that might cover their many sins.

The girls came down one by one, wearing silky sheathes over dirty jeans and under overlarge shirts. Their guilty faces were rosy and made up with too much makeup. They ranged in age from about fourteen to well on into their fifties. I gave them each a tight nod, offering them work at the mansion if they needed the money until they could find honest professions. I held the door open and warned them that if they were caught even drinking in this deserted place, I would hear about it. This way of life was over with, and they would make good use of the second chance, so help me.

I shut the door with a heavy sigh, waiting as the familiar clunk of heavy boots finally descended the steps. I could barely look at Bastien, unbathed and unshaved as he was. His usual scruff had grown into an inch-long beard that was scraggly and unkempt. He stank of sex and cheap beer, which wasn't a winning combination on even the hottest of guys. Gustav had his arm wrapped around Bastien's waist, with Bastien's limp arm slung across his neck, balancing my drunken man like the child he was.

Gustav sat Bastien down at a table and splashed a cup of water in his face, rousing Bastien enough to widen his eyes when they fell on my guarded expression. Bastien let out a loud belch, and then seemed to come to himself marginally. He spoke in only a string of swears until self-loathing closed his mouth in a mournful moan.

I couldn't be mad at him like this. I'd spent all my good rage on the dude who copped a feel. The whole thing just felt too sad or something. I wasn't about to push it under the rug, but I knew not to kick someone who was already so far down. Despite it all, I loved Bastien. Between Roland's stabbing and torture, I'd underestimated how very broken Bastien had become.

My hands found his dripping face, cupping his prickly cheeks so I could examine every chiseled angle. "Before you met me, you were content. You had your cabin in the woods." I saw the ache in his heart that shone through in his glossy eyes. "I shouldn't have taken you from your happy place. Your adventure isn't me. It's you, and there's lots more on your journey you need to figure out."

I tried to keep my legs strong and steady as I ducked under his other arm, working with Draper to get Bastien back to the mansion, where he could sleep it off. It was slow and painful, but each step marked a real growth in me. Even when I fell a few times, I picked myself back up and helped the man who had tried his best to be good to me. He was barely aware it was me who helped him along, but that trek taught me a little more about who I was. No matter what, I would be a person who was good to the ones I loved, whether they deserved it or not. I would be who I was, regardless of the way I was treated. I'd loved Bastien, and though I was torn up inside, I put my pain on hold to shoulder a bit of his. After everything, it was a comfort to know I was still Lane's daughter.

ABANDONED BY MY MONKEY

*T*he beauty of being a princess is that if you want to send your boyfriend home, there are people who can do that for you. It took a simple request from one of the stable hands, five minutes of dictating a letter for Draper to write down and shove in Bastien's pocket, and a heartbroken kiss on his sleeping cheek before Bastien was being loaded into a wagon to be taken back to his cabin in the woods.

The kitchen was empty at this time of night, and I was grateful to have it to myself after Faith, Hope and Mercy kissed my cheeks and left me to my creeping misery. I stared at my cup of water, knowing I should drink it, but unable to bring the ornately etched glass to my lips. Depression's funny like that.

"Is tha any way to say farewell to your strapping lads?"

I'd been so good at keeping my tears on standby, but when the meaning of Link's words resonated with me, the moisture started pooling in my eyes. My words came out choked with the suddenness of the pain that clinched my heart. "I didn't think... I guess it makes sense that you two would... You're really leaving me?" I couldn't turn around to look at him; I didn't want to debase myself in front of the seasoned warrior.

Link's voice came back gravelly. "Aye. We were here to help Bastien because he asked us to stay. If he's going back home, we've no reason to stay here."

I'm not a reason to stay, I said to myself as calmly and emotionlessly as I could, willing my tears to remain tucked inside of me until I was alone. *Of course I'm not. They don't owe me a thing. They're not really my friends. They're my boyfriend's friends, and I don't have one of those anymore.* "I don't want you to go. You're... You live here."

"We live wherever we put ourselves," Mad countered from behind me in the doorway of the kitchen. "And we aren't putting ourselves here no more."

I swallowed the lump in my throat and counted to three before speaking, so I didn't give my sudden swing of grief away. I wanted to argue. Part of me wanted to beg. But I knew that, just like my animals, I couldn't keep the people I loved in one place. I steadied my flood of anguish as much as I could before I opened my mouth. "Okay. Makes sense. Let me pack you two a sandwich for the road." I kept my back to them to make sure my face stayed out of view.

Of all the times I'd wished for Link to be a monkey and not catch onto anything going on around him, in this moment, I longed for his oblivious charm most of all. I didn't want him to see my bloodied and bruised heart. Link's voice was soft, and filled with too much understanding. "Rosie." His brogue wrapped around my name and made it sound like a sad song. After tonight, I was pretty sure those were the only kinds my name would be associated with. "Ye know we can't stay. Our duty is to the Brotherhood."

I waved my hand to let him know it was all fine, but I still couldn't turn around. "I get it. Bros before hos. It's cool. It was good to have you around here. You're welcome back anytime."

"Rosie," Link said again, this time with too much understanding.

"Go on, Link." I set to chopping an orange tomato, hoping my hand didn't tremble and make me cut off a finger instead. I hoped he'd gone, but I didn't dare check for confirmation.

I shut my eyes tight when I heard his footsteps coming up quick from behind me. His hug knocked the breath from me, but that seemed to be the way of things with Link. He was a giant monkey, and darn it if I didn't love his unpolished boyishness. He squeezed me from behind, his chin resting on my shoulder so he could kiss my damp cheek. "It'll be alright, wee Rose."

The tears were evident now. I was embarrassed, caught in my youthful indiscretion when I realized that Link and Mad meant far more to me than I ever had to them. I felt stupid for loving so freely, and for letting my heart soar so high without a safety net. I deserved this heartbreak, so I welcomed it for the life lesson it was. "Dammit, Link, get off me! Just go!"

He only squeezed me tighter, loving however he wished, which was his way. "Don't ye know tha we don't want to go? We have to see Bastien gets back on his feet. He's our brother."

"If you don't get out of here, I'm going to stab you with this knife, I swear!"

He chuckled at my threat. He gripped my wrist while keeping his other arm secured around my waist, and banged the knife onto the counter until it clattered from my grip. Most people didn't understand the rough hands of the Untouchables, but I did. Their calluses were a comfort to me, and their scars a beautiful map of all that made them the lost boys they were. The song that he'd made up for me was honey and acid in my ear as he crooned softly to me. "Rosie, I love ye. Rosie, I care. Rosie, without ye, my heart's in despair." His whisper was sweet, but it only broke me more. "It was a good thing ye did for Mad, getting him to open up like tha. I won't forget ye."

His words cut more than they healed, and before I knew it, a full-blown sob erupted from my mouth before I could stuff it back inside. My heart was breaking in slow motion, and Link was scrambling to hold me together as I fell apart in his arms. "I told you to go! I don't want you to see me cry like this!"

"Shh. I'm not seeing a thing. Ye were making me a sandwich, aye?"

I tried to nod, but my wet cheek brushed up against his, sealing my embarrassment that there would be no coming back from. "Don't tell him he hurt me. Don't tell him I cried."

Link's voice was almost as sad as mine. "I won't need to. He loves ye, Rosie. He knows he's pushed away the best thing tha's ever happened to him – besides me, tha is."

I sniffed and hiccupped my sadness, not sure if I was even coherent. "Losing all of you in one go? I'm not the one who cheated! I did my best to be good to him, but now I'm losing all of you. How is this how it ends?"

"Shh. This isn't the end for us. We'll be back for ye someday." He tapped the tattoo on the inside of my wrist with his thumb. "Our mark will keep ye safe until then."

I threw my head back into his chest and let out a mournful wail. "You all marked me! This was supposed to mean something! You were supposed to be the family who didn't leave me!" I struggled against him, throwing elbows to free myself. "Just go!"

Link was almost as stubborn as me, and held on tighter as I thrashed. "Settle, Rosie! I won't leave ye like this."

I fought with him until his strength exhausted me, making my fight painfully futile. When I was limp in his arms, he tried to scoop me up, but I came to myself marginally and wriggled down, breaking myself from his hug. "No." I swiped the tears from my eyes and did my best to stand tall a few feet away from him, bracing myself on the counter. "You can go now. Go be Untouchable."

"This isn't how we wanted to leave things."

"You want to leave, so you are. It's fine. I get it. You don't owe me a thing." I turned and saw Mad still standing in the kitchen doorway. His guarded expression gave nothing away. "Have a safe trip, Mad." I pretended my tears didn't exist, hoping if I wished it hard enough, it would be true.

"Aye." Madigan held out his hand to me expectantly, his eyes looking off to the side to avoid the raw emotion in mine. "My ring."

Link swore at the ill timing of it all, and started making apologies.

I blinked at Mad, his simple words taking a few beats to sink in. I don't know why my stomach dropped when I took the chain off my neck and plopped his heavy gold ring down in his open palm. It's not like we were actually engaged. The fakeness of my life hit me anew, pushing me down into an abyss I was certain I would never climb out of. "Thanks for saving me from getting raped by my uncle. Super cool of you. Have a good life, Mad."

Mad nodded as he slid his ring back onto his thick finger. "Aye. Ye were a good wife, Rosie."

I slammed into him with a hug that ended as quickly as it began. I tore myself away and waved my hand over my shoulder by way of a parting word. I wanted to beg them to stay, to help me through Avalon, and make our province stronger. I wanted him to stay for a million reasons, but knew none of them held a candle to the needs of the Brotherhood.

Not twenty minutes later, I watched from my bedroom window as the wagon rolled away, carrying three of the men I'd grown to love. I watched until the wagon disappeared through the streets, carrying the Untouchables far from the life I barely recognized as mine.

Love the book? Leave a review.
Otherwise Link dies.
I have that kind of power, you know.

Scan this code to sign up for my newsletter, join my book-of-the-month club and view my collection of books.

BROKEN GIRL

Enjoy a free preview of *Broken Girl*,
book 5 in your new favorite series.

SADNESS AND SCRAMBLED EGGS

"*Y*ou locked me out of your room last night," Kerdik accused quietly over breakfast. His chocolate-colored fitted slacks, crisp white dress shirt and charcoal vest were perfectly in place, making me look that much more disheveled in my jeans and wrinkled t-shirt.

I ate in the stone-floored kitchen with the staff, hoping they'd be normal and go about their day around me, but they ended up speaking in hushed whispers and being on their best behavior. I couldn't tell if they thought I would have a nervous breakdown and start bawling because my *Guardien* and my fiancé were gone, or if they were scared my temper was as sharp as my mother's – the dreaded Morgan le Fae. Or maybe they were terrified of Kerdik, whose displeasure was known to affect whole celestial orbs and throw nature into chaos. Either way, it made for an awkward breakfast, even a whole week after the Untouchables had left. I tried not to think about them, not to miss Link's goofy grin, Madigan's absence of a personality that only I found endearing, and...

I shuddered, reminding myself that I wasn't going to think about *him*. I vowed not even to say *his* name in my mind; it was too painful to hear it. I chewed on the toast, but it felt like sand in my mouth. "My locked door sure didn't stop you from breaking in."

"I was worried about you."

"Nothing to worry about. Sometimes things don't work out. Is what it is." I brushed the crumbs off my white t-shirt and stood. "I'm going back out to help with the wall."

Kerdik rubbed his hands over his face, exasperated with me even though the sun had barely risen. "You're still technically injured. I don't think manual labor is the right call."

"Maybe not, but it's my call. I want to help. There was a whole whorehouse operating right under my nose, but I didn't know a thing about it because I was laying around the mansion like a lazy bum."

"You're not lazy, you're injured!" As his tone rose, the servants scattered, fearful of his swinging rage. Two of the sisters who ran the kitchen, Faith and Mercy, whimpered, shoving each other to get out as quick as they could.

When it was just us on the tall stools at the stone island, I took my dish to the sink. I'd eaten half my breakfast, which felt like one brick too many sitting in my stomach. "Look, I need to keep myself busy, and I don't want to drop the ball on the whole princess thing. Lane should come back to a peaceful region with a wall in place."

Kerdik's nostrils flared. "You're shutting me out. I'm not the one who cheated on you."

I flinched at mention of the crime I'd specifically told my Avalonian BFF not to mention ever again if he valued his testicles. "You're not allowed to psychoanalyze me."

Kerdik raised his eyebrow, pursing his lips. "Being a brat to me isn't going to bring Bastien home."

I washed my dish with jerky movements, fuming. "I don't want him home. You seem to think I'm pining for the man who cheated on me in a whorehouse, who was so drunk, he couldn't lift a helping hand when I was attacked right in front of him. I am not so desperate as to ache over someone like that."

Kerdik stared at my black neck tattoo with unhampered attitude, as only the most intimate of friends could do. He'd laid in bed with me every night since Bastien had gone, so I think we'd achieved that level of closeness that kept me from shoving him when he spoke hard truth I didn't want to hear. "Actually, that's exactly what I think. I think you're waiting for him to come back with some amazing excuse that would make all the wrongs right again between the two of you." He shook his head. "It's not going to happen. He did what men who are unhappy often do. It's nothing more complicated than that."

"Do you want to wear that breakfast?" I steamed, eyeing his scrambled eggs and berries. My mood had been fouler than my usual cheery, shrug-it-off disposition, but everyone seemed to be giving me a pass. Somehow this only made me more irritable. "I told you that I don't need to hear his name, and there you go, just blurting it out like a foghorn. I know he's gone. I sent him away myself. This is me, moving on."

"You sleep fitfully now, when you do at all. You used to require eight hours a night, but you're barely down for two at a time before you're up and back at that wall. You're shutting out the animals, so your magic's not wearing down as much. You need them. They make you happy." He popped a berry into his mouth. "You called out for Bastien in your sleep again last night when I came in to check on you."

I inhaled sharply, my nostrils flaring at the verbal slap he would have been better off not mentioning at all. Instead of arguing, I scooped up a handful of his warm eggs and smeared them down his cheeks. I examined the sight that was Kerdik a mess, and looked with a satisfied sense of accomplishment at the beautiful picture. "Wow, I didn't think I could smile, but that sure did it. Thanks for being a jerk just so I could make you wear your breakfast."

Kerdik glowered at me, the stone floor beneath us rattling with his temper before he cooled down a few breaths later. "You're welcome. If I didn't mention you being a brat before, it goes double now. And you're not actually smiling, you know, so it wasn't even worth it."

"Oh, it was worth it."

"You haven't smiled in a week. That's not you. What's the point of being near you if there's no *you* left?" He said it as if he expected an answer.

"Then leave! I'm sure you could bunk up with the Untouchables, or go see Lane, who's still not back. Maybe you could go for a walk in the woods where I buried Abraham Lincoln and Hamish. Everyone else makes good use of the front door. Knock yourself right friggin' out, if this isn't the place you want to be."

"This isn't you." Kerdik squinted at me and tilted his head to the side, as if trying to size up something that was more complicated than a broken heart.

I pursed my lips, and then tried to calm down my frustration. Kerdik had actually stuck around, and I was lashing out at him for it. He was right; this wasn't me. "You're getting too I-know-everything about it all. He was my first love, K. It's going to sting for a while." I looked at the eggs I'd smeared on his cheek and winced. "Sorry about making you wear your breakfast."

He used the water he produced from his elemental magic, and ran his hands down his face, washing off the egg residue. "Do you want to talk about it?"

I shook my head. "I'm going out to the border. Send a magical bunny or singing telegram if you need me."

His nose crinkled. "You're a princess. You don't need to be building walls with a bunch of sweaty men."

I stretched out my back, which was sore from all the tossing and turning I'd done before Kerdik snuck in to cuddle me last night. "What I need is to work through some of this crap, and manual labor is a good way to do that. This is my province, so I should be out working in it. If hard labor is good enough for my subjects, then it's good enough for me."

Kerdik studied my face, and finally sighed. "Fine. If that's what you need, go on and do what you have to. Take Draper with you, okay? And don't work too hard. I mean it. Yesterday was too much, and you know it."

"Sure." Draper had been good about giving me my space after it all imploded. He was antsy without Lane around, so he stuck by my side that much more voraciously. Turns out, we both like to work when we're stressed, so neither of us gave the other one too much grief about it. Dad was well enough to take on most of the royal responsibilities, which was a relief to us both.

Kerdik stood before me and cupped my face, trying to warm my cold places. He pulled back and squinted at me, frustrated with my resigned nature. "Where are you, darling?"

"I'll be out on the border until Dad needs me to sit and hold court with him tonight."

"That's not what I meant."

I shrugged. "I know. I'm not really anywhere. I'll figure it all out. First broken heart. Where's the baby book, am I right? This one deserves a photo op." I ducked away when he tried to kiss my cheek. I didn't want to hurt him, but I saw the fresh wound there all the same. I shook my head, unable to look at him as I tapped my heart. "It's not you. You're perfect. Really, K. Better than I deserve right now. It's me. If you kiss me, it'll make me feel, and I don't want to feel right now. I want to nothing myself into oblivion. I need to be perfectly and utterly nothing."

Kerdik's eyes lit with that fire I'd seen build a cave out of a field in a heartbeat. He jerked me to him in a possessive way I wasn't altogether unfamiliar with, my breasts pushed against his firm chest. It rattled the feelings around inside of me, which was the exact opposite of the nothing I'd asked for.

His lips found mine so quickly, I scarcely knew what to do with myself. His hand pressed on the small of my back so that I was arched against him, my waist mashing to his hips in a way that was altogether carnal and probably not too ladylike. Confusion, indignation and a lust I didn't mean to feel rose up in me as my lips started to revel in the dirty dance they'd been invited to. The kiss was passionate, but lasted only a few agonized seconds. I felt more in those few seconds than I'd allowed myself in an entire week. He ripped a gasp from my mouth, swallowing it and making it his own.

When I finally had the wherewithal to pull away, my shriek was embarrassed. "What the crap, K?"

Then, so fast I almost fell over, Kerdik whirled me around, pressed my back to his chest and snatched an apple off the counter. He held it out in front of me as an ominous belch built up in my belly. I panicked when I remembered the last time we'd kissed, and the blaze that erupted from that carefully contained mess. I tried to slap my hands over my mouth, but Kerdik pinned them both down with an arm around my waist to secure me to him. "Let it come," he whispered, his lips tickling the shell of my ear.

The fire burst out of me much the same as it had before, aiming itself at the apple and toasting it as it lay in his palm. "I'm sorry!" I choked out when the fire died as quickly as it started. I was horrified that I'd hurt him.

"You can't injure me with fire. I'm an elemental, remember?" He moved the apple closer so I could see the crisp outer layer that had browned on one side. He buried his face in my neck, placing a kiss to a spot that was too sensitive to let him near without a shiver running through me. "People who are nothing feel nothing. You are not nothing," he reminded me, his fingers digging into my hip. "*You* are my fire."

I finally turned around in his arms, his fervor breaking through what had been a week of trying to numb everything with work and avoidance. I didn't like my bed without *him* in it. I didn't like the mansion without *him* bumming around, either.

There had been an ache in my chest since I'd sent his drunken butt off in a wagon with Link and Mad. With time, it seemed that hole only grew larger.

Kerdik held me, hoping I would break in his arms, but I maintained what little dignity I could scrape together, and remained in his embrace with a quiet demeanor. Finally, I leaned up on my toes and pecked his cheek. "I love you. No more kissing me, though. I'm already a mess. You shouldn't hitch your wagon to a dead horse."

He traced my lips like a man who knew exactly what to do with them. "I'll not apologize for it."

"How unlike you." I managed a... not quite a smile, but a lighter expression nonetheless, and squeezed his side, even though he wasn't ticklish. "See you tonight when you break into my room again." I sniffed his collar, my eyebrows pushing together in faux concern. "Hm. You smell like scrambled eggs. Might want to wash that off of you."

Kerdik was not amused at my joke, his eyes narrowing. "Leave the door unlocked tonight, or risk my displeasure."

"Dum-da-dum!" I sang ominously, mocking his almighty temper as I left.

Continue the series with *Broken Girl* today!

Find your next great read and sign up for the

newsletter at www.maryetwomey.com

Mary E. Twomey also writes contemporary romance under the name Tuesday Embers.

Visit her online at www.tuesdayembers.com.